THE REBOUND

L. STEELE

For the good girls who love
alphaholes
who buy them books and growl:
"STFUATTDLAGG"

I see you!

1

Solene

"You need to be punished for your indiscretion." He glares at her. "On your knees, hands behind your back, mouth open. You will take everything I give you without complaining. And— "

"Solene, are you here?" My mother's voice reaches me through the closed doors of the wardrobe. I press back into the wall and hold my breath.

The light slicing in through the slats in the door dips as her shadow passes in front of the door. I press my book close to my chest and wait... wait... Footsteps fade as he walks in the direction of the window.

"Where did she go?" That's my brother's voice. I freeze.

"Maybe she's out in the garden?" my mother replies.

"I checked before I came here," he snaps.

"Perhaps she's in the maze; you know how much she loves that space."

"I'll go check." Footsteps sound again, and the light through the slats disappears for a few seconds when my brother walks past. A second set of footsteps pad away. I stay frozen, my palms clammy, sweat pooling under my armpits. That was close. If my brother had caught me reading a spicy book, the two of them would have, have—I shudder. I don't dare to think of the repercussions, of how they'd react to the contents of my preferred genre of literature.

After my father died, my brother became the head of our family. Which means, he also took on the responsibilities of Mafia Don. And unlike our father, he has an archaic view on the role of women in the family. It doesn't help that he's fifteen years older than me which makes him practically a father figure. Thing is, he loves to boast that I'm a reader—which, in Mafia circles, makes me something of an anomaly. Thanks to the American nanny my sister and I had in our early years, we read and write English better than the rest of my Italian family. It's also why I prefer to read my smutty books in English. Of course, whenever my brother or my mother are around, I read only classical literature—with my smutty books hidden between the pages. On occasion, when I get tired of pretending to read the 'right' kind of book, I like to duck into the closet so I can read the kind of novel I prefer without having to hide it.

Silence returns. Some of the tension fades from my shoulders. I peek down at the book pressed against my chest, then at the shut door. I switched off my flashlight when I heard their voices earlier. I could switch it on and start reading again, b-u-t...

Maybe I should wait. Just a few more seconds to ensure my ma's left. And then, I can slip back into the land of my lead characters and that very detailed scene I was reading. Why did the MMC say he wanted to punish the FMC, and why did that feel so hot? I bite the inside of my cheek. And when he commanded her not to come until he gave her permission... Why did that send a pulse of heat racing up my spine? Something liquefies between my thighs. Ooh, that doesn't seem right, and yet it feels… right. It feels so good, surely, it can't be wrong.

I draw in a breath, then another, waiting until my pulse settles down. Until my heart stops beating so fast. Then I crack open the door and peer out. The room is empty. Thank god! I crawl out of the closet then jump to my feet. I glance down at the page where I stopped. "*—you hear me, little girl? Don't you dare come!*"

I walk forward, throw myself onto the bed on my front, then kick up my legs and peruse the words.

"Oh, master, I can't hold it, I can't," she groans.

"You can," he growls.

"Please, master, please— "

The book is snatched out from under me.

"Hey!" I look up to find my mother has the book in her hands. She looks at the cover—which is discreet, thank god. Not that it's going to help when she opens it up to the page where I was.

"No!" I jump up on the bed and swipe my hand out at the book. My ma steps out of reach, and I fall over on the mattress. I spring up again, reach for it, but she holds it away. She begins to peruse the contents, and my cheeks flame.

"That's my book," I cry.

She merely continues reading.

"Give it back!" I lunge for it, but she holds up an arm to fend me off. I throw myself at her, but she moves aside. I tumble to the floor. My knees hit the wood, and I cry out. Tears of frustration prick the backs of my eyes. I shove the pain aside, leap up to my feet. But Ma is taller than me. She holds the book high and continues reading. The blood fades from her cheeks. Her jaw tightens. The tips of her ears grow white. No, no, no, when that happens, it means she's really, really pissed off at me. Which means she's going to— her palm connects with my face, and I cry out. Stars burst in front of my eyes.

"What is this filth you're reading?"

"It's not filth."

She slaps my other cheek, and the impact carries me back. My heels slip on the floor, and once more, I hit it--this time, on my butt. I bounce up and reach up on my tiptoes. "Give me my book. That's mine, not yours. You have no right— "

She snaps the book shut and slams it down on my head. I cry out as black spots blink out behind my eyes. Bile boils up my throat. No, no, no, I can't be sick. I can't. If I am, she'll know that she's won, and I'm not going to let that happen.

"I hate you. Hate you!"

"You think I care what you think of me?" My mother lowers the book to her side. "How dare you read a romance novel."

"It's not a romance novel."

"Oh?" Her gaze grows more piercing. "Now you're lying to me?"

It's a spicy novel. There's a big difference.

My chest hurts, and my stomach ties itself in knots, "I... I'm n-n-not, lying to, y-y-you." I hate how my stuttering makes me sound weak.

"Oh, and now she stammers. You are incorrigible. You can't do anything I tell you to do. Then, you go against my instructions not to read romance novels. How many times have I told you, you should not read these sinful tomes?"

Tomes. Did she say tomes? She said tomes.

"It's not a tome," I snarl.

My ma curls her mouth. "It's a tome."

"No, it isn't."

The whiteness extends out from the tips of her ears to the lobes. Oh, no, that's bad. So bad. I've seen that happen only once, when she got so upset with my sister Olivia that she caned her.

I begin to back away, but my mother closes the distance between us and snatches me by my ear. She twists my ear lobe and pain slices through my head. "Let me go, you… you… witch."

"You mean bitch with a capital B, don't you?" my ma snaps.

"Yes, I do."

She stills. "What did you say?"

"I… I… I…"

She laughs. "Can't string two words together and wants to read romance novels. The way you're headed, you'll be losing your virginity before you're eighteen, and then your brother won't have a choice but to sell you into prostitution."

I stare at my mother in horror. "That's a terrible thing to s-s-say."

"It's what you deserve for reading these evil words."

"They are not evil."

Her smile widens. "But I can be when you don't obey me."

I hate her, I hate her, I hate her. Maybe she has a point. Maybe I am too young to read these kinds of books. Not that I looked it. Thanks to an early growth spurt, when I also filled out, I'm often mistaken for an adult. I certainly feel like one in my head and in my soul. Besides, all of my friends are reading them, too, and one of them loaned a book to me. How else am I supposed to find out about what happens between a man and a woman? My mother certainly isn't going to talk to me about it, and as for my brother... That would be creepy. My sister already left home; else I'd have someone to talk to about these strange goings-on in my body that I really didn't understand at all.

I drag the back of my hand across my face. My arm trembles. My palm hurts. I turn it over, stare at the slashes of pink that crisscross the soft skin. "She's a bitch with a capital B." My mother caned me. She dragged me to the kitchen, made me hold out my palms, then in front of all the staff, she brought the thinnest stick I've ever seen down on me.

I almost cried out. Almost. Thankfully, I managed to bite down on my tongue enough to draw blood. But I'll take the coppery taste over giving her the satisfaction of hearing me scream. Twenty strokes on each hand, and by the end, I was sweating and shivering. She'd finally stopped only to send me to my room and ground me without food for the next day.

I threw myself on the bed, had a good cry, and fell asleep. When I woke up, it was past midnight. I was starving, and my palms still ached. I drank water from the sink in the bathroom, which sated me for the moment, then washed my face. I headed back to my room, and unable to sleep, paced back and forth. I was still awake when the clock in my room struck two a.m. So, I crawled out of the window and down two floors using the branches of the tree that grows past my bedroom window. Then, I raced across the lawn, through the gate in the fence and down to the beach. I kept running until the house was out of sight. Only then, did I slow down. I walked until my feet were tired, finally sinking down on the sand under the moonlight.

It's late, but I couldn't stay in that house for one second longer. I needed to get out and run and pretend I'm free, at least, for a little while. Also, this is Naples, and everyone knows who my father was. It means anyone could recognize me and report me back to my family. On the other hand, no one would touch me. Not unless they want to incur the wrath of the local Mafia Don, which, face it, no one wants.

I bring my legs up, wrap my arms about them, and rest my chin on my knees. "I am going to run away and become a singer. I am going to be the most well-known pop star in the world. Everyone will want to hear me. I'll be rich and famous and—" I sniff. It's always a struggle to complete a sentence without stuttering when I get emotional.

The only exception is when I sing. When I close my eyes and allow the music to carry me away, I don't stammer. I don't trip over my words. I'm a completely different person. A beautiful woman, who is confident and bold, and who never has to worry about anyone catching her reading a spicy novel.

So what, if I'm a teenager? I understand what's happening between the pages... Most of it, anyway. And my imagination fills in the gaps. I love how the spice in the books makes me feel. All those tingles and trembles which imbue my lower belly, and between my legs, and send spurts of heat under my skin. It's weird, but also, strangely familiar. Like I've been waiting my entire life for something. Like I'm ready for it. I am.

I close my eyes and drop into that part of me which is only mine. I draw from that energy, then open my mouth and sing.

I let the words, the tune, the melody...carry me away. I pour myself into the rhythm, allowing the tune to subsume me. When I finally fall silent, I allow the sound of the wind to pour over me. The crash of the waves on the shore surrounds me. The sound of clapping brings a smile to my lips. I open my eyes and gasp. "Who're you?"

2

Solene

"Why don't you sing again?" the man asks me. He's a tall silhouette against the dark sky. And he's not alone. The guy next to him is broad enough to block out the view behind him. The whites of his eyes gleam in the moonlight. On his other side, a third man watches me in silence. The hair on the back of my neck rises.

"Who are you?" I snap.

The man who first spoke tilts his head. "Who're you?" he asks. His accent is different from what I hear every day. It sounds American. Like in the movies my mother sometimes allows me to see. Only the classics, and only the movies where there are no kissing scenes. Still, it's my only route to seeing a glimpse of the world outside my own, and while I may never get to travel, at least. this way, I know there's a reality outside the one I live in.

"I'm the daughter of the leader of the Camorra, which, if you were a resident, you'd know. Clearly, you're not."

The first guy looks me up and down. "You hear that, fellas? She's the daughter of the Camara."

"Not Camara; Camorra."

"You say po-tay-toe; I say po-tah-to." He takes a step in my direction. I slide back, bump into someone. I gasp and pivot to find a fourth man I hadn't noticed earlier. He cracks his neck. When he smiles, his teeth gleam in the darkness. My heart slams so hard into my ribcage, I feel faint. The blood batters against my temples.

"So, daughter of the Camara, you're a pretty little thing, aren't you?" He lunges toward me. I feint, then kick out and catch him in the shin. He grunts and stumbles, and it slows him enough for me to brush past him. I have to get out of here, have to. It was so stupid of me to think I could walk on the beach at in the middle of the night and get away with it. How could I have been so careless? I put on a burst of speed, the sand kicking up at my heels. Go, go, go. I lean forward, focus on a point in the horizon.

The next second, something catches me around the waist. I hit the beach. The breath rushes out of me. A heavy weight presses me into the sand. A panting sound fills my ears. Mine? That of the man who has his body pressed to mine? My pulse booms. Adrenaline spikes my blood. I begin to struggle, but he's so heavy, I can barely move. "Let me go," I yell, but it comes out as a muffled, "leh...m...g..."

Then the weight eases off of me. I'm turned on my back. I draw in a breath and the oxygen fills my lungs. My head spins. I spit out the sand in my mouth and crack open my eyes to find the man straddling me. He grins. "How many of us can you take in one go, little girl?"

What? No, no, no. What's he saying? Whatever it is, it's not good.

His lips curl, the intent in his eyes unmistakable. I try to pull away, but my arms are grabbed and held captive above my head. I try to kick out, but first one leg, then the other, is grabbed and held down. I can't move, can't breathe. I open my mouth, but nothing comes out. Fear twists my guts. My brain is trying to tell me I need to get out of here, but my body is seizing up. This can't be happening--not to me.

The man straddling me grabs the front of my night shirt and yanks. It tears down the front. The sound slices through the noise in my head.

I open my mouth and scream, "Help, help me, someone, ummmph —" He slaps his hand over my mouth and snarls, "I'm going to teach you what happens to little girls who draw attention to themselves."

Oh, god, no. No, please no, no.

He pulls down my pajama pants, and I scream, but the sound is stifled against his hand. He reaches down and unhooks his belt, then pulls down his zipper, the sound of which is ominous in the darkness.

I begin to struggle in earnest.

He leans his weight into me, and the feel of him between my legs sends a shiver of fear up my spine. My thighs quiver, and to my shame, a melting sensation—the same kind I get when I'm reading a smutty scene--fills the space between my legs. No, no, no, what's wrong with me? No, please, I don't want this. Tears leak from my eyes. He grabs the waistband of my panties, and a sob catches in my throat.

Not like this, please. I don't want to have my first sexual experience like this. I squeeze my eyes shut. If I lose my virginity like this, if my family finds out, they'll disown me. Oh, the shame. The entire community will scorn me and—

The weight is lifted off of me. I hear the sound of a body hitting the ground. The sound of a fist hitting flesh, a grunt, a man's scream. More sounds of a fight. I can't open my eyes. Can't move my arms and legs. Every part of me feels frozen. I lay there, trying to breathe, trying to inflate my lungs. Unable to do so. I choke, my chest rises and falls. I can't breathe, oh god, I can't breathe.

"Breathe," a new voice commands. "Breathe, dammit."

My body obeys him; oxygen fills my lungs.

"One more breath."

My lungs fill up with greedy gusts of air. The feeling is so intense, I feel lightheaded, like I'm dissociated from my body, floating away. Looking down on the scene, on the stranger who's leaning over me, while I'm fading...fading—

"Open your eyes."

I open my eyelids. The moonlight haloes his face and picks out the intense blue of his irises. A cerulean vastness, an ultramarine stain so vivid, so brilliant, it's captured me in its radiance and is penetrating through to my bones, my blood, my cells, the deepest, most hidden parts of me which I never even knew existed. All of it filled, embraced, burned with a flaming, glaring vehemence that sears me. Holds me captive. Pins me down to this plane. This earth. This. Here. Now.

"Take another breath, now," he orders.

I draw in a long, deep, life-affirming gasp, and energy surges through my veins.

"Good girl."

His voice fills the empty, hurting parts of me, turning me to mush, filling me up, turning me inside out, changing me forever. And ever. A trembling grips me. My hands and legs quake. My chest hurts. My stomach knots. I can't stop the quiver that unravels from the top of my head to my toes, then back again.

"She's going into shock," another man's voice says from somewhere above me. A small cry escapes me. No, no, no, I can't be seen like this by anyone else. I can't.

"Shh, you're safe." Blue Eyes gathers me into his arms, and I cower. I try to make myself small enough to fit in his embrace. I press into him, inhale the scent of dark chocolate with a dash of coffee. My stomach quivers. How can he smell both exciting and comforting at the same time? He begins to rock me, tucks my head under his chin, and holds me closer.

"We need to get out of here before they regain consciousness," the second man's voice says.

I must make a noise in my throat, for Blue Eyes pulls me in firmly against his chest and whispers, "You're safe, I promise. I won't let anyone get to you."

I believe him. I don't know who he is, but he won't hurt me. He was sent here to save me. My very own Prince Charming. I let out a sigh, cuddle in, and let the darkness overwhelm me.

I come awake with a gasp—my heart pounding, my mouth dry, my throat so parched it feels like I swallowed razor blades. I glance around a room illuminated with the early morning light streaming in from the open window. Glancing down, I realize I'm wearing my nightshirt and my pajamas. That's something, at least.

"How're you feeling now?" A hard voice reaches me through the semi-darkness.

A small scream spills from my lips.

A man unfolds his length from the chair next to the bed.

I sit up, then scramble back against the headboard. "Who… who're you?"

"Declan Beauchamp." He steps into the morning light, and his blue eyes gleam.

I swallow. "You saved me from those... those…" A shudder grips me.

He leans forward, and I shrink further back. He pulls the covers up and over me. I grab them from him and pull them up to my chin.

"Wh-what do you want?" I rasp.

He reaches for the bottle of water on the side table and holds it out.

I let go of the cover long enough to grab the bottle of water and tilt it to my lips. I chug down half of it, some of the water spilling down my chin and splashing onto the T-shirt. When I feel somewhat sated, I wipe the back of my hand over my mouth.

His gaze drops to my palm. I curl my fingers into a fist at once, but I know he must have seen the evidence of the caning, for his jaw tightens. "Who hurt you?" He growls.

I place the bottle on the side table and look away. The last thing I want to do is tell this man about the complicated dynamics of my family. I'm certainly not going to tell him my mother caned me.

"It's nothing," I murmur.

A nerve throbs at his temple. His shoulder muscles seem to bulge. Anger thrums off of him, a black cloud that presses down on my chest. "Who was it? Someone in your family?" he growls.

I firm my lips. "It's none of your business."

"You became my business when I saved you from those men."

I swerve my head in his direction, and he looks as surprised as I feel by his outburst. For a few seconds, we stare at each other. His gaze narrows. He searches my features then the expression on his face softens. "All I'm trying to say is if someone is hurting you—"

"They're not."

He clenches his jaw; a stubborn look comes into his eyes. *He's not going to let go of this, is he?* I blow out a breath. "It was nothing, I promise."

"Your palms are hurt and you're saying it's nothing?" he snaps.

"I bruised them climbing down the tree outside my room."

He opens his mouth, but before he can say anything else, I shake my head. "I promise, I'm fine."

He holds my gaze for a few seconds more. He doesn't seem very convinced.

"If you need any help—"

"I'm good. Really."

His eyebrows draw down. "You sure about that?"

No.

No.

I jerk my chin.

He runs his fingers through his hair, mussing those thick dark locks further. His eyelashes are full, his cheekbones so high it's a wonder they don't cut through the skin, and his mouth... Oh, god, his mouth. I hadn't noticed that pouty lower lip, the thin upper one, the overall shape so gorgeous. Combined with his broad shoulders, the pecs outlined by his shirt, the way his biceps strain the sleeves, and those veins that pop against his forearms... "You're gorgeous," I burst out, then wince. I didn't just say that. *I said that.*

A slow smirk curls his lips, and goosebumps shower across my skin. Liquid heat pools in my lower belly, and I glance away.

"Thank you," he murmurs in a low, deep voice that twists my insides further.

I peer up at him from under my eyelashes and say, "You're not from here."

"But you are."

I bite down on my lower lip, and his gaze grows heavy. That heat in my lower belly intensifies. It spreads to my extremities. My arms and legs tremble. *Oh, my god, why do I feel like I've been thrust into a sauna, then dumped into a vat of cold water?*

"I'm going to be a singer someday," I announce, then slap my hand to my forehead. "Forget I said that. I'm not sure why I'm babbling like this."

"A singer, huh?"

I lower my hand and scan his features. He's not laughing at my crazy pronouncement. Not like my family has every time I've stated it to them. Aside from my sister Olivia, who always encourages me to dream big, the rest of my extended family always looked askance when I talk about my dreams.

"I heard you earlier on the beach," he says slowly.

Heat flushes my cheeks. "You heard me?"

He nods, "You're good. Better than good. You have a certain innocence, yet a depth to your voice that's compelling."

I angle my head in his direction and ask, "You think I can sing?"

His smile widens. "I think if you pursued it, you could be famous."

Warmth pools in my chest. No one has ever told me that. No one has ever appreciated my talent. I've known it deep inside, of course, but to have someone else confirm it to me means so much.

"Are you a singer, too?"

He barks out a laugh. "Only in the shower, and badly, at that. No, I'm in the most narcissistic of all professions. I'm an actor."

"Ah." That explains his looks and that ripped build of his. I may only be a teenager, and a sheltered one at that, but even I've seen enough movies on TV to know that the man standing in front of me has the kind of looks and personality that would stand out on screen. "Have I seen you in anything?"

He smirks and replies, "Not yet, but it's only a matter of time before you do."

"You're confident of yourself," I scoff. He has reason to be, but still, isn't it difficult to be successful as an actor? Though if anyone can make it, it'd be this gorgeous guy.

"Your singing is what saved your life."

"Eh?" I scowl.

"I heard you singing and headed in your direction; that's when I noticed the men surrounding you and had to intervene."

"Th-th-hank you." Oh, no, not the stammering again; not now.

"What were you doing walking alone at two in the morning?

I frown. I've had enough of my family censoring my movements, without this stranger asking me about them.

"What's it to you?" I jut out my chin.

He arches an eyebrow. "You could have been," he pauses, "you know."

"But I wasn't."

"Pretty close."

I fold my arms across my chest, mirroring his stance. He's right, but I don't want to dwell on that. He saved me—it's true. And maybe I do owe him. The least I can do is answer his questions. But something about the arrogance that clings to him, that hooked aristocratic nose of his, the way he's watching me with a judgmental expression... It makes me want to defy him. "But I wasn't. You came at the right moment, and that's the point."

"That isn't the point," he growls, then lowers his arms to his sides. "I may not be there the next time. What then?"

"It won't happen again." I firm my lips.

"The confidence of youth," he snorts.

"You're not that old, yourself."

"Is that a sneaky way of finding out my age, little girl?"

"I'm not so little."

"You're what, eighteen?"

"Seventeen." The truth bursts out of my mouth before I can stop myself. Oh, shoot, why couldn't I have lied and pretended I was eighteen?"

"You're seventeen?" He takes a step back clearly wanting to put distance between us. "You're a teenager. My tastes run to women, and bloody hell—" He runs his fingers through his hair again. "You're distraught. Perhaps, still in shock."

"I'm not in shock. I know what happened, I know what those men wanted with me—"

"Oh, yeah?" He slaps his palms on his hips. "What do you think they wanted to do to you, pray tell?"

"Th-th-they…" I bite the inside of my cheek. I will not stammer, will not stammer. Oh, god, not now. Not when I want to appear grown up and wise beyond my years to this man.

"How old are you?" I ask.

He seems taken aback by my question, then lowers his chin to his chest. "I'm too old for you."

"How old?" I set my jaw. "You're what, twenty?"

"Twenty-one."

I flick my hair over my shoulder. "You're only four years older."

He scoffs, "And this is bullfuck."

H-o-l-y shit. He said, fuck... Aloud. I've read that particular swear word in my smutty books but never come across anyone who used it to swear aloud in real life.

He groans, "Don't tell me my swearing shocks you?"

"Of course not." I lie.

"You expect me to believe that?" He plants his hands on his hips again. "And don't change the topic. We're talking about why you were wandering on the beach at that time of the night dressed like that." He stabs a finger in my direction.

I look down at my nightshirt covered chest, over which the sheet is draped, then back at him. "So, it's my fault that I was attacked? That th-th-those m-m-men—" I burst out crying. *Oh, my god, how embarrassing!* I'm weeping bucketsful in front of this hot stranger who looks exactly like one of the guys from my smutty books. And he found me in such a horrible situation, too. I bury my face in my hands, and weep and weep.

At some point, he gathers me in his arms, and the scent of dark chocolate and coffee fills my senses. I turn my face into his shoulder, wrap my arms about him, and allow myself to cry. When the tears finally slow down, I hiccup.

"I've got you; I promise." He rubs his hand down my back in slow soothing circles.

I focus on his touch, on how my breasts feel heavy, on my nipples which are pebbled and pressing into his chest, on that strange, tickling sensation that feels like I'm developing an itch between my legs, on the hard column that presses against my inner thigh. My heartbeat kicks up, I angle myself so the space between my legs rubs against that thick rod, just to alleviate the itch, I swear. Goosebumps pop on my skin. My thighs tremble.

He must become aware of my actions in the same breath for he freezes and asks, "What are you doing?" He pushes me away and surges to his feet, looking down at me with a mixture of horror and disgust... and lust. It must be lust that makes his blue eyes darken until they're nearly indigo. Color splotches his cheeks.

"Fuck!" He begins to pace. "You need to leave, right fucking now."

My heart seizes. My chest hurts. A crushing sensation squeezes my ribcage. So, he doesn't want me. That's okay. There'll be others. Like the Mafia husband my family will engage me to when I'm eighteen. I hunch my shoulders. It's fine. I can deal with it. I still have my spicy books. I'll just have to do a better job of hiding them. My book boyfriends will never abandon me. They'll save me from my wretched life and love me enough to make up for all the disappointments in real life. I throw off the cover, then swing my legs over the side. My feet brush my sandals—thank god, I didn't lose them. I would have never been able to explain that to my mother—I slip my feet into them, then straighten.

"Fine!" I march past him toward the doorway and stop when he calls out.

"Wait, I'll take you."

3

Declan

"Fucking hell, she's only seventeen!" I drop down into another push-up, then another. Sweat drips down my chest onto the already sticky floor of the gym. It's a tiny underground space Knight and I discovered not long after arriving in Naples. A film role brought me here. The shooting wrapped up, but I decided to stay on, and Knight joined me. He decided to come out and visit me here in Naples before shipping out on his next mission. Then there's Cade.

Our friendship was sealed a few years ago, over the course of one memorable bender that lasted forty-eight hours. Knight, Cade and I had bar hopped every nightclub in London's East End and exchanged stories about the challenges we were facing in our chosen careers.

A month later, Knight left to join the army, I landed my first proper role in a movie, and Cade made reserve for the cricket team. The three of us have kept in touch since and hang out whenever we're in the same city. With Cade busy establishing himself on the cricket circuit, more often than not, the three of us catch up on the phone nowadays.

"Nothing happened though." Knight pauses midway through his push up, "Amiright?"

"You're right." I flow into the next push-up, and the next, then sink into plank position. "Nothing happened." Yet. And that's what bothers me. The fact that I even let things progress to the extent they had. The fact that I hadn't realized she was still a kid. Jesus Christ. She seemed so grown up with those fully formed boobs, and that dip of her waist, and those luscious lips. Her eyes though... The big green eyes with which she'd surveyed me, those fringed eyelashes, the way her pupils had dilated at my nearness—fuck, I should have realized she was an innocent. That she was younger than I thought.

"So, what's the problem?" Knight lowers himself into the plank position, as well, his biceps bulging, chest muscles already sculpted from the years he's already spent in the army. Asshole was huge to begin with, but after this last tour, he seems positively gargantuan. There's not a hint of fat on his body, either. Which is why I'm going to push myself until I can compete with him in the gym.

"No problem," I grunt. My triceps hurt, my shoulders shudder, but I stay planked. Knight—the fucker—on the other hand, has barely broken a sweat.

"The furrow between your eyebrows says otherwise. Or wait... Is that because the workout is too much for you?" He raises his leg, balancing himself on his elbows and on one foot.

Asshole. When he shoots me a challenging glance. I mirror his move. My arms scream in protest, sweat runs in rivulets down my throat. I grit my teeth, fix my gaze on his, and balance myself.

Sweat drips down my temples, into my eyes. I blink it away. I'm not going to give in.

"Stop trying to compete with me, arsewipe," he grunts. "Your fitness levels are not bad for a pretty boy"—he huffs out a breath—"but your endurance levels leave much to be desired."

"Go fuck yourself," I growl out and set my jaw.

Our standoff continues. My calves protest. My forearms feel like they're being shredded to pieces.

"You going to give up?" he growls.

"You first," I snap.

We continue to hold each other's gaze. My stomach muscles tighten. Bile threatens to boil up my throat, but fuck if I'm going to be the first to give up.

His breathing comes in choppy heaves, sweat drips from his chin onto the floor, the tendons of his arms pop, then he jerks his chin. "On the count of three, you wanker."

Finally, fuck. I nod in response. "One."

"Two," he joins in.

"Three."

Both of us collapse on the floor. My muscles scream in relief, blood rushing to the parts that I abused trying to hold myself up.

"Bloody fuck," Knight pants.

"Indeed."

For a few seconds, there's only the sound of both of us panting and drawing in huge gasps of breath. Then, I push myself up to sitting. He follows.

"Fuck, that felt good." He shakes his hair and the sweat from his forehead hits me in the chin.

"Don't want your fucking bodily fluids on me," I grunt.

He laughs. "You're a fucking pussy."

"Just being hygienic, man."

"You stay locked up with five other men in a bunker for days while you wait for your orders to move, and you'll know the true meaning of hygienic."

I wince. "You're a fucking saint."

"Or a hedonistic sinner." He tosses me another bottle of water. I uncap it, and chug it down, before wiping the back of my palm across my mouth.

"I dropped her off at her place and watched until she climbed up the tree to her room." I toss back the rest of the water, then arc the bottle into the waste bin.

She'd told me she was only seventeen, but the reality only sank in when I watched her sneak back into the house. She then stood at her window and angrily waved me off before turning and disappearing inside. I stood there, looking at her window for a few more minutes before I finally turned and left.

"So, what was she doing wandering around on the beach in the middle of the night? If you hadn't been there..." His voice tapers off.

"No shit." Truth is, I can't bear to think of what would have happened if I hadn't been there. "I didn't have a chance to find out why she was wandering outside at that time." I snatch up my towel and mop my face. "But I intend to find out."

I rise to my feet and walk toward the doorway, when Knight calls out, "She's part of the Camorra."

I pause, "Camorra?" I frown at him over my shoulder.

"As in, the Mafia."

"And you know that how?"

He lowers his arms between his knees, "We visited her family a few years ago. Her father's dead now, but her brother is one vicious, deranged motherfucker who can't be reasoned with."

It's no secret Knight's father is part of an organized crime syndicate. It's one reason he signed up for the army—so he could make up for the sins of his father. It's also why I have no reason to doubt the accuracy of his information.

I nod in his direction, "All the more reason for me to visit her and make sure she's okay."

"The Mafia don't take kindly to strange men visiting one of their women," he warns.

I scoff, "They're not going to find out."

"And if they do?" He scowls.

I thrust out my chest, "I'm going, and that's that."

"Obstinate arsewipe." He glowers back. "If I can't stop you—" He shakes his head. "If you're not back in an hour—"

"Two—"

He throws up his hands. "What-fucking-ever. Two hours. If you're not back within two hours, I'm coming after you."

"What are you doing here?" She gapes up at me from her bed.

I waited until past midnight, then climbed up the tree to her room. It's a warm summer night, and the glass pane as well as the shutters on the window have been left open—thank fuck—so I swung inside the room, then padded over to stand over her sleeping form. I admit, I stared at her sleeping, like the creep I'm turning out to be. What else would you call a grown man who snuck into a teenager's bedroom? Then, pissed off with myself, I shook her awake.

Now, she springs up, and the thin sheet she covered herself with falls about her waist. I take in the camisole she's wearing and notice the outline of her tits is visible. She follows my line of sight and pulls the sheet up under her chin again. "You shouldn't be here," she whispers and tips up her chin.

"No kidding," I whisper back. I cross my arms across my chest. "I need answers."

"And if I don't want to give them?"

I scowl. "You owe me."

"Doesn't explain why you're breaking into my room at this time of the night."

"You still haven't explained what you were doing out at 2 a.m. last night," I snap.

She sets her jaw. "You're really not going to leave until I tell you." It's a statement not a question, so I don't answer. She continues to look at me for a few more seconds, then heaves a sigh. She pushes off her cover and swings her legs over the side of the bed, before she straightens. She's wearing the camisole with a pair of sleep shorts and when she lifts her hand to run her fingers through her blonde locks, a strip of skin is bared at her midriff. My cock instantly thickens—fuck. This girl is going to kill me with how my body reacts to her.

"Well, what is it? Why were you out?" I demand.

She lowers her arm and shoots me a dirty look. "I had a fight with my mother, if you must know. She shut me in my room, without food for twenty-four hours. I got pissed off, and first chance I got, decided I was going to run away."

I scoff, "You were running away from home in your pajamas?"

"I didn't think it through, okay?"

"Clearly you're not accustomed to using your brain."

"No reason to be impolite," She flattens her lips.

"If I hadn't turned up—"

"I know," she groans and throws up her hand. "Spare me the routine. It's not like you care or anything. You couldn't wait to throw me out of your place yesterday."

"You're a child."

"I'm not."

"You're nothing but a spoiled teenager who's trying to get back at her parents for trying to discipline her."

She sets her jaw. "You have no idea what you're talking about."

"Oh?"

She tilts her head. Her eyes gleam. Then she grips the edges of her camisole and pulls it up and off.

4

Solene

"The fuck are you doing?" he hisses. His voice is half shocked, half angry, but his gaze... His gaze is one-hundred percent lust-filled. I knew it would be, since the evidence of his arousal prodded me in that sensitive space between my legs last night. Or perhaps, even before that, when he came to my rescue on the beach, and I first glimpsed those vivid blue eyes of his eating me up like I was cotton candy, and he had a sweet tooth.

I'm still wearing my sleep-bra, but the way his gaze sears my flesh, the way my nipples tighten into pinpoints of want, the way my flesh seems to swell, I might as well be naked. Those blue eyes of his deepen to indigo, and I know, without a shadow of a doubt, he wants me.

"You want me; that's why you came here to my room tonight." My words seem so loud in the silence. But I'm not going to take it back. "Admit it," I whisper. I know what I saw. What I felt when I pressed myself against him and felt his hardness stab into the apex of my thighs. Thank god for smutty books! Which I'm not going to be able to read anymore, thanks to Ma searching my room and confiscating each and every one of them. On the other hand, maybe this is the time to try out everything I've learned from the novels. I push out my chest, so my breasts thrust up. I don't need to look down to know my nipples are hard and pebbled, and oh, god, they're throbbing for his touch.

His throat moves as he swallows. He stares at my boobs as if he's entranced, then takes a step forward. I bring up my palms to cup them, and a groan spills from his mouth. It seems to shake him out of the stupor he's fallen into, for he jerks his head up. A nerve pops at his temple. The muscles at his jaw flex with such intensity, it's a wonder he hasn't cracked a molar.

"Declan, I—"

"Don't," he snaps.

His voice is so harsh, I can't stop the gasp that spills from my lips.

He glares at me for a few seconds longer. The expression on his face is angry and tortured and full of passion. So much passion and yearning and a fervency that I know I'll remember for the rest of my life. My head spins. My heart jumps into my throat. Strange sensations gather in the bottom of my belly, but before I can say or do anything else, he wrenches his gaze off of me. He bends, snatches my camisole from the floor, and thrusts it at me. "Put this on." He turns his back.

"What the—? What are you doing?" I swallow.

"I'm trying to do the right thing, which, if you had half a brain, you'd recognize as being for your own good."

My cheeks flame. I stare at his broad back, at how his shoulders stretch the fabric of his shirt. He's rolled up the sleeves, and when he raises his hand to rub the back of his neck, the veins in his forearms stand out in relief. That same melting sensation grips my lower belly. A heavy pulse beats between my legs. Oh, god, why is the sight of this man affecting me so? Worse, why is he rejecting me? Does he have a girlfriend? Someone older, more sophisticated, more experienced, perhaps? Is that why he doesn't want me?

"Get out," I snap.

"Are you decent?"

"Fuck off."

"Cover yourself up, please," he says in a subdued, long-suffering voice. And now, I feel like the little girl he's convinced I am.

I pull my camisole on, then for good measure grab my sweatshirt and shrug into it.

He must sense my movements, for he finally turns and stabs a finger in my direction. "Don't go cavorting on the beach at 2 a.m. again."

"I will, if that's what I want to do."

He sets his jaw. "You need a spanking, little girl."

My toes curl. A frisson of heat sizzles up my spine. *No, no, no, I surely can't think that is hot? What is wrong with me?* I wrap my arms about my waist and glance away, hoping to mask the desire I'm sure is visible in my eyes. "Please leave."

The words fill the space between us. He stares at me for a second longer, then takes a step forward. So, do I.

"I really think you should go," I murmur without conviction.

He nods but makes no attempt to move. The air between us grows heavy. My breasts hurt, my thighs quiver, and I squeeze them together. He glances down at the movement and his breathing grows erratic. He folds his fingers into fists at his sides, then turns and stomps toward the window. That's it. He's going to leave, and I'll never see him again. I'll never know how it feels to run my fingers through his hair, to drag my knuckles against his whiskered jaw, to push my breasts into his chest, to feel that turgid length between his legs pushing into that delicate space between my legs, to kiss him… kiss him. KISS HIM.

"K-k-k-kiss me," I burst out.

He pauses at the window, his shoulders bunch, but he doesn't turn.

"Please, just one last goodbye kiss. That's all I'm asking for."

Every muscle in his body seems to tense, and the planes of his back flex under his shirt. My fingers tingle, and oh, god, oh, god, I need to touch him, one last time. I know it's wrong. I know I'm too young for him. But I can't let him leave. Not without having something more of him to hold onto.

I walk toward him, my bare feet a whisper against the wooden floor. I reach him and press my palm into the center of his back. He flinches but doesn't pull away. The heat of his body reaches out to me, embraces me, pulls me close. I push my cheek in between his shoulder-blades, and his muscles are so hard, I might as well be pressing into a wall. A living, breathing wall of steel-encased flesh that's so full of coiled tension, the vibrations leap off of him and flutter through my body. My core clenches. Moisture trickles out from between my thighs. He must sense the effect touching him has on me because he becomes as immovable as a granite side of a mountain.

"Declan," I whisper. I'm not sure what I want, or what to ask for. I'm not sure I can put into words what I'm experiencing right now. This yawning pit at the base of my stomach. This need to reach for something that's out of reach. This feeling of falling and being out of my depth, of being on the verge of something so forbidden, yet something that feels so right, surely, it can't be wrong. Surely, when everything in me insists I want this, I need this, I yearn for this… I can have it, right?

"No," he says in a gravelly voice. "I cannot do this." He shakes me off and leans forward in preparation to shove his leg over the windowsill, when I throw my arms about him.

"Please don't go. Pease, Declan. Just one kiss, that's all I'm a-a-asking for."

He freezes. Maybe it's my stammering that stops him from leaving. Maybe it's the absolute desperation in my voice that reaches something inside of him, but he pivots, then glares down at me from his superior height. I tip up my chin and my gaze connects with his now indigo eyes. They blaze with so much passion, so much emotion, so much frustration and lust and everything I'm feeling that a sob catches in my throat. I throw myself at him at the same time he moves toward me. I'm on my tiptoes and he has his arms about my waist, pulling me up,

Our mouths collide and our teeth clash. The kiss is messy and fervent and a meeting of tongues, a collision of breaths, an intertwining of everything we cannot have. I push into him, press my breasts so they're flattened against his unyielding chest. I lock my arms around him, trying to memorize how it feels to have my thighs against his, my center cradling that heavy weight between his thighs, my belly melting against his lean waist, the scent of him, the taste of him, the sound of his heart banging against his ribcage, the thrum of his pulse that mirrors the unevenness of my own. I close my eyes, open my mouth, and melt into him.

A growl rumbles up his chest. He locks his fingers around the nape of my neck, tilts his head, and thrusts his tongue even deeper into my mouth. He's eating me up. I'm burning up. I'm going to combust, I—

I'm torn off him and flung aside.

5

Declan

One second, we're kissing; the next, she's taken from me. She hits the ground and screams. I jump toward her, but the man who threw her off, steps in between us. *How did I not notice him enter the room? How did I not hear him walk toward us? Was I so engrossed in her I didn't realize there was someone else in the room?*

"Who the fuck are you?" he asks in heavily accented English. His looks are swarthy, his hair cut close to his scalp. The shape of his face is similar to hers, and his eyes are the same color, too. He seems older than me, but surely, he's too young to be her father.

Solene jumps up and throws herself at him. "Diego, l-leave him alone."

He raises his arm and catches her in the face. She screams again and falls to the floor with a thud.

The sound slices through my head, my heart. Anger surges through my veins, and blood pounds at my temples. "You hurt her? You fucking laid a hand on her?"

I throw up my fist and catch him in the chin. He staggers back, and a fierce satisfaction blooms in my chest. I raise my fist again, and this time, bury it in his nose. I feel the crunch of cartilage, and blood drips from his face. I follow it up with a blow to his side, then his stomach. He bends over, and this time, I raise my fist and catch him in an upper cut.

He groans; his entire body snaps up and back. I raise my arm, close my fingers into a fist and pull back, but Solene throws herself between us. "Stop, h-he's my b-brother! P-please don't hurt him, p-please d-don't."

I glare at her, then at the man who straightens, then rolls his neck. Fucker's powerfully built; only reason he's still standing. A weaker man would be on the floor by now. He grabs her by the shoulders and shakes her. "What were you doing with him? Did you fuck him?"

Solene cringes. She glances from her brother to me, then back to him.

Diego's features darken. "Did you lose your virginity to him. Did you—"

"N-n-no." she shakes her head. "N-no, you're mistaken, I-I-I—" She draws in a breath, "I-It's n-nothing like that."

"Then how is it?" He thrusts his face into hers. "Talk to me, little sister."

The color fades from her face. Her entire body shivers.

"Solene—" I growl.

"S-stop, d-don't come c-closer." Her voice rings out, her stutter more apparent than ever.

She tips up her chin, squares her shoulders, then addresses her brother. "He…he c-came in through the w-window. I d-d-don't know who h-he is. I've never s-s-seen him before in my l-life. He forced me to k-k-kiss him… It's n-not my f-f-fault, I-I swear."

My heart somersaults in my chest. My vision tunnels. *She's lying. Why the fuck is she lying?* Anger twists my guts. "Solene!" I take a step in her direction, when two more men burst into the room.

It seems to shake her out of her reverie for she turns to me. Her green eyes are luminous, her lips trembling. "Run," she mouths at me. Then she squeezes her eyelids shut and a teardrop squeezes out from the corner of her eye.

"Get that *pezzo di merda* and teach him a lesson he'll never forget," Diego snaps.

I shove myself out the window, and leap toward the tree outside her room. I grab hold of the branches, turning at the last moment to see her staring at me with tears streaking her face. Then, the men crowd the window. One of them reaches over to grab at the tree as I half slide, half fall down the length of the tree trunk. I hit the ground and lay there, winded for a few seconds. The shower of leaves tells me the men are right behind me. I jump up, try to run, then growl when my ankle gives out under me.

"Fuck, fuck, fuck." I hobble forward, dragging my wounded leg. One step, a second. A thump, and I know the first of the men have hit the ground. Another thump, then footsteps thud in my direction. I try to speed up, make it another few steps before someone slams into me.

I hit the ground and am turned over. I throw up my arms to protect my face, and a fist smashes into my chest. Fire lights a path to my brain. I wheeze, keep my arms raised as fists pummel my side, my chest. I curl into a ball, then manage to pull back my uninjured leg and kick out, catching the guy in the face.

He falls back. I manage to jump up, but the second man swings at me. His fist smashes into my forehead. Pain slashes through my head. Sparks flash behind my eyes, and fucking hell—*not my face, you bastards*—I lower my head and manage to head-butt him.

He staggers back, crashes into the first guy who's already rightened himself. He goes down again and doesn't move.

The second man swings at me, this time, landing an uppercut. Sparks explode behind my eyes. Blood drips from my mouth. I manage to straighten, and he lands a punch in my forehead.

The force throws me back. My body arcs through the air, and I hit the ground. He races toward me and kicks me in the side. I yell, but he kicks me again and again. I manage to grab his leg and twist. He falls to the ground. I kick his head, and he stops moving, only a third guy appears from out of nowhere.

He charges toward me. I kick his leg out from under him, and he hits the ground, only to jump up again.

Fucking hell. I manage to stagger to my feet, then land my fist in his face. Fucker's bigger than me. He absorbs the blow and keeps coming. I block his next hit, then he smashes his fist into my nose. There's a breaking sound, and blood pours down my chin. White throbbing flashes of agony shudder out to my extremities.

I throw up my fist, miss. He lands his next punch in the side of my head. Black spots flash before my eyes. The world tilts. I look up to find I'm on my back on the ground. The second guy grins down at me. At least, blood smears his teeth. *Motherfucking bastard.* He raises his leg, I grab at it, tug, and he hits the ground and stays still.

My panting fills my ears, and blood thuds at my temples. Every breath I take sends spears of agony screeching up my side. I try to rise up, but my arms and legs don't seem to be cooperating.

Then, the first guy I felled hobbles over to me. He raises his leg, and sneers at me. "You dare touch one of our girls? You're going to pay for it, you *testa di cazzo*!"

He brings his foot down toward my head, and everything goes dark.

I come awake with a start. White. Everything is white. The scent of antiseptic clogs my nostrils. I try to move, but pain slices through my side. I must groan, for a face appears in my line of sight.

"Easy, ol' chap," Knight murmurs.

"What happened? Am I in a hospital?"

"Indeed. You're back in Blighty."

"How?" I cough.

Knight's face disappears from view, only to reappear holding a bottle with a straw. "Here."

I sip from it, and when I'm done, he places it on the side table. "It didn't sit right that I'd let you go on alone. Within an hour of you leaving I came after you. I found them beating the shit out of you, and fuck if I didn't return the favor."

"Motherfuckers," I breath through the next wave of pain. "I should have done a better job of defending myself."

"You injured them; gave me a fighting chance to get the better of them. It's what saved your life."

"He's being modest. If he hadn't gotten you on a flight out of there with doctors in attendance to patch you up, you might have popped it, buddy," a new voice growls.

I groan, "Fuck, don't tell me; it's the prodigal son, himself."

"You bet." Cade slaps my shoulder. Bursts of white and red flare behind my eyes. I grit my teeth, refusing to give him the satisfaction of hearing my groan.

"The fuck you doing here?"

"Heard you got beat up; had to come see how your pretty face was faring."

Face. My face. I reach up to touch my forehead, then wince. I have a bandage around my forehead, and oh, I'm in a neck brace. Fucking hell. "How bad is it?" I snap.

Cade and Knight glance at each other. Neither speaks.

"How bad? Tell me."

Something passes between the two of them, then Knight turns to me. "I won't sugarcoat it—"

"Don't."

"It's bad."

"Right." I swallow. I wasn't lying when I told Solene I was narcissistic. I only came into my looks when I turned eighteen. Until then, I was a too-tall-for-my-age, bespectacled nerd with an IQ so high, it was both a blessing and a curse. It meant I got into Oxford at thirteen; it also meant I got bullied for everything. From my relative youth to my too-large-for-my age form, everything was fair game. Until I took part in a university play, and everything changed. I discovered I could go on stage and forget about who I was. I could assume any persona I wanted and become that character. One not saddled with a brain so powerful it was more of a liability. From there, it was only logical that I pursue the one profession which depended on my looks and my acting talent. The only thing I ever wanted was to become a successful actor and now—now it seems even that might be out of reach.

"The wound on your forehead is likely to scar. You also have a smaller gash on your cheek, a broken nose—which, if you're lucky, will heal without needing any more surgery to fix it. You have three broken ribs, a sprained neck, a cracked femur, a broken ankle, many lacerations—"

"And a concussion," Cade pipes in.

"Thanks, man." I narrow my gaze on him. "Aren't you supposed to be playing in some tournament or another?"

"Yes, but I'd rather be sitting here gloating over your wounds than facing down a ball. Besides, the prize money wasn't that big for this one."

"You need it, though."

Cade's working his way up the leagues. His goal is to play for the English cricket team. Of the three of us, he's the one who comes from an unprivileged background. Which means, he's also always strapped for cash.

"No big deal." Cade shrugs.

"It is a big deal. You didn't have to do this."

"Yes, I did." He sets his jaw.

"You could, at least, accept some help from me and Knight—"

"Not in a fucking blue moon." He folds his arms across his chest. I take in his set features, then nod.

"Thanks for coming, anyway."

"This over a chick?" he drawls.

I shoot Knight a sideways glance, then wince when that causes a dull thud of pain to pool between my eyes. "You tell him?" I snap.

"Not me." Knight raises a shoulder. "He came to that conclusion all by himself."

"You're all beat up, yet you haven't lost the fire in your eyes. It's a chick, all right." He smirks.

"I haven't lost the fire in my eyes because I'm pissed," I growl.

Cade whistles. "Whoa, Romeo, what did she do?" Then he raises his hands and says, "No, don't tell me. She get her father to send his men to beat you up?"

"Her brother, and fuck you, dickwad."

"Ooh, pretty boy finally finds his spine, eh?" Cade leans forward in his seat. "What're you going to do about it? You going to take revenge?"

"Revenge?" Knight glances between us. "Hold on, she's just a kid."

"She's seventeen."

"Seventeen?" Cade's jaw drops, then he barks out a laugh.

"She looks older."

"They always do, man." He rubs his jaw. "So, you blame her for what happened to you?"

"Hell, yes. Her brother caught us kissing; she started it."

Both men look at me with disbelieving glances.

"It's true. She took off her sleep shirt—thank, god I made her put it back on—then threw herself at me as I tried to leave and begged for a kiss."

"It's the begging that got you, huh?" Cade's grin widens.

"Shut the fuck up, arsehole. She started the kiss, then I couldn't stop, and that's how her brother found us."

"No wonder he sent his men after you." Knight narrows his gaze on me. "If I caught a stranger with his hands all over my little sister, I'd beat him up, too."

Cade shoots him a glance. The expression on his face is one I can't read. Then he clears it from his features. "So, you're going to let it go, considering this could change the shape of your future?"

I draw in a breath. "I'll have to see a plastic surgeon and try to patch things up."

"Things will never be the same," he warns.

"You think I don't know that?" I glance away. The beauty from untouched skin is unparalleled, you can never replicate it by going under the knife.

"She probably panicked. She might look older, but she's still seventeen," Knight reminds me.

"Oh, she knew what she was doing. She told her brother she didn't know me, and that"—I tip up my chin—"that I forced myself on her."

"Fuck." Knight's voice hardens.

"Jesus!" Cade jumps up to his feet and begins to pace. "That's a right mess you got yourself into."

"No wonder, her brother wanted to kill you," Knight says slowly.

"And he would have if you hadn't come to my rescue," I murmur.

"What are friends for, huh?" Knight holds up his fist, and I manage to raise mine and bump it. Sweat beads my brow with the effort, but I ignore it.

"I'm not condoning what she did, but I still think she was too young to know better." Knight rolls his shoulders. "She gave in to her fear and wasn't fully aware of what would happen."

"Whose side are you on?" Cade slaps his thigh. "Check out his face. See how much he's going to suffer as a result of what happened that one night. His life is never going to be the same, you get me?"

I hear the pain and anger in Cade's voice. I know he's remembering something similar that happened to him. He's never shared the details, but I know there are things in his past he hasn't forgiven or forgotten, either.

Knight looks between me and Cade, then firms his lips.

"I take responsibility for what happened." My muscles bunch, and every part of my body seems to protest. "I shouldn't have gone to her room. I don't know what possessed me to do that. I just couldn't leave without seeing her one last time, you know?" I force myself to relax, then draw in another breath. "I understand she was spooked by her brother finding us and that she wanted to save herself. What I can't forgive is her telling him that she didn't know me."

"What else was she supposed to do? Tell him that she was the one who initiated the kiss?" Knight folds his arms across his chest. "Do you understand what that could mean for a girl who's part of the Mafia"

Cade stares. "Did you say, Mafia?"

"His girl's a Mafia princess." Knight nods in my direction.

Cade whistles, then turns to me. "You hit the bullseye, huh?"

At the same time, I protest, "She's not my girl."

"Let's keep it that way." Knight touches my arm. "It's best you put this behind you and move on. You need to focus on recovering, then on building your career."

"Or what's left of it," I scoff.

"Didn't take you for a defeatist." He frowns.

"Tell that to the casting agents who're looking for the next perfect face."

"Maybe the scars will add character, give you a depth the others don't have. Help you stand apart in the sea of symmetrical visages," Knight offers.

"Man here's an optimist, but in this case, I have to agree with him." Cade drums his fingers on his chest. "In any case, is a scar on your face going to stop you from pursuing a career in Hollywood?"

"Hell, no," I growl.

"That's what I thought." Cade's lips twitch.

"It's not going to be easy, but nothing can stop me from going after what I want." And that includes finding a way to get back at the Mafia princess.

6

A year later

Solene

"The weather is hotter than Naples." I place my hands in my lap.

Massimo glances up from his perusal of his phone. "I'll take your word for it." He goes back to texting.

O-k-a-y, when you have to resort to talking about the weather things are dire. But how else am I to open a conversation with someone I don't know at all? Someone who's much older than me. Someone who I met only a few days ago. Someone I'm engaged to and am going to marry very soon.

"It's so nice of you to organize this dinner with my sister and her fiancé," I offer. Yep, not only am I engaged, but Olivia, too, now has a fiancé, and this is supposed to be a get to know each other dinner, which Massimo took the initiative to plan.

"Nice?" Massimo tilts his head, without taking his gaze off that infernal phone. "Trust me when I say that was far from my intention in organizing this dinner."

"Oh." I hunch my shoulders. What do I say to that? What does he mean by saying his intentions were not what they seemed to be on the surface? I glance away, then back at him. "Palermo is much more beautiful than Naples," I murmur.

OMG, how pathetic. Now you're comparing the two cities. Of course, Palermo's a more scenic space; it's smaller than my hometown but has a lot more money. It's why crime is rife there and why my family was able to hold sway for so long. I drum my fingers on the table.

"I haven't seen much of the city. Do you think you'll have time to show me around?"

Massimo finally glances up at me. "I'm sorry, I've been a shit fiancé, haven't I?"

I blink, then look away. "It's fine, I know you must be busy with matters of the Cosa Nostra."

Yep, Massimo belongs to the clan who were once bitter rivals of my father's, which is how this engagement came about. I knew I'd be a bargaining piece, but I couldn't have predicted my wedding arrangement would carry this much significance.

He widens his stance. "I'm sorry you didn't get to have a say in who you're going to marry."

"Neither did you." I wince. I didn't mean to say that. I mean, that's what crossed my mind the moment I noticed Massimo didn't seem particularly happy at our engagement, but I should have learned by now that one does not go around voicing everything one thinks. You'd think after the pains my family took to drill that into me over the years, I'd have learned my lesson, but nope, the link between my brain and my mouth is often tremulous. It means, I tend to speak my mind at the most inopportune moment, like now.

"What makes you say that?" he asks slowly.

The fact that you couldn't stop looking at my sister, for one. Yeah, at my engagement, my sister Olivia burst in to congratulate me. My sister defied my mother to leave home to become an actress. That was when my father was alive, and he believed in her. But after my father passed away, my brother and mother ensured I submitted to the role of a Mafia princess. They made sure I didn't spend any extended periods of time with my sister, even when she visited. They wanted to use me in an arranged marriage to further Diego's ambitions within the organized crime syndicate network.

They impressed upon me how much they were depending on me to come through for them, since my sister couldn't be counted on. I was high-spirited, but when it came down to it, the need to make my family happy weighed heavily on me, which is why I agreed to this engagement. I hoped my fiancé might come to love me over a period of time, but that hope flew out the window when Olivia walked into my engagement party.

I saw how Massimo couldn't take his gaze off of her, how he followed her out of the room when she left, much to everyone's chagrin. My family were upset by what he did, but I didn't care. How could I, when not a day goes by that I don't remember Declan, when I don't regret what I did to him? I hoped his memory would fade with time, but his face is still the last thing I see before I fall asleep, and his name is my first thought every morning.

"I'm sorry; I didn't mean that," I murmur.

Massimo's eyebrows draw down, then he leans forward and says, "You're an obedient girl; you care for your family. It's why you agreed to their demands."

"I do respect my family, and I've been brought up in the ways of the Camorra. I know it's my duty to make a good match for them, however —" I place my fingers on his shoulder. My pulse rate shoots up, but I ignore it. I may have agreed to my parent's demands, but I'm never going to be someone who'll take things lying down. I tip up my chin. "Just because I'm a blonde doesn't mean I'm stupid."

His gaze narrows, then he laughs lightly. "You're not as compliant as you come across, are you?"

"Nope." I half smile. OMG, thank god, he has a sense of humor. He'll make Olivia a very good husband. A-n-d that's the issue. It's clear there's something going on between the two of them, but even if there weren't, I can't see this guy as my husband. I can't. I can't see anyone except the man whose name I will not permit myself to think of as my husband.

The hair on the back of my neck rises. I look up, and as if summoned from the depths of my subconscious, I meet a pair of azure blue eyes. The same eyes that have haunted my dreams and my waking moments and made me change my personality; change the trajectory of my life as punishment for what I allowed to happen to him. The same eyes I've seen on film posters in the city so I know he made good on his dream, which I knew he would, for I sensed that steely determination in him when we met.

His hair is shorter than when I met him, his jawline more pronounced. His cheekbones seem to have gotten more angular, if that's possible. There's also a scar across the right side of his forehead. That wasn't there the last time I saw him. It's also not evident in the posters I've seen with him on them. Guess he must use make up to cover the worst of it.

How did he get it, though? Did that happen when my brother's men beat him up? I clench my fingers together.

Not a day goes by when I don't regret what I accused him of. At least now, I can tell him. I begin to rise to my feet, but Declan's gaze narrows. His eyes widen in recognition, then harden until they become almost silver. Chips of ice that would jab me and freeze me. His jaw tightens. Even across the distance in the restaurant, I can feel the waves of hate that shimmer off of him. I swallow, and my butt hits the chair. Declan wraps his fingers around the wrist of the woman walking in front of him. *He's holding Olivia's hand? He's with my sister? No, no, no, this can't be happening.*

I track their approach toward the table, but when I glance at my sister, her gaze is locked with Massimo's. I turn my gaze on Declan to find he still hasn't looked away from me. I swallow. Oh, god, this is not what I was expecting. Why did I agree to this dinner? They come to a halt in front of our table, and for a few seconds, no one speaks. The tension is so thick in the air, it presses down on my shoulders. The band around my chest tightens. A heavy weight sinks to the bottom of my stomach.

This is it; all my sins come home to roost. I've often wondered what it would be like to meet Declan again. What would I tell him? What would he say? Would I ever throw my arms about him and climb him like I wanted to that day? I never thought when I met him again, I'd be engaged and he… He'd be with my sister. Declan is engaged to Olivia, and oh, my god, is this the universe's way of sticking it to me?

Is this my punishment for what I did to him? He could have been killed, but I was so worried about saving my own skin that I didn't think about what could happen to him. And why does he look even more gorgeous, bigger, wider, taller? His shoulders look like they are going to burst out of his suit jacket, his biceps stretch the sleeves, and his pants cling to his powerful thighs like they were stitched using him as a live model.

He shifts his stance, and I glance up to find he's smirking at me. His eyes though... They're cold, hard, merciless. What happened to the man I met? That softness in him that had called out to me. That empathy I sensed in him when he assured me he'd never hurt me. That sensitivity that touched his features and declared that he was a romantic at heart. That...gentleness in his eyes with which he surveyed me like I was the most exquisite creation he'd ever seen.

The silence stretches, and my nerve endings chafe. My muscles are so tight, a headache begins to knock behind my eyes. Every part of my body feels like it's so tightly wound up, I'm surely going to explode unless I do something to defuse the situation. Say something, anything. I jump up to my feet. "Livvy, you look beautiful," I burst out.

My sister's face breaks into a smile. "And you look angelic." She moves around the table, takes me by the face and kisses me on both cheeks.

"This must be your sister," Declan says from behind her. That low, deep voice sends my pulse-rate sky high. My toes curl. No, no, no, I can't have this reaction to him. Not when he's my sister's fiancé now. I risk a glance at him, and his lips curl. There's a look of satisfaction on his features. Damn him, but he's aware of exactly how much of a disadvantage I am at here. Did he know I was Olivia's sister? Was he aware he would meet me when he agreed to this dinner?

Olivia takes a step back, and still holding my hand, turns to him. "This is my sister Solene. Solene, this is Declan, my—"

"You're Declan Beauchamp, the movie star." I tip up my chin. He may have taken me by surprise, but damn, if I'm going to allow that to silence me. "Livvy, why didn't you tell me your fiancé was someone famous?" I tug my hand out from her grasp and hold it in his direction.

It forces him to let go of his hold on her—good. He touches my hand, and sparks of electricity shoot up my arm. My stomach ties itself up in knots. Liquid heat shoots through my veins. Heat flushes my face, and I try to look away, I do, but it's as if my gaze is locked with his.

Something sparks deep in his eyes. Those blue eyes of his turn indigo. The way they did that night when I realized he was attracted to me. He must feel the same sensations I do, for the tendons of his throat flex. He holds my gaze for a few seconds more, then one side of his mouth curls. He chuckles, as if it's all one big joke, then bends and kisses my fingers. "At your service."

My blush intensifies. Declan straightens, an intense expression sparking in his eyes. The seconds stretch, then Olivia clears her throat. I blink. Declan's jaw hardens. He releases my hand and turns to Massimo.

"You must be the lucky man," he growls.

Massimo ignores his proffered hand. "I still don't see a ring." He directs the comment at Olivia. Huh? Did they already have a conversation about her engagement ring?

She nudges Declan, who raises a shoulder. "Uh, yeah, we don't believe in a ring to be engaged," he murmurs.

Massimo's gaze narrows. "I thought you said your ring was being resized?"

"Eh?" Declan blinks rapidly.

Olivia nudges him again, and he coughs. "That's what I meant. The ring is being resized. But whether she's wearing a ring or not is not the point. We don't need it to proclaim the veracity of our love, do we now, darlin'?"

"Exactly what I meant, darling." She wraps her hand around Declan's bicep, then meets Massimo's gaze. Massimo glances down at where she clutches at Declan. A muscle leaps at his jaw. A nerve throbs at his temple. He looks like a man on the verge of committing a crime. That's how angry he is with the suggested intimacy between my sister and Declan. I sneak a sideways glance at Declan to find he's glaring at me. Oh, hell, this is going to be interesting. Downright messy, I suspect.

Olivia gestures toward the chairs. "Let's all sit down, shall we?"

"It's you and me now, huh?" I glance toward Declan, then wish I hadn't, for he's glaring at me with a look that implies he's really pissed off with me. Not that I blame him.

As the dinner progressed, Massimo and Olivia dropped all pretense that they were both engaged to someone else and had eyes and ears and words only for each other. This escalated until they had a conversation where they couldn't stop taking digs at each other. Then Massimo excused himself, apparently, to go off and cool his temper, and Olivia rushed after him.

The silence stretches. Declan continues to glower. I open my mouth, then shut it. What am I going to say anyway? That I'm sorry for what I did? Is it going to make a difference, at all?

I take a sip of my ice water, then glance at the bottle of wine with longing. Now is the time I could do with something more to shore up my courage. But I've never drunk alcohol before. My mother and brother forbid it—except for the occasional family celebration where everyone received a few sips to join the toast. And let's face it, it made the gatherings more bearable. Even then, I sometimes found myself getting a little tipsy from those mouthfuls. So, I'm not sure now is the time I want to start drinking; not when Declan is scowling at me from across the table.

"Are you really engaged to Olivia?" I venture.

"What do you care?" he growls. A vein pops at his temple. The muscles below his jawline flex and, good god, if he grits his teeth any harder, he's going to crack a molar.

The tension between us ratchets up. The air is so thick with unsaid emotions, it seems to press down on my chest. Sweat pools under my armpits. My nerves are so stretched, my teeth are so on edge, I'm going to scream any moment. I squeeze my fingers together in my lap , "That's not fair. You know I did care about you."

"We hardly knew each other. We met, what was it, once?"

"Twice."

"Oh, yes, the second time is when you told your brother that you didn't know me, and I had broken into your room with a view to hurting you."

I flinch. "Don't say that, please."

"It's true, isn't it? That's what you told him—that I was forcing you against your will."

"I didn't mean it."

"Sure you did," he leans forward in his chair. "I was beaten up so badly by your brother's men, I needed twenty stitches and reconstructive surgery on my face to revise the worst of what the blemish left behind. Not to mention, the broken ribs, a sprained neck, a cracked femur and the broken ankle I sustained. I was in the hospital for weeks, then needed physical therapy for months to regain full movement."

I flick my gaze up to the scar on his face, then back at him. "I'm so sorry, Declan. I didn't mean for that to happen. I saw my brother and was so afraid he'd be angry at me. If he knew that I was willingly kissing you, there's no telling what he would have done to me."

"Instead, you decided you didn't care what he and his henchmen did to me?" he snarls.

"I didn't think he'd set his men on you—"

"Lies, all lies." He slaps his palm on the table and the plates jump. One of the forks slides off and hits the ground with a clash. I flinch again.

"Stop acting like you're this innocent princess, when we both know that's not true."

"I don't know what you mean."

"Oh?" He bares his teeth. "You took off your top and came at me. You threw yourself at me. You begged me to k-k-k-kiss you, don't you remember?"

Tears prick the backs of my eyes. My heart feels like it's going to shatter. Is it because he's mocking my stammer and how I begged him to place his lips on mine? Or is it because he's nothing like the gentle, tender, protective man I remember? Physically, he's so different. So much harder, so much more solid and inflexible and impenetrable. Even his face looks meaner, the scar adding a world-weariness and cynicism that wasn't there. Is it because of what I did? Because I accused him of something he didn't do? Because I was too afraid of my brother to bear the consequences of my actions? Because I couldn't bear the thought of more punishment? Because I couldn't bear for my brother to think I was spoiled goods. Because I wanted to gain my family's approval? My entire life has been dedicated to making them happy. So much so, I pushed away the only man I knew could have meant something to me.

"I was a kid. I got scared. I'm sorry I told him I didn't know you. I panicked, okay?"

He draws in a breath, then runs his fingers through his hair. "I'm sorry I wasn't around to help you out. What happened to me that day wasn't your fault. I knew you were a kid. I know a lot of what happened wasn't your fault. It was mine. I came to your room. Me, a grown-ass man, and I came creeping into your room because I couldn't leave without saying goodbye. That was my mistake."

"No, it wasn't. I'm glad you did. I would have been devastated if you'd left without seeing me one last time."

He lowers his hand, then places his fingertips together. "I'm not sure changing the trajectory of my career was worth it."

"Wh-what do you mean?"

"Thanks to this scar, which not even plastic surgery could remove completely, I couldn't get leading man roles. It's what brought Olivia and me together."

Of course. Olivia suffered an accident that inflicted a scar on her face. As a result, she, too, has struggled to find roles. And now, he's engaged to her and—I glance up at him. "You didn't answer my question."

"Not sure I owe you any answers," he drawls.

"You do, on this one." I hold his gaze, "Olivia... Are you really engaged to her?"

7

Declan

Yes, say yes. Say you are engaged to her sister. "No, I'm not," I say through gritted teeth.

A breath whooshes out of her, some of the tension in her shoulders seems to fade. I glance down at the ring on her left hand. "You, however, are engaged to the man she loves."

She blinks, but other than that, there's no other visible reaction on her features. Did she already know? Did she suspect that Olivia loves Massimo?

"You don't seem surprised?" I place my palm flat on the table.

She looks away, then back at me. "I saw the way they looked at each other, so no… I'm not surprised."

"You're still going to marry him?" Anger squeezes my chest so hard I see flashes behind my eyes. Jesus Christ, why is the thought of her marrying someone else winding me up so much?

"I—" She lowers her chin. "I'm not sure what to do."

"You still trying to do what your family asks of you?"

She jerks up her head. "They're my family. I love them. Of course, I'm going to follow what they say. Besides, it's not like I have a choice.

I'm dependent on them. If I refuse what they ask of me, they'll disown me."

"Would that be so bad?"

Something sparks in her eyes, lending them the brilliance that had entranced me from the beginning. Then, just as suddenly, it fades away, leaving a bleakness. "Yes. No. I don't know. This was supposed to be the happiest time of my life—being engaged, planning my wedding, looking toward the future—now I'm not so sure."

Her eyes gleam with moisture, and my heart stutters. A hot sensation twists my insides and a hollowness yawns in my stomach. Goddamn her. From the moment I came across her fighting to get away from those men on the beach, a part of me has belonged to her. I knew her only for thirty-six hours, but it was enough to change the course of my life. I raise my hand and touch the jagged scar on my forehead. I wasn't lucky that day. The injuries I suffered that day left their mark on me, in more ways than one. It's why I'm here—to make her pay. And I can't forget that—no matter how much her proximity affects me.

"Don't bother with those fake tears. They don't affect me."

"They're not fake," she sniffles.

"They were fake that day when you thrust yourself between me and your brother, when you accused me of something I hadn't done."

"Y-you're never going to let me forget that, are you?"

"Nope." I make a popping sound at the end of the word. "Not as long as I live, babe."

She swallows, then locks her fingers together on the table. "I deserve that. What I did to you was wrong. But I was only seventeen."

"Older than the age of consent in your country, so clearly, you knew what you were doing when you tried to climb me like a tree."

"It was teenage hormones," she bursts out.

"And is it hormones that's making you want to continue your engagement with a man who's in love with another?"

"Th-that's duty." She sighs. "B-besides, what choice do I have? I can refuse to marry him, but that's not going to make a difference. It's not like I c-can run away."

It's the first time her stammer is evident. I noticed it when I went to her room that day, but assumed she'd overcome it. Apparently, it only arises when she is in a state of high emotion, like now.

"And if you could?" I drag my thumb under my bottom lip. "What if I gave you a way out?"

"Eh?" She scrutinizes my features and asks, "What are you saying?"

"You wanted to become a singer, if I recall."

"Childish dreams," she scoffs.

"I heard you that day on the beach. You have a unique voice."

She raises a shoulder. "Lots of people are talented; doesn't mean they all get to use it or make a career out of it."

"I don't know about them, but I do know this"—I reach forward and place my hand over both of hers—"it would be a pity if you didn't share your voice with the world. It would be wrong if you hid away here, and spent your life married to someone who doesn't want you. It would be a serious error if you didn't take this opportunity I'm offering you."

"You're offering me an op-p-p-portunity?"

I nod. "Come with me to LA."

"What?" She gapes at me. "W-what do you mean?"

"Just that. Come with me to the city where dreams are made. Try your luck. I'll even use my contacts and introduce you around to the right people."

"You're j-joking."

"I'm not. This is your chance, Solene, to make all of your dreams come true." When I mentioned LA to her the first time we met, I saw her eyes light up. Not that she'll necessarily go for this proposition, but my instinct says the fiery girl who stepped between me and her brother—before pretending she never met me—had too much determination in her to not want to do something with her talent. And I didn't lie when I told her how distinctive her voice was. I fully intend to introduce her around to the right people in LA. Of course, she'll have to trust me enough to come with me and live with me, which means, she'll be at my mercy. And while I'll support her efforts, whether she'll be successful in making a career out of her singing or not will be up to her hard work and luck. She changed the trajectory of my life; it's only right I do the same for her.

"Why should I trust your offer? Why should I come with you, especially after you made it clear you hold me responsible for what happened to your face?"

I curl my lips. "Because your fiancé prefers your sister over you."

Her face falls. My heart lurches at the look of hurt that crosses it, but I push aside my emotions. This is right. I'm doing her a favor by offering her a ticket to LA. I'm giving her a chance to fulfill her dreams, after all. And if, along the way, I have the opportunity to take revenge for what she did to me, then that's a fringe benefit. She owes me, after all.

"If you stay back, you lose face. You're spoiled goods. No one is going to marry you now. You don't have a choice." I push back my seat and begin to rise, but she swoops down and grabs my arm. "W-where are you going?"

"To find out what's keeping *your* fiancé and *my* fiancée."

"Olivia..." She narrows her gaze. "Did you befriend Olivia so you could get to me? Did you know she was my sister when you met her?"

I allow myself a small smile. "Now, that would be telling." I try to pull away, but she tightens her grip.

"How dare you pretend to be engaged to her! How dare you play with her life? It's me you have a grudge with, not her."

I stare at her fingers, then back at her face.

You'll address me as Master when it's just the two of us. You will keep your eyes lowered, unless I give you permission to look at me.

She releases her grasp at once. Good. It's important she know her place in the scheme of things. She may still pretend to be an innocent Mafia princess, but I've changed. My inclinations and proclivities have changed, thanks to that one incident which altered the course of my life.

I set my jaw. "My relationship with your sister is separate from my non-relationship with you."

She winces.

"Olivia is my friend, and I'm only helping her out —against my better judgment—because she asked me to." I roll my shoulders. *Why the hell am I justifying myself to her? I don't owe her anything.*

"She asked you to—" Her forehead clears. "I see, she's trying to—"

"Make Massimo jealous enough that he'll break up with you? Yes."

She opens and shuts her mouth. "I don't understand. Why didn't she just talk to me?"

"For the same reason you didn't confide in her? I assume she's as petrified of your brother as you are."

"With good reason. If Diego gets wind of the fact she's pretending to be engaged to you, he'll be furious."

"We'll let Massimo deal with that, shall we?"

Her frown deepens. "Do you know something I don't?"

I raise my hands. "What are you talking about?"

"For someone who's walked into the middle of a business arrangement, you're too calm."

"I've come too far for things to not go my way." I smirk.

"You're awfully confident that I'm coming with you to LA."

"That's because you're thinking of it right now. You know this is your last chance to make something of your life. You're not going to let go of it."

She juts out her chin. "You don't know me at all."

"I know when you set your mind on something, you'll do everything in your power to get it."

She half laughs. "All this based on our very limited interaction."

I've seen you up close, Solene. I've smelled the scent of your arousal. I've tasted your lips. Felt as you ground yourself on my cock. If I'd let you that first night, you'd have come all over my tented crotch and created a mess. You'd have gone down on your knees and sucked my dick and begged me to empty myself down your throat, if I'd allowed you to.

"You took off your camisole and threw yourself at me. You kissed me—"

She swallows. "You kissed me back." Her lips part. She's remembering that kiss. So am I. The fusing of our lips. The clash of teeth. The sweet scent of her arousal that sank into my skin and haunted me for days.

I scoff, "And there's not a single day I don't regret it."

She sets her jaw. "Well, I don't."

"You should. I had no business being in that room with you."

"But I wanted you there." She leans forward in her seat. "And I'm sorry I lied to my brother. If I could go back and change things, I would."

"And been beaten up along with me? No, you did the right thing. I was bitter for a long time afterward at what happened..."

"And now—?"

"Now? I wish I never came with Olivia."

The color leaches from her face. "You don't mean it."

"I only found out you were Olivia's sister when she called me for help. She wanted me to pose as her fiancé. I couldn't say no. I thought knowing I was going to see you beforehand would help steel me against the impact of seeing you again, but—"

"But?"

"But, seeing you is bringing back just how stupid I was. You were a child then, and while you're eighteen now, you're still innocent in many ways."

She lowers her chin to her chest. "All the more reason I shouldn't come with you."

"All the more reason you should come with me." I allow my lips to twitch.

"Why's that?"

"I'm probably the one man who won't take advantage of you."

She firms her lips. "I'm not that innocent."

I scoff. "The very fact that you're trying to claim otherwise tells me you are."

Color flushes her cheeks. She opens and shuts her mouth as if she's unable to form the words she's thinking in her head.

"You're safe with me. Our relationship will be strictly professional."

She narrows her gaze. "Why do I not believe you?"

I raise a shoulder. "Believe what you want. One thing is true though..."

"What?"

"I'm your one shot at making something of yourself, which is why you're coming to LA with me."

8

Solene

I got on the flight with him to LA.

Not that there was ever any doubt I was going to do that. It was my dream come true. What I've wanted since I turned five and burst into song, which surprised my mother who promptly told me, no way, was I to sing in front of anyone else. Singing as a profession is right up there with prostitution, if you were to believe them. She'd already decided my future lay in becoming a compliant Mafia wife. A part of me resented being told that. I rebelled against it in my own way… Until my actions resulted in Declan's beating. I took that as a sign to give up on my dream and make my family happy instead. Meeting him again unleashed the real me—the part I'd subsumed for all these years.

Then, there's the fact that Massimo and my brother Diego got into an altercation and Massimo shot him point blank. Y-e-a-p, that happened. I should be shocked. Only, growing up in the Mafia, death is no longer a stranger. Still, to see him crumple to the ground in front of my eyes was enough to convince me I had to get out of that place.

After Diego's death, Massimo decided to marry Olivia, and make no mistake, I'm happy for the two of them. Going by how they couldn't keep their gazes off each other throughout the wedding ceremony and reception, it was clear the two were destined to be together. They love each other and I'm not going to stand in their way.

As for me? My destiny is somewhere far from this place. Whether it's with Declan or not is something I'm going to find out. For the time being, he's afforded me passage to a future I've dreamed of, and I'd be a fool not to accept it. I can't wait to get away from my family and their underworld connections and start afresh. Moving to a country a continent away where no one knows me sounds perfect. We waited until the end of the ceremony, then Declan told me we were leaving. I was already packed and ready.

Now, I glance out the window of the private jet he ushered me onto. To think, I've never been on a plane before; but even with my limited experience, I can tell that my surroundings are plush. The carpet is thick, the fittings gleam, and the seats are covered in leather so soft, they seem to mold to my form.

Since boarding the plane, Declan hasn't said a word. He's in the seat next to me, despite the rest of the plane being empty. The heat of his body is a furnace that draws me in; that dark chocolate and coffee scent of his permeates my senses. He's a large, solid presence—immovable, unshakable, and currently, asleep. He closed his eyes and seemed to drift off before the plane began its taxi.

I drag my gaze over the contours of his upper lip, which somehow, seems thinner and meaner than when I saw him last. Fine lines bracket his mouth. I can't remember him having them. Of course, they only add to his presence, giving him a look of worldliness tinged with cynicism that lends him an air of tantalizing experience.

His neck is thicker, the veins more pronounced. Has he been working out? Duh, of course he has; he's a movie star. And it shows, given the outline of his pecs through the sweatshirt he changed into before we left.

His waist is definitely narrower, and his thighs—OMG, his thighs are more powerful, the muscles sturdier, like he's been doing tons of squats or whatever it is men do to bulk up their lower body. As for the tent over his crotch, I swallow. Was that area so pronounced? I can't remember. To be honest, there's not much left of that young man I met on the beach in Naples. This one would have beaten the stuffing out of my brother's bodyguards. The man I remember has been replaced by an older, more mature man of the world who's also famous. Good thing, too, or my brother might have recognized him.

"Wanna touch?"

"What?" I jerk my chin up and find those iridescent blue eyes fixed on me. This close, I can make out the dark center surrounding the pupil, which is almost as black. And the black striations of his irises, combined with the scar on his forehead, and those high cheekbones, lend him a chillingly mean appearance.

I swallow. This is Declan—the man who'd saved you from being assaulted, after all. He may pretend he's changed, but surely, inside, he's still the same man. The one you fantasized about under the covers with your fingers between your legs. Since every one of my spicy books was confiscated, the only thing I had left to go on was my imagination, and it's amazing how creative one can get when left to one's devices for so much of the day. I wrote out many of my thoughts... rambling lines and words that I strung together into tunes I hummed to myself in the privacy of my shower. If my mother or brother had caught me singing, they'd have punished the heck out of me. I wasn't taking that chance, not after what happened that day with Declan.

I learned my lesson. I knew then, my fate was sealed, and it was futile to resist. I decided I was going to conform and follow the plan laid out for me by my family. I never thought things would change, that I'd have the chance to pursue the dream I had as a young girl. Not until Declan came back into my life.

Something sparked in me then. The ghost of that defiant girl I thought I'd banished forever emerged and insisted I follow my inclination. It was now or never. And with my brother gone, there was no one to hold me back. Sure, my mother wasn't happy that I decided to leave, but without my brother's support, and with Massimo taking over as head of the family, she couldn't stop me. So here I am, enroute to LA with my childhood crush. Who hates me.

"My cock? Do you want to touch it? Isn't that what you were thinking?" Declan drawls.

I gape, "Wh-what do you mean?"

He smirks, "You were staring at my crotch, and your thoughts were plainly written on your face."

"Was not."

His lips curl. "All your emotions are reflected on your features. You can't hide what you're feeling. Which is probably your only saving grace."

I firm my lips. "So, this is why you wanted me along? So I can become your personal punching bag?"

"Among other things," he drawls.

"Oh, my god, you don't even have the decency to deny it?"

"Why should I? You'll always get the unvarnished truth from me... babe."

I open my mouth to tell him off again, but what's the point? With the mood he's in, he'll probably only turn it around and make it all my fault.

"You still didn't answer the question."

"What question?"

"Wanna touch my— "

"No." I cross my arms across my chest. "I thought we weren't going to... you know— "

"Fuck?"

My cheeks heat. "Exactly."

"No fucking doesn't mean no touching."

"What?" My blush deepens.

"A-n-d I rest my case about how innocent you are." He pulls out his phone and begins to scroll down the screen.

Guess I've been dismissed then.

I glance out the window at the cityscape far below. *Why don't I feel a shred of apprehension leaving with this almost-stranger? Why don't I feel down about leaving my home-country behind? Why am I not more scared about the future? Why do I feel like I have only now started living? Not being held back by my family, or the oppressive society I grew up in?* I draw in a deep breath and my lungs inflate. The oxygen rushes into my blood and my head spins a little. It's as if I've been reborn. Emerging from a womb where I was sheltered and controlled for too long. I shoot a sideways glance and take in the scar at his forehead. *How deep was the wound that caused that? How much did it hurt?*

"It didn't hurt that much. Unfortunately, that didn't stop the scar from forming."

I stiffen. "I didn't ask."

He glances up at me. "You were thinking so loudly, I could hear you."

"You don't know what I'm thinking.'

"You're nothing, if not predictable."

"Oh?" I tilt my head. "What am I thinking about right now?"

He peruses my features. "You're thinking how much you want to get on your knees and suck my cock."

I flush. Heat twists my belly. A heavy pulse springs to life between my legs. Oh, god, his filthy words are better than the ones I read in those books. Now, I remember why I liked those novels so much. All those dirty talking, morally grey heroes made me feel funny in my lower regions. But none of them turned me on as much as Declan, with his hard, gravelly voice, that mean look in his eyes, and a demeanor implying he hates me so much, he's going to turn my life to dust. I swallow, then square my jaw. "You're wrong."

"Oh?" He smirks.

"I'm not thinking it; I'm doing it right now."

9

Declan

With that, she unhooks her seatbelt and drops to her knees in front of me.

Interesting. I should be shocked. No, I am shocked by her forwardness, but only because this is Solene—the girl I thought was innocent, the girl I know was a virgin when I last saw her, the girl responsible for turning my life upside down.

I've had plenty of women since then. I tried to drown out the lure of those green eyes by burying my cock in as many warm holes as I could find, but nothing helped. I need closure. I need to face that specific ghost from my past and put it to rest. Which is why I offered to take her to LA with me. I'm helping her find herself; but more importantly, I'll finally get over my obsession with her. Seeing her every day will be a kind of exposure therapy. Soon, I'll be able to flush her out of my system. That was my rationale. It didn't include her kneeling in front of me with a half-eager, half-terrified look in her eyes.

"The fuck you doing, Solene?" I growl.

Take it out. Now, squeeze it from base to crown and lick off the precum. Good girl. That's it. Now take it all the way, until you choke on it, until I can wrap my fingers around your neck and feel my shaft ensconced by the walls of your throat.

Without taking her gaze off my crotch she gulps. "I...I...I..." She squeezes her eyelids shut. "I'm so pathetic I can't even do this properly." She jumps to her feet, then races down the aisle. The bathroom door opens, then closes behind her.

I blow out a breath. Jesus, that was close. If she had touched the snap of my jeans, I'd have been a goner. I wanted to watch the reaction on her face when she was greeted by the sight of my fully erect cock. A cock that throbs and extends and presses painfully against the fabric of my crotch, determined to get out. I widen my stance to accommodate my erection, then throw my head back against the seat and groan.

Did I make a mistake inviting her to come with me? I'll admit, I saw something in her. I recognized how lost she was. How she's floundered to try to find a path for herself. I think allowing herself to be trapped in an arranged marriage was her last effort to find some meaning to her life.

But I've heard her sing. I've seen how terrified she was of her brother. That was not the life for her. Her talent needs to be shown to the world. And it's only a few phone calls for me to arrange to introduce her to the right people. I know, I know, I was planning to seek revenge, but instead, I did the right thing for her, decided to be the bigger man. I invited her to come with me so she could pursue her dreams. Clearly, I didn't think this through. I was sure I was over her. That I'd be able to resist her. I hadn't realized that gorgeous girl had blossomed into a sexy siren.

I rise to my feet and walk toward the bathroom. I push it, and the door opens. There, in the fairly spacious room—because, private plane, duh—she's standing with her back to me. She has the fingers of one hand pressed onto the lip of the sink. Her head is thrown back, and in the mirror, I can see her eyes are screwed up in concentration. And here's the important bit... She has the hem of her dress pulled up and the fingers of her other hand are stuck down her panties.

I step in, and the door swings shut behind me with a whisper. Silently, I step toward her.

"Declan, oh god, Declan," she breathes heavily.

"Are you touching yourself while thinking about me?"

Her eyelids snap open. Her gaze connects with mine in the mirror. Her fingers are still down the front of her panties. I close the distance to her until my chest is flush with her back. She shudders. Color heightens her already flushed features. Her eyelids are heavy, her lips slightly parted. She looks like a woman who just masturbated. It was thoughts of me that spurred her on. Satisfaction fills my chest. I grip her hip, and she shivers.

Pull up your skirt, take off your panties, then present me with your arse. Your every hole is mine to fill. Mine to take and possess and use in any way I deem fit.

I wrap my fingers around her wrist.

She flinches but doesn't pull away.

"Have you been fingering your pussy, Solene?"

Red stains her cheeks. Delightful. She's not as innocent as she looks, yet she's undiscovered. Untouched by the world. And fuck, if I don't want to keep it that way.

She tries to pull her hand away, but I tighten my grip. She stills. Her breathing grows rough. She swallows and the pulse that flutters at the base of her throat speeds up. The scent of her fear leaches into the air, and mixed with it, the unmistakable tang of need, of want, of lust. I bring her fingers to my mouth and suck on them.

A moan spills from her lips. Her pupils dilate until only a circle of green remains around the circumference. My dick stabs into the fabric of my crotch, and I widen my stance to accommodate it. The movement sends a shudder through her. "Declan..." she sighs.

Her soft voice reaches some part deep inside of me. A part I forgot about in my rush to get to the top of my chosen field. I release her hand and step back. "I came to make sure you were okay."

On your knees, arms behind your back. Open your mouth, press down your tongue. When I thrust my cock down your throat, you'll take it without gagging.

"I'm okay," she whispers.

I'm not. And if I have my way with you, you won't be, either, and fuck, if that doesn't make me hornier and even sorrier for inviting you into my world. I smirk. "Didn't sound like you were okay. Sounded to me like you were masturbating with my name on your lips."

She blinks. "You m-must be m-mistaken."

"Oh?"

She nods. "I-I wasn't... m-masturbating."

"So why do your fingers smell like your cunt? Why does the taste of your cum still coat my tongue?"

She flushes. Through the dress, her nipples are pointed. Goddamn.

She's wearing a bra; I'm sure of that, but it hasn't stopped the tight little buds from being outlined against the fabric. *Take off your dress, then bend over so I can squeeze your breasts as I take you from behind.*

She lowers her chin so her hair falls over her features. "You don't have to talk so filthy."

I laugh. "When I start talking filthy, you'll know."

"Oh?" She peeks up at me. "How's that?"

"You won't be able to stop yourself from climaxing."

She gapes. "You're joking."

"Nope. But you trying to convince me you weren't masturbating while thinking of me is."

She shuffles her feet. "Fine, I was so turned on I tried to relieve myself, so—" She holds up her fingers and waggles them at me.

"You could have told me your problem, and I'd have taken care of it."

"I don't need your help," she scoffs.

"Put your fingers back in your cunt."

"What?" She gapes.

"Pull up your dress, Solene," I tell her.

She scowls. "I may be a Mafia princess, but don't think I'm a pushover."

I look her up and down, then fold my arms across my chest. "Pull. Up. Your. Dress." I lower my voice to a hush, and she shivers. "Now," I snap.

She reaches down, and inch by inch, pulls up the hem of the dress.

"Good girl."

She shudders. Her cheeks flush. She continues to raise her dress until her pale pink panties come into view. My already erect cock grows thicker. I lean in so the bulge at my crotch presses against her. She gasps and her eyelids flutter down.

"Eyes on me."

She raises her heavy eyelids, the green of her eyes reduced to a thin circle around her dilated pupils. It's how she looked at me that time when she was unable to stop herself from grinding on my cock. She was too young then to realize what she was doing. Now, she's grown up. She's still innocent, though. Despite her defiance, she's inexperienced. And I promised myself I wouldn't fuck her. Dammit.

I release her and curl my fingers into fists at my sides. "Now slip your fingers inside your panties."

She swallows, then obeys me.

"You're doing so well, Rabbit."

Her lips part. The color on her cheeks deepens. She definitely likes it. Whaddayaknow? The little princess has a praise kink.

"Now part your legs and slide two fingers inside your channel."

She increases the distance between the pale flesh of her thighs. Without taking my gaze off her, I know she obeys me, for she gasps, "I'm so—"

"Wet?"

She nods.

"And tight and soaking and saturated in your cum."

A whine slips from her lips, her knees seem to buckle, and she leans a hip against the sink for support.

"Now fuck yourself."

"Wh-what?"

"Move your fingers in and out of your sopping cunt."

The flush blooms on her neck. Then she complies. Her spine curves. Her entire body jerks. "Oh, god, oh, god." She opens and shuts her mouth; her eyelids flutter.

"Don't look away; stay focused."

She holds my gaze in the mirror, and her features reflect the pleasure that her body's feeling. For the first time. I'm sure of that. And fuck, if my chest doesn't grow heavy with satisfaction.

"Now, pinch your clit."

She blinks, then purses her lips. "I... I can't do that."

"Why not?"

She shakes her head.

"Don't defy me, Rabbit."

She swallows, "Don't make me d-do something I won't like."

I frown. "How do you know you won't like it?"

"I... I just know, okay?"

I frown "You're not making any sense."

"Too bad." She firms her lips.

She was ready to follow my instructions. In fact, I was sure she was loving every moment of my directing her on how to pleasure herself. And my instincts are never wrong. So, what's the problem here?

"What is it?" I tilt my head. "You can tell me what's bothering you."

She hunches her shoulders. "I can't."

"Try me."

She looks away, then mumbles, "I don't know where my clit is."

"Excuse me?" I gape at her.

Her cheeks flush. She pulls her hand out of her panties. "Get out."

"No fucking way."

She lowers both hands to her sides, and her dress falls to below her knees again. "Leave already."

"How do you not know where your clit is?"

She lowers her chin to her chest. "Oh, my god, this is so embarrassing," she whines.

"Explain this to me... Please."

She stiffens, then slowly, her shoulders droop. "I was brought up in a strict environment. I went to an all-girls convent school. And sure, I gathered some knowledge of how things are supposed to be between a man and a woman thanks to the women gossiping in the kitchen, but I don't know all the details."

My jaw drops. I knew she was innocent, but to think she doesn't know the parts of her own anatomy? Let's just say, I didn't see that coming. "You do know how babies are made, right?"

"I was sheltered; doesn't mean I'm stupid." She scowls at me over her shoulder. "I know what a clit is; I just don't know where mine is located, okay?"

Her cheeks turn even more fiery. She slides out from between me and the sink and, walks over to the wall, and pushes her forehead into it, grumbling, "Somebody kill me already."

I chuckle.

"It's not funny, you *stronzo*," she snaps.

"It is from where I am."

She turns around. "I knew you'd laugh at me."

"I'm not laughing at you." I spoil the effect with the chuckle that cracks out of me.

She firms her lips. "Sure looks like you are."

"I'm not, I swear." I hold up a hand. "I'm just surprised. You're so—"

"Confident? Outspoken?" She raises a shoulder. "Trust me, it got me into a whole lot of trouble, too."

"I know," I murmur.

She must sense I'm remembering her run in with Diego for her features soften. "I never got a chance to experiment down there."

"You mean you've never—"

"M-masturbated before? N-no," she whispers.

This time, I don't bother hiding the surprise on my features. "You're kidding."

She folds her arms across her chest. "Can I go now?"

10

Solene

"Nope, no fucking way. Not until we fix this thing," he drawls.

Madonna santa! For the love of all that's holy, this asshole is intent on stripping me of all vestiges of self-respect.

"What do you mean fix this thing?"

"I'm going to show you where your clit is."

I back up until I'm flush against the wall of the bathroom. "No way."

"Yes way."

"I'm not letting you touch me."

"I'm not going to touch you," he says with conviction.

"Right, that whole thing of making me 'come'"—I make air quotes—"without you touching me."

"Correct." His lips twitch. "Now take off your dress."

"What? No!"

The smile vanishes. "You will do as I say."

I scowl at him, and for some strange reason, I want to stamp my foot and yell at him. But that would only confirm to him that I'm young and inexperienced; and while that may be true, I'm not going to reinforce that image to him.

"Solene, take off your dress."

His hard mean voice ricochets off my heart and arrows straight to my core. I tremble. Something knotted inside of me eases and a pulse flares to life between my legs. With trembling fingers, I shrug off the dress and let it drop to the floor next to me.

His breathing grows rapid, the rise and fall of his chest increasing in intensity. Other than that, there is no other change in expression on his face. He merely folds his arms across his chest, then nods toward my panties.

"Slip those off." His voice brooks no argument.

This time, I don't even try to protest. There's something about his assertiveness that elicits a response from me I'm not able to control, something about the confidence in his stance, about how relaxed he still is, like this is an everyday occurrence, that both puts me at ease and makes me want to question exactly what it is that's happening here—though, perhaps that's a thought I'll save for later. For now, it's almost a relief to hand over control to him.

"Take off your bra."

I do.

"Now slide your legs apart."

I do.

"Touch the slit between your legs."

I slide my fingers between my thighs, and the pulse in my lower belly intensifies.

"What do you feel?" He rumbles.

I hesitate, he arches an eyebrows.

I glance away, then back at him. "Uh, it's so moist." Heat flushes my skin. "And so hot. I... I'm dripping." I squeeze my eyes shut. Did I *say* dripping? I said *dripping*.

He clicks his tongue. "Did I give you permission to close your eyes?"

I snap my eyelids open and shake my head.

"You will do *only* as I say."

I jerk my chin.

"Scoop up some of your cum then hold your fingers up and over the topmost part of your pussy."

My *cum?* The pulse in my belly drops to my core and every part of me seems to be focused there. I follow his lead, then touch my pussy lips.

"Did I tell you to touch yourself?" he growls.

"B-b-b-but—"

He glares at me, and the words die in my throat.

"Did I, Solene?"

I shake my head slowly, before raising my hand and letting it hover over my core.

He nods, "*Now,* touch the part at the top between your pussy-lips."

I slip my fingers between my pussy lips at the top and a spark of pleasure zips out from the point of contact.

"Oh," I gasp.

"Indeed." He smirks. "What do you feel?"

"A… spongy bud… that's… growing?"

"Harder, more stiff, more swollen?"

I nod.

"That's your clitoris."

"Clitoris?"

"Or your clit. Now, move your finger around and see what feels good to you."

"My clit." I trace the little button-shaped part of me and tendrils of pleasure zip out. "Oh, god." *How did I miss this? It seems so obvious now.* My eyelids flutter but I manage not to close them. The fact that his now-indigo eyes are fixed on mine insists I stay in the moment. I continue to rub my clit, and my thighs clench. Heat zips out from where I'm touching myself to my breasts. My nipples are so tight, so hard… I need to squeeze them, need to massage my heavy breasts, need to... My fingers tingle, the pulse between my legs intensifies and seems to spread to my wrists, my breasts, and even behind my eyeballs. But I don't stop. I keep fingering my clit.

His eyes flash. His features form into an expression of approval, and every pore in my body seems to pop in response.

"You're doing so well," he croons.

A quiver of heat streaks through my veins. What is it about his praise that gives me such a primal thrill? Maybe, it's the fact that I never received any growing up. I continue to rub my clit and feel a tickling sensation further back. I ease my finger back and discover more moisture gathering between my thighs. I move my finger back toward my clit, and it slides even more easily over the bud, so I speed up my actions. That heavy throbbing feeling grows thicker, deeper, swirls in on itself. The coming of a storm. The tension in the air before lighting hits. That sense of something teetering, looming over the horizon.

"Slide the finger of your other hand inside your hole."

I moan. He called my entrance a hole, and that feels so wrong. And so right. A-n-d I slip a finger inside myself, but it still feels so empty. I wriggle my hips, and when that doesn't help, I can't stop the whine that spills from my lips.

"Still empty, huh?" He scans my features then, before I can reply, he adds, "Slip another finger inside yourself."

I do.

"Better?"

When I don't reply, his lips curl. "Add a third finger."

Wha—? Did he say a third finger? My pussy clamps down on my fingers, but something's still missing. Butterflies take wing in my stomach. Sweat beads my upper lip a-n-d, *fine, I have nothing to lose, do I?* I stuff a third finger inside my pussy, stretching myself around the girth, and *whoa—! S*ensations crowd my skin. My scalp tingles. *That's so good. Sooooo good.*

My movements slow down and he snaps, "Don't stop kneading your clit; keep at it."

"B-but I feel like"—I lower my voice to a whisper—"like I'm gonna pee."

"Don't worry. You won't."

I study his face to see if he's telling the truth, and he nods. So, I go at it again, sliding over the swollen bud and stuffing my fingers in and out of myself, in and out. The tension builds, knots, folds in on itself. Sweat pools on my upper lip. "Declan, I can't."

"You can."

"Declan, please, please..." *What am I begging him for? What do I want?* Liquid heat spurts through my veins. My breathing stutters, but I continue to stroke my clit, keep on skating my fingers in and out of myself, in and out, and all the while, I'm holding this gaze. I'm looking into those startling, now midnight blue eyes of his. He's guiding me, leading me, pulling me toward that goal I can't get to fast enough. *Keep going. Don't stop.* A trembling sweeps up from my toes, my knees... My thighs tremble. My inner muscles clench.

"Dec-lan," I gasp.

"You will not come, Rabbit."

"Wh-what?" I stare at him, continuing to pump my fingers in and out of my sopping wet pussy. Every brush of my fingers against my clit sends a fresh burst of sparks shooting up my spine. *Something* is lapping up against my nerve-endings, threatening to overwhelm me. It batters against my will, threatening, pushing, dashing, battering against the last barriers of my sanity. "Please, please, Master."

His gaze intensifies. Those midnight blue eyes deepen in color until they're almost black. The scar on his forehead stands out against his skin. He draws in a breath, then jerks his chin. "Come," he growls.

And the orgasm—because, surely, that's what this is—crashes over me. The climax goes on and on, and he still doesn't release me from the tractor beam of his gaze. I pull my fingers out and begin to slump against the wall.

That's when he closes the distance between us. He shoves his hand between my legs, cups my pussy in a possessive grasp and holds me up. My inner walls contract, and I shiver again. Every movement of his seems calculated to impress on me the mastery he has over my body. With his free hand he circles my wrist and brings my fingers—now stained with my cum— to his nose. "The sweet scent of your freshly orgasmed cunt… Is there any better scent in this world?"

Oh, my god, that's so dirty. And hot. Why are his filthy words such a turn on? Before I can voice my protest, he lowers my fingers to his mouth. And when he closes his lips around my digits and sucks them clean, that melting sensation that gripped me when I'd climaxed overwhelms me. My eyelids flutter, and I give in to sleep.

When I come to, I'm horizontal on a bed. Muted light streams in from one of the windows. I hear the hum of the engines, so I know we're still up in the air.

"How're you feeling now?" a hard voice asks from beside me.

A small scream spills from my lips, and for a second, I'm transported back to that moment when I woke up in Declan's bedroom in Naples. And when he unfolds himself from the chair and walks over to stand next to me, I wish I could go back in time and fix everything that happened after.

"I'm sorry Diego's men beat you up. I didn't think it through. I didn't realize…"

"Shh…" He picks up the bottle of water on the bed stand, uncaps it, and holds it out.

"I really do mean it.".

"I know, Rabbit." He urges me to accept the bottle of water, then insists I drink half of it before he allows me to put it down.

"I'm good."

"Let me be the judge of that."

I fold my arms over the sheet and realize I'm still naked.

"My dress?"

He angles his head in the direction of a dresser on the far side where my dress is folded up along with my bra and panties. "You sure you're okay?"

I take in the crease in his forehead, the worry in his voice, and can't stop the slight curve of my lips. "I had an orgasm, and I was tired from all the events of the past few days, but other than that, I'm fine."

He surveys my features. "Good."

"I'll be out of your hair as soon as I figure out how to launch my career in LA."

"Hmm." He holds his fingers under his nose, and oh, my god, he's smelling me. He's sniffing at the remnants of my cum on his digits. That's gross. And strangely, romantic. Ugh. I didn't think of that as romantic, did I? Because he's still wearing me?

"The evidence of your arousal smells even better a few hours later. Like aged, fine wine whose bouquet grows more potent with time."

I swallow. "What are you trying to do, Declan?"

"What do you mean?"

"This—" I point to the space between us. "I was sure you wanted revenge for what happened but now, I don't know."

He slides his hand inside his pocket and frowns down at me. "Neither do I." He seems taken aback by his confession, then he sets his jaw. "Very insightful words for a weak society princess, who's only accomplishment was agreeing to an arranged match."

It's as if he's plunged a hot knife into my chest. He gave me my first orgasm, gave me so much pleasure, I'm sure my brain cells are going to take a while to recover from it and now, he's injured me so much it hurts to breathe. My emotions must show on my face for he swears aloud.

"Fuck, didn't mean to say that."

"Yes, you did."

"Fucking hell." He drags his fingers through his hair. "You tie me up in knots, you know that?"

We stare at each other for a few seconds. The silence stretches and the mixed-up feelings inside me are mirrored on his face, and that eases some of that tight feeling around my ribcage.

Then he inclines his head. "Why did you call me that?"

"What?"

"Back there in the bathroom, you called me Master."

"Did I?" I frown.

"You know you did."

I lean back against the pillows. "It seemed... right. When you use that tone of voice, you seem to know what you want. And it makes me want to—"

"Make me happy?"

I nod slowly "Yes. It makes me want to do everything you ask, and—" I stiffen. "How do you know that?"

"Lucky guess?" This time the smile on his face is secretive. Does he know something I don't? Before I can ask, he heads toward the doorway, only to stop.

He looks at me over his shoulder and states, "This doesn't change anything, Solene."

11

Solene

"Your room's on the second floor, to the right of the stairs."

Declan stalks toward the doors at the far end of the living room. They open to a view of an infinity pool, beyond which the sea stretches out to the horizon. The sight is breathtaking.

A few hours ago, we landed at a private airstrip and boarded a limousine. We pulled away and drove through the city of LA, then through the hills. Throughout the ride, a hoodie-wearing Declan stayed glued to his phone. I tried to ask him which part of LA he lived in, and he said Malibu. That's the only word we exchanged during the entire two-hour journey. Apparently, distances in LA are five times the normal distances one covers during a journey in my home city of Naples. A sharp pang of something twists my guts. No, surely not. I can't be homesick. Not already. I'm simply missing the familiarity of things, that's all it is.

When we arrived at his place, a man emerged from the house and carried our suitcases up the stairs. The man driving our car had introduced himself as Rick, Declan's bodyguard. When Declan glowered at him, he looked at me in apology before driving off.

Now, I glance around the living room. There's a massive sectional placed diagonal to the back doors. Opposite is a massive TV, while in the center there's a coffee table. That's it. There's so much space here, one could get lost walking from one end of the floor to the other. Okay, I'm exaggerating… somewhat. The space doesn't seem very lived in or homey.

I spin around and head toward the curving staircase we passed earlier. Heading to the second floor I glance left. There's only one set of double doors at the far end of the corridor. Is that his bedroom? I turn, and head toward the only door on the right.

When I walk in, I gasp. The entire space is massive, like five times the size of my room back home. That's not an exaggeration. Sunlight pours in through the large windows that cover one wall of the room. Another thing to get used to. The sheer brightness of this place. It's like all the sunlight in the world has been directed through a prism at this city. It's more than a little overwhelming.

There's something about California that's all new-world, hopeful and optimistic. Maybe a little too optimistic, a little too chirpy for my liking. It touches everything with a golden glow and makes the impossible seem possible. I've never been here, but perhaps, I sensed it from all those miles away. Getting out of my comfort zone has shown me how much of the world is left to be explored.

I walk toward the large floor-to-ceiling windows and look down. I have a view of the infinity swimming pool, the pool house on one side, and the beach beyond. The entire vista is overwhelming in size, in beauty, and in luxury. I may not have traveled and have very limited knowledge of Hollywood movies, but even that confirms the scene in front of me is luxurious, larger-than-life, and uncommon. How big a star, exactly, is Declan?

As if my thoughts have conjured him, he walks out of the pool house. He's wearing a pair of swimming trunks that mold to his hips. His shoulders are corded, his chest planes are defined. And is that a ten-pack, nope, twelve-pack. I swear to god that's a twelve-pack. Is that even possible? The twin grooves on either side of his concave stomach dip down to disappear under the waistband.

Even at this distance, I can make out the shape of that thick column between his thighs. My belly flip-flops. A thousand little sparks seem to light my veins. *Ohmygod, I'm not even that close to him, and yet, I can't stop my body from reacting to him. And I almost touched that part of him. Almost had my fingers around his c-c-c-cock! Oh hell, now I'm stammering in my head? That's never happened before. Is that how much he unnerves me? How's that going to help me?* I need to resist this attraction to him. Otherwise, I'm going to be too distracted to focus on the reason I came here. There's only one thing to do.

I walk out of the house and toward the pool. My heart hammers in chest. My pulse stutters at my throat. I can do this. I can do this. I need to do this. I can't let him walk all over me. This is the new me. The Solene who will not let anyone intimidate her. I've had enough of that to last a lifetime already.

My brother used my loyalty to my family to make me conform to his demands. My mother used my love to negotiate a marriage for me. An arrangement I was freed from thanks to Massimo and Olivia, but also to Declan for giving me a way out. I'm grateful to him for that. Doesn't mean I'm going to let him walk all over me. I need to stand up to him if I want to have any hope of him treating me as an equal. And that's how I'm going to live my life from now on.

When I come to the edge of the pool I stop. He cuts through the water, his arms knifing through the surface, his legs propelling him forward toward me. As if he senses my perusal, he reaches the edge of the water and surfaces. He folds his arms over the lip of the pool and shakes the water out of his hair. Droplets of water cascade over my ankles, my feet. He rakes his gaze up my legs, my hips, my chest, then tilts his head back. A smirk curls his lips. *Jerkass.*

I shrug off my robe to let it pool around my feet and have the satisfaction of seeing the smile disappear from his face. His jaw drops. He opens and shuts his mouth, but nothing emerges. Good. I may be an innocent but this... This shows I haven't lost that fire inside me. The fire that consumed me when I first met Declan. The fire that was banked by my brother and mother for the past few years but meeting D—which is a moniker that suits him well, considering the monster D he's packing—has rekindled it. He looks me up and down, and his gaze widens further.

"The fuck, where's your swimsuit?"

"I don't have one. And the weather's too nice to miss out on a swim, huh?" I shoot him a smile then dive in over his head. Being in Naples with nothing else to do, I spent a lot of time honing my swimming skills.

It's the one thing my family didn't stop me from doing. Of course, I was only allowed to use the small pool in our backyard, and only when there were no men around. Still, it gave me time to hone my swimming enough that I execute that dive perfectly.

I swim to the surface then strike out toward the other end. Confession: I've never swum naked. And definitely not with the heated gaze of a man I've kissed following me as I reach the end of the pool then push back—and gasp. For he's right in front of me.

Holy hell, he's right here, and I slam into the unforgiving wall of his chest. The heat of his body slams into me. That familiar scent of dark chocolate laced with coffee, which has haunted my dreams, is laced with chlorine, but it's just as potent. It sinks into my blood, heading straight for my core. My toes curl. I begin to go under, but the next moment, he grips my waist and pulls me up. I break the surface, draw in a breath, and oxygen floods my lungs. My head spins, but maybe that's because of his nearness.

The sun's rays slant over my head and halo his. The color of his eyes deepens into a piercing indigo, and I'm transported right back to our first encounter on the beach, when he saved me. I became his then, and the fact is, I've never been anyone else's. However much I've tried to deny the effect he had on me when I saw him in my room, I already knew I belonged to him. It's why I accepted his invitation to accompany him back to LA, knowing there were no guarantees. The opportunity to pursue the career of my dreams is a bonus. I want it, but I want him even more. I found him again, I'm not going to give him up that easily.

I lean in so my nipples brush his chest. His shoulder muscles bunch. His chest planes seem to writhe like an electric current is running through his veins.

His hands land on my hips and he pins me in place. I tip up my chin and gasp. His eyes… Those gorgeous blue eyes of his are so dark they could be black. Flecks of indigo spark in their depths. Such hypnotic eyes captured me the moment my gaze clashed with his. And in a way, they've never let go. He entrapped me then, like he is now.

My throat dries. My chest tightens. A heavy beat settles between my thighs. I lean in even closer until my breasts are crushed between us. I wrap my legs around his waist, and my naked core cradles that hard column in his swimming trunks. Sensations sizzle up my spine. My head spins. I reach up to try to kiss him, but I'm too short. So, I settle for sinking my teeth into his throat.

He shudders. The muscles of his shoulders bunch. "What do you think you're doing?"

"Trying to tempt you to break your self-imposed restriction."

He glares down that patrician nose. "It's for your benefit."

"How is that?"

"If you're known in Hollywood as another arm-candy girlfriend, no one will take you seriously. And your talent is too important for anything else to act as a diversion."

I scowl. "You expect me to believe that?"

"I don't care what you believe. What you need to understand, though, is that I'm too much man for you to handle."

I open my mouth to protest, but he thrust his hips forward. The column of his shaft stabs through his swimming trunks and into my melting core. My entire body seems to seize up. Goosebumps pop on my skin. Despite the fact that the pool is heated—Hollywood, eh?—I shiver.

His smirk widens. "That's what I thought." He releases his hold on my waist, pushes me away, and taps my head. "Run along now, like a good little girl."

He moves past me, hauls himself out of the pool, and begins to walk away. I should let him go. I should cut my losses and go back to my room, but that impulsive part of me that has always gotten me into trouble, the part that insisted I rebel against my mother and run out of the beach at two a.m., surges forward. I shove myself out of the pool with less grace than him, then call out, "Hey, jerkface."

12

Declan

The fuck? Did she just call me—? I pivot, and she throws herself at me. In what's a repeat of that scene in her room that got me into trouble in the first place, she literally climbs me like a tree. Instinctively, I cup her behind to stop her from falling. She hooks her ankles about my waist, throws her arms around my neck and rears up. Poised with her lips just a hair's breadth away from mine, she demands, "Kiss me," then waits.

I pull back enough to be just out of reach.

"Damn you, kiss me, asshole."

"My, my, what a potty mouth you've developed, little girl. And to think, you were expecting to go into an arranged marriage?"

"I'd have won him over eventually, and—"

"Don't fucking talk about him." I wind her hair around my palm and tug, so the beautiful column of her neck is bared for my appraisal.

"You jealous of him?"

"Don't talk about any other man when we're together."

"Is there a 'we' then?" She looks at me from under hooded eyelashes.

"There's no 'we.' I'll never belong to only one woman, and definitely not to a young, virginal Mafia princess—"

"I'm not a virgin."

"What a little liar you are."

"I might have been sheltered, doesn't mean I didn't get around, and—"

I pull on her hair, and she flinches. "You're hurting me."

"Better get used to it," I growl. Then, because I fucking can't help myself, and because the sight of her slick, naked body fills my vision, and because my cock is seconds away from bursting through the barrier of my swim trunks and burying itself in her hot tight pussy, and no way, will I allow myself to go there—yet—I run my nose up her throat.

She shivers, and her nipples tighten into points that dig into my chest. My dick extends and thickens, and the blood drains to my groin and—fuck this, but I'm fast forgetting why I thought it a good idea to declare I wasn't going to shag her.

I draw in a deep breath, filling my lungs with that sugary sweet scent that is her. My heart seems to swell in my chest; my balls harden. I open my mouth and sink my teeth into the side of her neck, mimicking the bite she placed on me earlier. Only, I go a step further. I break the skin, so the coppery taste of her blood fills my palate.

My eyes roll back in my head. Fucking hell, I knew she'd taste as sweet as she smells. My heart seems to expand until I sense its beat in every cell in my body. Until I can feel her pulse racing in tandem with mine. Fucking hell, this is dangerous. This is why I didn't want to mess up the lines I drew earlier. My proclivities are the kind she would never be able to bear. And to think, it's her actions that created those needs in me. I lick the skin I broke, and the depression of my teeth marks on her neck sends a primitive thrill down my spine. Which, in turn, warns me that if I didn't put distance between us, it's going to be too late. It is too late. Too late.

"Declan?" She searches my features. "What's wrong, you—"

There's a flash from the side. I turn my head in that direction, and another flashbulb goes off.

"Motherfucker!" I take a step forward toward the pool and drop her.

"What the hell, Dec—" The rest of her words are swallowed up by the water closing in over her.

I turn and race toward the bushes, where the photographer's hidden. I leap over the hydrangea, then push through the assorted flowering bushes planted there. I reach the perimeter of the garden to find a man racing across the beach and away from the house. Fucking fuck. I turn and find her right behind me. The good news? She's wearing her bathrobe. The bad news? I'm pissed with her.

"The fuck did you follow me here?" I roar.

She gapes, then swipes out her arm. Her palm connects with my cheek, and fuck me, my pulse rate goes through the roof. The blood drains to my groin. "You've done it now," I growl.

The color fades from her face. She gulps, looks to the left, then the right. Well, she's not going to find any help there.

I take a step toward her. She yelps, then pivots and races back in the direction of the house. *Scamper along, little rabbit, there's no place for you to hide that I can't find though.* I prowl past the swimming pool and back to the main house. I hadn't carried my phone with me, hoping to carve out a little more time offline, but that's at an end now. I head inside, my bare feet slapping on the hardwood floor. I snatch up my phone and video call Rick.

"Declan?" He picks up on the first ring.

"A pap got a picture of us—"

"Us?"

"Me and Solene."

"Ah." He smirks.

"What was that 'ah' for?"

"Nothing boss, just a figure of speech."

"The fuck you calling me boss? You served with Knight. I trust you as much as my closest friends. It's why I took on your company to provide my security detail."

"And insisted I become your bodyguard."

"No one else I'd trust with her life."

"Aha!"

"No, stop there. No more. There was a paparazzi—"

"I'm on it."

I blink. "You are?"

"Have eyes everywhere, and one of my men is already chasing him down as we speak. So, you want me to become her security detail after this?"

"You go where she goes."

"Hmm."

I scowl. "Okay, had enough with your sound-effects. You have something on your mind, man?"

"Me? Of course, not. Maybe it's your guilty conscience—"

"The fuck would I have a guilty conscience for?"

"Do you have a guilty conscience?"

"Fuck you, man!"

He laughs. "Keep your shirt on. If I didn't fuck with you, Knight would never forgive me."

"Speaking of, have you heard from him recently?"

His features shadow. "Not in the last week."

"Hmm," I stroke my chin, "Let me know when you do. By the way, you ever going to share what your real name is?" Ever since Knight found out Rick's real name and was sworn to secrecy by him, it's been Cade's and my mission to find this out.

"You ever going to share why you decided to bring a young, innocent girl with you to LA?"

I scoff, "Innocent, my arse. You have no idea who she really is."

"A Mafia princess you saved from an arranged marriage?"

I pause then ask, "That's not a guess, is it?"

"You know better than to ask me that."

Of course. Nothing could stay hidden from a hardened ex-military guy who retired after he was awarded the Victoria Cross—the equivalent of the Purple Heart in the US.

"Well then, you'll also know that I have the contacts in LA to give her singing career a head start."

"Hmm," he frowns.

"There you go again—" I glare at him. "Out with it, mofo. I hate your measured glances and considered pauses."

"I didn't say anything."

"I wish you would and get it off your chest, so I can get on with my life."

"You sure you want to hear this?" His eyebrows draw down.

"Wouldn't ask if I didn't, asshole!"

"You sure you'll be able to withstand all the attention coming her way when they discover her talent?"

I lower my chin. "So, you've heard her sing, I take it."

"I wouldn't be co-owner of the leading security agency in LA if I couldn't find out all the details of the principal I've been charged to look after."

I glance away then at him. "If you want the truth, it's going to be bloody difficult to share her with anyone else, in any form, but if I'd known what was good for me, I wouldn't have inserted myself back into her life the way I did, either."

13

Solene

I run my hands down my dress. Why are my palms damp? And why does my stomach feel like I swallowed a massive rock? I don't need to be nervous. If there's one thing in the world I can do, it's sing. So why does it feel like I'm going to be sick? My stomach heaves. Bile laces my throat. I race to the bathroom, drop to my knees and bend over the toilet bowl. The scant contents of the dinner I ate last night spurts out. Gross! I reach up, flush away the remains, then grab some of the toilet paper, wipe off the seat and flush that away as well. By the time I collapse against the wall of the bathroom, I'm trembling.

Last night, after I made a fool of myself by trying to seduce Declan and failing—oh, except for being caught by that paparazzo on camera, the photos of which I haven't yet seen on social media, thanks to not having a phone—I marched to my room and shut myself up there. I refused to come out for dinner, and when I finally peeked out my door, I found a tray of food left outside for me by of the staff. I haven't seen them around, but I'm sure he has an army of helpers all trained to do their work and keep out of sight.

I ate the sandwich, drank the milk, then, surprisingly, fell asleep. I woke up to banging on the door and Declan telling me to get ready for an audition; and with a leading talent manager, no less.

Sweat beads my brow. I lock my fingers together and bring my knees up closer to my body. *Maybe I shouldn't do this. Maybe I was a fool to think I could go after my dream. What was I thinking? Everything I've lived so far has taught me to keep my head down, to not draw attention to myself. And while I'd tried to keep that flame of rebellion burning inside of me, my mother's and brother's indoctrination must have snuck in under my skin anyway. Right now, I feel like the biggest fraud in the world. Trying out to be a singer? Leaving home to come with a man I barely know to the talent capital of the world in my attempt to pursue my childhood ambition? I must have been smokin' something.* Only I hadn't. I was flying high on reconnecting with the man of my dreams, on knowing I didn't have to marry a man I knew my sister was in love with. I felt like I could throw off the shackles of my past and forge forward... Into nervousness and anxiety and imposter syndrome. I squeeze my eyes shut and lean my head back against the wall. *Oh, my god. Maybe I should have refused to go. Why did I think I could accomplish this? I can't. I can't. I—*

There's a knock on the bathroom door. "Solene, it's getting late," Declan calls out.

I bury my head in my hands. No, no, I'm not ready. I'm not.

"Solene?" He bangs on the door with a little more force. "We have to leave in the next five minutes to get there on time."

I bite the inside of my cheek.

There's silence, then, "Solene, are you okay?"

No, I'm not. Not that it's any of your problem. It's your fault I'm in this position. If you hadn't extended the invitation for me to come to LA, none of this would have happened. It's your fault, asshat. At least, my knowledge of words didn't suffer as a result of my strict upbringing within the Mafia. Turns out, Mafia women have potty mouths and colorful vocabularies they aren't above using when they're cooking and away from the menfolk. And I'm a good listener. And an even faster learner. Except when it came to realizing that I am absolute shit at singing in front of others. *A bit late to realize that, isn't it? After you've upended your entire life to pursue it?*

"Solene, open up." Declan bangs on the door again. "Solene. Open. The. Door. Now." He lowers his voice to a hush and the force of his personality shudders through the space. There's something strident, something so demanding in his tone that I automatically rise to my feet. I walk to the door, unlock it, and he pushes it open. His big frame fills the doorway. His shoulders are bunched, his jaw set so hard, he's probably already cracked a molar. His nostrils are flared, and his hair is tousled like he's run his fingers through it. He glares at me; I tip up my chin.

"The fuck is wrong with you?" he growls.

I firm my lips. "The fuck is wrong you?" I yell, then slam my hands into his chest. *Stronzo*'s bigger and stronger than I remember, and I haven't grown a centimeter since I reached my five-foot-four-inch height at seventeen, but I must take him by surprise, for he stumbles back a little. I brush past him and am almost free when he grabs my arm and swings me around to face him. I lower my head, so my hair falls over my features. Not that it makes a difference. He pinches my chin and applies enough pressure that I have to tilt up my face. I glance away to avoid meeting his eyes.

"Have you been crying?" he demands.

"What's it to you?"

"Have you, Rabbit?"

I wince. "I wish you wouldn't call me by that nickname."

"You resemble a very uncertain rabbit right now, one trying to hide from the world by locking yourself up in the bathroom and feeling sorry for yourself."

I brush the wetness from my face. "I'm not feeling sorry for myself."

"Hmph." I sense him continuing to appraise my features. "Want to talk about it?"

"Want to let go of my chin?"

"You first." His grip on my chin is unyielding. The angles of his body settle into a pattern that tell me he intends to wait me out.

"We're going to be late," I point out.

"Our appointment can wait."

I swivel my gaze in his direction, and at once, those hypnotic blue eyes snap on mine. Mistake, mistake. Now I won't have a choice but to tell him about my fears. When he looks at me with his all-seeing eyes, I can never hide anything from him. "That's a very influential person you're talking about," I say softly.

"Don't change the topic, Rabbit."

I blow out a breath. "I'm nervous, okay? I've never sung in front of an audience before."

"Eh?" He seems taken aback. "When I saw you on the beach, you were singing aloud."

"To myself, with the waves for company, not to mention those jerk faces who decided it would be fun to jump me."

"And me," he reminds me.

"A-n-d you," I agree.

"Do you want me to tell you again how fresh and different your voice is? Is that what this is about? If you're looking for an ego-boost..."

"I'm not, you douchebag. I'm simply telling you why I'm out of sorts. I've only sung in front of my family or in the shower before this."

"In the shower?" His eyebrows knit.

I resist the urge to roll my eyes. "My family forbid me to sing in front of strangers, so yeah, the only way to get practice was to sing in front of them or when I was alone, and I much preferred to do so when I was on my own."

"So?"

"So?" I slap my palms on my hips. "So, this will be my first audition, you *pezzo di—*"

He glares at me, and I slap my lips together. Fine, maybe that particular insult in Italian is a step too far, but he deserves it. He holds my gaze for a second longer then nods. "Fine then, let's practice before we leave." He releases my chin, but I'm too shocked to move.

"Eh, wh-what do you mean?"

"You're nervous. You think you haven't practiced enough. You're not sure how you're going to sound, so go on, sing."

He steps back, leans a hip against the wall and says, "Go on, then."

"Piss off," I snap.

"For a sheltered Mafia princess, you sure have a colorful vocabulary."

"If you only knew." I toss my hair over my shoulders. "And I'll be damned if I'm going to sing for you here."

"Either you sing for me here and get practice, or we head over to our appointment, and you can sing for the leading talent manager in the business."

14

Declan

She opted to audition for Harry Baldwin directly. Not that I was surprised. Not that I wouldn't have loved to hear her sing just for me. Not that I hadn't given her that choice, knowing full well she'd opt out of giving me a private audience.

I shove my hands in the pockets of my jeans and rest my shoulder against the wall on the far end of the studio.

Her voice fills the air, and in the sound booth, she squeezes her eyelids shut as she sings the coda of her original song. The notes soar, and the emotions in her tone paint the atmosphere with a raw sensation that cuts through the walls I've put up around my heart. Once more, I'm transported back to that beach, the scent of the sea in my nostrils, that sweet scent of her that laced the briny air and drew me toward her. An arrow toward a bullseye. I've been headed in her direction all this time, and now I have her. Except, I can't let myself have her. Not in the way I want. Not when my own tastes have changed so much over the years.

I brought her to LA for one reason only. To allow her to find herself. To give her talent a stage. Yes, I might have started out thinking I wanted to punish her for what she did to me—and maybe the emotional part of me still wants to—but the more rational part of me knows she was a kid. She made a mistake. Anyone in her position would have done the same thing to save herself. I did hold a grudge against her, but I also share the blame for what happened.

Her voice rises on the last note, and the hair on the back of my neck rises. Goosebumps pop on my skin. She pulls off the headphones, opens her eyes, and her gaze connects with mine through the glass wall of the sound booth.

Her green eyes are large, luminous; her cheeks are flushed. Her blonde hair is in a cloud about her shoulders. With her simple white dress and ballet pumps on her feet, she looks like the young eighteen-year-old she really is.

Then she smiles at me, and my breath catches in my chest. My heart seems to drop into my stomach. Her voice is every bit as pure as I remember, but it has added depth now, a huskiness that speaks to her awakening as a woman. Her lower notes are darker, more erotic; her timbre is feminine, more sensitive and mature than what I recall.

She's blossomed into a talent ripe for the picking. A soprano the world is going to welcome with open arms. One I'm going to step away from. To my right, Harry jumps to his feet and claps. A-n-d that is a first. I've never seen the man this excited in all the time I've known him. He strides to the door of the recording booth, twists open the handle, and steps through. She tears her gaze off of mine and turns to him with a smile.

He throws up his arms and waves them around. "Incredible. Your voice, the lyrics, the pitch, the impressive breath support and ability to hold notes for extended periods without wavering. All of it has blown me away." His voice reaches me through the open doorway. "Did you say you wrote the lyrics yourself?"

She nods.

"And the melody is yours?"

She nods again.

"Excellent." He claps his hands. "It could do with a few minor tweaks to make it more approachable to the audience overall—"

She scrunches up her eyebrows.

"But nothing that's going to take away from your unique mix of rich dark notes and bright upper range. You're a darker Taylor Swift, my dear. A lighter Lady Gaga. You're in that perfect sweet spot between them. You're the next big—"

I push away from the wall, head to the door and walk out, then pull out my phone and dial Rick's number. "Stay with her," I say when he answers.

I head down to the reception, then jerk my chin at the girl behind the counter.

"Keys to Baldwin's Ducati."

She blinks, opens her mouth as if to protest.

I arch an eyebrow and color flushes her cheeks. "Yes, of course, Mr. Beauchamp." She reaches under the counter, then hands the keys to me.

I head for the parking lot of the studio, then toward the bike parked in the corner. Fringe benefit of being a well-known star? No one refuses you. I snatch the helmet hung around the handle, plant it on my head, then straddle the bike. I thumb the start button until it roars to life, before turning it around and heading for the exit.

She comes running out of the building and plants herself in my path.

Goddamn it. I slow down and come to a stop. The throbbing of the engine mirrors the beating of my heart.

She heads closer, her mouth moving as she speaks. I rev up the engine and shake my head. I know, arsehole move. She scowls up at me. Her lips continue to move. I shake my head again, indicating I can't hear her. She stamps her foot, then punches my shoulder. Fucking adorable. And I thought she was a subservient Mafia princess. She's going to be a handful. I stay in place, one foot on the ground balancing the bike. She slaps my chest, then indicates to me I should raise the screen of my helmet. I shake my head.

She leans into me, and I swoop my arm about her waist and throw her across the fuel tank. The hem of her dress flips up, so her arse is exposed. With each vibration of the motorcycle's engine, her thighs quiver. My cock instantly thickens. She writhes around, and I lean one arm over the small of her back. She continues to buck, and I bring my palm down on her butt. She must be shocked, for she stills. I take advantage of her temporary compliance and spank her left arse cheek, then right, then left again. She begins to squirm and thrash around. I bring my hand down on her butt one last time, and her entire body shudders. Her thighs quiver and fuck if she isn't aroused. Which wasn't my intention…

Or maybe it was, but not consciously. I simply wanted to teach her a lesson for her sass. I was planning to get away from her—that's why I came down here—until she thrust herself in my path and threw me off kilter. Again. But I've learned my lesson. I'm not going to let her subvert me again.

I pull her off the bike and plant her back on her feet. Her features are flushed, her hair awry. Eyes dilated, there's only a circle of green left around her pupils. A tear slides down her cheeks, and she brushes it away. She opens her mouth, but before she can speak, I give her a mock salute and drive off. In my side mirror, I catch a final glimpse of her giving me the Italian chin flick, and I laugh even harder than before.

I drive up the Pacific Coast Highway, allowing myself to breathe for the first time. Cloistered in that studio hearing her sing, being witness to how her voice and natural innocence seduced one of the most powerful men in the industry was bittersweet. It's exactly what I predicted. I should feel vindicated for having spotted her talent. Instead, I wanted to bury my fist in Harry's face, then snatch her up and take her to my place, lock her up and never let her out.

And that kind of possessiveness is strange and new, and yet, also reassuring. It shows me I can still feel. That I'm not turning into a one-track, hit-making machine for whom only money and fame matter, though they do mean a lot to me.

The next big success at the box-office is what I'm aiming for. That's the one thing I know how to work toward. It's safe and predictable, in as much as a favorable outcome can be predicted in this fickle industry. It's why I came to this city in the first place. And that I've managed to make, it despite the scar on my face, is testament to how hard I've worked. How much I've manipulated people and circumstances into giving me what I want. I made people accept my flawed face as the norm. I turned my weaknesses into a competitive strength. It's how I stand out in the sea of perfectly sculpted profiles.

Knight was onto something all those years ago when he pointed me in this direction. In a way, I owe my career to him. Now, if only I can avoid screwing things up by letting myself get sidetracked by a pretty face.

I bypass the turn-off that would lead toward my place, and instead, head toward the only other place that's offered me refuge over the years. A place where my identity is protected and where I can indulge my need for release.

Another forty minutes of riding, and I draw up to the familiar black gates. They open as I approach, and I drive through. I park my bike, hook my helmet over the handle, then run up the steps. The door opens and a silver-haired, distinguished-looking woman shoots me a smile. "The usual?"

15

Solene

"Where is he?"

I pace back-forth-back in the living room of Declan's place. After he spanked me, then drove off without a word, I was too stunned to move for a few minutes. That's when Rick ushered me back to the limo that had brought us to the studio. As soon as I got home, I ran straight up to Declan's bedroom and peeked inside.

It was my first time in there, and the sight of the massive bed draped in black sheets in the middle of a room twice the size of mine took my breath away. I walked in, the view out the windows up there was astounding. On one side, floor-to-ceiling sliders lead to a deck and a stunning view of the ocean and the horizon that stretches out for what seems like forever. The room itself is sparse. Hardwood floors, a fireplace on one side with armchairs placed in front of it, an end-of-bed bench, a table pushed up against another wall with a laptop on it. The bed was made and there were no clothes in the laundry basket on the far side of the room, so his staff must have been in here to clean up. Still this room felt more lived-in. There was spare cash on the dresser, books laying open on the nightstand. The door to the closet was half-ajar like he pulled on some clothes and stepped out without closing it fully.

And curled into a cubby in the wall next to the bed was a whip. I swallowed. A whip? *Why did he have a whip?* I should have walked out right then. Instead, I edged toward it and drew my fingers over the braided leather. *What would it feel like to have it slither across my skin? To have it lick up the curve of my butt and—*I immediately stopped that line of thinking. *Where had that thought come from anyway?*

Standing there, I closed my eyes and drew in that dark scent of his. Some of the tension faded from my limbs.

Looking into his room felt like getting a peek into his mind, although I confess, I still don't understand his motivations in offering to take me with him to LA. He said he wasn't going to sleep with me, yet that spanking had definite sexual undercurrents. Not to mention, how he spoke to me on the flight over. Our encounters, so far, have been filled with erotic overtones. yet he continues to keep his distance from me.

He's already making good on his promise to introduce me to the most important people in the music business; Harry Baldwin indicated he's more than happy to sign me. Declan had been gung-ho—rattling off the names of the labels he was going to pitch me to. Of course, I was thrilled. To hit success on my first try is more than I'd anticipated. Only when I turned toward Declan to share my excitement, he was gone. I excused myself and rushed down the stairs and out the front door, where I found him ready to leave without me. And he didn't stop for me. Not really. The douchebag pretended he couldn't hear me over the sound of his bike. Wait, was that his bike? He arrived in the limo with me. Whatever. Was he pissed off with me? Was he unhappy I'd impressed Harry? I have so many questions for the man who hasn't returned home hours after he, inexplicably, drove off without me.

Now I turn on Rick, who's positioned himself near the doorway of the living room. "Where's Declan? I'm sure you know."

There's no change in his expression. He's a big guy, as big as Declan. His hair is dark, and unlike Declan, his eyes are a steel gray. He's just as classically handsome, but without the scar. In some ways, he's even more good-looking than Declan, but somehow, he does nothing for me.

I march up to him and tip up my chin. "Where did he go? And don't tell me you don't know."

"I do know, but I can't tell you."

"Why is that?"

"Declan's orders."

I groan in exasperation.

A phone rings from somewhere behind me.

"I believe that's for you?"

"I don't have a phone," I scowl.

Yep, Diego and my mother refused to get me a phone in their bid to keep me 'innocent.' Little did they know, I had access to my friends' phones in school.

"You sure?" For the first time, a hint of a smile curves Rick's lips. I glower at him, then turn and march over to the origin of the sound. Sure enough, there's a phone on the coffee table. The name on caller ID says Olivia. Huh? I pick up the phone and accept the FaceTime call.

"Solene, how are you?" My sister's face appears on the phone. "Are you okay? I was so worried about you."

"How did you get this number?"

Her eyebrows draw down. "Declan gave it to me..."

"Of course."

She scrutinizes my features. "Are you okay? How's LA treating you? And how about your meeting with the talent agent? How did that go?"

"You knew about the— Don't tell me; Declan updated you." I roll my eyes.

"He did."

I scowl.

"He and I are friends, Sol, and trust me, I've been giving him grief about whisking you away to LA without giving any of us a chance to think. But I knew this is what you wanted, so I didn't stop him."

I hunch my shoulders. "It is what I wanted. It's just—"

"What is it?" My sister's features grow concerned. "Has he been treating you okay? If he tries any funny business, I'll..."

"You'll fly over here and give him a piece of your mind, I know." I half smile. "And he's treating me... the way I want to be treated."

"Hmm." She purses her lips. "I'm not sure what to make of that, but I'm not going to ask you for more details, either."

"Wise choice." I chuckle. "How's married life?"

Her cheeks redden. "Uh, it's good. I'm good. Massimo is—"

"Better than you expected?"

She clears her throat. "Yes, to that. He's much gentler than he comes across. He cares for me, Sol. He loves me." Her gaze grows dreamy.

"We're moving to London so he can help his brother legalize the Cosa Nostra business."

I snort. "Is that what they're calling it nowadays?"

"They're serious about it, Sol. Michael, his brother and the Don of the Cosa Nostra, is expecting his first child with his wife. He's determined for the child to be born into an environment that's safe."

"So, he's going to what, kill all his enemies?"

"Or buy them off and make peace with them." She nods.

"For someone who hated the life and ran away from it, you sure are re-adjusting to it very quickly."

Her brow furrows. "I am, right? It's because of Massimo. When I'm with him, I feel safe. When I'm in his arms, nobody else in the world exists. When I'm looking into his eyes, I know he'll do everything in his power to keep me protected." She sighs. "Look at me, getting all sentimental and sappy. Did you ever think you'd see the day?" She laughs.

A heavy sensation grips my chest. My stomach ties itself in knots. I'm not jealous. I'm not. "You deserve every happiness, Olivia."

"So do you. You do know Declan has feelings for you, right?"

"He feels... something for me." I shuffle my feet. I never told my sister about how Diego found me and Declan in that compromising situation. To be honest, I'm not sure I want to bring it up to her right now, either. Diego is no more, and the past belongs to Declan and me. It's up to us to figure out how to get past it... Or not.

"You sure he's treating you okay?"

"He's already introduced me to the best talent agent in town who's taking me on, so yes, he's delivering on his promise—the reason I came to LA with him in the first place."

Once more, she peruses my features, then nods. I hear someone calling her. She glances up and the big smile that lights up her features indicates it's Massimo talking.

"I gotta go. We're heading off on our honeymoon. But if you need anything—"

"I'll call, I promise. Now go, before your new husband loses his patience and decides to throw you over his shoulder and carry you out of there."

She laughs. "Bye, darling." She blows me a kiss, then the screen goes dark.

I turn to Rick. "I don't have the number to this—" My phone vibrates. I glance down to find a message:

. . .

Declan: This is the number of your new phone.

Clearly, he keyed his number into the phone book. I slide the phone into my bag, then brush past Rick, and toward the entrance. I push open the heavy double doors and step into the bright sunshine. No surprise, I hear his heavy tread in my wake. I begin to walk down the front steps, and he catches up with me at the bottom.

"Where are you going?"

"In search of Declan." I walk past the limo and down the driveway.

"How do you think you're going to find him?"

"I don't know, but I'll think of something." I continue down the drive, and he keeps abreast.

"This is LA, you can't walk anywhere."

"I come from Napoli. We walk everywhere."

"You don't have any money on you."

I scoff, "I can catch a lift."

He blows out a breath. "You're not going to give up, are you?"

"Nope."

"Fine. Wait here." His footsteps fade away. The next thing I hear is the car starting up, then he slides the limo to a halt next to me.

Yes! I round the limo and slide into the passenger's seat next to him. "So, where are you taking me?"

16

Declan

He brings down the whip and red welt blooms across her back. Droplets of blood blossom in its wake. The man scoops up the blood and brings it to his mouth. He sucks on his fingers. The coppery taste would fill his palate right now. Bet, he's turned on and can't wait to cover her pristine butt with his markings. The woman is naked. She's bent over a whipping bench, on her elbows and knees, with her torso resting on the elevated portion of the bench. Straps encircle her forearms, calves and waist, restricting her movement. Her arse is in the air, her knees far enough apart that, even at this distance, I can see the moisture glisten down her inner thigh. I shift in my seat on the other side of the one-way mirror. The two are in an exhibition room at the Club. Yep, that's what we call it because it doesn't have a name. It's one way of guaranteeing absolute privacy to members. If the place doesn't have a name, then everyone refers to it by a very generic name, which diminishes the chances of snoopy paps stumbling onto its existence.

I'm seated in the private viewing room as the sounds of the Dom and his Sub carry to me over the speakers. Normally, I'd be the one on the other side of the glass.

I'd be the one to raise my whip and snap it, making her wince, before bringing it down on her back, then below her butt, and across the backs of her thighs. I'd be the one to pause and scoop up her cum and drag it over the freshly broken skin. I'd be the one to widen my stance to accommodate the thickness between my legs. I'd be the one standing over her, working her over, wearing only jeans.

I came here with that intention, anyway, but when I saw her stretched out and ready for me, I couldn't proceed. Her shape was wrong. She was too tall, too pale, her hair too dark. Her little sounds of anticipation were all fake. And her scent—it completely destroyed any chance of me feeling anything. In short, that little siren has spoiled me for any other woman. So, I contented myself with assuming the position of an onlooker.

He whips her again, and she groans. The sound should turn me on. It should thicken my cock, ratchet up my pulse. It should make me want to stalk over, grab the whip from the Dom, and whip his sub myself, but it's not her. I curl my fingers into fists, then bow my head.

I need a release. I need a bloody release, so I can get thoughts of her out of my system. So, I can set her free to pursue her future. So, I can allow the world to discover her. It's why I brought her with me, after all. So why am I finding it so difficult to let go of her?

I squeeze my eyes shut, then pull up my T-shirt, open my fly and shove my hand down the front of my pants. I pull out my cock and squeeze it from base to crown and again. I think of her eyes, those gorgeous green eyes that welled up with tears when I spanked her. She was aroused; I'm sure about that. Though I hadn't meant to lose my temper that way. I hadn't meant to punish her, but I couldn't stop myself. I allowed myself that one slip, and damn, if I didn't sense that inner submissive in her.

Am I fooling myself? Does she have an inner need to be dominated by me? Would she be sickened by my proclivities, or would she find them intriguing enough to want to experiment with me? I massage my swelling dick, spreading my legs wider as I begin to pump myself. Up-down-up.

I will not corrupt her. Will not allow my tendencies to mar her. She's young and innocent, and while she may be spirited, there's little doubt she has no idea what BDSM involves. And if I had an iota of decency, I'd keep it that way. Doesn't stop me from imagining it though.

My balls harden, blood fills my shaft. I continue to squeeze my cock, again and again. Sensation radiates out from my crotch. My limbs grow heavy. *On your back, thrust out your chest, bare your tits for my cum, you slut.*

"Oh, fuck, Rabbit, I'm going to come." The tension tightens at the base of my spine, then explodes out. I come right there in my pants, my cum splattering in thick strands on my stomach.

A gasp reaches me. I turn to find Solene standing not a foot away, staring at me. Her gaze is locked on my crotch as I continue to squeeze myself. Her breath rises and falls; her chin trembles. *How the hell did she get here?* Before I can ask the question, she licks her lips, and my dick attempts a quick resurrection.

In the adjoining room, the woman groans. There's a snap of the whip, and she squeals.

Solene jolts, then jerks her head in the direction of the sound. Her gaze widens. Her jaw drops. The sound of the whip connecting with the woman's arse fills the space. Solene's body shudders. Color flushes her cheeks. When the woman moans loudly, she swallows.

"Such a good little submissive, you are," the man growls.

Solene stiffens. Shock flashes across her features. Then she brings her knuckles to her mouth and bites on them. She squeezes her thighs together. Goddamn, but she's aroused. Does seeing the couple together and how he dominates her turn her on?

I should stop right now and ask her to leave. I should find out how she tracked me down here, but the lust painted on her features stops me.

"How badly do you want my cock?" the man demands. He throws down his whip, then grabs her hair, forcing her head back. "How much do you want me to fuck you?"

"So much," the woman gasps.

"Ask for it, you whore."

Solene lowers her arm to her side. Her eyes grow even bigger. She seems taken aback, but clearly not enough for her to run out of here. She shuffles her feet, yet keeps her legs pressed together. I can only imagine the hot melting sensation between her legs at this very second. My thigh muscles lock, and my balls tighten.

In the next room, the woman whines, "Fuck me, please. Please, fuck me, Master."

I don't need to take in the scene unfolding in the room. When Solene draws in a sharp breath, I know he's thrust into the woman. The sound of flesh meeting flesh reaches us. I reach for a tissue from the side table, clean up the mess on my stomach, then I button myself up, rise to my feet and walk over to stand behind Solene.

Through the one-way mirror, the Dom curls his fingers about his sub's neck.

I curl my fingers about Solene's neck. She shivers.

In front of us, the woman's back arches in response. She pushes her butt back, taking him in even deeper.

A quiver runs up Solene's body.

"Does that turn you on, little Rabbit?" I whisper as I haul her close, until her back is flush with my chest.

She draws in a sharp breath.

"Does watching them turn you on? Do you want to be dominated like she is?"

Solene doesn't reply. Her gaze is riveted to the tableau.

I push my hips forward so my cock is nestled against the curve of her butt, then tuck her head under my chin. "Do you like what you see, baby?"

She swallows hard.

"There's no shame in admitting you're discovering the submissive inside of you."

Through the one-way mirror, the man pounds into the woman with such force, her entire body lurches forward. She throws her head back and a keening cry emerges from her mouth.

Solene rolls her neck, and the back of her head connects with my chest.

"Ohmygod," she moans.

I slide my palm up her dress and dip inside her panties. When I cup her pussy, she gasps, then parts her legs, giving me access. I slide my finger inside her sopping channel. She arches against me, pushing her butt back against my still erect column. I add a second finger, and she throws her arms about my neck. "Declan, I want—"

"Shh, baby."

I curve my fingers inside of her, and she arches up on her toes. "Please, please, please," she groans.

"Stay with me, Rabbit."

I move my fingers in and out of her. In and out. I add a third finger, and she huffs. I press the heel of my hand into her swollen clit, and she cries out. "I can't take it, I can't."

"You can and you will."

Ahead, the Dom unstraps his sub and pulls her up so she's kneeling on the bench. He pinches her nipple, and she wails. The sound bounces off the walls and surrounds us. The air seems to grow heavier. A bead of sweat slides down the side of Solene's temple. I bend my head and lick up the drop, then drag my tongue to the curve of her ear. I bite down on her ear lobe, and she flinches.

I pinch the swollen nub of her clit, then thrust four fingers inside her.

She cries out, I tighten my hold around her throat enough to cut off the sound and her breath. Her gaze widens. She glances up at me, a hint of fear in her gaze.

"Do you trust me?"

She blinks.

"Do you trust me, Rabbit?"

She holds my gaze for a few seconds, then nods.

Finally, fuck. I increase the pressure about her neck just a fraction. Enough for her body to twitch. For her nails to dig into my forearms. Then I increase the pace of my ministrations, in-out-in. The quiver starts from her toes and vibrates up her legs, her hips. She thrusts out her pelvis, taking my digits deeper into herself, then curves her back. Her eyes roll back in her head. I press my lips to her ear. "Come," I snap, then release my hold on her throat. Her mouth opens, she sucks in a breath and the color rushes to her face, and she cries out. Moisture bathes my fingers as she comes and comes, then slumps against me.

I continue to weave my fingers in and out of her, finger fucking her through the aftershocks of her climax. Her knees seem to give out, and I pull my fingers out of her, then sweep her up in my arms. I stalk back to the chair and sit down and pull her into my lap. She cuddles closer, and I place my fingers against her lips.

Even though her eyes are closed, she opens her mouth and curls her tongue around my digits. Sensations pool in my chest. A current of electricity zips down my spine. My balls grow heavy, and I'm sure she must sense the insistent pressure against her hip. She stirs, then raises her heavy eyelids. "What happened to you, Declan?"

17

Solene

His eyebrows furrow. There's a conflicted look in his eyes. He seems so uncertain, so approachable, so much closer to the man he was when I met him, so much more the Declan I dreamed of being with. A melting sensation pools in my chest. I raise my palm to cup his cheek.

"Tell me, Declan, what made you change so much?"

The sound of my voice seems to shake him out of his reverie. His jaw hardens.

"None of your business."

I stare. Of course, he had to shut down, just as I thought I was getting through to him. Every time I think he's softening toward me, he seems to find that alphahole part of him and draw that persona over himself like a cloak. He's hurting, and I think it's because of what my brother and his men did to him, and yet—it's not like he's blaming me completely for it. He's certainly punishing both of us for it, though.

"You know it is. We are very much each other's business since the day we met."

"Is that right?"

I nod. "It's why you brought me here to LA. You can tell yourself it's because you wanted me to find myself, carve out a career and showcase my talent to the world, but really, it's because you want me near you."

"Interesting theory." He smirks.

"Oh, please, don't mock me. You know I'm right."

His eyes gleam. "What I couldn't have guessed is what a filthy little hussy you are."

My nipples harden. My stomach flip-flops. I will not let him speak to me like that; I will not. "Take that back." I try to sit up, but he wraps his arm about me and holds me close.

"You're not leaving until I share some truths with you."

I search his features, see the resolution in his eyes. "O-k-a-y." I nod.

"Okay." He glances up. I follow his gaze to where the man has the woman he fucked earlier in his arms. She is curled into his chest, a look of contentment on her face. He rises to his feet and walks out of there.

"Where is he taking her?"

"Aftercare."

I turn my face in his direction. "Is that what this is?" I point my chin in the space between us.

"I didn't whip you," he points out.

"Do you—" I swallow. "Do you want to whip me?"

"Do you want me to whip you?"

I search his features. His expression is almost bored. It's as if he doesn't care about my answer. Then his left eyelid twitches, and I know it's the opposite. There's a part of him that's very much invested in how I reply.

The silence stretches. What should I tell him? Then before I can reply, his brow furrows.

"What are you doing here anyway?"

Ah, that. I raise a shoulder.

"I'm going to have Rick's arse for this," he says grimly.

"No, it's not his fault, uh—" I glance away, then back at him. "I might have thrown a fit and not given Rick a choice but to bring me."

"He's a bloody security guy. He should know how to deal with his principals."

"It's not his fault."

"Hmm." He scans my features. "I take it that's a no, then."

"To what?"

"My earlier question."

"You mean about the, uh, the—"

"Whipping," he smugly supplies.

"I'm not sure what I think about it. It's not something I've ever thought about. It didn't look very pleasant there." I stab my thumb in the direction of the now empty room.

"And you saw how much she enjoyed it. For that matter—" He curls his fingers around my neck lightly. "So did you."

I flush. It's true. I came so hard I blacked out for a few seconds.

"What you did—" I place my fingers over his. "When you—"

"Choked you?"

"Choking? Is that what it was?" I ask slowly.

"Did you enjoy it?"

"I enjoyed the orgasm, but for a few seconds there, I panicked," I confess.

His gaze intensifies. "You held on, you rode the wave, you had the mettle to see it through."

A warmth bleeds through my veins. Why does his praise feel so good?

"I had a feeling you knew what you were doing," I finally say.

"I did."

"So, you've done this with other women?"

In response, he brings his digits—the same ones he had inside me, the same ones I sucked on—to his mouth and sucks on them.

Heat flushes my skin. He licks each of his fingers in turn, then wipes them on my cheek.

I flinch. "You're filthy."

"Took you long enough to realize that."

"You—" I firm my lips. "Did you do that to change the topic?"

His gaze shutters. "It's time we got you home." He rises to his feet.

"Now, you're definitely changing the topic."

His lips curl. "Not aware we were discussing anything."

"You're so full of yourself." I huff.

"I'd rather you be full of—" He stops and firms his lips.

"Why don't you complete the sentence, huh? What were you going to say?"

"It doesn't matter."

Was he going go to say he'd rather I be full of him? I wrinkle my nose. That's hot. Also, that's a bit ugh. But still hot. If only I'd had access to my spicy novels, my education would have been more rounded. Instead, I had to glean information from the gossiping between the women in the kitchen.

More often than not, they complained about the act itself and how it was a duty for them to open their legs when their men climbed into their beds. I wanted to tell them it needn't be that way. That if their men were a little less selfish and more focused on their pleasure, they'd know that having sex needn't be the chore they made it out to be. Unfortunately, my ma made sure no additional spicy novels reached me. In fact, she impounded the non-spicy fiction novels Olivia managed to sneak in for me on one of her visits home.

"What's wrong?"

"Eh?" I blink up at him. "What's wrong is that you're carrying me like I'm a child when I am perfectly capable of walking on my own two feet."

"You just came so hard you could barely stay upright. Not to mention, I wasn't exactly gentle with you—" He shoots me an annoyed glance, as if that orgasm was my fault. "So no, you don't get to walk."

"So, I have to look completely foolish so you can assuage your conscience?"

His arms tighten around me. He doesn't reply, simply strides through the corridor, then down the flight of steps I used not long ago. He heads past the reception. The woman behind it doesn't even blink an eye. Guess she's used to women being carried out of here. I frown. *That's not good, is it? On the other hand, if it means women are having such strong orgasms, they're unable to make it out on their own steam, then that's good, right?*

Declan walks out the main door. He waits for only a few seconds before the limo drives up. Rick rounds the car and opens the door to the backseat. "Is she okay?" He frowns at Declan.

"I'm okay."

"She's not," Declan says at the same time.

"Hey, I'm good, I—"

He drops me in the passenger seat with just enough force that I blink. He follows me in, and I scoot over.

"Why are you in such a mood?"

"I'm not in any mood." He hits a button, and a panel rises, cutting us off from the driver's seat.

He pulls out his phone and busies himself.

"I forgot to say thank you."

He stills. "For the orgasm?"

Heat flushes my face again. Damn, I'm not a shy kinda girl. I'm not, I swear. But my lack of exposure to the world, and definite lack of experience when it comes to O's, is catching up with me. I refuse to show it, though. I tip up my chin. "That, too. But I was talking about the cell phone."

"Hmm." He settles back into the seat and continues to scroll through his phone.

"Are you checking your social media?"

"I leave that to the minions."

"Minions?"

"My team. I have a team that takes care of all that." His tone is impatient, but at least, he's answering my questions, eh?

"Isn't it better if you do some of it hands on? You know, be authentic and all that."

He shrugs. "The fans will be happier if I focus on my next film."

"You sure?"

"It's worked for me so far, hasn't it?"

"That's before you had a hit. Now you're hot property and all—"

He shoots me a sideways glance.

"What?"

"You saw my last film?"

I glance away. "I wasn't allowed to see movies or have any access to popular culture."

"Hold on, you weren't allowed to see movies?"

"Only some of the classics, like "The Sound of Music," and even then, I had to close my eyes during the kissing scenes."

He stares at me. "So, no movies?"

I shake my head.

"No music—"

"Italian opera. I wish I could have learned to play musical instruments, but my family was against it."

His eyebrows knit. "What else weren't you allowed to do?"

"No eating out in restaurants, lest I was tempted to flirt with the waiter or worse, run away with one of the other patrons."

"You're kidding."

"Do I look like I'm kidding?"

He puts down his phone; his forehead furrows.

"What about going to a nightclub?"

I scoff.

"Picnics?"

"Only in the company of women."

He tilts his head. "Gaming?

"Please. I didn't have my own phone, let alone, access to the internet. Not that it stopped me from using my friends' phones or sneaking down to the family computer in the study after everyone went to sleep."

He opens his mouth, and I raise my hand. "I learned how to wipe out all traces of my searches."

He seems to relax a little.

"And no books, of course."

"What?" He gapes. "No books?"

"Not the kind that matter. I did have access to the books in school, and the classics and non-fiction. Just not the right kind of books, you know?"

"What do you mean?"

"The kind of books that matter?" I make air quotes.

"Sorry, you lost me."

"Spicy books."

His frown deepens. "You mean books about cooking?"

I burst out laughing. "Oh, my god, that's classic. I mean it is about cooking, but not the kind of cooking you're thinking of. The kind with steam and interesting positions, and vegetables which are of the right shape, and— "

His brow clears. "You mean, erotica?"

"I mean spicy books."

He looks me up and down. "I see."

"There you go, getting all judgmental." I stab my finger at him. "So, men can watch all the porn they like, but if women read spicy novels we're judged, huh? And what about men objectifying women, as they've done for centuries. Not to mention, marrying us off in arranged alliances, then expecting women to spread their legs, receive their sperm, and produce children for them. But when it comes to us women seeking pleasure between the arms of book boyfriends, you get all smirky and snicker at us, and— "

"Whoa, whoa, hold on, I'm not judging you."

"You were judging me right then."

"I wasn't."

"You were!"

He blows out a breath. "Can I prove otherwise to you?"

18

Declan

"OMG, OMG, OMG." She stands in front of the shelves of books in the biggest bookshop in the city, her palms clasped together. "This is... These are..."

"The spicy novels you couldn't stop talking about?"

She opens and shuts her mouth, then runs her fingers through her hair. "How did you know—"

"Where to find them?"

"Umm, yes?"

"Lucky guess, I suppose?" I raise a shoulder.

She reaches out and runs her fingers across the spines of the books. Her features soften; her lips part. Her entire body leans into the books. It's as if she's making love to the bookcase. A sharp sensation stabs my chest. My guts knot. What the—? I can't be jealous of the books, can I? Her chest rises and falls. Her lips curve. She pulls out one book, then another, and another. The last begins to tip over from her hold.

I bend and catch it then, looking around, I grab a basket and deposit the book inside. I hold it. "Drop your books in here."

She glances down, slides her books into the basket, then looks up at me from under her eyelashes. "Thank you."

"You're welcome."

"You're being very polite."

I smirk. "Does that surprise you?"

"It does, considering how you've been blowing hot and cold with me since we reconnected."

Drop down to your knees, lock your hands behind your back. You will not move until I give you permission.

"Declan?" Her brow furrows. "Are you okay?"

"How many books can you get in the space of ten minutes I wonder?"

"Is that a challenge?" Her eyes gleam, then she stiffens. "I don't have the money to buy these books."

"Consider it a gift."

She sets her jaw. "I don't want to accept any favors from you."

"You'll be doing me a favor by getting these books."

"How's that?"

"It will help you understand my lifestyle."

She tilts her head. "Your lifestyle."

"Best if you read the books first." I reach past her, pull out "*Fifty Shades of Grey*," and drop it into the basket.

"Is that a good one?"

"It's the mother of all your spicy books."

"O-k-a-y?"

"How about?" I pull out a few, read the blurbs on the back, then choose two more and drop them into the basket.

"You sure seem to know a lot about spicy books?"

"I know… enough."

"Have you read any of them?"

"Don't need to." I roll my shoulders. Not when I'm living the scenarios depicted in many of them. Spicy authors know what they're talking about. Some of the books are prescribed reading for both Doms and subs in the Club. Not that I needed it. I went through my own journey to get here.

She folds her arms across her chest. "I am a bit confused as to why you're doing this. Also, I really don't want to accept another favor from you."

"Once your first song releases, you'll be rich enough to pay me back for the books."

She tips up her chin. "Not only the books. I'll pay you back for putting me up in your house."

"It's not like there'd be anyone else occupying your room. But if it makes you feel better, sure—"

"It does."

"Now that's settled..." I nod toward the bookshelf. "How many books do you think you can pick in ten minutes?"

An hour later we walk toward the front of the shop. I'm carrying four—yes, four—baskets, two in each hand, all of them loaded with books. I refused to let her carry any of the baskets. She protested at first, then finally relented when I told her it would save me time as I'd include it as part of my daily workout routine. She was disbelieving until I explained to her I have a daily workout routine to stay in shape for the screen. Heaving the weight of these books would help me offset some of the time I'd have otherwise spent at the gym. And I'm not lying. My biceps strain and my triceps protest. A burn tugs at my calves. *Who knew carrying books would provide such a work out? Maybe I should replace my weights with spicy novels?*

"Hey, hold on, we haven't paid yet," she calls out.

I glance over my shoulder to find she's stopped in front of the cashier's counter.

She looks around. "Why is there no-one at the cash desk?" She frowns, then straightens. "For that matter, why are we the only ones in the store?"

I chuckle. She was so entranced by the books, it's the first time she's noticing we're the only ones in the store.

"It's paid for," I explain.

"I didn't see you pay for it."

"Believe me, it's taken care of."

She purses her lips. "I'm confused. There's no one here, but the store is open because nobody stopped us from coming in. Also—" She presses a finger to her cheek. "I thought you were famous?"

"I am."

"But no one stopped you for autographs, because there's no one in here, because..." she draws down her brows. "What's happening, Declan? What are you not telling me?"

"Can we have this conversation after we get home?"

She looks past me and her brow clears. "I see."

"What do you mean?"

"There's no one in here because they're all out there."

I turn around, and sure enough, there's a crowd of photographers clustered around the entrance on the other side of the double doors that lead out of the bookshop.

"Bloody fuck." I reach for my phone when it rings. Rick's name shows up on the screen. "There are—"

"—paps in the front. Come around to the back door. I'm waiting with the limo."

Motherfucker's on the ball when it comes to issues of security. I made the right decision hiring him, unlike my dubious idea to bring her with me to LA. The jury's still out on that one.

I pivot and walk back toward her. "Come on." I want to grab her hand, but I'm still holding the baskets with her books. So, I jerk my chin in the direction of the back door. "Rick's waiting there." I march ahead of her, then glance over to find she hasn't moved.

"The fuck, woman? Can't you do what you're told to do, for once?"

Her lips thin. "If I wanted to be ordered around by an asshole of a man, I could've stayed back and married another Mafia guy."

"And you knew what you were getting into when you agreed to come with me."

She blinks rapidly. "If I'd known you were going to give me whiplash at every turn, I might not have."

Flashes go off outside the glass doors at the entrance.

"We need to go before the paps decide they'll risk breaking into private property. Or figure out we're headed to the back door."

She glances over her shoulder then back at me. "But don't we have to pay for the boo—"

"Fuck the books. I own the bloody bookshop, so I don't need to pay for anything in here. Are you satisfied?"

She gapes. "Y-y-y-y-you own the shop."

"The entire chain actually."

"H-h-h-h-how?"

"I'll tell you in the car, okay? Let's go now... Please?"

The p-word seems to do it, for she nods and strides forward. I follow her through the shop to the exit at the back. We walk out and head toward the idling limo. Good man, Rick. He's kept the engine running. A flash goes off—of course, there's always that one photographer who breaks away from the pack and takes a risk.

She falters, but I head past her and toward the back door. "Get in."

To my relief, Solene obeys. Rick opens the door for her, and she slides in. I shove the first two baskets inside, then the next two. A couple of books fall out.

"Leave them," Solene cries.

I bend and pick up the books, and more flashes go off. I throw the books inside the car and straighten to find there are now five paps. All clicking away and, moving closer by the minute.

"Are you buying books for your new lady love, Declan?"

"Who is your new girlfriend, Declan?"

"Is it true she's an up-and-coming singer?"

"Is she an old flame?"

"Is it true you have a piercing on your unmentionable?"

I scowl, then realize they're probably throwing out all of their hypotheses in the hope of getting a rise out of me. It's how they push us to react, so they can carry the outburst as a news item.

I turn my back on them, and one of them jeers, "You moving onto ugly waifs who look like they've never had a decent meal in their life?"

Anger sizzles through my veins, and tension builds in my muscles so fast, spots of black spark in my line of sight. He's trying to get me to make a move; he's taunting me to take a bait.

I begin to slide in, when the same guy laughs. "Lost your balls?"

My vision tunnels. He's so close now, I think I can feel his breath on my neck.

"You're an action star on screen, but in real life, you're unable to come to the defense of your lady love, eh, you—"

I turn around and smash my fist into his nose. Blood blooms from his face. Flashbulbs go off. I grab his collar, pull back my arm again, but Solene yells, "Stop, Declan!" She throws herself across the seat and grabs at my shirt. "Please, let's go."

More flashbulbs go off.

I release my hold on the man, who stumbles back, then slide inside the car.

Before I've shut the door, Rick accelerates and drives away. No one breathes a word. I lean back against the back of the seat, when she leans toward me. "You have a piercing?"

19

Solene

He definitely didn't have piercings at twenty-one. Not that I remember. Not that I saw him completely naked then to draw that conclusion, but it didn't seem possible that gorgeous, wholesome-looking man could have piercings. This growling, grumpy—still achingly handsome, but also slightly older and scarred male, though? Yeah, he could have a piercing. Or several. But I didn't notice any that day at the Club. But then I didn't get a full-frontal view of his cock, either. I wasn't standing that close, and his body was wreathed in shadows.

"Where is it?" I burst out.

"I've no idea what you're talking about."

"That journalist, he said you had a—"

"He's not a journalist." His jaw tics. "He's a celebrity-baiting, privacy-invading gutter guppy who's on the lowest pecking order of the food chain. He's worse than a cockroach; he survives on other people's misfortunes; he thrives on their anger and outbursts. I fucking hate him and his ilk."

I gape at him. "What's a guppy?"

He blinks, then barks out a laugh. "You're one of a kind, you know that?"

Heat flushes my cheeks. A gooey sensation puddles in my chest. A different kind of moisture forms between my legs.

He shakes out his hand, and I glimpse the reddened skin over his knuckles. I take his hand between my much smaller ones. He's so much darker than me, and it's not fake tan either. Before I can talk myself out of it, I pull his hand closer, then bend and kiss the distressed skin.

A shudder runs up his arm. Without glancing at him, I wrap my lips around his knuckle and suck. He inhales deeply. "What are you doing?" he asks in a low voice.

In answer, I bite down on the already injured skin until a drop of his blood oozes onto my tongue. I suck on it, and the coppery taste seeps into my palate. My core clenches. My thighs quiver. What am I doing? I'm not sure, except it feels so right.

"That was so hot." I turn toward him. "You, losing your temper because he insulted me."

He searches my features, then pulls his hand from my grasp. "I'd have done that for anybody in your position."

Anger crackles across my nerve-endings before I retort, "I don't believe you."

He pretends to yawn. "Not my problem." He pulls out his phone and begins to play with it.

The anger erupts into a full-blown volcano that pulses through my veins. I grab the phone from him, then hit the button to lower the window on my side and toss out the device.

There's silence in the vehicle, broken only by the sound of my window rolling back up. Tension thrums from his body. The air in the back of the car grows thick. His muscles are knotted so tightly, I can feel the tautness that writhes under his skin. I begin to slide away from him and toward my door.

"Scared, Rabbit?" he growls in that low, hard voice that sends a shiver of apprehension up my spine...combined with something else—an expectation, a frisson of excitement that makes me shiver. My lower lips swell. My nipples tighten. Gah! Why does his anger turn me on? I'm not afraid of him. I'm not. I tilt up my chin, then toss my hair over my shoulder. "Of course not."

"Hmm."

He swipes out his hand, and I yelp. Only, he plucks a thread from my dress and flicks it aside.

I laugh, and the sound is so tentative, so nervous, I firm my lips.

"You wouldn't be laughing if you knew what I was going to do next."

"W-w-w-w-what's that?" Aargh, this stuttering. I was sure I was rid of it, but apparently, being turned on triggers it. Note to self: Do not let yourself be turned on by Declan. Hah! What a joke. Like I have any chance of resisting this man's influence, his charisma, the sheer dominance of his presence that pushes down on my shoulder and pins me in place.

There's a soft whirring sound and the screen behind the front and back seats rises. So does the fine hair on the back of my neck. I draw in a choppy breath. Don't do it. Don't do it. Unable to resist the pull in his direction, I turn my head. And meet that raw, chilling gaze of his. Oh, god, oh, god. His eyes have an unholy look in them. One side of his lips curls. He knows exactly how this building anticipation is beginning to affect me. He looks down at his lap, then at me.

Oh no, no, no, no. I set my jaw. He arches an eyebrow. His gaze narrows, and I can't stop myself from swallowing. Can't stop the slow, heavy pulse that blooms between my thighs. My panties are soaked, and he hasn't even touched me.

He lowers his chin. His nostrils flare, and he pats his thigh. Once. Instantly, I scoot over and lay across his lap.

"Good girl."

His hard voice pours over my skin, leaving little sparks of fire in their wake. I squeeze my legs together and grip the edge of the seat. Oh, my god, why is every cell in my body responding to his praise? What does it mean that I was so quick to obey him? Not that I could have refused, even if I'd wanted to. Which I didn't.

I might put up a show of defying him, but really, it's an act. I wanted his complete attention on me. This is what I want. The touch of his palm as he flips up my dress and cups my butt cheek through my panties. The stroke of his hand as he continues up the arch of my back, making me stretch.

"You like that, huh?"

I nod. Of course I do. I'm trying to locate that inner rebel that helped me survive all those the years of confinement with my family. And mostly, I'm convinced I have enough of that spark inside of me to fan it into a full-blown fire of opposition. But when it comes to Declan, and the forbidden side of him that he's hinted at, there's no resistance.

"You know what you are?"

I shake my head.

"A brat."

"A brat?" I tilt my head.

"And you know what happens to brats?"

His fingers graze the seam of my panties and I whine. "What?" I swallow. "What happens?"

"They don't get what they want."

"I don't want anything from you, I—" I huff, for he's slipped his fingertips under my panties and grazed my throbbing clit. Just a touch, but it's enough to send a flurry of sensations streaming up my back.

But then, he pulls away his hand. The next second, he grabs my waist and swings me up and onto the seat next to him. My butt hits the seat. I blink, then turn on him. "What's the meaning of this, why didn't you—?"

"Fuck you?" He laughs. "I don't fuck virginal little girls."

"I'm not a—" I pause.

His smirk widens. "You going to deny that?"

"Fuck you," I snap.

"Not likely. My tastes run to the extreme, and you'd never be able to take it."

I open my mouth, then shut it. He's right. I'm out of my depth. I have no idea what I'm dealing with here. He may have bought me books—correction, he bought the chain of bookshops, but it's probably small change for him. And he's right. At heart, I'm that scared little, virginal Mafia princess. No. I fold my arms across my chest. I'm going to show him how wrong he is, if the last thing I do.

The car draws to a halt. I glance out to find we're in front of a restaurant.

"What's this place?" I scowl.

"Wouldn't you like to find out?"

20

Declan

Maybe it was a bad idea to bring her here. I scowl at the waiter, who can't take his eyes off of her as he uncorks the bottle of wine. He pours a little into my glass. I take a sip and nod my approval. He leans over to pour some into her glass, which means he has to move closer to her and —I jump to my feet. "No wine for her!"

The waiter's hand jerks. Drops of wine stain the white tablecloth. In two strides, I reach him and take the wine bottle from him. "Leave." I jerk my chin in the direction of the kitchen.

He half bows, then scurries off. "Asshole," I grumble as I put down the wine bottle, then snatch up the bottle of water and top off her glass with water.

"Umm, what was that?"

"What was what?" I place the bottle of water on the table, then move over to fill my glass with wine before taking my seat.

"You know, the way you sent that poor man scurrying off?"

"He was standing too close to you."

"He was trying to pour me some wine."

"And now, he isn't."

She gapes at me. "Are you feeling okay? Maybe that run in with the pap upset you more than I realized."

"I chew through them in my dreams, so don't worry your pretty little head about it."

She sets her jaw. "Don't treat me like that."

"Like what?"

"Like a woman who has no idea what's happening around her. I admit, I'm in a different country and still getting used to my environment, but I learn fast."

"You don't say." I raise my glass. "Here's to you."

She glances at her glass of water, then at me. "But I want to drink wine."

"You're not yet twenty-one, so no wine for you."

"But in Italy, the legal drinking age is eighteen," she protests.

"We're not in Italy. We're in the U.S. and the legal drinking age is twenty-one."

She pouts. "But I wanna drink wine."

"And I wanna bend you over the table and fuck you right now, but I'm not going to, so I guess we're even."

She gapes at me again. I can't stop the chuckle that wells up. "Doesn't take much to shock you."

"Ha!" She tosses her hair. "Enjoy it while you can. I'm a fast learner." She takes a sip of water from her glass, then sets it back on the table. "Thank you, by the way."

"For what?" I raise the glass of wine and sniff its bouquet.

"For the books earlier, then for defending me from the paparazzi. And now, this." She waves a hand in the air. "It would be a lot better if I knew what you wanted from me, but I guess I can't have everything, huh?"

She looks, and I hold her gaze. "I'm not sure what I want from you, either. I was really pissed at you—not so much for this scar..." I gesture to my forehead. "Although admittedly, that did alter the course of my career. But hey, being a villain in Hollywood is not so bad, I'm finding out."

"I'm so sorry, Declan."

I wave my hand. "It's not your fault your brother sent those guys after me. I should have anticipated the encounter ending like that. I was angrier that you implied to him that I'd forced you."

She swallows. "I didn't know what else to say. Diego... His anger was not pretty. He'd have punished me, and I was scared."

"I understand that now."

"You do?" Her gaze widens.

"You were seventeen, a kid. And while seeing you again reignited a need for revenge, which I admit, was on my mind when I first asked you to join me in LA, I quickly realized the error in my thinking."

"So, you… forgive me?"

I tap my fingers on the table. "Let's just say, I don't blame you anymore for what happened."

"Okay."

"Okay."

"So, is this a truce?" She holds up her glass of water

"It's a… beginning of our friendship."

"Friendship?" Her forehead furrows.

"Friends. You and me." I clink my glass with hers, then take a sip of the wine. "Not bad." For the most expensive wine on the menu.

"Can I take a sip, please? I've never tasted wine before."

"Never?"

She shakes her head.

"Hmm. Since this is an evening of firsts for you—" I slide my glass across the table. "A taste won't hurt I suppose."

She snatches up the glass takes a sip then coughs, "Ugh, it tastes like vinegar."

I laugh. "You get used to it."

She takes another sip, swirls it about her mouth, then makes a face, but swallows it down without flinching.

Take my dick down your throat. Breathe through your nose. I prefer it if you gag. I want to see the saliva drool down your chin. I want the tips of your teeth to scrape over my shaft and—

Footsteps approach, then, "Declan?" Rick's voice cuts through my thoughts. I turn to find he's walking next to a tall, skinny woman with pinched lips, hollowed-out cheeks, and hips which might almost look good if she put on five more pounds.

"Giorgina," I say with resignation.

Rick shuffles his feet, "Sorry, she was throwing a fit outside, and short of hauling her away physically—"

"Don't you fucking touch me, you prick," she snaps.

He doesn't bat an eye. "I know you didn't want to be disturbed. It would have been worse if I'd stopped her from coming in."

"Damn right." She marches over to the table and throws down her phone, screen face up. "Care to explain this to me?"

"No, and you're interrupting a private dinner."

"It's fine, really, I can go—" Solene begins to rise, but I glare at her.

"Sit down."

Her butt hits the chair, but she looks thoroughly pissed about it. A chuckle wells up, but I manage to stop it. Damn, if it doesn't send a signal straight to my dick when she obeys me like that. Her body knows who her master is, her mind and emotions have yet to catch up though.

"Is this your new plaything?" Giorgina looks down her nose at Solene. "Shoo, can't you see the adults are talking?"

Solene stares, then a mutinous expression comes over her face. She leans back in her seat and tips up her chin. "Who's this skinny bitch, darling?" She drawls.

Giorgina scoffs. "Well, in comparison to your puppy fat, yes, I guess I'm skinny."

"Puppy fat?" Solene's gaze narrows. "I'd be careful what you say next, you anorexic Barbie-lookalike."

"I'll take that as a compliment." Giorgina sniffs.

Solene looks taken aback, then a reluctant chuckle leaves her mouth. "You have a sense of humor for a dried up—"

Giorgina lowers her chin to her chest, and Solene shuts her mouth.

"So, this is the woman for whom you decked a paparazzo, huh?" Giorgina looks her up and down.

I reach across, and take my glass of wine, then take a sip. "What took you so long?"

"I've been trying your phone non-stop, but it kept going to voicemail."

"Ah." I smirk at Solene. "I wonder why that's the case, hmm?"

"Never mind about the phone." Giorgina plants her hands on her hips. "We need to release a statement about why you went all kamikaze on a pap, while you were trying to defend—"

"Solene," I helpfully supply.

"Solene." Giorgina looks between us. "Someone care to tell me what's happening?"

"Nope." I half smile.

"Jesus, Declan, this doesn't look good."

"Adds to my bad boy persona. Given directors only approach me to play the villain, this makes it seem like an extension of my on-screen image, which won't hurt."

"The asshole pap wanted to press charges, but I bought him off," Giorgina sniffs.

"Of course, you did."

"He also wants an exclusive."

"Not happening." I drain my glass of wine.

Solene looks from me to Giorgina. "So, you're his—"

"Long-suffering PR manager," Giorgina snaps without taking her censorious gaze from my face. "You could be a little more subtle about this date you—" She glances around the restaurant, "Did you buy out the restaurant? Where's everyone else?"

Solene whips her head in my direction. "Did you buy out the restaurant?"

"Nope." I pour more of the wine into my glass, then take a sip. "I bought *the* restaurant."

"You *bought* the restaurant," she blinks.

Solene stares. "*You* bought the restaurant?"

"That's what I said."

The color drains from Solene's face. She opens and shuts her mouth, then reaches across the table toward my glass of wine. I don't stop her, so she snatches it up and takes a sip, only to cough.

"Ugh!" She makes a face, places the wine down, and instead, reaches for the water.

I shoot her an I-told-you-so look, and she scowls back.

Giorgina throws up her hands. "Can the two of you stop whatever it is you're doing and focus on the fact that, when the news of his sale is bound to get out and—"

"The owner signed a non-disclosure agreement."

"Which only means the news is delayed by a few days. I suppose I should be grateful for that reprieve."

"I also bought a bookstore chain."

This time, Giorgina whips her head around to stare at Solene. "You did that for her?"

"It was a good investment." And this way, wherever she travels in the U.S., she'll always have a bookstore where she can walk in and get her spicy books.

She rocks back on her heels. "This is going to cause a media furor."

"That's why I'm paying you, aren't I?"

"Absolutely." She cracks her knuckles. "So, we release a statement informing the press about your new girlfriend, and— "

"I'm not his girlfriend," Solene interjects.

At the same time, I growl, "She's not my girlfriend."

She looks between us. "Suit yourselves, but it's best we stick to this story, and— "

"Absolutely not. I will not drag Solene into this. Besides, she has her own talent manager who also manages her PR."

"She does?" Giorgina straightens, then once, more turns to Solene. "And what is it you do?"

"I'm a singer."

"A very talented singer who will be famous very soon," I murmur.

Solene's face flushes. She looks down and begins to play with the hem of the tablecloth. "Thank you."

"You're welcome."

"O-k-a-y…" Giorgina fans herself. "You may insist there's nothing between the two of you, but the sparks between you two say otherwise, alright?" She looks to Rick, who hasn't moved from his stance beside to her.

He looks taken aback, then slowly nods. "Much as it pains me, I have to side with her."

"I'm always right, if you'd only admit it." Her eyes gleam.

He scowls. A nerve tics at his temple. Interesting. Apparently, my PR manager has the ability to rub him the wrong way.

"Anywho,"—she turns to Solene—"if you can put me in touch with your manager, I'll talk to them, and we'll figure out our stories so we don't contradict each other."

"Oh, I don't know his— " Solene begins.

"Check your phone," I murmur.

She blinks, then pulls her phone from her bag which she placed on the floor behind her. "Ah, his number is— "

Giorgina snatches the phone from Solene. Her fingers fly over the screen. Then her phone, which is still face-up on the table, buzzes. She hands over Solene's phone, picks up her own and a few seconds later, it's Solene's phone buzzing.

"Now, we're connected." She taps at her phone, then slides it inside her handbag. "I'll leave you two lovebirds alone."

"We're not— " Solene begins, but Giorgina pivots.

"Come on, then. Chop, chop." She beckons to Rick, then flounces off.

Rick's features grow thunderous. The tendons of his throat pop. He curls his fingers into fists at his sides and glares after her.

"Easy, big fella, you don't want to make things more difficult for yourself," I drawl.

He snorts. "Speak for yourself." Then he half bows in Solene's direction. "Pardon the intrusion." He turns and stalks after Giorgina.

"Uh, they don't like each other?" Solene glances in his wake.

I chuckle. "That's foreplay."

"What?" She turns to me. "You're kidding, right?"

"Nope. We'll see how long they hold out against each other."

She moves around in her seat.

I stare at her with interest. "Your butt bothering you?"

She tosses her head. "What do you think?"

I can't stop the smirk that curls my lips.

She stops fidgeting, glances around the restaurant, then reaches for her wine glass, and curls her fingers around the stem. "Why did you buy this restaurant?"

"I wanted privacy, and this was a good investment."

"And you made sure no one else dined here? That doesn't seem like sound business sense."

"It was worth it."

She flushes again, takes another sip of her glass. "I really don't understand you."

"You don't need to understand me; you simply need to focus on your career as a singer."

"Which I will, but what about this afternoon?"

"What do you mean?"

The waiter, a woman this time, wheels in the food and slides the plates in front of us. "Enjoy," she smiles and backs away, pushing the serving cart.

Solene glances down at her food. "You ordered pizza for me?" She looks up. "How did you— "

"You're from Napoli. Not rocket science to make the connection with pizza."

"Still, you kept in mind I'm from Napoli and ordered a dish that is a specialty of my hometown." Her gaze grows dreamy.

I frown. "Don't go reading too much into it. It's our one evening together. I thought you should experience everything you've missed out on over the years, and what you've been missing since you left home."

"Everything I've been missing, huh?" She picks up a slice of the pizza. "Nothing compares to the pizza in Napoli, and— " She bites into a slice of pizza, then moans.

My dick twitches, and blood rushes to my groin. Fucking hell, she's enjoying her food. That's all it is. Some of the olive oil smears her chin. She doesn't wipe it off. She finishes off the slice of pizza, then starts on the next. Then the next. After the fourth piece, she looks at my plate. "You're not eating?"

"I'm full already." And I am. Watching the sheer joy and satisfaction on her face is a thrill like no other. Interesting. *When did I last find such joy in giving?* Maybe when I brought my grandmama a pashmina shawl. But other than that? Nope, I've been too focused on myself and my career. Too focused on building up my roster of films. A couple of hits don't mean anything in Hollywood. Sure, I'm well known, but it's not enough. And while I come from a privileged background, I've never touched my father's money. I've always wanted to make it on my own.

Power, fame, fortune—I thirst for them, but I want to earn them myself. And I know I'm talented. From a very young age, all I ever wanted was to act. And the scar on my forehead only made me more determined to succeed. Indeed, it fired me up in a way nothing had before. That, and the thought that, one day, I would take revenge on her. I now know the second wouldn't make me happy. But the first? The chance to lose myself in a character was the biggest aphrodisiac in my life, until I ran into her again.

I watch her polish off the rest of the slices of pizza, then she leans back with a groan. "That was *buonissimo*." She puts her fingertips together and brings them to her lips. "It was almost like being back in Napoli."

Her features fall a little, and she lowers her arm. "I don't really miss home. I mean, I couldn't wait to get away. I still can't believe I made it out, so I'm not sure why I said that."

"It's still home."

She glances up at me. "Where's your home?"

"London, I suppose." It's close to where I studied and where most of my friends are.

"And your parents?"

"My mother's no more, and my father runs a business based in a city called Lille in France, just across the channel from England."

"So, you're French?"

"In origin."

"Do you speak French?"

"Only when I'm fucking."

She flushes, then tips up her chin. "You can't embarrass me."

"Then why are you blushing?"

"I'm not."

"You are."

"It's the wine." She reaches for my glass then tosses back the dregs. She doesn't cough this time, nor does she make a face. Sigh. They grow up so fast, don't they?

When she places the glass down on the table, her cheeks are beet-red.

"You're going to pay for that, you know?"

"Maybe." She shakes her hair back from her face. "But I need courage."

"For what?" I scowl.

"For this."

21

Solene

I jump up to my feet. My head spins a little, probably due to the wine I've consumed, but I ignore it. I push aside my empty plate and clamber onto the chair. I have the satisfaction of seeing his gaze widen. I pull up the hem of my dress then get down on my hands and knees and crawl across the table to him. He swoops down, and I flinch, but all he does is slide his plate and cutlery out of my way. Then, he leans back in his seat, tracking me with his gaze. I inch closer, never taking my gaze off his face. I may have initially surprised him, but the expression on his face indicates he's more curious than anything else about what I'm up to. I pause in front of him; he watches me steadily. A bead of sweat slides down my back. A heavy pulse flares to life between my thighs.

The fact that he's not making a move, but instead, waiting for what I'm going to do next, infuses me with a sense of power. Oh, I have no illusions; he's very much in control, but for this moment, he's willing to wait for me to take the initiative and that...is almost as hot as him taking the lead. Almost as much of a turn on as watching him spread his legs wide to accommodate the unmistakable bulge at his crotch. And make no mistake, the column in his pants is huge.

My mouth waters, my thighs clench, and I want more. I want him to throw me down on my back on this table and fuck me. I want him to shove that big monster cock inside of me and rid me of this empty sensation I've carried in my core for so long.

I move forward until I'm at the edge of the table, then lean in. I'm close enough to brush my nose against his neck. Close enough to inhale his scent and hold it in my lungs until every cell in my body seems to fill with his essence. I flick out my tongue and lick his skin; a growl vibrates up his chest.

"You have no idea what you're doing," he warns.

"Don't I?" I glance up at him from under my eyelashes to find his blue eyes have turned into that blazing indigo, which tells me he's not unaffected by my nearness, either. It gives me the confidence to open my mouth and sink my teeth into the side of his neck.

The next second, he plants his heavy hand around the nape of my neck and pulls me back so he can see my face. I freeze, then flick out my tongue and lick the drops of his blood which cling to my lips. His gaze narrows. His pupils dilate. All expression is wiped clear from his face, so it feels like he's wearing a mask. A cruel, mean mask that gives me no clue to what he's thinking. Except, his chest rises and falls, and the veins at his throat are so tense they could burst out of his skin any moment. His nostrils flare, and I'm sure he's inhaling my scent, too. It gives me the courage to place my lips over his. My breath brushes his mouth, and a pulse flares to life at his jawline.

"Be very careful, Rabbit, you might not like what's coming next."

"That's my problem, isn't it?" I dig my teeth into his lower lip and pull down with enough force to draw blood again.

"Fuck!" His tone is frustrated and angry, and also, lust-filled. He tightens his hold around my neck and hauls me back, but not before I flick out my tongue and lick the droplets of blood off his lip. I swallow; his gaze is fixed on my mouth.

"The things I want to do to you." He shakes his head as if to clear it. "I know what you're doing. I can see I misjudged you badly when I invited you to accompany me. You're smart and a quick learner, but you haven't seen the world."

"Unlike you?" I scoff.

"Thanks to you, I grew up fast."

I swallow. "I'm—"

"No, don't apologize. I owe you a debt. It's because of what happened to me that I appreciated what I had. It's because I kept getting turned down for roles that I made up my mind to fight harder, smarter, and be more strategic than anyone else. It's because you showed me the error of my ways that I knew I couldn't afford to dick around anymore. That entire encounter made me stronger, more focused—"

"Less sensitive."

"Sensitivity is overrated."

I frown. "You're an actor. Shouldn't you be in touch with your emotions?"

"Is this the conversation you want to have while you're on your hands and knees with your pussy dripping all over the tablecloth?"

I swallow. More moisture slips out from between my legs. "Oh, god," I breathe.

"You mean Oh, Declan, don't you?" He smirks.

I scowl. "Your confidence should make me want to hate you. Instead, it turns me on more, and I really don't understand why."

"Don't you?" He leans forward until his eyelashes kiss mine. "Want me to spell it out?"

"Spell what out?"

"You're a submissive, little Rabbit. You want a Dominant who can tell you what to do and take all choice from you. You're a brat who wants to be spanked and put in her place and denied her pleasure until she learns her place. You're a—"

"I'm nothing like that." I try to pull away, but he holds me in place.

"You will listen to me."

"I—"

He glares at me, and a shiver oscillates down my spine. That pulse within my belly is a full-blown pressure pit that seems to draw every emotion I hold in my body. I stare at him, unable to move, transfixed by the authority written into the angles of his face. I'm mesmerized by the force of his dominance that forms a force-shield around us. A cloud of heat seems to spool off of him and slam into my chest. I gasp.

He's going to subjugate me, control me, hold sway over me, influence me. He's going to make me bend to him, and I will... Just, not yet. My breath comes in uneven waves, I dig my knees and my palms into the table for support, then shake my head.

His gaze widens. "The fuck was that?"

"I—" I clear my throat. "I'm not giving in to you."

"You will."

"Maybe, but right here, right now, I'm issuing a challenge to you."

His eyes gleam. He cants his head, and the movement is so like that of a predator that my arms and legs tremble. My heart is racing so hard, I'm sure he can hear it. The pulse thuds at my temples.

Strange, it's the fact that I'm looking into those laser sharp eyes of his that anchors me and gives me the confidence to say, "You'll never make me submit."

"And when I do?"

"You won't!"

His lips curve. Those white teeth of his flash. "Game on!"

A ripple of apprehension runs down my spine. My stomach flip-flops. A heavy pulse descends between my legs, and I know then, I shouldn't have challenged him. I wasn't thinking clearly. If I had been I would have realized the chase is what excites the beast in him; or maybe, I did. Maybe I knew that about him from our earlier interactions. Maybe I wanted to turn our encounter into one he wouldn't forget easily. I want to stand out amongst the women he's met. I wanted to earn back his respect, his trust, even. I set my jaw. "It's not a game," I say through gritted teeth.

"Everything is a game, baby. And when I win—and I will win—you will do everything I want. You will become the perfect little submissive. You will yield to me and allow me to make you mine."

"Make me yours?"

He blinks, then scowls. "I mean, you will defer to me in every aspect of your personal life."

"And my singing career?"

"That's not within the scope of our agreement."

"So, only my non-professional life?"

"I don't repeat myself," he drawls.

I look between his eyes, then nod. "And if I win?"

"You won't."

"What if I do?"

"What do you want?" He smirks. *Jerkface is so confident, huh? We'll see how that goes for you, Mr. SmirkyPants.*

"Then, you'll do whatever it is I want."

He raises a shoulder. "It won't come to that, so… Yeah, sure, what-fucking ever."

I hold out my hand. "Deal?"

22

Declan

She fooled me. She deceived me. And I was so caught up in the moment, so filled with lust and want and that absurd need to be inside of her and possess her that… I forgot my promise to not have a relationship with her. If I'm being honest, that commitment to myself flew out the window the moment we got on the flight to LA. It was wishful thinking on my part that I'd be able to stop myself from getting involved with her.

There's a very thin line between hatred and love, and I've never really hated her. I'd thought I wanted to take revenge for what she did, but really, that was an excuse to hold onto her memory. It was my way of justifying why I spent so much time thinking about her. None of which makes it easy for me to stomach the fact that she got to me.

She threw down the challenge, and of course, I was going to accept it. The only thing that had allowed me to keep my distance from her was the fact that she was an innocent. The fact that she'd never be able to understand my darker proclivities, never be able to comprehend my lifestyle and the taste I've acquired for BDSM.

But she turned up at the Club and didn't run out screaming after what she saw. If anything, she seemed to be turned on by the thought of being dominated, which gave me pause for thought. And then, this evening, when she clambered onto the table and crawled toward me... It was easy to forget she's an innocent. With her slumberous eyes, flushed cheeks, and breasts that invited me to squeeze them and caress them, she's turned out to be a siren. A sexy, seductress who can, surely, take everything I inflicted on her and deliver on my demands.

I rub the back of my neck and stare into the dregs of my whiskey glass. After arriving home, I escorted her to her room. I drew her a bath and ordered her to soak herself until her aches and pains subsided.

I wasn't half as hard on her as I've been on any of my other subs. But she's not any of the other subs. She's... Solene. She's the one woman who's been on my mind since I first saw her. The one I still can't believe I ran into after all this time, and brought to LA. The one who's going to be the next big pop star—of that, I am sure.

I spanked her today and left my prints on her creamy arse. I marked her. I squeeze my fingers around my still full glass. I caused her pain, and it's my job to ensure I provide her after-care. The trip to the bookshop and the restaurant—and buying them—was a spur-of-the-moment decision. When you have money, it's interesting how quickly you can get things organized. It was worth the effort to see the smile that lit up her face.

But I still had to take care of the physical pain I caused her, which is why I insisted on the bath. I made sure to choose a book for her from the pile we brought home and handed it to her to read in the tub. I left before I'd be tempted to hang around and see her strip, which, in itself, is a warning sign. I've never had trouble disassociating my feelings from my need to dominate; this is the first time the two worlds threaten to merge, and I'm not sure how I feel about it, at all.

I fled, like the coward I'm turning out to be, then headed down to the bar adjoining the gym on the first floor of my house. I poured myself a drink, and now, I'm not sure I need it, either.

When my phone buzzes, I reach for it with relief. The number is blocked, which means it's from someone I don't know or— I answer the call. "Knight?"

There's silence on the line, then he laughs, "Good guess, buddy."

"Not too many unknown numbers I'd answer, but I had an instinct this was you."

"The perils of being a famous Hollywood star, eh?"

I wince. "Still the same ol' man who couldn't stay out of a girl's room when he should have."

He blows out a breath. "When will you forgive yourself for what happened?"

"A little difficult when the girl who changed your life is now a full-grown woman and reminds you at every turn of your mistakes."

"You think what happened was a mistake?"

I hesitate.

"That's what I thought." He lets that sink in. "When are you going to stop fooling yourself about your feelings for her?"

"Feelings?" I laugh. "I thought I wanted revenge for what happened, but turns out, it's—"

"—more complicated?"

I rub the back of my neck. "You seem to know an awful lot about relationships."

He stays quiet, then, "When you see death closely every day, I guess it makes you grow up real quick."

"Fuck. There you are, defending your country, and here I am, whining about what, in the big scheme of things—"

"Is probably the most important decision you'll ever make."

"Decision?" I frown.

"You going to tell her how you feel?"

"Not likely."

"What are you waiting for?"

I let go of the whiskey glass and rise to my feet. "In all honesty, I'm not sure. Maybe I'm not ready—"

"Oh, you're ready."

"Maybe I'm not a relationship kind of guy."

"You're the man who hired a private jet and surprised your grandmother on her birthday. You're a relationship kind of guy."

"Gee, thanks for shooting down my excuses," I snap.

"You're welcome." I can hear his smirk in his voice. "You—"

"You hiding, Beauchamp?" Rick walks into the den, then pauses when he sees me on the phone. I wave him forward, put the phone on speaker. "Guess who—"

"Rick, you fucker!" Knight booms.

"How's it going there with you, arse-wipe?" Rick drawls.

Knight draws in a breath, "It's... going."

The tension in his voice is evident. I frown. "Everything okay? The enemy troubling you guys?" I ask.

"It's coming to a head. I'm expecting to be pulled up for a mission soon."

"You sound worried." I frown.

There's silence, then Knight barks out a laugh. "Not more than usual. But enough about me, how's it going with you two? Not tired of seeing your face up on the screen yet, pretty boy?"

I smirk. "I'm an actor. I love seeing myself on screen."

"At least he's honest about it." Rick chuckles.

"And you, Rick? Has going private been everything you thought it would be?"

"The money's much better." He rubs the back of his neck. "Can't say I don't envy the action you and your team get to see."

"Action?" Knight scoffs. "At the moment, it's all waiting around for the orders to come through." His voice grows pensive. "Never know when the other shoe is going to drop."

Rick exchanges glances with me, then turns to the phone. "Whoa, you not getting enough pussy? Is that why you sound so... repressed and lonely?"

His ploy at distraction works, for Knight laughs. "That's one area where I don't have any complaints. You, on the other hand, I believe have been having trouble getting it up, hmm?"

"Eat shit, douchebag," Rick growls.

"Fuck you, too, with knobs on," Knight retorts.

Rick smiles widely "Your parents are definitely related, you son of a—"

"Okay, jeez, it must be true love that has you two trading such sweet endearments," I butt in.

"If you prefer, we can spend the time insulting your scarred-yet-pretty face, but my call time is too precious. Also, I need to call my sister, so au-revoir, motherfuckers." Knight disconnects the call.

"Was it me or did he sound more preoccupied than usual?" I scowl at the phone.

"He definitely sounded like he had a lot on his mind. Not unusual. Sitting around waiting to hear what his next mission is going to be about can't be easy."

"Yeah," I rub the back of my neck. "Not that it's the same but waiting around between shots on set can be tedious, too."

"Course, anytime you want to break the monotony with a fight—" Rick slams his fist into his palm.

"Not that I'm not tempted at a chance to bash in your already broken nose but—" I raise my hands. "I have a shoot coming up, and I can't scar my face more than what it already is."

"You mean that?" He stabs his finger at my forehead. "Only Hollywood would call that a scar."

"Doesn't look the same on a close-up when your face fills a fifty-foot cinema screen."

He winces. "Why you would put yourself through that, I don't know."

"I don't know… Must be the money and the fame that comes with it, not to mention the free pussy?" I smirk.

He raises a shoulder. "Whatever floats your boat, man. I came by to tell you I'm leaving for the night, but the security cameras are all working, and I did a final check. Also, the night shift of armed guards is in place to patrol the perimeter."

"Thanks, man." I hold up my hand and we do a clasp then a fist bump. He turns to leave, then pauses. "You know, Declan, life is unpredictable. When you have what you want within arm's reach, you should grab it and hold it close. You never know when or if you might get another chance." He holds my gaze for a few moments, while I search my brain for a response. Turning, he leaves.

I stare after him. Apparently, my friends are far ahead of me when it comes to figuring out what's right for my love life. Maybe they have a point? I pour myself another glass of whiskey, then walk up the stairs toward my room. When I reach the top, I change directions, push open her door, and walk in. That's when she steps out of the bathroom. Naked.

23

Solene

"You?" I freeze.

He rakes his gaze from the top of my hair that I've piled in a messy bun on the top of my head, to the drops of water that cling to my décolletage, to my waist, down between my thighs, and to my feet. By the time he raises his gaze to my face again, I'm flushed and melting. My fingers tingle. I want to wrap my arms about myself and shield my nakedness, but to do that would mean to give away how exposed I feel. He'll take it as a sign of weakness. He'll use it to bring me under his control. He'll use my emotions against me. He'll make me bend to his will and I…

I'm going to love it. I may be inexperienced, but my instincts tell me he knows how to please me. He'll satisfy me. He'll make me feel like one of the characters in my smutty books. The book he chose for had the MMC introducing the FMC to the pleasures of being dominated. If that's not a sign of what he intends to do to me, then I don't know what is.

His gaze narrows, and a considering look comes into his eyes. Then, he reaches behind him and locks the door. The sound of the lock clicking into place sends an explosion of sensations down my spine. My core clenches, my toes curl, and a thousand butterflies take flight under my skin. I take a step back and he smirks. "Scared, Rabbit?"

I tip up my chin. "Of course not."

"You should be."

I gape. "Are you trying to scare me?"

"Am I succeeding?"

He is, but I'm not going to let him know that. "What are you doing here?"

"What do you think?"

"Thought you were going to keep our relationship professional?" I scowl.

"Is that why you challenged me to make you submit?"

I shuffle my feet. "I didn't think you'd accept that. I thought your promise to keep our interactions professional—"

"—will still be valid."

"Eh?" I blink rapidly. "You lost me there, considering you broke the promise the moment you walked into that bathroom on the plane and—"

"I didn't touch you then," he reminds me.

I scoff. "You made me orgasm. You showed me how to find my clit, then made me climax for the first time in my life. I'd say we broke more than just professional boundaries then."

"You should know, I will not get emotionally involved with you," he warns.

"Will not or can not?"

"What's the difference? You're on the verge of launching your career. I'm about to head into months of grueling shooting for my first role as the lead hero of—"

"Lead hero?" A burst of happiness blooms in my chest. I race toward him and launch myself into his arms. "Oh, my god, Declan, that's amazing."

Only, when he cups my bare bottom and fits me over the thick column at his crotch do I realize that I'm naked and he's aroused. Very aroused.

"I do believe you're excited for me," he murmurs.

"I do believe you're excited for me, too," I manage to choke out.

"What are we going to do about that, hmm?"

"What do you want to do about it?" I gasp.

In answer, he drags me up and down that monstrous pillar he's sporting between his thighs. My core clenches. My belly bottom outs. A line of fire seems to ignite from our point of contact to my extremities. I lose my hold on him, but he grips my butt tighter and pulls me close. "So much sass. Who'd have thought that shy, virginal Mafia princess would turn out to be so feisty."

"Maybe I'm not a virgin," I scoff.

His brows draw down. A fire ignites deep in his eyes, turning them into stormy rain clouds. It's an expression I haven't seen on him before.

"Are you jealous?" I burst out.

He seems taken aback by my question. "Why should I be jealous?"

"Because I might have been with someone else?"

His scowl deepens. "Have you been with anyone else?"

"Only one way to find out."

A growl rumbles up his chest and the vibrations sink into my blood. My nipples tighten, and my clit throbs. Since he taught me how to touch myself, I've been so much more aware of my body. So much more aware of my attraction toward him. So much clearer… I wanted him. I link my arms about his neck, and the muscles of his shoulders jump.

"You have no idea what you're doing."

I tip up my chin. "On the contrary, I know what I want. You, on the other hand, seem to think you have to protect me."

"You want me to fuck you, is that it?"

This is what I wanted to hear. And yet, hearing it from him, I can't stop my features from heating. Still, I manage to nod. Not that it convinces him.

"I don't do relationships, Solene."

"I heard you the first time."

"And I won't make a habit of this, either."

Which means, he's been thinking of making whatever's happening between us a habit. Pleasure blooms in my chest, but I don't let it show on my face. Instead, I tilt my head. "Are you going to fuck me, then?"

He searches my features. "I want you too much not to, but I don't do vanilla sex, either."

"Think I don't know that after that little scene at the Club?" I scoff.

"You shouldn't have been there, but I suppose it's good you were. This way, you know what's coming next."

"You mean you're going to take me over your lap and spank me?"

"Did the scene in The Club involve spanking?"

I shake my head.

"So, what did it involve?"

I bite down on the inside of my cheek, then whisper, "Whipping."

"Say it aloud."

"Whipping," I hurl the word at him. "Happy now?"

"Not quite. I need to ask you, do you agree to be whipped by me, Solene?"

"Wh-whipped?"

He nods.

"Wh-why do you want to whip me?" I look between his eyes. "It's the blood, isn't it? That's what turns you on, the blood?"

24

Declan

Not anyone's blood, but your blood. That's what I want to say, but I don't. Instead, coward that I am, I answer her question with a question. "Does this mean you agree to be whipped by me?"

She pales, then slowly nods.

"Good."

She laughs, and the sound is nervous and edged with fear, but goddamn me, it goes straight to my balls.

"I'm not sure it's going to be good for me," she mumbles under her breath.

"I'm going to make sure it's good for you, baby." I turn around, unlock the door, and stalk out of her room, then up the corridor and into my bedroom.

Her gaze goes straight to the whip I have curled on the wall, but I pinch her chin and put enough pressure, so she has to turn her gaze back on me. "I'm not using that one."

"Ah." Some of the tension leaves her body.

"I have a bigger one in my closet."

"What?" She cries out, "A bigger one?" She begins to struggle, and I squeeze her closer. "Relax, I was joking."

"Joking?" She stares at me, then buries her fist in my shoulder. "How could you do that? You *pezzo di merda*. You *testa di cazzo*. You— "

I lower my head and close my mouth over hers. She continues to wriggle in my arms, which means she bounces against the rigid erection in my pants, which grows even thicker. Her movements slow, and I continue to kiss her. She parts her lips, and I thrust my tongue into her mouth. She shudders. I tilt my head, deepen the kiss and inhale her breath.

She moans, stops struggling. Her eyelids flutter closed. I know the exact moment she stops fighting, for she pushes her breasts forward and into my chest. A pulse flares to life in my belly, in my chest, even behind my eyeballs. I've never felt this way before. I've never kissed a woman this deeply before, either. Without taking my mouth off hers, I walk to my bed and lower her onto it. When she opens her eyes, I hold her gaze as I straighten and step back from the bed. She begins to cover herself with her arms, but I shake my head.

She lowers her hands to her sides. Once more, I drag my gaze down her body to her pink-tipped toes. I've met and acted with some of the most beautiful women in the world, but none of them come close to her perfection. I reach over to unhook the whip from the wall near the headboard.

Her eyes grow wide, and she follows the motion of the whip as I snap it out. Her shoulders jerk. "A-are you going to use that on me?"

Spread your thighs. Hold open your cunt for me, so I can fuck you with it.

"D-Declan?"

"Turn on your front, Rabbit."

She swallows, then flips over on her front. She pillows her face on her folded arms and glances at me through the curtain of her hair. "What are you going to d-d-do?"

"Hush now." I drag the whip down her spine and goosebumps pop on her skin. I draw it over the curve of her butt, and she clenches her arse-cheeks.

"Relax," I order.

She draws in a breath, then millimeter by millimeter, the tension drains out of her.

"Good girl."

She shivers. I jerk my gaze to hers to find her lips are parted. Her eyelids are heavy, the look in her eyes a combination of fear and anticipation. I trail the whip over the valley between her arse-cheeks, and she swallows.

"Part your legs, baby."

She does. And her ready compliance sends liquid lust shooting through my veins. My dick pushes against the fabric of my jeans, begging to be let out. *Fucking hell.* At this rate I'm going to come in my pants. I haven't been this aroused since... She threw herself at me and kissed me in her room before her brother interrupted us. *What does that mean?*

I raise my arm and bring the whip down across her butt.

She yelps.

"Steady now."

I drag the whip across the line of red that blooms across the creamy globes. The lust in my veins catches fire. Sweat beads my forehead. I raise the whip and snap it down, thwack-thwack-thwack, laying a line of welts from just under her tailbone to the crease at her thighs.

She gasps out, her breath coming in pants. When she tries to wiggle away, I place my arm across the small of her back to hold her in place.

"Declan," she yells.

"Did that hurt?"

"What do you think, you *faccia di merda*?"

"I think if I touched your pussy, I'd find you wet."

She stills, and when I glance at her, there's a guilty look on her face.

"I'm right, aren't I?"

"That's so strange." She swallows. "It hurt when you whipped me. Not too much, but just enough to stimulate my clit."

"Your new favorite word, I see?"

She rolls her eyes. "You can blame yourself for creating a monster."

I frown. Clearly, she's enjoying our interaction. If she decides to find her release elsewhere after this— That's not my problem, is it? I tighten my hold on the whip. One night. I get this one night to fuck her out of my system, and then, I'm going to make sure our schedules conflict, so we don't run into each other.

I'll ensure all of my contacts are aware of the brand-new talent on the pop culture scene. And yeah, I'll make sure the known sharks in the industry steer clear of her, and that her manager—who owes me—always has only her best interests at heart and ensures she doesn't commit the same mistakes I did when I started out in the industry. But other than that, I'm going to make sure we don't meet face-to-face at all.

I raise my arm again, and this time, when I bring it down, the sound echoes through the room. She mewls, and when I spy the single drop of blood that pops against the white of her skin, heat grips my chest. I bend, then lick away the scarlet dot, and the coppery taste goes straight to my head. I'm losing myself now. A-n-d it's too late to stop this slide into hell, or heaven, or the combination of both that is her body. I toss the whip away, reach over, cup her arse cheeks, and begin to massage them.

"Oh, god, that feels... That feels— "

"Good?" I ask.

"It shouldn't." She winces as I squeeze the abraded flesh. "But it's only making me more wet."

"Oh, fuck." I bend over and lick the line of red from one side of her arse-cheek to the other. A groan bleeds from her lips. Her entire body shudders. I kneel between her legs, then bend and run my tongue up her slit, all the way to her arsehole.

"What are you doing?" She gasps.

"Shh, let me taste you." I grip her inner thighs and spread them apart, then stab my tongue inside her channel.

"Declan," she huffs. "Oh, god, oh, god, that's so— " She gasps when I curl my tongue inside her. Then I slip my hand under her pussy and begin to rub her clit.

She groans, then pushes back, riding my tongue. I circle her clit, and she whines. And when I press my heel into the swollen nub, her thighs quiver. Her back curves. Convulsions work their way up her legs, and her inner walls contract.

Oh, fuck! The sensations grip me, my cock now in so much pain, black spots spark around my line of sight. But this is about her. Her pleasure. I want to make sure she orgasms before I take her. I want to make our first time together so unforgettable, everything and everyone coming after me will pale in comparison. My shoulder muscles bunch, my entire body seems to seize up. If she dares fuck another man, I'll... I'll...

Do nothing. She's not yours. She can't be. Not when the whipping today is barely the tip of what my tendencies lean toward. I'm not the right man for her, which is why I need to make this night one she'll remember for a long, long time.

I increase the intensity of my movements, then slide my tongue in and out of her sopping wet pussy.

The vibrations grip her. Her panting is so loud, the sound echoes the beats of my heart. That's when I straighten.

She stills and turns to glance at me over her shoulder. "What are you doin—"

I haul her hips up, then slap her pussy. "Come right now."

25

Solene

I instantly orgasm. The climax crashes over me. My eyes roll back in my head. As the aftershocks pulse through me, he pulls me up, so I'm balanced on my arms and knees. He reaches over to grab a condom from a drawer in the bedside table. I hear the clink of his buckle, then the r-r-rip sound of his zipper being lowered. Then something blunt teases my opening.

I flinch. I can't help it; it's an involuntary reaction. Despite the fact he's made me come, and I've felt his fingers inside me, it's clear the size of what he intends to breach me with is... Much bigger. Broader. A trembling ladders up my spine.

He must sense my apprehension because he wraps his fingers about the nape my neck. "Shh, I promise I'll make this so good for you, baby."

He bends over me, the edges of his zipper abrading my skin and sending more sensations pouring through my veins. I grit my teeth against the pleasure that follows in its wake. The cells of my body seem to be awakening, my brain cells firing non-stop at the onslaught of feelings that percolate through me.

When he increases his grip on my neck, some of the apprehensiveness fades away. My body seems to recognize him, even as my mind and heart are trying to catch up. Moisture pools between my legs, my inner walls preparing for his intrusion. And when he skims his cock over my pussy-lips, the warmth in my lower-belly spills over. With the fingers of his free hand, he strokes my clit, and all my nerve-endings seem to flare at once. That's when he breaches me. One minute I'm empty, the next, he's there, pushing through the tightness.

I freeze; so does he. He stays there for a second, then another. Tension rolls off of him. I sense his muscles coil, and his thighs that hold mine apart seem to turn to stone. His fingers around my neck tighten around the front, constricting my breaths, until my lungs burn. Then he circles my clit once, twice and plays with my pussy lips.

"Let me in, Rabbit." His breath curls around my ears, the tone of his voice reassuringly an order. A command. A directive that brooks no resistance. One that demands I obey. One my body wants to obey. I widen the space between my thighs, there's a pinch of pain, and he powers through the barrier. His thickness stretches me, fills me, throbs against my inner walls. I'm so full, so crammed with him. I throw my head back and gasp.

"Breathe, baby," he growls.

I shiver. Goosebumps pepper my skin. More moisture bathes my insides as he stays where he is. He stays. And stays. Some of the tension leaks out of my body.

He pinches my clit. I gasp. He rubs against it, and that now familiar liquid heat rushes up my legs, my hips. That's when he slips in another inch, and another. A groan rumbles up his chest, vibrating up my back at the same time.

My nipples grow so hard my breasts hurt. "They hurt, they hurt," I whine.

He releases his hold on my clit, only to weigh my tit in his palm. He squeezes my breast and another moan spills from my lips.

"So gorgeous, so beautiful." He licks the shell of my ear. I'd collapse if not for his hold on my neck. Plus, his cock is holding me up.

"You're nothing like I imagined you'd grow up to be, Rabbit. You're so much more, in every way."

His praise destroys any last doubts I might have had. I curve my spine and thrust out my butt. He slips in further.

"That feels so good," I murmur.

"It'll feel even better once I'm in."

I pause. "Umm… you are in," I point out.

He laughs. "Not completely, baby."

"What?" I try to look over my shoulder, only his hold on my neck prevents the movement. "Are you joking?" I demand.

In reply, he pulls out of me, and in the next breath, he pumps his hips and sinks into me. He repeats the movement again and again. Each time, he slides in deeper and deeper. Each time he enters me, sensations blaze up my spine, fill my blood, go straight to my head.

All my attention is focused on where we are joined. On how he holds me by my neck like I'm his. His. Oh, god. I'm falling for him. Correction. I've always been in love with him. I thought it was a childhood crush, that I didn't know him well enough. I still don't know him well enough. But it doesn't matter. What the heart wants, and all that. Or as people in my country say, a *colpo di fulmine*. A strike of lightning. That's what I felt that night when I saw him. I've been trying to deny it ever since, but given the emotions I'm experiencing, it's clear I never got over him.

He pulls out of me again, this time, pausing at the rim of my entrance. Then with a low growl, he thrusts forward, burying himself so deep inside me, his balls slap against my pussy. I cry out, more from the shock of feeling him in a place which feels impossible for him to access, than from any pain. I try to speak, but no words come out. All I can do is stay. Stay. And take everything he's pumping into me.

His chest rises and falls against my back. His grip on my neck seems to tighten even more, then he licks my cheek up to my temple before kissing it. "I'm going to fuck you now."

That's all the warning I get before he begins to fuck me in earnest. In-out-in. Each time he slams into me, my entire body moves forward. The headboard slams into the wall. Something crashes off to the side. Sweat beads my brow. My arms hurt with the effort of holding up my weight. My thigh muscles scream at this new position I've assumed for too long. Too much. How much more can I take? How much—oh, god! Pleasure spirals up my body, turning everything it touches into golden sparks. Flashes of lightning go off behind my eyes. I'm coming, coming.

"Wait for me." His voice anchors me, holds me, restrains me as he propels forward and into me one last time then, "Now. Come with me. Right-fucking-now."

That's when I shatter. The orgasm seems to go on and on. I'm aware of someone screaming— Is that me? That doesn't sound like me. That sounds like a woman who is at the very end of her pleasure-pain cycle, one who's coming so violently she sounds more animal than human and — Oh, god it's me. It's me. Then the pleasure crashes over me, and I give in to the tidal wave of feeling.

Something cold is pressed between my legs. The sore feeling at my core abates somewhat. I sigh. Then I'm turned over onto my front, and a soothing touch pats across my butt-cheeks. There's a slight stinging sensation, followed by relief. My muscles relax. Any remaining tension fades from my shoulders. My entire body feels like it's turning into a gooey mess. I burrow into the bedclothes, push my cheek into the pillow, which smells like dark chocolate and coffee. So yummy. My stomach growls. I want to open my eyes, but my eyelids feel like they are weighted down. I pillow my head in the softness and float off.

What seems like a few seconds later, I'm being shaken awake. I open my eyes to find I'm still in bed, on my back. Those aquamarine blue eyes hold mine. His hair is mussed, and a day's old growth shadows his chin. I reach up and drag my palm against his whiskers. The chafe of his stubble against my skin sends a sizzle of heat straight to my core. I trail my fingers up to the lightning shaped scar over his forehead.

The skin around his eyes tightens, but he doesn't pull away.

"You're gorgeous," I say softly.

His lips quirk. "You're still high on endorphins."

"Is that from the fucking?"

His brow draws down. "You need to be disciplined."

"Are you offering?"

He shakes his head. "I truly have created a monster."

"Are you going to fuck me again?"

"Are we going to talk about what happened first?"

I scowl. "Do we have to?"

He searches my features. "I took your virginity, Solene."

"Good. It was an inconvenience, and now I'm glad I don't have to worry about it anymore. Also—" I rush to get the words out before he speaks, "Also, I wanted you to have it."

His eyes flash. "I'm your first, Solene. Do you know how that makes me feel?"

I swallow. "H-how?"

"It makes me want to tie you to this bed and not let you leave until I've fucked you over and over again. Until I've lost myself in you and imprinted the shape of my dick in between your legs, so with every step you take you remember me."

"Hmm." I fold my arms behind my neck. "What's stopping you?"

He seems taken aback by my question, then a smirk curls his lips. "You're a brat."

"And you like that."

He pauses, then nods slowly. "More than I expected." He says the words under his breath. It feels like he's talking aloud to himself. "I suspected you were a virgin, considering you were going into an arranged marriage. But the way you acted was at such odds with what your character should have been, I couldn't be sure."

I smile a little. "You liberated me, Declan. You took me out of there, and it's giving me a chance to be myself again. I can't even begin to explain how free I feel now that I'm here." I glance around his massive bedroom, then back at him. "And I don't mean the money and the private jet and this amazing house and pool, although"—I waggle my eyebrows—"all that helps, too."

"Definitely a brat." He snatches his shirt from the floor and hands it over. I shrug it on, then watch as he prowls over to his closet. He reappears a moment later, a pair of grey sweats in his hand. His chest is bare, the dents between his twelve-pack making me want to run my fingers over them to feel the steel under his gleaming skin. His biceps are thick enough to rival the size of my thighs, not that I'm skinny.

I am, by no means, curvy, but I also like my food and have never stopped myself from eating, so I'm definitely on the healthier side. But compared to this man, I'm half his size. His thigh muscles ripple and oh…

Between them, his massive cock juts up. He's already erect? Again? Is it possible for someone to recover that quickly? Even with my limited knowledge of the male anatomy, I'm fairly certain men need time to recover between rounds. But not Declan, apparently. I gulp. Also, there's a flash of metal at the tip of his shaft.

"Is that—?" I point at his dick. "Is that your piercing?"

"If you're referring to my *Apadravya*—"

"Your what?"

"My piercing." He says patiently. "It's called an *Apadravya*."

I stare at the barbell like jewelry which passes vertically through the glans from top to bottom and wince. "I'd call it painful."

"It was." He shrugs.

"So why did you get it?"

"Because I could?"

I shake my head. "That's not an answer."

He squeezes his cock from base to head. "I got it because I wanted to prove to myself I could. I was tired of fighting for my roles in film. Tired of the constant rounds of auditions. Tired of feeling defensive because of my scar."

I glance up at the silvery line on his forehead. "I'm sorr—"

"Don't apologize." He cuts his palm through the air. "I wanted to do something that made me feel in control."

"So, you got a painful piercing."

"Made me feel like a rockstar... Once the pain wore off. Also, it enhances sexual pleasure for the woman." He smirks. "For both the front and rear entry."

O-k-a-y. I widen my gaze. "I can't believe I didn't notice that earlier. Also, I have no idea how that... that monster cock of yours fit inside me."

"That's because you were too busy being fucked, baby." His smirk widens.

The ego of this man. But considering the baseball bat-sized cock between his legs, it's probably justified. A cock whose length and girth I've felt intimately. My inner-walls clench. I squeeze my thighs together, but he must notice the movement, for he smirks. He stalks over to me, but before I can say another word, he's bent and scooped me up in his arms.

I yelp. "Where are you taking me?"

26

Declan

Turns out, I like watching her eat. I like cooking for her—something I don't do very often, since I'm never home long enough to use the gleaming appliances in this kitchen. What I like even more, though, is watching her squirm around in the chair trying to find a comfortable position. No doubt, the welts on her butt are causing her an inconvenience. She's feeling every one of those thin red marks I put on her unmarked backside.

And the blood. The sight of that one drop of blood turned my world completely upside down. I've blood played before, but to see the blood I drew on her backside caused my heart to stutter. And when I saw her blood on my dick, I swear it stopped for a second. A primal, foreign sensation took a hold of me.

I cleaned her up, took care of her hurt backside, but I wasn't able to leave. I stood over her and watched her as she slept, and then her stomach grumbled. I knew then, I couldn't leave... Not yet. *One last meal is allowed, right? She's still my guest. And for tonight, at any rate, my sub. I can take care of her. It's the right thing to do. 'Course, now I'm justifying myself.*

Which is not like me. It's also a clear sign I need to get the hell away from her. After I fuck her one more time. Just once more is allowed, right?

"You done?" I nod at her plate.

We're seated at the breakfast table by the window.

Outside, it's still dark. The lights of the city twinkle along the curved shore of Malibu on my right. Ahead, the sea stretches out, a black void. Like my life before she came into it.

Across the table, she shovels more food into her mouth. When's the last time I ate with that kind of relish? For me, food is more than a fuel or something to enjoy. It's primarily a means to reach the kind of physique demanded of me for my movies. Not that I'm complaining. The hard work required to maintain the build that gives me an advantage over others is something I enjoy. The working out, the sweating, the grunting, the discipline of waking up at four a.m. and completing my workout is something that anchors me and grounds me. It reinforces the effort needed to hold onto the position I carved out at the top of the Hollywood food chain. So, it doesn't explain why I'm ready to throw everything aside, throw her over my shoulder, and take her back to bed. A-n-d, I need to seriously stop this train of thinking, right-fucking-now.

She finishes the last morsel of food on her plate and sets her fork down. "I am now."

I slide the glass of milk toward her. "Drink that."

She eyes it with distrust. "You want me to drink milk?"

"You're going to need the energy."

She scowls at me. "And if I refuse?"

"Drink. The milk. Solene."

She reaches for the glass and drains it. "Happy?" She places the empty glass on the table with a snap.

"Definitely bratty."

She sticks out her tongue at me.

I smirk. "You're going to be doing that again, and on command."

Before she can say anything, I push my chair back, then spread my legs. "On your knees."

"Excuse me?"

I glare at her. She pales, then sets her lips together. "Whatever."

"I'm going to fuck that sass out of you, baby."

She scoffs. "I'd like to see you try."

"Oh, I'm going to do more than that."

"Crawl to me."

Her cheeks pink. "What do you mean?"

"Don't make me repeat myself."

Our gazes clash and whatever she sees in mine must make her realize how serious I am. She pushes back her chair and lowers herself to her knees, then places her palms on the floor. She inches forward on her hands and knees under the short expanse of the table until she reaches me. When she pauses, I nod toward the space between my legs.

"Come closer."

She shuffles forward until her shoulders touch my thighs on either side.

"Good girl."

She shudders. The pleasure the words bring her is so evident on her features. She gazes up at me with a trusting look on her face, even as there's confusion in her eyes and a hint of obstinance to the set of her chin. It's this push-pull within her that echoes the struggle inside me, which makes our interactions so addictive. I want to own her, consume her, break down the stubbornness that makes her so alluring. I want to crush her defiance, so she'll obey me without hesitation. I want to... Build her back up in a way that mirrors my devotion to her. The kind of woman I've looked for my entire life knowing... Always knowing, I'd already met her. I thought I'd lost her, but she's right here in front of me.

I reach down and place my thumb on her bottom lip. I apply pressure, and she closes her mouth around my digit. She sucks on it, and I feel the pull all the way down to the crown of my cock. I pull it out, then jerk my chin. I drag my gaze over the jut of her breasts covered by my shirt—she's wearing *my* shirt, and fuck, if that doesn't send the blood draining to my groin again. Her chest rises and falls. Her breathing roughens. She bites down on her lower lip, and fuck, if I don't feel that at the crown of my cock.

"You want me to fuck you, Rabbit?"

She nods.

"You're fucking perfect." I wrap my fingers about her nape, then bend and kiss her forehead.

"You have another virgin hole left. Will you let me have it?"

She swallows. Some of the color pales from her cheeks. The seconds stretch, then she nods.

"Are you sure? You don't have to—"

"I'm sure."

Turn around, push your forehead into the ground, then pry your arse-cheeks apart and present yourself to me.

"I appreciate you agreeing, but you're not ready yet."

She stills. "I'm ready."

"You're ready when I say you are."

"And when will that be?"

"You'll know it." I weigh her breasts through my shirt before circling the outline of her nipples, finally planting my palms on her hips and setting her aside.

She whines. "Are you going to fuck me now?"

I shake my head.

"Why not?" She pouts.

"Because." I raise a shoulder.

"That's not an answer," she cries.

"That's all your brattiness is getting from me." I rise to my feet and begin to walk away. For a few seconds, there's silence. Then, "What the —" I hear the slap of her feet on the floor, then footsteps coming toward me. I turn in time to catch her as she flings herself at me.

"You're getting predictable." I smirk.

She sets her jaw, narrows her gaze, then she slaps me.

27

Solene

My palm print stands out against his cheek. *Madonna Mia*, how hard did I slap him? His blue eyes lose color, turning so pale they almost seem silver. The scar on his forehead turns white. Oh god, that's not a good sign, is it? And I'm clinging to him with my arms about his neck, since I decided to throw myself at him and climb him like a tree... Again.

"Umm, you can let me down now."

His lips draw back in the semblance of a smile. Correction, it's not a smile at all. It's more of a statement of intent. He moves toward the breakfast table, his movements slow, deliberate. A thrill runs down my spine. My stomach ties itself in knots. My throat is dry. All the moisture has drained to that spot between my legs where he planted his cock inside of me not too long ago.

"What are you doing?"

He laughs. The *stronzo* laughs.

"If you think you're scaring me, you're not."

"You will be."

He says it with such conviction, my heart begins to race. What the hell is he going to do? What does he have in mind? Whatever it is, I'm not going to like it. What's even more frightening is the thought that I will. Well, I have only myself to blame.

To be fair, he patted me on the head and told me he wasn't going to fuck me today. But his gesture inflamed me. It felt like he was treating me like a child which I'm not. Of course, that's exactly how he wanted me to feel. *Bastardo*.

I'm on the verge of something big. Something monumental. I can feel it. And tonight, this night when I lost my virginity, I want more. I want to be with him. I want to... push him until he loses control and shows me the younger version of himself I met. The man who had emotions running through his veins, before he found a way to hide that authentic part of him. I want to feel his unfettered self, want him to bare himself to me and show me how he really feels. Want him to not hide anymore or hold back, as he's been doing so far.

He reaches the table, then lowers me to my feet in front of it.

"Declan, what—"

"Shh." He grips the ends of the shirt and yanks, pulling it apart. The buttons pop off. A small cry escapes my lips. That tightly leashed violence in his actions sends a spurt of expectation swirling down my legs. My knees turn to jelly, but his hold on my shoulder prevents me from sliding to the floor. He holds my gaze. "Do you want to leave?"

I look between his eyes. The silvery sparks are now intertwined with swirls of blue and green. Impatience clings to him. His chest muscles are so tense they could be carved out of marble. With that flawed beauty of his, he looks like he belongs from another dimension. Almost a god. No wonder he owns the silver screen. No wonder I could never get over him.

"Solene?" He looks down at me from his much taller height. "Last chance. If you want to leave, then do it now."

I slowly shake my head.

"You want to stay?"

I nod.

"If you do, I'm taking your arse."

I shiver. Goosebumps crop up on my back. My pussy clenches, even as my hindbrain warns me of the repercussions of not leaving. Run, now. No. I will not run. I want this. I want to feel alive. I want to feel everything he's going to offer me. After being caged for so long, I'm finally free. "I want you to."

His eyes flash. The next moment, he spins me around. The plates and cutlery on the table hit the floor with a crash. I flinch. The next second, he applies pressure at the small of my back. I bend, pressing my cheek into the table. He wrenches my arm behind my back, then the other, then shackles them with his thick fingers. Before I can react, he kicks my legs apart. Cool air strikes my center. Moisture oozes out from between my pussy lips, and I moan.

"Fuck, you're loving this, aren't you, Rabbit? Your cunt is still swollen from earlier, you carry my marks on your butt-cheeks, yet you can't wait for me to shag you."

A moan spills from my lips. My lower belly spasms. My core quivers. He scoops up the cum that trails down my inner lips and smears it around my puckered hole.

Instantly I clench.

"Relax, baby—or not. It's only going to hurt more if you don't."

I blow the hair out of my face and stare at him.

He smirks. "That got your attention, huh?"

"I'm beginning to remember why I hated you."

"You never hated me. You were attracted to me. You couldn't keep those big doe eyes of yours off of me from the moment we met."

I stare at him, and he holds my gaze. For a few seconds we're engaged in a face-off, then I look away. "You're right. From the moment I saw you, I couldn't look away. There was something about you that told me you were important to me. That you were going to play a leading role in my life. Which is probably why, when you whipped me, I orgasmed. Despite the fact that my mother caned me—"

"Hold on, your mother caned you?"

I jerk my chin up. "The night we met… I'd jumped out the window of my room and decided to walk the beach because I'd been caned earlier. Those marks on my—"

"Palms. The one's I asked you about. You told me you got them from sliding down the tree."

I raise a shoulder. "I wasn't about to admit I got a walloping from my mother for behaving badly."

"Behaving badly?" He frowns.

"She caught me reading smutty books and lost it."

His shoulders seem to swell. A pulse throbs at his temple. "She whipped you because she caught you reading your spicy books?"

"She was worried I was going to get corrupted and that I'd get ideas about boys and—shock, horror—I might even sleep with one of them and lose my virginity—"

"Instead, you lost your virginity to me," he says in a strange voice. His gaze narrows. Those gorgeous blue eyes of his turn a deeper shade of indigo. That's the only indication he's turned on, because his expression is one of anger, but also, frustration.

"I wanted it to be you." I tip up my chin.

"Whatever the reason, it was wrong of her to cane you," he growls.

"But *you* can whip me, huh?"

He chuckles. "Ah, but that's with your consent." He grows serious. "Only I can hurt you. Only I can touch your skin. Only I can order you to obey me, to do as I command." His gaze intensifies. "You belong to me, Rabbit, you understand? You are mine!" His chest rises and falls.

A thrill engulfs me. My core quivers. When he goes all possessive, it's the most erotic thing ever. Better than reading about my book boyfriends, and th-a-t's the biggest compliment ever.

The air between us thickens. His nostrils flare. It's as if he can sniff the response of my body on a primal level. He releases me suddenly, only to turn me around to face him. He takes my hands in his, lifts them up, and presses his lips to the insides of my palms. His gesture is so tender, the feel of his lips on my palms so soft, so full of meaning, tears prick the backs of my eyes. I blink them away.

"It happened a long time ago," I say softly.

"I knew something was wrong that day. I should have probed harder. I should have pushed you to reveal what had actually happened."

"No way was I going to tell you what had happened. I mean, I meet this hot man and the last thing I'm going to do is tell him about my problems at home. Not when I'm trying to come across as all grown up."

He shakes his head. "I can't believe I thought you were eighteen."

"Well, I'm eighteen now." I flutter my eyelashes.

"And you're trying to distract me."

"Am I succeeding?" I lick my lips, and that's when he swoops down and closes his mouth over mine.

28

Declan

I stare at her sleeping features and can't stop the smile from curling my face. This woman... She's unique. She's exquisite. There's no one like her around. No one who can tie me up in knots and make me feel out of sorts, and at the same time, make me laugh.

She fluttered her eyelashes at me, and I was unable to resist. I've had Hollywood's most beautiful actresses throwing themselves at me, and none of them turned me on the way a come-hither look from my very own siren does.

And I didn't take her arse after all. I kissed her senseless, then carried her into my room. I placed her on the bed, then proceeded to make love to her... missionary style. I told her I don't indulge in vanilla sex, but clearly, I lied. I looked into her eyes as I buried myself inside her and proceeded to slowly, torturously sink my dick, inch by inch, inside her tight, very-recently-virgin cunt, over and over again. At least I wrapped my cock.

I was tempted not to. I wanted to feel her with no barriers between us. Just the fact I even thought of that shook me. I managed to don the condom before impaling her in one smooth move. The force of my penetration made her entire body jolt. She gasped, then wound her arms and legs around me and held on.

Tears squeezed out from the corners of her eyes, and I slowed my movements further. I allowed the tension to build in my balls and reveled in the melting walls of her pussy as she clamped around me, as I lifted her hips and tilted my pelvis so I could hit that secret spot deep inside of her.

Once-twice-thrice. She gasped for air, her pupils dilated, and she dug her heels into my back and buried her fingernails in my shoulder-blades. Color rushed up her chest, her cheeks; her entire body jerked. She fluttered around my shaft, and I knew she was so very close. That's when I thrust into her one last time and ordered her to come with me. And she did. She opened her mouth and screamed as the orgasm tore through her. I pressed my lips to hers, shared her breath, and absorbed the sounds she made as she climaxed.

Then I pushed my knees into the bed and rammed into her, stuffed my dick into her cunt one last time, and emptied myself into her. The entire time, I held her gaze and it was the most intimate experience I've ever had. Sweat poured down my temples and my shoulders. The heat from our bodies wrapped us in a cocoon of lust, of need, of everything I've ever wanted from a woman and didn't even know it.

She moaned as she came down from her high. Her body twitched one last time, then her eyelids fluttered down and she slipped into slumber.

I pulled back enough to watch her sleep, my cock still nestled inside her. I stayed there until my cock began to recover. Then, changing the condom for a fresh one, I proceeded to fuck her slowly without waking her. She orgasmed in her sleep with little sighs and moans that made me instantly come inside her. Then I pulled out, cleaned myself up, then her, and held her until the sun's rays slid into the room.

Now, I push away from the bed. Taking care not to wake her, I dress, pack a bag, and force myself to leave the room without a last look at her. Having texted Rick earlier, I now meet him outside the house at my car.

"You sure you want to leave?" Do I detect a hint of censure in his voice?

"What do you mean?" I slide into the driver's seat, then slap the button on the visor to raise the garage door.

"You're not taking her with you?"

I raise a shoulder. "She's a big girl."

"She's new to this city; she doesn't know anyone."

"She has her manager—"

"And we all know how trustworthy that breed is. He may protect her career interests, but he'll do it to the detriment of her personal life."

"She wanted this career. She needs to learn to navigate the waters."

I try to shut my door, but he grips the top and refuses to let go.

"The fuck?" I glower up at him.

"She's still young; she could do with a helping hand."

"That's why I've deputized you to stay here as her bodyguard."

"She doesn't need a bodyguard; she needs a—"

"A—?"

"A friend."

"I'm not a friend." I rotate my shoulders. "I don't have her best interests at heart."

"That's why you bought out a chain of bookshops, so she could buy her books in peace? Then paid upfront for controlling interest in a restaurant so you could take her to dinner without any eyes on the two of you?"

I narrow my gaze. "James Hamilton is a friend. His restaurant is solid. It's a good investment."

"You did it for her, and you know it."

"If that's how you choose to interpret it, I can't stop you."

He glares at me. "You're being an ornery douche-wipe. Also, you're running scared."

Now, he's really starting to piss me off. "Me? Running scared? You must be mistaken."

"So, that's not why you're creeping away at"—he checks his watch and raises one eyebrow—"at 6 a.m.?"

"I always planned to leave early in the morning. Which reminds me, it's getting late."

He scrutinizes my features. "You've made up your mind?"

I set my jaw.

"You're going to lose her, and only then, will you realize the mistake you've made by leaving her. By then, it might be too late."

I straighten and look ahead through the windshield. "You can't lose what you never had."

29

Two weeks later

Solene

"There you are!" Olivia exclaims. "I've been trying to reach you for so long."

"Sorry, sis, I've been busy. New career and all that, you know."

She purses her lips. "You've been too busy to text me and tell me you're okay?"

"I'm telling you now, I'm okay." I paint my mouth with the gloss, then smack my lips together. "In fact, I'm off for my first recording today."

"The recording of your first song?"

"It's only a demo, but yeah, I'm recording it." I can't stop the grin that stretches my lips.

"Whoa, that's amazing." Olivia's smile matches mine in intensity. My sister really is happy for me. She's always supported me. Well, as much as she could, considering she wasn't always around when I was growing up. She managed to escape our family at the right time and, clearly, marriage suits her. Not that I begrudge her. She knew what she wanted early on and went after it. She had the courage to fight for her convictions, to never give up, and to follow her dreams. And as a result, she has succeeded. That's something I wished I could have done then... Something I'm doing now, thanks to Declan.

"How's the acting career going?"

Her smile widens more. "It's slow, but I've landed a new talent agent who believes in me. Regardless of whether I'm scarred or not."

I cap my lip gloss and place it on the table. "That's what I've always loved about you, Livvy, you don't let challenges get you down."

"Oh, I was down after the accident that left me with this." She points to the scar on her face. "But you know, Massimo was there with me that day at the hospital. He stayed with me the whole time, and that's when I knew I was falling for him. But I knew he was part of the Mafia, and the last thing I wanted was to marry a Mafia guy, considering I left home as soon as I could precisely so I couldn't be trapped into an arranged marriage with one of them."

I stare at her, and she flushes.

"I didn't mean anything by that comment. I wasn't trying to find fault with your agreeing to one in the first place."

"I know. And honestly, the place I was in, I thought my only way out of that family was by getting married." I bite down on my lower lip. "When I think of it now, I can't believe they brainwashed me into believing that was the only way forward for me. But when you're in that situation with our family, it's difficult to think you have choices. If I hadn't met Declan when I did— " I shake my head.

"Speaking of, where is he?"

"He's on a shoot."

"And you didn't go with him?"

My guts twist, but I manage to paste a smile on my face. "I do have my own career to launch."

"Is he going to be around for your first recording?"

Isn't that the question? Fact is, I haven't seen or heard from him since he left me asleep in his bed. The *stronzo* didn't even leave me a note. Which, honestly, is not what I expected. Especially not after how he held my gaze as he came inside me. There was this intensity to his movements, a desperation in how he took me, a possessiveness that bled through his touch into my skin, the way he painted my insides with his cum as if he were marking me as his... Or maybe, that was my imagination playing tricks on me…

Maybe the speed with which he changed his mind about keeping our relationship professional and then taking my virginity is what made my head spin.

And the asshole left it to Rick to convey the news that he'd left for his shoot. *Coward.* I curl my fingers into fists. Not that I'm going to call him and find out where he is. Or when he plans to come home. I'm not going to stalk him on his social media or keep an eye out on the tabloids or the film publications for news of where he is either.

"Solene?" Olivia's voice pulls me out of my meandering.

"No, he's not going to be at my recording. Or if he is, he hasn't mentioned it to me. He's a busy man. A top-rated Hollywood film star, for chrissakes. Of course, he's not going to be around for something as trivial as this."

She stares at me.

"What?"

"You said chrissakes."

"I did."

"If Ma were to hear that—"

I scoff. "I'd never say that in her presence."

"Being away from home has been good to you. Not that I ever doubted it. But you sound like the Solene of old again."

I sober. "I feel like I'm regaining all that exuberance and courage of my youth, which I thought I'd lost. Turns out, it only needed the right circumstances for it to resurface."

"Hmm." She opens her mouth, when someone calls her name. "Oh, hey Karma!" Olivia waves at someone off screen. "Yes, I'm talking to my sister. Do you want to say hi to her?"

What? Before I can protest, Olivia's flipped the screen, and the face of a dark-haired woman wearing dark lipstick and dark eyeshadow, and definitely channeling a goth princess, fills the screen.

"Hi, Solene. I'm so sorry we didn't get to know each other better at Olivia and Massimo's engagement and wedding."

"Right." I rub my forehead. "You're Michael's wife?"

"Correct," she flashes me a smile.

"Michael is Massimo's oldest brother, and the Don of the Cosa Nostra, eh?"

"Ex-Don. Also," she leans in closer, "They don't use that term anymore, since they're legalizing the Cosa Nostra."

"They are?" I stare. The Cosa Nostra is one of the oldest Mafia families in Italy. The Mafioso blood runs in their veins, and they're thinking of switching to the right side of the law?

"I know, the love of a good woman, and all that," she smirks. "Now that the Sovrano brothers are getting married, they want to ensure they and their wives are safe. Plus, they want things to be safe for the kids when they come, so— " She raises a shoulders.

"Right, wow, okay then."

"Anyway, enough about me, I hear you're going to be the next big thing in pop-music?"

"Umm, I'm going to need a lot of luck for that to happen."

She takes in my features. "From what Olivia tells me, you're someone who's determined enough to make it happen. And while I haven't heard you sing, I'm sure you're enormously talented."

"Thanks." I laugh. "I can do with all the good wishes."

"Speaking of— " Her eyes gleam. "There are a few women I want you to meet."

"Umm, I don't think— "

"Relax, they're not from the Mafia. Neither am I, though Michael did kidnap me— "

My eyes bug out. "He kidnapped you?"

"Oh, don't sound so surprised. You know these Mafia guys. Once they want something, they go after it. Not that different from your guy."

"My guy?" I blink. This woman is flitting between subjects like a butterfly between flowers.

"Declan?"

"He's, ah, not my guy."

"Pfft— " She waves a hand in the air. "The two of you meet. The next thing we know, you're running off with him to LA— "

"Only because he's a big star and he has all the contacts and— "

"—there was no need for him to share his contacts with you."

"I suppose not," I murmur. Now is not the time to tell them about how Declan and I already met. I should have told Olivia about it, but I've kept putting it off, and now, I'm not sure it makes a difference, to be honest. What happened is between Declan and me.

"You're right, he did want me here. And he's been helpful. And perhaps, he feels something for me, but I'm not sure what." I raise a shoulder.

She glances to her right, exchanging a look with Olivia.

"Have you made any girlfriends in LA? Anyone you can speak with and bounce your thoughts off of about your love life?"

"This is LA."

She blinks.

"This is LA. And I've been here a very short period of time, but I can tell you, no one here is your friend." It's what Declan tried to warn me about, but being on my own for the past two weeks is already making the reality of my situation clear. Trust no one, and your manager even less. That has become very clear to me already. Harry doesn't give a shit about me as a person. To him, I'm an asset, and it's his job to make me earn as much as possible in as little a time as possible. That's how he makes his money. Of course, I make money for myself, too, but I have to watch out for my own best interests. I'm still building my career, so I don't mind Harry putting me out there for every possible gig and pushing me to record this demo, so he has something to share with influencers and record companies. Given a choice, though, I'd rather just sit in my room and pen new lyrics for my songs and come up with new tunes. For now, though, I have no choice but to follow Harry's lead.

"Solene, did you hear what I said?"

30

Solene

I blink and Karma's excited features come into view. "Uh, you were saying something about your friend, Isla?"

"Yes, yes." Karma nods with enthusiasm. "She's not married—or pregnant— unlike the rest of us old farts."

"Wait, you're pregnant?"

"Not showing yet." She tilts the phone down and pats her belly. "But only eight months more until I officially join the leagues of sleep-deprived but pretending-to-glow-mothers."

My head spins from the info dump.

"Not that I'm old. It's a manner of speaking."

I nod. Best to let Karma exhaust herself... She has to run out of words eventually, right?

"Olivia and I are older than you, and we're married. Isla isn't and is going through something similar."

"She's trying to become a singer?"

Karma scoffs. "No, I mean on the 'matters of the heart' front."

"Ah, sure. Although, I don't know how useful it's going to be for us to message each other without meeting face to face."

"I'm sure you two will get along really well."

My phone buzzes:

Harry: You're going to be awesome today. I can feel it. Can you feel it? Remember best to leave two hours before your appointment time. LA traffic!

Mama mia, why does everyone I meet sound like they belong in a failed American sitcom? Probably because the characters in the sitcom are based on people like them in the first place. Also, why is getting from one part of LA to the next an exercise in patience and fancy car maneuvering? Not that I dare to navigate the traffic. I leave that to Rick.

How I miss the breezy half-hour car rides to any destination, which is all it took to get anywhere in Napoli. Or better still, walking everywhere. A concept that was met with horror from Harry. Welcome to my reality, folks. Guess I'll have to take his advice and use the treadmill.

Of course, there's the beach, but apparently, celebs don't use the beach because—paps. I pointed out I wasn't a celeb, to which Harry responded I needed to act like one so I would become one. A logic I don't quite understand. Either way, he convinced me it's best to use the gym in Declan's basement, and no, I'm not complaining. Just adjusting. That's all. I paste a smile on my lips and wave at the screen. "I've gotta go, girls."

"Okay, I'll put you in touch with Isla and—" Karma begins, but Olivia cuts her off.

"Solene, you should contact Abby."

"Eh?"

"Abigail Warren. Remember, you two used to keep in touch?"

Abby has a Mafia background like me, and we bonded when we met once on her family's trip to Italy. We've kept in touch but moving to LA disrupted that.

"I haven't messaged her since I came to LA," I admit.

"Exactly. And I don't mean to just pull names out of a hat and insist you friend them. I want to make sure you know you have a virtual circle of women rooting for you."

"We all are." Karma pops her head in front of Olivia. "Can't wait to see you hit the big time!"

"Thank you so much, you two." Tears prick my eyes. *Ridiculous. I'm fine. I'm going to be fine. I'm living the life I've always wanted. I'm here, trying to make it big in my chosen field. I'm going to be more than fine. I'm going to be great!* I swallow down the ball of emotion in my throat and blow them a kiss. "I really do need to leave, guys!"

I disconnect the call, drop the phone into my bag, and walk out of the room. Taking the steps two at a time, I head out the front door. Rick has the door of the limo open for me already.

I pause and wrinkle my nose. "Can't we use a smaller car?" I hold up my palms facing each other and bring them together. "Something more compact?"

He laughs. "This is LA. Everything is bigger than normal. Also, this car is safer for you."

"Safer?"

"It's bulletproof."

"Oh." I blink rapidly. I come from a space where it's not uncommon to hear of random shootings, and I remember walking into the kitchen to see my mother sewing up my father's wounds when he was alive, but to find myself at the receiving end of the protection is disconcerting.

"You sure I need that?"

"Just following orders."

"Ah." So, Declan hasn't forgotten about me completely? He may not speak with me, but he's left instructions for my safety. Is that good or bad? Either way, I'm simply happy I'm able to leave the house. I'd spent the last few weeks focused on writing and creating music—and Declan helped here, too. He had Rick show me to a studio he'd set up for me in the basement of his place. All of which is so confusing.

The man cares for me—he has to with everything he's done—but he's still avoiding me. I slide into the backseat. Rick shuts the door behind me, then takes the driver's seat and eases the car forward.

"That was good!" Harry claps from his position behind the producer in the control room of the studio. I slip off the headphones and crack my neck. I've been recording, or trying to record, for the last six hours. We've stopped for breaks, and the producer has stopped often to steer the direction my voice was taking. Which isn't something I'm used to.

Singing itself, is not the issue. I've been singing since I was five. It's following his directions as he tries to change the natural trajectory of the melody I'd planned. Oh, and he's not happy about the lyrics. He finds them too niche. Yep, niche versus mainstream is an argument I'm already becoming too familiar with.

"Was it really?" I scowl at him through the glass wall that separates the recording booth from the rest of the studio.

"Umm, uh, it's better than what you started with," he offers.

"I still don't understand why you want me to change my lyrics and the arrangement I had in mind."

"Because it's not—"

"Mainstream enough." Yeah, I got that. The hair on the nape of my neck rises. I glance around the recording booth. Nope, can't see any cameras in here. So, why does it feel like I'm being watched? Must be my imagination. A chill runs up my spine, and I shudder. "I think I've had enough for today."

I place my headphones on the narrow counter then walk out of the live room.

"We're not done yet," Harry cries.

"We are for now."

"But—"

I walk up to him and plant my palms on my hips. "I really am thankful you're taking a chance on me. I am. But if I can't record the song as I imagined it, then I'm not sure I want to do it, anyway."

"I have more than twenty years' experience in this field. I've built some of the biggest names in this business from scratch. I—"

I hold up my hand. "You're a genius when it comes to creating stars from singers. I understand. What I'm questioning is if that's what I want to be."

He stares at me for a few seconds, then bursts out laughing. "Everyone wants to be a star."

"I'm not saying I don't want it. But I don't think I want it enough to get it by being something I'm not."

He searches my features, then takes a step back. "I've seen a lot of young girls come here with dreams in their eyes. I've seen most fail. Very, very few succeed. The ones that do are not always the ones that work the hardest, but it's the ones that work the cleverest. The ones who know where to focus their efforts. The ones who know how to play to the lowest common denominator so they're accessible to as many people as possible."

I narrow my gaze. "You mean, the ones who are eager enough to give up their true selves and change, until they don't know what they stand for anymore?"

He raises a shoulder. "I've heard all the arguments. Ultimately, it's about what the audience wants—"

"Exactly, and how do you know what they do or don't want if you don't even try to show something new to them?"

He blows out a gust of breath, and his jaws shake. With his short stature and pot belly, not to mention, the bald head, he looks like someone's adorable uncle. Except for his eyes, which are bright and shrewd... The look of a man who's seen a lot. He has the experience to know what works, I'll grant him that. Only, I'm not sure if it works for me. I open my mouth to tell him, but he holds up his hand. "It's only our first day working together. And perhaps, I pushed you too much—"

"It's not the hours or the hard work that bothers me. It's trying to become something I'm not. It doesn't feel right."

"There are many a principle you'll have to bend to get to the top," he warns.

"Not from where I am. I had to make enough compromises to become someone I wasn't growing up. I didn't leave that only to come here and conform to someone else's idea of what I should sing or not."

His features soften. "I'm almost touched by the courage of your conviction and your ideals. It's good to have them. Just know, they may cause you to miss out on a lot of big opportunities."

"Then perhaps those opportunities are not for me."

He half smiles. "It's late; you're tired. Sleep on it and see what you make of it tomorrow, huh?"

"But—"

"Trust me on this. Don't make any decisions when you're exhausted. Wait until you've mulled it over, okay?"

I nod slowly, then grab my bag and leave.

By the time I reach home, I'm both pissed off and upset. That didn't go the way I wanted it to at all. I'm sure Declan's housekeeper left me food in the fridge, but the thought of another dinner on my own? Nope, not what I want right now. I head up to my room, pull out my phone and call the person I've been meaning to speak to for a few days. The call is answered on the first ring.

"Hello?"

"Abby, it's me."

"Solene?" She accepts the video call, and her familiar features fill the screen. I swallow down the ball of emotion that clogs my throat. Gosh, I've missed her. It's great to have a sister like Olivia who's so concerned about me, but she's Declan's friend. Not that she'd empathize with him more, but I'm uncomfortable about keeping Declan and my previous association secret from her. I appreciate her and Karma putting me in touch with Isla, and I do intend to connect with her, but Abby? She's not only an old friend, but also neutral territory. If there's anyone I can unburden myself to, it's her.

"Abby," my voice cracks. I clear my throat. "It's so good to hear your voice."

"Girl, don't go disappearing on me like that again." She looks around herself and says, "I'm at work. Let me find a room where I can talk to you." She rises from her seat and walks across the floor and into what looks like a conference room. She shuts the door behind her, then looks into the phone screen. "Are you okay? Where have you been? I've been trying to reach you."

I wince. "I'm sorry, there's so much I want to tell you."

"Wait, let me guess. Did you get married?"

"Umm, no."

"But you've met someone?"

I hesitate.

"I knew it. Is he the same man who appeared in your room and then got beat up by your brother?" Her face falls a little when she says, "Also, sorry about your brother."

"Me, too." I begin to pace. "You know how Diego was forever shooting his mouth off. He had no restraint. And in his line of work, that doesn't bode well. It was only a matter of time before he overstepped the line."

"It must still hurt; he was your brother."

I bite the inside of my cheek. "Would it be terrible if I said I'm relieved he is gone? It makes me feel like a free woman."

She nods slowly. "I understand. It's how I felt when I finally shored up the courage to leave home."

"It's why you're my role model. When I grow up, I want to be just like you."

She laughs. "My life is far from perfect. When I turned down my father's help, I didn't realize it meant living in a small one-bedroom place, scraping by from paycheck to paycheck."

"But you're happy."

"Very," she says softly. "I was lucky my father didn't stop me when I turned eighteen and made my bid for freedom. I was so worried that you wouldn't get that chance."

"I almost didn't. If it hadn't been for Declan, I might never have had the courage to leave, either."

"Declan huh?" Her eyes sparkle. "So that's his name? And you're with him now?"

I laugh. "Yes, and yes. I'm in LA—"

"LA huh?" She blinks rapidly, "So, he became an actor after all?"

"Quite a famous one, actually." I bite down on my lower lip and say, "His full name is—"

"Declan Beauchamp?!" she bursts out.

Then, seeing the guilty look on my face, her gaze widens. "OMG, you really are with Declan Beauchamp, the villain in the last Bond Film?"

"Not with him; just staying in his house."

"He asked you to come along to LA, then invited you to stay in his house. You're *with* him."

I drag my fingers through my hair. "I'd rather not discuss him with you right now."

"I'd rather not discuss anything else but that with you, but—" She holds up a hand. "I respect your wishes. So, why is it you called?"

"I have this conundrum. Should I perform the songs as I love them, or as my manager thinks I should?"

"What does your gut say?"

"That I sing them the way I imagined them."

She raises a shoulder. "There you go."

I laugh. "He'll never let me perform them that way."

"The internet," she declares.

"Eh? Not sure what you mean."

"You have a phone, don't you? Record your song, upload it to the internet, and let your listeners vote with their ears."

"I can do that?"

"Solene, please. I know you've been cloistered by your family, but surely, you've had a phone all these years?"

I glance away.

"You didn't have a phone?"

"The old-fashioned kind, attached to the wall, where everyone in the house can hear you? I had one of those."

I peer up from under my lashes to find she's looking at me with sympathy. "Shit, and I thought my family was bad."

"They didn't want me to end up like Olivia."

She draws in a breath. "I'm a PR professional babe, so you came to the right place. I'm gonna tell you exactly how to do it."

31

Declan

"You're where?" Knight's forehead wrinkles.

"I don't know. Somewhere over Mexico?". I yawn, then throw off the cover and sit up in the bed of my private jet.

On my way to the shoot, I used the plane, only to be inundated with memories of her. I left the plane with the taste of her on my lips, the scent of her crowding my senses, the feel of her clinging to the tips of my fingers, the warmth of her pussy surrounding my dick. That last? It hasn't left me in all the weeks I've been away. I've heard about a phantom limb aching after being cut off, but what do you call a phantom pussy that never lets go of its hold on your cock?

I drag my fingers through my hair. I'm losing it. I've been away from her for two weeks, and the shoot is far from over. But the first weekend I have off, I've decided to hop on the plane—risking being swamped by the memories of her that cling to this plane—and go to her. I have no idea how she's going to greet me. No clue if she'll hit me or welcome me with open arms. Probably not the second, but even if it's the first, it's okay. At least she'll be touching me.

I squeeze the bridge of my nose. That's how desperate I've become;

flying thousands of miles to see a woman on the off chance she'll deign to acknowledge my presence.

"The fuck you doing away from LA?" Knight's voice pulls me out of my meanderings.

"The last I heard, I'm a working actor. And contrary to public opinion that we sit around on our arses all day, waited on hand and foot, I wake up at four a.m. most days to work out, and then head to location for make-up, prep and shoot."

He laughs. "You also fly around in a million-dollar private jet that emits up to ten times more carbon dioxide than a normal commercial flight."

I wince. "Look, I know it doesn't make up for it, but I also donate the equivalent of what it costs to fly on one to off-set carbon omissions."

He blinks. "You do?"

I rise to my feet and pad over to the adjoining bathroom. "You sound surprised."

"Knowing you, I shouldn't be. You're the most generous person I know."

"Not like you don't do more than your share with your inheritance." I prop the phone on the counter, then flip up the lid of the commode and shove my sweatpants down.

"It's only money." He raises a shoulder.

"You only say that because you were born with it." The sound of my stream of urine hitting the porcelain fills the air.

"As were you."

"It's why we're happy to give it away. Now, if we'd been like Cade and born with not a penny to our names—"

As if summoned, my phone vibrates with a notification that indicates Cade is waiting to join the call.

"I'm patching him in," Knight warns.

Cade's face appears on screen. "Hey, motherfuckers."

"And here I'd hoped I didn't have to see your butt-ass ugly mug for a little longer," I groan.

"Aww, did you miss me, honey?" He makes smooching noises. "Catching you with your wiener in your hand, too. How appropriate."

"Go fuck yourself," I grumble, then pull up my sweats and flush.

"Heard you're having girl problems?" Cade smile widens.

"Heard you're having performance issues?"

Cade whistles. "Descending to that, are we? It must be love," he sings out.

"Shut the fuck up, wankface."

"I've seen Trappist monks look happier than you, bro," he offers.

"This is what you get when you wake me up in between time zones and countries." I scratch my unshaven chin.

"So, you get a day off and decide to hop a flight to go see your lady love?"

"What's it to you?" I scowl.

"Since you're the first of us three to decide to settle down—"

The blood drains from my face. "Who said anything about settling down?"

"You're doing a twenty-four-hour turnaround to go see her. Hence..." He raises a shoulder.

"Hence nothing. A man's entitled to go back home, isn't he?"

"Keep fooling yourself into thinking that," he chuckles.

"Is there a point to this call, you mofos?"

"Yeah, don't screw it up," Knight growls.

"Screw what up?" I pad out into the main cabin and toward the small galley where a buffet has been laid out. I ignore the food and pour myself a cup of coffee.

Cade jumps in. "Your chance at happiness, you dumbass. Not that I'm a proponent of marriage. But you've been mooning over this girl for months—"

"So have you."

He blinks. "Ex-fucking-cuse me."

Ha, got ya, asswipe.

"You've been carrying around a torch for this woman and you haven't bothered to acknowledge it, so don't preach unless you can follow what you teach, and all that."

"Huh? Do I know what you two are talking about?" Knight lowers his eyebrows. "Anyone I know?"

"Yes," I say at the same time Cade growls, "Nope."

"Which one is it?" He glances between the two screens with our faces.

"It doesn't matter." Cade walks into what looks like a dressing room. "Wankface here is trying to distract us by drawing attention away from him." He places the phone on a bench, then begins to strip.

"Fuck, I could do without the sight of your arse filling the screen."

"You showed me your pecker. Only fair I up the ante."

Knight groans. "I did not get on a call with the two of you to be treated to a display of your private parts. Trust me, I get enough of that from my fellow team members."

"It's what happens when the three of us are so strapped for time that the only time we get to meet is when one or the other of us is getting undressed."

Cade carries the phone with him into the shower. "I have five minutes to get clean and join the team manager for a press conference, which is why I jumped on the call, by the way."

"And here I thought it was because your week wasn't complete unless you jumped on a call with the two of us," I scoff.

"That, too." He switches the phone to his other hand. "Other than my sister, you two are the only family I have. The least I can do is get on a weekly call with you guys. Even if it means I have to suffer through the puppy dog eyes of Mr. Lovesick here."

"That's it, I'm gonna sign off—" I begin, but Knight cuts me off.

"The press-conference, what's it for?"

Cade hesitates, then, "Not much. You're looking at the new Captain of the English cricket team, is all."

"Knew it. Congratulations, douchebag," Knight says warmly.

"For once you're being almost modest. It must mean a lot to you, huh?"

Cade glances away, which, in itself, is unusual. The man's ego rivals mine, if that were possible. He's hiding something.

"It's a culmination of everything I've worked for since high school," he murmurs.

"It's fucking great news. I'm chuffed for you." I hold up my fist, and Cade virtual bumps it.

"It's brilliant." He cracks his neck. "Of course, it's only the beginning."

Knight laughs. "Of course."

"World domination and all that, huh?" I can't hold back the tinge of sarcasm coloring my words.

Cade smirks. "Now, now. It's what you want, too, which is why you've been chasing the top spot in Hollywood all these years. And it's not about the money, considering how loaded your folks are."

"You're right. It was never only about the money. Although, I prefer to be independent and support my lifestyle without drawing on my father's wealth. There's a different feeling when you spend your own money. It's about—"

"Don't say creative satisfaction. The three of us know that's what's driving you to see yourself on the big screen."

"Creative satisfaction. What's that?" I drum my fingers on my chest. "I'm not naive enough to believe I can follow my heart's desire and also make it to the top of the food chain."

"And that's more important?" Knight sets his jaw.

"You mean being number one? Of course it is," I snap at the same time that Cade says, "You bet your balls it is."

Knight's lips thin. "You wankers have got it all wrong."

"Your morality compass is on a different level, Knight. You believe in the power of right. That good always prevails. That doing the right thing pays dividends." Cade hunches his shoulders. "At least you still have a conscience, which is more than I can say for the two of us fuckers."

"It's how I'm wired. It's why I joined the army," Knight confesses.

"And we count on you to hold onto your path." I quirk my lips. "Between Cade and me, we have enough transgressions; we need you to balance out the scales."

"Whoa, hold on. You're making me sound like a saint."

"Compared to the two of us, I reckon you are." Cade laughs.

"You two give me too much credit. You have no idea how many times I question why I took this route." A haunted look comes into his eyes. "Some of the things I've seen here would..."

"Surely, give us nightmares. And yet, you persist. Damn, if I don't have the utmost respect for that, too." I tip my chin.

"When you're in it every day, it doesn't feel like a path to be respected or that it's right. There are enough moments where I'm in a grey area, when my sanity takes a beating and I wish I were a hundred miles away. And then, something else happens, and it makes everything worthwhile." His features soften.

"I wish you could share more with us. It's crazy you're not allowed to talk about what you go through."

"They do have shrinks for that," he replies and tilts his head. A beeping sound starts up on his side. "Guess my time's up—" He blows out a breath. "I need to get on."

Cade jerks his chin. "Anytime you need to talk, bro, you know where to find me." He raises his middle finger at the screen. "Also, before I forget, congratulations Mr. Action Hero."

"You follow the entertainment news?" I ask, taken aback.

"Uh..." He reddens. "I might have an online alert on your name for industry news."

"Aww, should I be touched?" I blow him a kiss.

"Fuck you, too, asshole. You take care of yourself, Knight." His screen goes blank.

"Cocky wankface. He's going to take a hit one of these days, and then things will never be the same." I scoff.

"Pot, kettle, and all that." Knight touches his fingers to his forehead. "I gotta go. Talk next week?"

He signs off. I toss back the rest of the coffee, then place it on the counter. I head back into the stateroom, take a quick shower, then pull up the script I need to memorize before I land in LA.

A secret no one tells you about actors? It helps if you can speed read, and even more, if you have a near photographic memory. The first I've learned, the second I've cultivated, and it's especially helpful when it comes to remembering fight choreography. It's amazing what the human mind can do when you set your mind to it. For the next few hours, I focus on the script and have memorized another hundred pages when the pilot announces we're landing. A sensation very much like happiness fills my chest.

Los Angeles has always been a pit-stop, a place to sleep in between shoots, somewhere to call a base because it's convenient since it's where the Hollywood decision-makers are based. This is the first time I can remember, I'm actually happy to be here and looking forward to going home. Home? Because she's here.

I rub my temple. There's no cause for this sense of anticipation that fills me. Nope, it's not about her. It's not. I'm just exhausted and looking forward to sleeping in my own bed. That's all it is.

The jet taxies to a stop. I head down the stairway and toward where my car is waiting. The person standing next to it is someone I don't recognize.

"Where's Rick?" I scowl.

"He said to give you this." He holds up his phone.

I glance at the screen, then swear. "Take me to her."

32

Solene

Keeping my body flat against the wall, I peer sideways and out the window of my room. From my vantage point, I can make out the small crowd of paps gathered outside the gates of the house. Initially, there were only a couple of them—and I recognized them as journalists from the massive zoom lens cameras hung around their necks. As I wondered about their presence, my phone rang. It was Rick, telling me to stay away from the window. He asked me if I'd checked the video I'd uploaded earlier. I told him yes, and asked him how he knew about that, but instead of answering, he directed me to take another look at it. Then, he warned me again to stay hidden. Before I could ask him any further questions, he disconnected.

I rush to pull up my phone and check the video I uploaded. It's a song I recorded shortly after talking to Abby. I was unable to sleep and decided to put my newfound insights to use. Honestly, I didn't think anything would come of it... but holy hell. If I'm reading the video views right, and I am, the song already has a million views. A million in a matter of hours. No, I'm not kidding. It's my first video on a handle I set up after Abby showed me how. That was a few hours ago.

I uploaded the video and fell asleep. Then woke up to my phone buzzing. Abby screeched down the line and asked me to check the response to my video. At first, I didn't comprehend what I was seeing. I saw the number of views, and I had to ask her a few times if the number was what I thought it was. Abby was so excited, she could barely speak. She tried to tell me how difficult it is to get ten thousand views, let alone a million, and in such a short period of time. I explained that it was only me, singing my heart out, acapella. Just me, my voice and my words.

She insisted it's the lyrics that elicited that kind of response. The lyrics I scrawled in the one notebook my mother didn't find. The lyrics I've polished over the last two weeks and set to the tune Harry wants me to change. I just sang the song as I heard it and saw it in my mind's eye, and apparently, people love it.

Now, I alternate my attention between the video views on my social media handle and the growing number of people joining the circus outside the gates of Declan's house.

At some point, the number of people swells to what looks like a fifty-strong crowd. Some have parked their cameras on stands trained at the house. The number of views on my video keeps growing. When it hits two million—holy shit, two million—three vans, each with the sign of a popular news station's logo on the side, drive up in quick succession and join the fray

Then, one of the paps must notice my movement at the window—this, despite my taking extreme care not to be seen. He trains his camera squarely at me, and the rest follow suit. The hair on my forearms rises. A sensation of my stomach bottoming out assails me. I push away from the window, walk to the bed, and sink down onto it. I'm not sure exactly what's happening. No, that's a lie. I have a very good idea what's happening; I just can't believe it. They love my song. No, they adore it. They can't get enough of it. I peek down at my phone and revel in the comments on the video:

@sonic: Gorgeous Voice

@tunelover: Holy shit, this is the best thing I've heard since forever

. . .

@cynic: Okay, you've won me over

@mysticboom: OMGOMGOMGOMG

@delflower: those lyrics, that voice, how do you do it?

@lokithedog: what color lipstick are you wearing?

Abby told me to reply to as many comments as I could. I keep my fingers poised over the screen but... What do I say? The phone buzzes; it's Harry. He's tried to reach me at least twenty times so far, and I've ignored every call. I mean, what am I going to say to him? He'll probably be pissed off that I released the song online. Also, I didn't follow his instructions when it came to modifying the tune. So... Yeah. No, I definitely don't want to talk to him. I let the call go to voicemail, then drop the phone by my side. What am I going to do? What can I do? If only Declan were here, I could ask him. If only—

"Solene, are you okay?"

I glance up, and it's as if I've conjured him out of thin air. A fierce happiness blasts through me. My feet barely touch the floor as I race over to him. I leap into his arms and throw mine about his neck. "You're here!" Then I burst into tears.

"Shh, baby, it's okay." His one arm is under my butt supporting me. With the other, he rubs soothing circles over my back. "Let it out, darling, let it all out." I'm dimly aware of someone else—Rick—stepping back and closing the door.

Then, Declan walks over to the sofa on the other side of the room and sits down with me in his lap. Damn, damn, damn, I need to stop blubbering all over him. At least, he's not wearing one of his fancy-ass suits, which would make this worse.

And I'm not going to apologize for falling apart like this. Or for soaking his sweatshirt. I'm allowed to have a good cry, given the emotional rollercoaster of the last month, aren't I?

He draws his palm down my hair and his touch is so gentle, so unlike how he was with me before he left that I cry harder. All the pent-up worry and frustration and anger I've stored seems to bubble up and pour down my cheeks. I'm aware of him rocking me, and somehow, the way he's offering me comfort and caring for me only makes it all worse.

He left me without even a note. He simply disappeared without a word. And now, he comes back, and I fall apart in his arms. How pathetic am I? I try to pull away, but he tightens his grip about me. His arms are steel bands around me. The familiar scent of dark chocolate and coffee envelopes me. His chest is broad enough for me to bury my face in it and cry my heart out. When my sobs finally subside, he presses his lips to the top of my head. "Feel better now?"

I nod, then promptly hiccup. Oh, god, someone kill me.

He leans over, grabs the glass of water on the end table, and passes it to me. I gulp down half of it, then place it aside.

"It's a little overwhelming, huh?"

I clamber off his lap, and he loosens his grip enough for me to sit next to him. He keeps his arm about my shoulders and tucks me into his side. I pull up my legs and allow myself to draw comfort from his big body. "You saw the video?" My voice cracks, and I swallow down the bubble of emotion that seems to have lodged itself there.

"You're brilliant in it, as I knew you would be. And now, the world knows."

I peek up at him from under my eyelashes. "You think it's good?"

"Good? It's the fucking bee's knees!" He growls.

I bite the inside of my cheek.

"I'm not the only one who thinks so, by the way. So do the three million people who've viewed it."

"Three million?" I shake my head. "The last I checked—"

"Here." He pulls his phone from his pocket, swipes the screen, then hands it over.

I glance down at it, then gulp. "Wow, that's another one million in half an hour?"

"It's growing in popularity. Seems you're unstoppable."

I hand the phone back to him and tuck my face into his armpit. "I have no idea what this means."

"It means, you've been discovered. You're going to be an overnight star."

Something in his voice makes me glance up at him. His features are soft, those blue eyes of his blazing with some kind of inner turmoil I can't interpret.

"What's wrong?" I ask.

He shakes his head.

"Tell me." I dig my elbow in his side. "Please?"

He pulls his arm from around me, and the cool air makes me shiver. A chill runs up my spine, and I wrap my arms about my waist. "Declan?" I murmur, "I'm so happy you're here with me."

He shoots me a sideways glance. "I'm glad I'm here with you, too."

I reach up and drag my finger down the crease between his eyebrows. "So, why are you frowning?"

"I'm not."

"You are."

He holds my gaze for a second, then rises to his feet and begins to pace. "I'm pleased for you, I really am—"

"But?"

"But I wish I could have had you to myself a little while longer. I knew it was only a matter of time before you'd be discovered. Hell, that's why I put you in touch with Harry, but I hoped I'd get a few months to have you to myself before the world, in all its craziness, asked to have a piece of you."

A buzzing sound fills the air. We turn toward the window where I hadn't drawn the drapes to find a device hovering there.

"What's that?" I gape.

"A fucking drone. It has a remote camera."

He stalks over to the window and pulls the drapes shut, then walks over to the next window and repeats the action, and the next, until we're closeted in the room with the sunshine now blocked by the curtains.

"Jesus." I lock my trembling fingers together.

"And it's only just beginning, babe."

"I… I'm not sure I can cope with it."

"You can, baby. You're tougher than you give yourself credit for."

"I… I'm not sure."

"I am." He walks over and squats in front of me. "Look at me, Solene."

I glance up, and his gorgeous blue eyes lock with mine. "I'm here for you. I'll help you navigate through the madness. I'll protect you from the worst of it so you can focus on your craft. At the same time, I'll ensure you enjoy your rise to fame."

My heart begins to race. My pulse kicks up so I can hear the blood drum in my ears. "Why?" I swallow. "Why would you do that?"

"Because I'm falling for you."

33

Declan

Her lips part. Her pupils dilate. Color floods her cheeks. She leans in, and I'm sure she's going to kiss me. Instead, her palm connects with my cheek. My face snaps to the side, not because there's much force behind it but because she caught me by surprise. Anger thrums at my nerve endings. That mean ugliness that I manage to rein in most of the time swirls to the surface.

Take off your top. Pull your breasts up above your bra-cups. Hold them together so I can fuck the valley between your breasts.

I shake my head to clear it. "The fuck is wrong with you?"

"The fuck is wrong with you?" Her green eyes blaze fire. "You leave me without a word. There's no phone call from you. I have to get updates of your whereabouts from your bodyguard—"

"*Your* bodyguard, actually."

"There's nothing on your social media."

"Oh, so you scanned my social media?" Some of the anger abates and is replaced by an emotion very close to exaltation. Huh?

"Stop smirking, you *stronzo*. You took my virginity, and then you didn't have the decency to talk to me after that."

"I thought you'd need time to recuperate from how—"

"How?"

"—how rough I was with you." My neck heats. I'm not going to apologize for taking her virginity. It's who I am. I want something, I grab it for myself. I don't wait. It's who I am. So why do I feel regret for not taking it slower with her? I rise to my feet, and she jumps up onto the couch.

"Are you apologizing?" She arches an eyebrow.

"What if I am?" I scowl.

"Then you need to say it aloud."

I fold my arms across my chest. "I'm not sorry I took your virginity. I'm glad I was your first."

She tips up her chin. "I still don't hear it."

"I'm sorry if I wasn't gentle with you. But I'm not sorry if it caused you pain."

"What?" She gapes. "You're not?"

"The more the pain, the more the pleasure, don't you know that?"

"Is that the story you sadists tell yourselves?" She huffs.

I look at her with interest. "You been reading the spicy books I bought you, Rabbit?"

She flushes. "They're *books*."

"And hopefully, they provided you a quick education, which"—I widen my smirk—"I do believe they have."

She plants her palms on her hips. "I thought this was an apology?"

"I'm sorry I left you so suddenly and that I didn't contact you. And I'm sorry you had to find me in the Club with no introduction to that part of my life. But I'm not sorry for fucking you."

Her flush deepens; her lips part. The pulse at the base of her throat picks up speed. Fucking hell, she's aroused. And all because I used that four-letter word? I tuck a strand of hair behind her ear, and she shivers. Yep, definitely aroused. I move closer, until my torso brushes against hers. A tiny whine spills from her lips.

"If I were to push my hand between your legs, would I find you wet and aching and throbbing for me?"

"Guess you'll have to find out."

She tips up her chin, and I lower mine. At the sound of buzzing, she stiffens. "That's my phone," she murmurs.

"Ignore it." I cup her cheek; her chest rises and falls.

I brush my lips over hers, share her sweet breath, and the blood drains to my groin. I grip her butt and pull her into me. She yelps, then grips my shoulders to right herself.

The buzzing fades away.

I bite down on her lower lip. She opens her mouth, and I sweep my tongue over hers. She digs her fingernails through the fabric of my sweatshirt and into my skin. I feel the pinch all the way to the crown of my cock. I tilt my head, kiss her deeply, sucking on her tongue, drawing in the honeyed taste of her. A groan rumbles up my chest. She pushes her pelvis into the hard column in my crotch. She chafes against it. I squeeze her arse-cheeks, and another shudder ladders up her spine.

"Fucking hell, Rabbit, I missed you."

"I missed you, too."

I release my hold on her butt, only to pinch her chin and hold her face in position as I deepen the kiss. The scent of her, the taste of her, the need for her twists my guts. That's when the buzzing of the phone starts again. I ignore it, continuing to suck on her tongue. My heartbeat ratchets up. The pulse bangs at my temples. *Bang-bang-bang.*

Bang-Bang-Bang. There's a knock on the door. "Declan, we need to speak." Rick's voice cuts through the sexual haze that grips me.

I manage to drag my mouth from her and lean my forehead against hers. "Fuck." I stare into her dilated pupils. "We'll continue this later."

She stares up at me.

"You okay, baby?" I murmur.

She nods.

I brush my lips over hers again. Our mouths cling. I deepen the kiss when—"Declan! It's urgent." Rick bangs on the door again.

I tear my mouth away from her again. "One second," I yell in the direction of the door, then step back and look her up and down. "Where's your dressing gown?"

"Eh?" She blinks. "I'm wearing a perfectly decent pair of shorts and T-shirt."

"Your shorts are too short."

"What?" She gapes.

I pivot, walk over to the closet and survey the contents. Shit, I should have taken her shopping before I left. Well, this time, I'm going to do things right. I turn, pull off my sweatshirt and walk over to her, pulling it down over her shoulders. She must be too dazed from the kiss—not complaining about that—for she thrusts her arms through the sleeves. I smooth the fabric down over her hips. It comes to mid-thigh and engulfs her.

"I look ridiculous,"

Her phone stops buzzing, then starts again.

"You look…" *—like mine*. "Good in my clothes."

She scoffs, then rolls up her sleeves, before jumping down from the couch. I walk over to her bed and scoop up her phone. Disconnecting Harry's call, I head toward the door and swing it open.

"Finally, fuck." Rick looks from me to her, then takes in the curtained windows. "The drones are taken care of."

"Good."

"We have bigger problems," he warns.

"Ain't that the truth." I hold out my hand to her. "Ready for what's coming?"

"No, absolutely not." I glare at my team. "I'm not putting her in front of the cameras."

We're in my living room, and thanks to some quick thinking on Rick's part, we've managed to get injunctions against any kind of aerial intrusion of my airspace. Fucking hell, I've never had an issue with the paps using drones to monitor my movements, but even if they had I wouldn't have cared about it. But I've never had to protect someone else from their encroachment, either. Turns out, I'll do anything to protect her from that bunch.

Giorgina folds her arms across her chest. "Newsflash: She's already put herself in front of the cameras. It's what caused this entire pisspot of a disaster."

"Hey, don't talk about me like I'm not here." Solene jumps up from the sofa where she's seated next to me. "I can make up my own mind about my future."

"Can you?" Giorgina looks at me then back at her. "You might want to talk to your boyfriend about that."

"He's not my boyfriend," she bursts out.

"Not what the evidence suggests," she drawls.

Harry pushes the door open and steps in. Rick who's been positioned next to the doorway, steps in front of him.

"I'm her manager." Harry's jowls shiver as he swallows. "I... I was invited to join the meeting."

"He's right, I texted him." I wave my hand, and Rick steps aside.

"You texted him? You texted my manager?" Solene turns on me.

"Much as I hate his weaselly arse, he is the best in the business, and you need someone to watch out for what's best for your career."

"I can't believe you'd speak to my manager without consulting me."

"Don't think I'm going to consult you before I do what's best for you," I growl.

She narrows her gaze on me. She's standing over me, and considering how pint-sized she is, it doesn't give her much of an advantage in height.

"Give me my phone." She holds out her hand.

I widen the space between my legs and throw my arms over the back of the couch.

Her lips thin. "No one decides what's best for me. Not you. Not Harry. I decide for myself. Only I know what's on my mind; not anyone else."

I scowl at her. "I know this city and this industry. I've been in showbiz for almost a decade. I can help you navigate the fallout from your overnight success."

"And I don't doubt that. In fact, I welcome it. I'm more grateful than you'll ever know that you flew out in the middle of your shoot to come see me. You're here when I need you most, but—" She squares her shoulders. "But the final decision is mine. Not my manager's, or my boyfriend's, but mine."

"Ah, so you accept that I'm your boyfriend?"

She flushes then stabs her sneaker-clad toes into the floor. "I'm living with you. I put up a video, and the paps traced me to your home. I'm not sure what else to call you."

I hold out my hand, palm face up. She glances at it for a few seconds, then slowly places her much smaller palm in mine. I tug on her hand, and she tumbles into my lap. She yelps and tries to pull away, but I wrap my arm about her shoulders. "I'll never say or do anything that will hurt you. I'll do everything in my power to ensure you're protected. I'll put an end to anyone who dares do anything to compromise you. This, I promise."

Her eyes grow bright. She sniffles and whispers, "Th-th-thank you."

"You're welcome." I pull out her phone and hold it out. She pockets it, then throws her arms about my neck and presses her lips to mine. Of course, I deepen the kiss. I tilt my head, open my mouth over hers and suck on her tongue.

Harry clears his throat. "That's touching, but we still haven't worked out how we're going to deal with the fallout from her going against my recommendations."

She breaks away from the kiss and glances at him. "You mean the eight million and counting views of my video?"

He runs his finger under his collar. "It's an unprecedented accomplishment, I grant you, but it might have been even better received if you'd followed my advice."

"Are you referring to your recommendation of making my song more mainstream?" She scoffs.

Harry swallows, then squares his shoulders, "I stand by what I said."

"And I appreciate it. I do, but..."

"But?" he scowls.

"But—"She jumps up from my lap, pulls down the sweatshirt—my sweatshirt—over her hips, then walks over to him. "Who am I?" she asks him.

"Excuse me?"

"Who am I, Harry?" she asks in a voice dripping with exaggerated patience.

"You're Solene."

"And what am I in relation to you?"

He frowns. "My client?"

"Bingo. And you're my manager. And if you want to get the credit for being the person who discovered the hottest talent in town, then I recommend you shut your trap and understand, while I value your advice, the final word is mine."

He seems taken aback, then slowly nods.

"*Benissimo*, I think we finally understand each other." She leans in and plants a kiss on his cheek.

Harry flushes, then thrusts out his chest. "Of course we do."

"*Bene*." She turns to me and asks, "What's next?"

34

Solene

"I didn't think this is what the photoshoot was going to turn out to be." I pout up at my boyfriend. *My boyfriend.* I'm still getting used to calling him that. To think, less than a month ago, I was headed for an arranged marriage. And today, I'm on the brink of launching my own album, and I have the man of my dreams wrapping his arm about my shoulders and pulling me in.

Giorgina set up this event overnight. She and Harry convinced me it was a good idea to do a joint photoshoot with Declan for the paps. She had a point when she said it was better to do that, and control the narrative, rather than have them trying to tail us and sneak pictures of us. They'll probably still do that, but at least we'll be ahead of the curve by releasing the first picture of the two of us on our own terms.

I'm a novice at this game, but her rationale made sense. However, I didn't anticipate it would turn out to be such a circus. There are at least a hundred—I kid you, not— a hundred photographers lined up to photograph us on the steps of the most exclusive boutique on Rodeo Drive.

I glance at the lenses, which instantly flash and flinch.

"Look at me, baby." Declan tucks a strand of hair behind my ear, eliciting another ripple of flares going off.

I know I'm safe. Declan's with me, and he's positioned Rick and more of his security team on either side of us, keeping the camera guys at bay. Still, the anticipation of those assembled is a palpable sentiment. It's not unlike the salivating of beasts in the zoo when it's feeding time. A shiver of nervousness judders under my skin. He must sense it, for he notches his knuckles under my chin and tips up my face. "You're safe, baby, I promise. It's like ripping off a band-aid. Power through it, and it will be all over before you know it."

"Promise?" I raise my gaze to those heady blue eyes of his and am instantly snared. A hot flush oscillates under my skin, and my stomach flip-flops. There's something in his eyes I've never seen before. A tenderness, a protectiveness, and it's mixed with another sentiment I can't quite place. Maybe a mix of pride and surprise? He's as bemused as I am by the interest this impromptu photo session has evoked among the journalists.

"Kiss her, Declan," one of them calls out.

"Kiss!" Another one cries.

"Kiss."

"Kiss."

More voices join in.

Without taking his gaze from mine, he pulls me up to my tiptoes. The blue in his eyes deepens to indigo. The pulse at his temple beats faster. The thought of kissing me is as much of a turn on for him as it is for me.

He dips his chin, and without closing his eyes, brushes his lips over mine. Soft. Almost adoring. And so romantic. Not words I ever thought I'd associate with this man. His eyelashes entwine with mine; his breath interlaces with mine. His hold around my waist is a heavy weight that seems to brand me. My thighs seem to melt, and my core heats up. I push into that thick column between his legs, and something flashes in his eyes. He deepens the kiss. I open my mouth.

We're being watched by the media. Everyone is going to see just how much I am into him, but I can't stop myself. He asks and I give. That's the way it is. I can protest. I can put up a fight. He wants me to put up a fight. But we both know it's only because it makes my final surrender so much sweeter. So much more arousing. So much more satisfying for both of us.

He sweeps his tongue over mine, kissing me with the kind of passion I've only dreamed about. The kind of desperation I sensed when he fucked me earlier. When he made me come so hard, I saw stars. And oh, god, I can't wait to feel his hands on my body, his cock nestled inside me as he takes me again. My heart begins to race, and a thousand little fires seem to light up under my skin. His kiss deepens further until it feels like he's consuming me. Branding his taste into my heart. Marking me with his scent, ensuring I'll never feel the same again. Then, he tears his mouth from mine, his chest heaving, the pulse at his neck mirroring the agitation I feel inside me.

"How much do you love her, Declan?"

I blink, becoming aware of the flashlights still going off around us, lighting up his face until it feels like we're in the path of a storm.

"Do you love her, Declan?"

"Yes," he says without taking his gaze of mine. "Yes, I do love her."

Wha—? Before I can formulate my question, he turns and nods his chin at the assembled group. "That's all folks."

Instantly, the speed with which the flashbulbs go off intensifies.

"Look here, Declan."

"Here, Solene."

"One more picture, guys."

He threads his fingers through mine, turns and stalks into the boutique with me in tow. The door shuts behind us. I turn to find Rick taking a stance in front of it. Another of his security detail draws the blinds, shutting off the sights and sounds.

In the sudden silence, I sag against him. "Whoa, is it always that bad?"

"I've had worse, but I admit, the persistence of the reporters took me by surprise."

"They like the two of you together." Giorgina flounces in from wherever she's been lying in wait. Harry puffs as he tries to catch up with her.

"It's mayhem. They're already uploading to social media sites—" He waves a phone at us.

"Later," Declan growls at the two of them.

"That was a success, and that kiss!" Giorgina fans herself. "You guys are going to be on the front page, dominating the headlines of all celebrity news blogs and tabloids. Of course, you know what you need to do, is shoot a follow up to your now ten million viewed post and, with him and—"

"Giorgina. I said. Later." Declan's voice booms around the empty boutique.

She blinks, seems to shake herself from whatever PR fevered vision she was having and nods. "Of course. You two did a great job. Now go enjoy your reprieve." She blows us a kiss and walks off.

"Yes, you two were marvelous, you—"

Declan makes a growling sound deep in his throat. Harry pales—"I'll uh, I'll take myself out of here." He turns to leave, then glances at me. "I need you at the studio, recording the rest of the songs."

"Rest of the songs?" I blink.

"You had a taste of one going viral. The record labels are tripping over themselves to sign you up, and—"

"Harry—" Declan takes one step forward. "Leave."

Harry yelps, then turns and breaks into a jog. His body fat jiggles under his too tight jacket as he disappears around the corner that leads to the back exit.

"Finally, fuck." Declan releases my hand, then cracks his neck. He stalks over to the side and through a doorway. I follow him and find myself in a spacious room. There's a floor-to-ceiling mirror in one corner. Next to it is a curtained entrance which must lead to a dressing room. On the other side is a row of dresses on a movable rail. He stalks over to a wet bar at the back of the room and pours a glass of whiskey for himself. He grabs a bottle of water and walks over to the couch facing the mirror.

"Did you mean that?" I burst out.

"What?"

"Don't act like you don't know." I stomp over to him. "You said you love me."

"I did."

"Did you mean it?"

"It's what they expected to hear from me."

"Oh." Some of the fight goes out of me. "So, you didn't mean it?"

He surveys the bottom of his glass of whiskey. "I have feelings for you. I feel something for you. Else you wouldn't be here. And I wouldn't have flown down at the first chance I got to be with you. But is that love? Honestly, I don't know."

I hunch my shoulders. At least he's being honest, so there's that. Not that it makes me feel any better. Not like I expected him to fall in love with me so quickly, either. Not that I love him. I mean, I've always thought I did, but maybe I was in love with the idea of him. As for the real Declan, do I? I feel secure with him. I'm glad he's here with me when everything around me is changing so fast. And he's only helped me so far. He's responsible for changing the trajectory of my life. As I did for him. A shiver of trepidation runs down my back. I dismiss it. The one thing I can be sure of is he wants me to succeed in my career. Everything he's done so far points toward that. As for what there is between us, it's something I need to work out.

"Okay." I lock my fingers together.

"Okay?" He frowns. "You're okay with that?"

"It's not ideal, but I'm not sure what I feel for you, either, so we're even."

He seems taken aback, then barks out a laugh.

"You surprise me at every turn, Rabbit."

I allow my lips to curve. "Is that good or bad?"

"It's good. In fact, it's my turn now."

"Your turn?"

"To catch you unawares."

His eyes gleam. One by one, his muscles relax. The way he looks at me, it's like a lion regarding his prey, or a rabbit he has in his sights. I swallow. My stomach bottoms out. That familiar hollowness in my core intensifies. I squeeze my thighs together, and his lips curl.

He takes a sip of his whiskey, places it on the side table, then twists open the bottle of water. "Thirsty, Rabbit?"

35

Declan

"I assume the question isn't as straightforward as it seems?" she murmurs.

I tilt my head. There she is. My smart Rabbit who knows my most innocent questions are also the ones that are filled with landmines.

"It's whatever you want it to be."

She shifts her weight from foot to foot. A considering look comes into her eyes. Then she nods. "I'll take it at face value, for now. So yes, I'm thirsty."

I crook a finger at her. She moves toward me without hesitation, then sinks down on her knees in front of me.

"Good girl."

A shudder runs through her.

"Open your mouth."

She blinks, then obliges. I take a mouthful of water, then lean forward and dribble it into her mouth.

She stiffens. I'm sure she's going to spit it out, but instead, she swallows. Every. Last. Drop. Fuck, if her acquiescence isn't the most erotic thing I've experienced.

"Want more?" I murmur.

Again, she nods without hesitation, and my cock stabs against my zipper. Once again, I take a sip of water, then place my mouth over hers. I allow the water to seep onto her tongue, then wrap my fingers about her throat. "I want to feel my cock down your gullet when you swallow."

Her breathing speeds up. Color smears her cheeks. "Do it then. I want to feel the shape of your shaft on my tongue."

"I see your vocabulary has expanded in the little time I've been away."

"You have no idea," she replies and angles forward, or tries to, for my hold on the back of her neck prevents her from moving.

"Why are you stopping me?" she whines.

"Because first, I need you to try on those clothes."

"And I need a new wardrobe, why?" she calls out from behind the curtain.

I glance up from the script I've been trying to focus on since she grabbed a dress and strode into the dressing room.

"Because you're the next big thing and you need to dress like one," I say patiently.

"So why couldn't I have gone to a mall? Or to one of the department stores?"

"Because you'd have been mobbed."

"That's seriously the most ridiculous thing I've ever heard. Those photographers were there for— "

"You and me." I half-smile. "The two of us together, we're clickbait, baby."

"I saw the throng of paps with my own eyes, but I still can't believe they wanted to photograph me as much as you." She pushes the curtain aside, walks out, and my breath leaves my lungs. I take in her hair, which flows about her face, and the shoulders left bare by the dress. A blush pink in color, it clings to her curves, nips in at her waist, then flows down to end just above her knees. With her thigh-high black boots, and the dewy freshness of her skin, she looks like every man's wet dream come true. She looks like the kind of girl every red-blooded male would want to turn over his lap and spank, then fuck, then take home to meet his mother.

I accepted Giorgina's help arranging for the wardrobe, and I gave instructions for how I'd love to see her dressed. What I hadn't considered is that everyone else would see her, too, as soon as she starts appearing more in the public eye. Too late. She's already in the public eye, and everyone who hasn't heard of her will very soon. This is, likely, the last weekend I'll have her to myself. Soon, she'll release her album and be swept away in the adulation that will accompany it. She'll find success, fame, the life she wants...

As for me? The movie with me at the helm will, hopefully, cement my place in the annals of Hollywood. We'll each be free to go our own way. This weekend, though? She's mine. And while I'll never unleash the full brunt of my depravities on her, I'm still going to fuck her. I'm going to bury myself inside her pussy, where no one else has been but me, and have my fill of the woman who's haunted my dreams.

"Take off your dress."

Her face falls. "Don't you like it?"

When I continue to stare at her, she huffs, "What?"

"You heard me. Don't make me repeat myself."

She firms her lips. "I don't know what crawled up your arse, but I already told you I didn't come here to be treated like a—"

I angle my head.

She hesitates.

"Like a? Go on, don't stop now. Say it, Rabbit."

"Like a whore," she spits out. "There, happy?"

"Not until I show you how much you want to be one for me."

"I know you like these domination-submission games—"

"Not a game, baby; this is my life."

"Whatever—" She raises a shoulder. "And I appreciate the crash course you afforded me by buying me those spicy books, all of which I've read, by the way. And I understand, somewhat, what you like. In fact, I'll be the first to admit, I don't mind playing along... Up to a certain limit."

No limits. No safe words. You'll do as I say. You'll take my cock as I deem fit to give it to you. In your mouth. Your pussy. Your arse. One after the other. And you'll take it. You'll take it and be happy, and when I'm done, you'll thank me for having given you my attention.

"Do you want to leave?"

"What?"

"Do you want to go back to the house? I'll have Rick take you."

"And where will you go?"

"I won't fuck another woman,"—I place my foot over the knee of my other leg—" if that's what you're worried about."

She sets her jaw. "But you'll go to the Club and watch other women being fucked."

"Does that bother you?"

"Of course, it bothers me, you *stronzo*. You just told them you love me. Next thing, you're turning up at the Club and watching some other woman being railed. If you think that doesn't bother me, you don't know me."

"Jealous, Rabbit?"

"Not jealous. Possessive." She plants her palms on her hips. "But you know what? Forget it. You go do what you want, and I'll go find someone else who can give me what *I* want." She turns on her heels and stalks off toward the dressing room.

"The fuck?" *Did I hear that right? Did I hear her say she'll find someone else? It's going to happen—eventually.* My stomach tightens. My guts churn. I shove the sinking feeling in my chest aside and jump to my feet. "Don't you move another step."

She snorts, then raises her middle finger over her shoulder.

A-n-d, that's it. She's done it now. My vision tunnels. Adrenaline laces my blood. I stalk over to the dressing room, shove the curtain aside, and step inside to find her meeting my gaze in the mirror.

"Doesn't feel good when I throw your words back at you, huh?" She scoffs.

"I told you I wasn't going to fuck another woman."

"And I told you I was going to find someone else who'd give me what I want. I'm not going to indulge in penetrative sex, either, if that's what's bothering you."

"It doesn't bother me," I lie through gritted teeth.

"Okay." She begins to unzip her over-the-knee, fuck-me, heeled boots.

"Leave them on," I snap.

"The heels are too high to wear on a daily basis."

"But they're the perfect height for you to lean over and grab your ankles when I fuck you."

36

Solene

I freeze, then slowly straighten. This time, when I meet his gaze in the mirror, I flinch. Those blue eyes have turned into frigid chips of ice. His gaze is sharp enough to cut through my skin, and pierce through any barriers I might have erected around my feelings. His jaw tics. His left eyelid twitches. He looks pissed. Very pissed. So pissed, I'm surprised he hasn't grabbed me and turned me over his knee and spanked me.

Goosebumps pop over my skin. And oh, god, I'd like that so much. Too much. There's no redemption for me. I wasn't lying when I said I don't want him to treat me like a whore. I just want to be treated like I'm his whore. His slut, who takes any punishment he bestows on me, and asks for more.

When did I turn into such a masochist? How did he loosen that part of me and allow it to rise to the surface? How did he know how much I wanted to be possessed by someone as strong, as forceful, as dominant as him? And how long can I keep up this pretense of not wanting everything I sense he can do to me? Everything he's mentioned, as well as everything I've glimpsed in his eyes, but which he's never voiced to me. How long can I hold onto that part of me I refused to give up through all the years I was controlled by my family? Isn't this just another kind of subjugation, though? So, why do I crave it so much?

"You can turn around and leave now, but if you stay, I'll take it that you want what I'm going to do to you."

Liquid heat thrums through my veins. *I want it. I want it. I. Want. It.* I tip up my chin and force myself to hold his gaze. "I'm done running."

"Then, say you want what I'm going to do you."

I swallow. "I want what you're going to do to me."

"Good. Now bend over and grab your ankles."

I hesitate.

"Now."

I comply. Like a bow he's strung to his specifications, I widen the space between my legs, then curve my back, thrust out my butt and circle my boot-clad ankles with my fingers.

Through the space between my legs, I watch him approach. He stops so close behind me, the heat from his body curves around me. It cocoons the two of us in a halo of anticipation, of expectation, of the degradation I know he's going to unleash on me. And I welcome it.

He grips my hip, then yanks off my panties. I cry out. My thighs clench. Moisture pools between my legs, and to my horror, a fat bead of cum slides out of my slit and down my inner thigh. He instantly scoops it up. I hear the pop as he pulls his finger out from between his lips. Heat sweeps through my skin. My blood pumps harder. *Whoosh-whoosh-whoosh.* The noise of my pulse drums in my ears.

He stays silent. Unmoving. Waiting. Waiting. *For what?*

My muscles tighten. My stomach twists itself into an infinity shape. A heavy pulse settles between my legs. My clit seems to have attracted all the blood in my body. My nerve-endings stretch. My hearing is tuned into the slightest change in his breathing. I wait. Wait. Yet when he moves, I don't see it coming. All I feel is the sting between my legs when he slaps my pussy. I squeal. And instantly, orgasm.

"Fucking hell."

His hold on my hip is the only thing holding me up. I shudder and pant as the orgasm slams into me. Black spots prick my vision. The gushing sensation between my legs intensifies. I sway, and he plants his heavy hand on my other hip, helping to right me. The aftershocks pulse through me. My consciousness seems to have separated from my body, and I'm looking down on this spectacle. As if from a distance, I hear the clink of his buckle, the r-r-rip of his zipper being lowered. Then the crinkle of a condom. In one thrust, he impales me.

I groan as the blunt crown of his cock slams into that spot deep inside me. Through the thin membrane of the condom, his piercing digs into the sensitive walls of my pussy. Shockwaves of sensation zip up my spine. My head spins and I scream, "Declan!"

"I'm here, Rabbit. If you could see how your pussy is molded around my shaft, how your swollen clit is begging for me to abuse it, how the puckered hole between your arse cheeks is ready and waiting for me to violate it, you'd know that I'm not letting you go until you orgasm at least three more times."

"You're crazy," I gasp, then yell when he pinches my clit.

Sparks of sensation sear my pain centers. Then, he stuffs his digit into my back hole with no preamble, no warning—Okay, so he did state his intention, but honestly, I didn't think he'd go there again so soon after the last time, and—he pulls out of me until he's balanced at the edge of my slit, then thrusts forward with such force, my entire body moves forward.

His hold on my hip is firm enough that I don't unbalance. He begins to fuck me. Fast. Hard. In-out-In. Every time he slams into me, he grunts, growls and swears. "Fuck, Rabbit. Fuck." He picks up pace, going even faster. He begins to pluck on my clit, circling it, pulling at it, chafing it, knowing exactly how to send signals to my pleasure center that my body is not mine anymore. It's his instrument to do with as he desires. To take me. Use me for his pleasure. To inflict the kind of agony that will only heighten the next orgasm, which sweeps out from where he's slammed into me again.

I yell as I come. I swear I see stars this time. Sweat beads my hairline. My limbs tremble. "I can't. I can't. No more," I groan.

"Three more."

I blink. It takes a few seconds for his words to sink in.

"That's what you said last time, you *pezzo di merda*," I yell.

In reply, he spanks my arse. Once-twice-thrice, in quick succession. I groan as the pain from the contact arrows to my center. My clit hurts. My insides shudder. That's when he adds a second digit to my puckered hole.

I groan. My thighs spasm. And he's still fucking me. The man's a machine as he pummels into me again and again. He doesn't stop. He's not even out of breath.

"Dec-lan," I gasp.

"Come for me, Rabbit. Right fucking now."

And I do. This time, the orgasm blooms in my center, then spreads to my extremities like a gentle rain. Pleasure flickers across my brain. A soft sigh leaves me. I sway like fruit on an peach tree. Ripe and ready to be plucked.

And still, he thrusts into me. He releases his hold on my clit, only to wrap those fingers around the nape of my neck. I shiver. And yet, I feel grounded. Tethered to this plane, to him. Tuned into his every command. His needs. Mine. His. So, when he puts his cheek next to mine and licks the shell of my ear, I shudder. He pulls me closer, twists his fingers inside my backchannel, then tilts his hips and drills into me in such a fashion that his balls thwack into my clit. Shudders of pain and pleasure alternate through my veins. I gasp, and hear him growl, "Come."

And I do. Again. The orgasm envelops every part of me. My cells are filled to overflowing. My scalp tingles. My legs hurt. Even my toenails are flushed with the pleasure-pain he's jolting through me with every flick of his fingers and stab of his cock. Then, his hold on my neck tightens. I try to breathe, but my lungs burn. My entire body shudders. I release the hold on my ankles and claw at his wrist. Darkness streaks across the fronts of my eyes. A part of me registers that he's pulled out of me again and that he's waiting, poised at the entrance of my channel. And then he sinks into me, all the way in, deeper than he's ever been before. He hits a part of me I didn't even know existed.

"Come with me." He loosens his hold around my neck. Oxygen inflates my lungs and dilates my cells as I gulp down air. I hear someone screaming, then realize it's me, and I shatter. The last thing I remember is his groan as he empties into me.

I black out after that. I have a vague recollection of Declan pulling my sweatshirt over my dress, then carrying me out the backdoor and to the car. Thankfully, there are no paps to witness my sex-hazed state. Along the way, he speaks to one of the shop's assistants and orders them to deliver all of the clothes and shoes in the dressing room to his place. Guess everyone in that shop heard me scream when I climaxed earlier. I flush. To see the expressions on their faces, you wouldn't guess, though. Guess they're paid enough by Declan to ignore the goings-on.

I fall asleep in the car and wake only when he carries me to his room. He strips me of my clothes, fucks me again—very slowly this time

—then spoons his body around mine before pulling the covers over both of us.

I wake to find him moving about the room getting dressed. He walks over, kisses me and orders me back to sleep. I want to ask him where he's going. A part of me knows he's leaving. But I can't not obey him. Besides, I'm exhausted, and when he tucks the blankets around me, I fall asleep again.

When I awaken, I'm alone with a slim rectangular jewelry case and a note addressed to me on his pillow.

37

A month later

Declan

"So, this is where you're hiding out?" Knight kicks out his legs and glances about the 7A Club. It's situated in the heart of London yet tucked away from intrusive eyes, thanks to the tree cover in front of its impressive facade. The pre-war heritage building has become my home away from home. I'm now renting a room above the club house… on an ongoing basis.

"I'm not hiding out."

I'm hiding out.

"You're hiding out," he says with finality.

"I have no idea what you're talking about."

"Oh?" He places the tips of his fingers together. "Then what are you doing here, instead of being in LA?"

"I knew you were coming here, and it's been so long since I've seen you, I thought I'd spend some quality time with you."

He lowers his chin and fixes me with a disbelieving look. "We're good friends, and I like your company, but if I had a woman waiting for me, you bet your arse, I'd be with her instead of choosing to put up with your ugly face."

"Aww, now you hurt me." I slap my hand over my heart in an exaggerated gesture. "And here, I thought this was our chance to make up for some of the time we've lost over the years."

He chuckles. "You poor sod. You're running scared, huh?"

"I don't know what you mean." I snatch my mug of coffee and take a sip.

"Did you realize you were falling for her? Is that why you've stayed away?"

"Falling for whom?"

He reaches over and claps me on the back of my head.

"Ow, what was that for?" I place my cup down on the table, then grab a paper-towel and dab at the stains on my sweatshirt.

"Stop pretending you don't know who I'm referring to."

"Fine, I do. And no, I'm not falling for her."

"You prefer to fly halfway around the world to London instead of going to LA when you get time off, and you're going to tell me it's not because you have feelings for her."

"First, the shooting of the film has moved to Europe, which is why it's easier to come to London rather than LA. And two—" I ball up the towel and dunk it in the bin. "I'm not falling for her because I've already fallen for her."

He blinks. "Hold on, so you're saying that—"

"I have feelings for her, yes. Which is why I need to stay away from her."

"You're not making any sense. You discovered you have feelings for her, so you're putting distance between the two of you?"

"Isn't that what I just said?"

He rubs his chin. "So, you're running scared."

"I'm not scared," I scoff.

"So why aren't you in LA telling her how you feel?"

"Why do you care either way?"

"Because you're my friend. Also..." He trails off as he shuffles his feet. "Abby, may have mentioned it to me."

"Abby, your sister?" I tilt my head.

"She and your girl are good friends. We met the one time my father explored the possibility of striking a business arrangement with Solene's father. A notion he later dropped." He raises a shoulder. "Abby and Solene hit it off, though, and kept in touch."

"What are the odds, huh?" I prop my ankle over the knee of my other leg.

"The organized crime world is insular. Doesn't matter if you live in another country; elements of the syndicate keep in touch with each other. As the law has grown more savvy, so have they.

"I hinted to her that I was developing feelings where she's concerned," I admit.

"You don't sound happy about it."

"I'm not." I drag my fingers through my hair. "I'm not ready to be tied down. Then, there are my proclivities."

"Is she aware of your tastes?"

"She came to the Club—"

"You took her to the Club?" He stares.

"Of course not. She managed to coerce Rick into bringing her."

Knight barks out a laugh. "Sounds like she's keeping you on your toes."

"You have no idea."

He leans forward, interest shining in his eyes. "Sounds like she's good for you, so why are you running from her?"

"I'm not—"

He narrows his gaze on me.

I blow out a breath. "Yes, okay, I didn't expect to develop these emotions where she's concerned."

"So, she *is* aware of your fondness for BDSM?"

I hesitate, then nod slowly.

"I repeat, what's the problem, then?"

I rub the back of my neck, "She's young and her career is just beginning. I'm not going to sully her with how far I want to take things."

"Maybe she's not as naive as you think she is. She comes from the Mafia. Surely, she's aware of what happens in the wider world."

"I can't impose my inclinations on her."

Though everything, so far, points to the fact that she might enjoy the lifestyle. But once I take it that far, there's no returning, and I can't risk getting so involved with her that I wouldn't want to let her go. And that's exactly what could happen. What might already have happened.

"You need to give her a chance. You can't decide for the both of you."

I toss back the coffee, then slide my cup on the table. "What makes you such a relationship expert?"

"I'm not. But I've seen death close enough to appreciate you don't always get a second chance."

"Seems I'm in time to lift the mood of this par-tay." Cade's voice reaches us a second before he slips into the vacant chair around the coffee table. A waiter appears at his elbow with a tumbler of whiskey. "Thanks, mate." The waiter steps away, and Cade raises his glass. "You pussies still sticking to tea?"

"It's coffee," Knight says mildly.

"Also, it's not even six p.m.," I add.

"It's six somewhere in the world."

"The saying is, it's five o'clock somewhere in the world," Knight chides him.

"Even better!" Cade raises his glass, then takes a sip. "JJ keeps the best whiskey in town." He's referring to the man who runs 7A, a reformed Mafia Don the three of us know well.

"High praise, coming from the new captain of the English cricket team," a new voice booms.

"Speak of the devil..." Cade turns to greet the newly arrived man. JJ claps Cade on his shoulder. "I'm rooting for you to take the team all the way to the finals of the next World Cup."

"You bet." Cade smirks.

JJ barks out a laugh. "Cocky as ever. And hell if I don't appreciate that."

"Haven't seen you in a while, Knight." He and Knight clasp hands, then bump fists. "How long are you in town?"

"Shipping off tomorrow."

"Another secret mission?" JJ surveys him with a shrewd look in his eyes.

Knight's lips quirk. "You could say that."

"I respect what you do to keep us all safe. I wish I could do more to show my gratitude."

"You do a lot." He glances around the table. "You all do, and the men are grateful."

He's referring to the fund JJ started, and which we all contribute to monthly, the proceeds of which go to helping military vets find jobs after they leave the forces.

"Not enough. Not when your men give their lives for a cause. You have my respect. In fact—" JJ snaps his fingers and another member of his staff appears with a bottle of amber liquid and fresh glasses. JJ holds it out to Knight, but Cade intercepts it.

"Macallan 50?" He whistles. "Impressive and accepted with thanks." He opens the bottle, picks up a fresh glass, and splashes some of the liquid into it.

Knight laughs. "I second Cade; and thanks, JJ."

Cade rises to his feet and shakes the other man's hand. "We've had our differences, but the work you're doing for the vets is irreplaceable."

"I'm committed to using my resources for the greater good." He jerks his chin at me. "As for you, don't you think it's time to tell that pretty girlfriend of yours how you really feel?"

My jaw drops. "The fuck you talking about?"

He chuckles. "The look on your face is that of a man caught in a web of his own making."

"Your imagination is running away with you in your old age." I snort.

"And now, he resorts to using cheap insults." He clicks his tongue. "You're definitely in a quandary."

"What's it to you?"

"What can I say? I'm a sucker for a good love story and a happy ending." He smirks.

"Neither of which I'm looking for," I snap.

"Nonsense. Everyone's looking for love."

"Not me."

"Especially those who protest they're not," Cade pipes up.

"That includes you, asshole." I stab a finger in his direction.

He chokes on his drink, then begins to cough. Knight reaches over and slaps him on the back. When the coughing subsides, Cade shoots me a nasty glance and snaps, "We're not talking about me."

"Your time will come, boy," JJ says and slaps his thigh.

"Like yours did?" I scoff.

"And I'm the happiest man in the world for it." His face lights up.

"Even though you got together with your son's girlfriend?"

The skin around JJ's eyes tightens, then he bares his teeth. "Jealous because I went after what I wanted? You could learn a thing or two from it."

"What-fucking-ever."

JJ laughs. "The famous refrain of a man who knows he's lost the argument. Mark my words. There'll come a time when the two of you are gonna have to come to me for advice."

"Advice?" I growl.

"Ad-fucking-vice?" Cade looks at JJ like he's crazy.

"Laugh now mofos, but when it's time to learn how to grovel to win back your ladyloves, know that I'll be here, ready to give you an earful."

"Grovel?" I exclaim at the same time as Cade.

The two of us exchange looks.

"I'm not gonna fucking grovel to anyone," I declare.

"Is this a sign of early senility?" Cade scoffs.

"I'll have the last laugh," JJ says with such supreme confidence it sends a pulse of anxiety down my spine.

"Anyway, what about him?" I stab my thumb in Knight's direction.

"What about him?"

"You didn't include him when you gave your 'learn to grovel' speech." I make air quotes with my fingers.

"I didn't, huh?" JJ rubs his finger under his bottom lip. "It's probably because the man's got a lot more devils to deal with than the two of you put together."

Both Cade and I glance toward Knight, who's wiped all expression off his face. Apparently, JJ touched a nerve there.

"But let's not get ahead of ourselves, eh? I reckon it's the two of you jokers who're going to bite the dust first."

Cade scoffs, "Not in your bloody lifetime."

"A-n-d, my prediction is, he's going to be the first to fall, but time will tell, eh?" With a wave of his hand, he moves off.

The three of us are silent in his wake.

"You believe what he was nattering on about?" Cade looks between me and Knight with a wary look in his eyes.

"Not unless there's something you're not sharing with us?" I narrow my gaze on him. "Is there, Cade?"

In a moment of weakness, he confessed to me about his love-hate relationship with Knight's sister Abby. Something he hasn't told Knight about, and rightly so. Knight would have his head if he did. But that's not my concern.

"Of course not." He glances away, then back at me. "And you? You contemplating the ol' ball and chain anytime soon?"

"No fucking way." I rub the back of my neck.

Knight smirks. "Why does it feel like you're protesting this too hard. Both of you."

Cade stiffens, his muscles tense. It's clear there's something on his mind. Then, his forehead clears. He squares his shoulders, a determined expression on his face. "I think it's time we celebrate Knight's one night of freedom, don't you think?"

"I think—"

"Declan, you selfish piece of shit!" A woman's voice—a familiar and very angry woman's voice—snaps.

I turn to find Solene heading in my direction. Without breaking stride, she grabs the bottle of whiskey and pours it over my head.

38

Solene

"The fuck?"

He glares at me, a look of surprise and anger on his face. The scent of alcohol permeates the air. I promised myself I wouldn't lose my temper. Told myself I was going to talk to him reasonably and ask him for an explanation for why he simply cut off all communication with me. But the moment I saw him, relaxed and kicked back in his armchair, talking with his friends like he hadn't a care in the world, something shattered inside of me. My gaze narrowed, adrenaline emptied into my blood stream, and before I could stop myself, I stomped over to him, grabbed the bottle of whiskey, and upturned it over his head.

"That was a very expensive whiskey," he growls.

"You can afford it."

"Oh?" He tilts his head.

There's a chuckle behind me, cut off quickly when I turn to find the two men with him surveying the proceedings with big smiles on their faces.

One of them looks familiar and also sports a military haircut. He rises to his feet and holds out his hand. "I'm Knight, Abby's brother."

"Of course. I thought I recognized you."

His grin widens. "She'll be pleased to see you."

"I can't wait to see her, either. In fact,"—I place the now empty bottle of whiskey on the table—"since my work here is done, I think I'll head over to say hi to her right away." I turn to leave.

"You're not going anywhere," Declan growls.

I turn back to scowl at him. "I'd like to see you try to stop me, asshole."

"Ah, I think I'm late for my next appointment." Knight steps back from the both of us. "Good to see you again, Solene."

"Likewise," I call out.

Knight claps the back of the head of the other guy. "Time to go, shitstain."

Charming.

"And just as it was getting interesting." The other guy slowly rises to his feet. "I'm Cade." He holds out his hand.

I go to take it, when Declan makes a warning sound at the back of his throat.

I ignore it, move toward Cade and take his hand. When he brings my fingers to his lips, there's a full-on growl from somewhere behind me. The next moment, Declan marches over and stands between us.

"Unhand her," he snaps.

I gape at him.

Cade smirks, but he releases my hand. "A pleasure, Solene. Not so much, arsewipe." He nods in Declan's direction. "Also, you stink."

He pivots and follows in Knight's footsteps.

"Don't know why you're getting all possessive when I haven't seen you in over a month."

"I called you," he protests.

"Twice, you *stronzo*. You called me twice."

"I did message you."

"Like that counts," I huff.

"I've been busy. You know how it is on set." He raises a shoulder.

I stare. "And on your time off, you came here to meet your friends?"

"So?"

"So?" I take in the lack of regret on his face. *Oh god, he doesn't care about me at all.* It's why he hasn't been in touch. And like a fool, I ignored it. And I tracked him down—with Rick's help—and here I am, foisting myself on him when he, clearly, doesn't want anything to do with me. I swallow. "I made a mistake. I don't know why I bothered coming here to talk with you."

I turn to leave, but he locks his fingers around my wrist. "Fuck, I'm sorry Solene. Truly. You took me by surprise, is all."

"That gives you no right to hurt me. And you do, Declan, more than you know." I keep my face averted. "I was taking a risk that you'd walk all over me when I came here. I wish I'd paid more attention to my instincts and stayed away."

"I'm glad you didn't."

I will not look at him. Will not. I try to tug my arm out his grip, but he pulls me in.

"Please, Solene, please forgive me."

"Fuck you," I spit out.

"I very much want to."

"If you think I'm going to let you, you're sadly mistaken. Not after you treated me like I mean nothing."

"It's not that you mean nothing to me. You're crawling under my skin. You're occupying my thoughts, my every waking moment. I'm not even able to concentrate on shooting the most important movie of my career because I can't focus on anything but you."

"Well, boohoo, like I give a damn."

Once more, I try to move away from him, but he tugs on my arm. I yelp and stumble against him. He wraps his arms about me and pulls me up to my toes and into him.

"Ugh, you're all wet and stink like a distillery."

"And whose fault is that, huh?"

"Yours, of course. You pissed me off," I retort.

"So much sass, so much fire. So much everything. It makes me want to—"

"What?" I tip up my chin. "What, huh?"

A gleam comes into his eyes.

Uh, oh. This is not good. Not good at all. I poured the whiskey down his shirt, and he's not going to allow me to walk away without making me pay for it. I try to move back, but his hold around me tightens. The column in his pants stabs into my lower belly, and a treacherous heat coils there.

"It makes me want to throw you over my shoulder and carry you out of here to spank you, then fuck you, until you remember never to do that again."

Oh, my god! My pussy clenches. My toes curl. "Don't you dare—"

He clicks his tongue. "I wouldn't complete that sentence if I were you."

I set my lips. "I'll say what I want, when I want."

"Is that right?" His gaze intensifies.

"Yes, and can you please let go of me now?"

He does. Only, before I can move away, he bends, and the next moment, I'm hoisted over his shoulder. *What the—* Before I can catch my breath, he's marching off.

"Let me go!" I yell.

In answer, he spanks my behind. My clit throbs in response. It's like there's a direct connection from the point of contact to my core. I'm so turned on, and hell, if that doesn't make me even angrier. I writhe and struggle, but his hold on me tightens. My hair hangs over my face, blocking my line of sight.

I feel so helpless, and so small, in comparison to his superior strength. My nipples harden, and my thighs shudder. I continue to buck and heave. I lock my fingers together and bring my joined hands down on his back, but he doesn't even flinch. I hear the sound of voices, then he's out of the club, heading down the steps and through a corridor. The lights change to a harsh fluorescent from the warmer glow of the club, and his footsteps echo through the space. He must be taking the back exit. Sure enough, I hear more voices, then he shoulders open a door and steps into what seems to be an alley. The next second, I hear the sound of a car's engine, and he tosses me into the back seat of the same car Rick drove me here in.

I instantly straighten. "I hate you." I throw myself at him as he slides in behind me, and he catches me and holds me against his chest. He slams the button in the door, and the partition behind the driver's seat begins to rise. I catch sight of Rick focused on the road a second before the panel shuts us off.

"How dare you!" I open my mouth, only his lips are on mine. I try to yell, but he absorbs the sound. I slap at his shoulder, but he locks his arm about my waist and yanks me into his lap. I wriggle, squirm, twist my body and try to pull away; my butt pushes into the thickness at his crotch and I freeze. That size of him, that solidness, that absolute maleness of his—oh, how I have missed this. Yes, he did message me and call me, but that's no substitute for actually being here, in his arms, on his lap, grinding on the column on his cock. *It feels so good. Soooo. Good.* I moan into his mouth.

He tightens his grip on my hips and pulls me down so he's stabbing into my core. Even through the fabric of his pants and my jeans, I feel his shaft throb. I groan, and this time, he deepens the kiss. He thrusts his tongue inside my mouth, then begins to thrust up and into me. Each time he pistons up, he hits the nub of my clit. Flickers of sensation reverberate up my spine. My breasts seem to swell.

He releases his hold on my hips, only to cup my breasts. He massages them, and I huff. He twists my nipples between his fingers, and fire zips down to my clit. My pussy clenches, and he must feel it, for he tears his mouth from mine. "I need inside of you."

I reach down between us, unzip my jeans, and rise up to my knees long enough for him to yank them down with my panties. I shrug them off, along with my sneakers, then look down to find he's shoved his own zipper down. His cock springs free. It juts up—hard, thick, veiny, precum oozing from the head.

He pulls me onto his lap and holds my hips, so I'm positioned right over his shaft.

"Take off your top and your bra."

I comply.

"Now, look at me," he orders.

I glance up; our eyes meet. Once more, I'm locked into the tractor beam of those gorgeous blue eyes. He applies pressure, and I push down and over his cock. When he breaches me, we both groan.

His chest rises and falls. The tendons of his throat flex. I lean in, bury my nose in the curve of his neck and breathe. My lungs fill with Declan. Notes of dark chocolate and coffee. Temptation. Complex. Erotic. Filling. He yanks on my hips, I slide down, and he impales me completely. I throw my head back and moan. The sensitive skin of my inner thighs chafes over the hair at the base of his shaft. "Oh, god, Declan."

"Eyes on me, Rabbit."

I lower my head, once more meeting his gaze.

"I'm going to destroy your pussy."

39

Declan

I thrust up and into her. Her gaze widens. And again. And again. Color flushes her cheeks. Her pupils dilate, her breathing intensifies, and that pulse at the base of her throat goes into overdrive. *Fucking hell.*

I squeeze down on her hips, knowing I'm going to mark her. Hoping I mark her. Wanting her to carry my imprint on her skin. I hold her in place then, once again, drill up and inside her. I hit that part deep inside her that I know sends her over the edge, and she doesn't disappoint. Her lips part. A low keening sound emerges. I instantly lock my mouth over hers and absorb it. I keep my eyes open and stare into hers as I, once again, spear into her. Her entire body shudders. Her pussy clamps down on my dick, and her thighs tremble. She holds onto my shoulders, her fingertips digging into my skin through the fabric of my shirt, and I know then, she's marked me, too.

I slide my palms down her butt and tease the puckered hole between her arse cheeks. Her eyes grow enormous. She begins to pant, tries to writhe away, but I hold her in place. I slide my finger inside her back hole, then push up into her again. Her back curves. She thrusts out her breasts. I bite down on her lower lip, and she moans.

I curve my finger inside her back channel, then push my dick up and into her, increasing my pace, hitting that part at her very core, again and again and—

"Dec-lan, I'm going to—"

"Come with me, baby."

She groans. Her eyes roll back in her head. Moisture bathes my shaft. I thrust into her one last time, then pull her up and off my cock before I come. Threads of white paint her chest, her throat, her breasts. She begins to slump, but I hold her upright, then massage my cum into her breasts, and across the skin of her stomach.

"Wh-what are you doing?"

I drag my cum stained fingers across her lips. She flicks out her tongue and wipes them clean. And when she finally looks up, I brush my mouth over hers, tasting myself on her. The blend of her taste with mine goes straight to my head. My cock thickens again, pressing into her lower belly. She chuckles, and the sound ignites my nerve-endings.

"Ready to go again so soon?"

I pull her closer, and she snuggles into me. I tuck her head under my chin, breathe in her sweet scent. She yawns, and her eyelids flutter down. Outside, the sights of Central London flash by. I grew up here, skipping classes and hanging out with my friends, first in the coffee shops, and then in the pubs of Soho. Now, I'm driving through it with a woman I won't let myself keep in my arms.

"What are you doing in London?" I finally ask.

She yawns so widely, I hear her jaw crack.

"I had to meet a label. Also, I wanted to see you."

"You've seen me now."

"Umm, I'd say we've more than seen each other." Her lips curve in a smile.

"When does your tour begin?"

She stills. "How do you know about the tour?"

"I may not have been physically in LA. Doesn't mean I don't know what's happening."

She digests this, then asks, "You're in touch with Harry?"

"Also," I admit.

"And Rick's been updating you?"

"You know he is."

Her muscles stiffen. She tries to push off my lap, but I don't let her go. *It's okay to hold her for a few more seconds, isn't it?*

"That's why you left him behind? So he could spy on me?" she snaps.

"I left him behind to protect you."

"Why do I need protection?"

"Because you're new talent in LA. You don't know how the system works."

"And Rick does?"

"I do."

She looks at me. "So he *is* spying on me."

"He's keeping me posted on your whereabouts, so I can make sure no one takes advantage of you."

Her forehead crinkles. "So, if I'm meeting someone who you think is going to 'take advantage' of me"—she makes air quotes—"you, what? Call them and threaten them?"

I glance out the window.

I sense her taking in my features. The silence stretches. A beat. Another. Then, "Oh my god, you do call and threaten them, don't you?"

"I call them, yes, and let them know you're with me."

"That I'm your kept girl? Your mistress? Your lay?"

"My girlfriend," I correct her.

She shakes her head. "You confuse me, you know that? You fuck me and leave without a word, except for this." She holds up her hand.

I touch the silver bracelet encircling her wrist, the one I left on my pillow after spending the night with her in my bed in LA.

"You barely call me, but you ensure you're there to run interference in case anyone is being an asshole to me."

"I'm invested in making your career a success," I murmur.

"You say I'm your girlfriend— "

"For the benefit of the media," I remind her.

She balks, but continues, "—but you don't stay in touch with me."

I look down at where my dick is nestled against her, then up at her face.

"That's not what I mean, and you know it," she exclaims.

"This is the life of an actor. I go where the shooting is. I need to be on set for months at a time. I need to get under the skin of the character to give it my all."

"And what do I get?"

I stay silent.

"An occasional fuck in the car, is that it?"

"It is what it is. Besides, soon you'll be touring and on the road for weeks on end."

She doesn't reply, but something in her eyes makes my breath catch. There's a softness, that just-fucked heaviness in her eyes, a lazy contentment that clings to her features that I put there. Her cheeks are flushed, and her hair is in a cloud about her shoulders. She looks exquisite, gorgeous, a siren who's ensnared me. She looks like she's mine.

"Declan..." She swallows. "Ask me."

I hold her gaze, unable to look away.

"Please, ask me. Ask me to come with you."

"I can't," I murmur.

"You can; you just don't want to."

The car pulls onto the highway and the city zips past.

"You're right. I'm not that selfish. Your career is just starting. Your voice is just beginning to be recognized. You're only just starting your journey." *The one I can't accompany you on.* "I may not be there with you in person, but I'll always be there to ensure you don't take a wrong step."

"I'd rather be with you," she whispers. She sniffles, and my heart feels like it's going to break.

My fingers itch to wipe away her tears, but I resist. *This is good. This is right. This is how it should be. I shouldn't have fucked her but... enclosed with her in this tiny space, it was bound to happen. I need to find a way to ensure it doesn't happen again. I need to find a way to put distance between us, so come what may, neither of us is tempted to repeat this mistake.*

"You'll see, in retrospect, this was the right thing to do."

"What was?" She frowns up at me.

I tuck a strand of hair behind her ears, then reach down and retrieve her clothes. "You need to get dressed."

She looks at me for a second longer, before reaching for the tissues in the car. She wipes herself then pulls on her clothes. I tuck myself back in, zip myself up. When I glance up, she's looking at me with parted lips. Her cheeks are flushed, her breathing slightly erratic.

"Fucking hell, Rabbit, don't look at me like that." I pull her into my side. When she snuggles in, I dip my chin and kiss the top of her head.

She pushes her nose into my armpit and breathes deeply.

I laugh. "You sure you want to do that?"

"You always smell delicious."

"Yeah?" I chuckle.

"Like a dark chocolate drink laced with coffee," she replies with a nod.

"Right now, I smell like a brewery."

"The whiskey does add a certain appeal; it goes right to my head."

"That's my proximity making you dizzy, baby."

She scoffs, "I forget how big your ego is."

I open my mouth, and she holds up a hand. "Nope, no cheap shots about what else is big."

"You said it." I grin down at her.

She peers up at me and a small smile curves her lips. We look at each other for a few seconds until the car pulls to a stop. She's the first to break the connection. When she glances out the window at the jet parked on the tarmac, she looks confused.

"Are we at your private jet?" When I don't reply, she turns to me, her eyes sparkling. "Where are we going?"

"*We're* not going anywhere."

Her shoulders slump, and she looks away. "You're leaving?"

"I had less than forty hours off. I need to get back."

She swallows. "How long is the shoot going to be for?"

"Eight months."

She gapes at me. "Did you say eight months?"

I nod.

"And when were you going to tell me that?"

She sees the guilty expression on my face. Not that I try to hide it, to be honest. I could have, if I'd wanted to, but a part of me wants her to see I'm doing it on purpose. This is the only way for her to realize the kind of man I am. She'll never come first. And what a load of bull that is. *She is first. She deserves better; it's why I'm doing my best to push her away. If only she'd understand that.*

Her face falls. She seems stricken for a few seconds, then recovers enough to swipe out her arm. I'm anticipating it, so I grab her wrist and stop her palm from connecting with my face. I twist it behind her back and haul her close enough that I can make out the specks of gold in her eyes. "It's my prerogative what I share and don't share with you about my life, do you understand?"

"Fuck you."

"Not for a long time." I release her, then shove open the door. My heart hurts; there's a band around my ribcage getting tighter by the second. I slam the door shut behind me.

Rick's standing there, his gaze narrowed on me. He opens his mouth, and I shake my head. "Not right now."

"You don't deserve her," he snaps.

I laugh. "You're preaching to the converted."

I stalk toward the jet, intent on embarking it and flying the fuck out of here. Still, I'm not so distracted that I don't hear the tap of her footsteps behind me. I turn just as she throws herself at me. I catch her, swing her up, and she wraps her legs around my waist. "Don't go. Please, don't go. Don't do this."

I push my forehead into hers. "I have to."

"You don't have to do anything. You don't have to choose this way of life." She swallows. "You can stay here with me, Declan. You can make that choice."

And I almost do. I almost say 'fuck off' to the movie shoot and damn the consequences. Almost. As I look into her tear-filled eyes, my heart stutters. My stomach ties itself in knots. I lower my forehead to hers, and for a few seconds, we look into each other's eyes.

In that moment, I know, if I decide to stay, my life will change. Everything I've worked for, all of the challenges I've overcome, will be for nothing. And... I can't do that. And I can't take her with me. It would destroy her burgeoning career, and I can't do that to her. This is her dream. Besides, I'm not the man for her. I'm not the person she thinks I am. I'm not the younger version of myself she met. The one she's never forgotten. The one she's in love with. I've changed. And so has she. And she needs to understand that.

"I choose—" *You.* My voice cracks. A ball of emotion blocks my throat. I manage to swallow it away, then firm my shoulders. "I—" I swallow. "I choose to leave."

I lower her to her feet and take a step back. As I straighten, I see the intent in her eyes, see her raise her arm. And this time, I have no intention of stopping her. Because I deserve it. Her palm connects with my face the same time as a flashbulb goes off.

"Motherfucker."

I feel her palm print on my cheek, and a sliver of pain threads through my blood. I welcome it. I deserve her hate. I deserve her slapping me. And so much more.

I step around her and close the distance to the pap who continues to click away. Fucking feeders of the lowest order. I grab his camera from his hand and raise it, intent on smashing it on the tarmac.

The man yells as Rick grabs my arm. "Don't, man. You'll only make it worse."

The journo's lips twist. "Lover's quarrel, huh?"

"Fuck off."

His grin widens. "Is that your comment?"

"Oh, I have a comment for you." I grab his collar with my free hand, haul him close to my face and snarl, "Come near her again, and I swear, I'll kill you."

40

Solene

"Whew, the two of you are catnip for social media," Harry glances up at me from his phone.

I glance out the window of the plane. Not a private jet, but a commercial airliner, though we're flying business. Harry'd mentioned to me it was only a matter of time before I'd get upgraded to first. In all honesty, it doesn't matter to me that much. I'm just glad to be out of LA, and the house that reminds me so much of him.

After Declan threatened the pap, the man claimed he'd sue Declan for assault. Declan laughed in his face. Then shoved the camera at his chest, before he pivoted and stalked past me to the waiting jet. He avoided me completely. Pretended I wasn't there. *Stronzo* blanked me. He threatened the pap and told him to stay away from me. Then, he didn't have the decency to say goodbye before he got on the plane, which subsequently taxied down the runway and took off.

The pap continued taking photographs of me until I threw myself into the back of the car. The tears began flowing down my face before I could completely shut the door, and that, along with the one of me slapping him and the one with my legs wrapped around his waist, are the ones being splashed across the media.

Rick drove me to Abby's place, and the two of us proceeded to get stinking drunk. For me, it didn't take much. She, wisely, didn't share any of the social media pictures with me. The next morning, I managed to make it to the airport, driven by a silent Rick who told me Declan had arranged for a private plane to take me back to LA. I almost refused to get on it, but given I needed to be back for meetings with the label, I decided to accept the gesture. For now.

In all honesty, I've given up trying to understand the rationale behind the man's actions. I slept most the way back to LA, then met up with Harry the next morning. The rest of the day was taken up with meetings with labels. I hoped our pictures would stop circulating online by the next day, but apparently, twenty-four hours later we're still headline news.

"I don't know what's going on between the two of you, but this on-again, off-again relationship theme, is fucking amazing PR." Harry nods in my direction.

He's been briefing me about the rest of the meetings he's set up for me.

"Is it, though?" I bounce my sneaker-clad feet on the floor. "Am I not being seen as simply another pretty face and a Hollywood star's girlfriend?"

"Any PR is good PR." His tone is serious. "Also, this way, your face continues to be in the news, which is going to be amazing for when your record drops."

I hunch into the oversized sweatshirt. *His* sweatshirt. I borrowed it from his closet. Even though it was washed, I'm sure I can smell him on it. I miss him so much today, I wore it to my meeting with Harry. Yep, I'm pathetic. The man, clearly, doesn't see me as a priority in his life, while I wear the sweatshirt he wore because it makes me feel closer to him. Loser with a capital L, that's me.

"When are you meeting him next?"

"Meeting who?"

"Declan?"

"I have no idea."

"Hmm..." Harry purses his lips. "I could check with Giorgina and let you know."

"No thanks." I jerk my face in his direction. "I don't want her thinking I don't know what's going on with Declan. If he wants to see me, he'll reach out to me. And then... I'll think about whether I want to see him."

He frowns. "That's not going to help your profile."

"Fuck my profile." I glance at my phone, which I use mainly to record my songs.

"You wouldn't be saying that if you knew how many views the video of your song racked up."

"How many?" I ask, pulling up the playlist of the tunes I've recorded. I need to listen to them and figure out how to improve on them. Harry found me a band on short notice, and it's lucky we clicked on the very first try. That's what happens when you're a singer who can't play a musical instrument. You'd think my mother would have allowed me to play the piano. After all, it's a musical instrument that fits right in with her traditional outlook of a woman's role in society, right? But nope, the only pianist available locally to train me was a man, so that was ruled out. Didn't matter that he was old enough to be my father. That's how sheltered an upbringing I had. That's when I decided to make my voice my instrument. Which is fair—but as he pointed out, and this time he was right, if I was going to perform on stage, I'd need a band. So, I agreed to let him help me put one together.

"Twenty million views."

"What?" My phone slips from my nerveless fingers onto my lap. "B-b-but the last time I checked, it was five million."

"A second wave of listeners came in. It happens sometimes. I'm sure the headlines with you and Declan didn't hurt."

"O-k-a-y." I lean back in my seat. "So, that's good, right?"

He nods.

"Which means, I don't have to worry about additional PR and stuff?"

Harry laughs. "It doesn't work that way. You've got some massive momentum going, but you need to build on it. And the best way to do that is to be seen with Declan and—"

"Not happening." I hook on my earphones and scroll down my list of recorded tracks.

"But the press is going crazy for the two of you—" He waves his phone at me. "Forty-eight hours since that pap clicked the two of you, and they still can't stop talking about #Declene."

"#Declene?"

"Yeah. Declan plus Solene equals Declene. You have your own couples' hashtag."

"O-kay?" I raise a shoulder.

"That's all you have to say?" He stares.

"Actually, I'm not sure I like the sound of it."

His jaw drops, then he seems to collect himself. "Nonsense. You're the biggest thing since Bennifer and Jelena."

I look at him blankly, then shrug. "Who are they?"

"What?" His eyes bug out even more. "You don't know who they are?"

"Of course I do," I lie.

Shit, all that time spent hidden away in Napoli under my mother's careful scrutiny hasn't helped my pop culture knowledge. But it has meant I've had a lot of time to write, and enough lyrics and song tunes to fill many records. And thankfully, I sang. In secret... A lot. To keep myself company but also, because deep inside, the dream of becoming a singer and using my voice in some form never went away. But becoming a popstar? Nah, that never factored anywhere in my realm of possi-bilities.

Unaware of my racing thoughts, Harry continues to talk, "Then you'll know that the fact they're comparing you and Declan to these gods of the zeitgeist is huge."

"The gods of what?"

"The zeitgeist, the defining spirit of our times."

"O-k-a-y." I pull the hoodie up over my head and forward, so it cuts out his face.

"You have a good thing going here, Solene. It's a one-in-a-million opportunity. Don't screw it up."

Three months later

"You sure you're going to be okay?" Abby's worried voice cuts through the noise in my head. I take a deep breath, then another. I can do it. I can. I'm only facing a crowd of ten thousand. No problem. So what, if this is my very first live performance, ever.

"Of course I'm going to be okay. I've been practicing for this," I place my phone on the side of the dresser then stare at my reflection in the mirror. I'm in the dressing room of Staples Center, one of the leading live performance venues in Los Angeles.

I take a sip of water, and my stomach heaves. It's probably because I took my back pain medication on an empty stomach. Not only have I lost my appetite since I started prepping for my live performances, but I've also found that being on my feet non-stop seems to strain my back in a way that has never happened before. I should probably consult a doctor, but who has the time? For now, the over-the-counter variety of ibuprofen will have to do. I place the bottle on the vanity counter, then practice my deep breathing to help calm down.

"You've been practicing in front of a virtual audience. Performing in front of a real one is bound to be daunting," Abby murmurs.

Y-e-p, from someone who didn't know what social media was four months ago, I've turned into someone who spends every second not recording plugged into the online space. Turns out, they love me. They really do. I have close to a million fans following me on my main social feed, and they love to hear me perform. I have women swooning over my voice and my looks, and men proposing to me every day. And boy, does it soothe my ego to have my virtual friends hang onto my every word. Especially since, my so-called boyfriend has been AWOL since he walked onto the plane.

I know, I'm trying to fill the Declan-shaped void in my life with the adulation of fans, but hey… At least they want me. They love my singing. They can't get enough of me. And if this is where I'm going to get love, then why shouldn't I embrace it?

"A lot of my virtual fans have promised to be there in the audience to cheer me on."

"Well, that's sweet of them. And I'm sure you're going to do a stellar job. All I'm saying is, it's okay to acknowledge you're nervous."

My guts churn. Bile boils up my throat. I fix a smile on my face and swallow away the acrid taste coating my tongue. "Nervous? I'm not nervous." My stomach gurgles. My guts heave. "I'm not—" The sour taste intensifies in my mouth. "Oh, god, I'm going to be sick."

I race toward the tiny ensuite bathroom and drop to the floor in front of the commode. I empty the contents of my stomach—which wasn't much to begin with. I was too nervous to eat breakfast or lunch today. An apple and a snack bar are about all I was able to force down. I heave the meager contents, then flush and sit back on the floor, panting. Sweat beads my forehead, and my heart is banging so hard against my ribcage, it feels like it's having its own concert in there. A chuckle escapes me, the sound loud in the tiny space.

"Solene, are you okay? Solene?" Abby's voice reaches me from the phone screen in the other room.

I shake my head to clear it, then rise to my feet. My knees knock together but I manage to stay up. I stagger to the sink, drink water from the tap, then glance at my flushed appearance in the mirror. My skin is pale, my eyes too bright. There are hollows under my cheeks, but really, that only adds to the ethereal look of my appearance. I'm wearing a silvery dress that comes to mid-thigh, paired with rhinestone, over-the-knee boots with heels that are, at least, eight inches. Fortunately, they're platform heels—I insisted. No way am I stumbling onto stage and then face-planting, which I still might do if I don't get a hold of myself.

"Solene, if you don't tell me you're okay, I'm going to call Declan right now and—"

I turn and step out into the dressing room, then yell across the room before I grab the phone. "Don't you dare, you—"

"There you are," she says with relief.

"Don't mention the name of that *testa di cazzo* in front of me."

She scowls. "Then don't scare me the way you did just now."

"Sorry, babe, didn't mean to. I just had a moment there, but I'm fine now."

She searches my features. "You don't look better; you look a little feverish."

I roll my shoulders, then swing my arms and jump about a little. "Just trying to psych myself up, is all."

Luckily, my make-up is largely intact. It took a team of hairdressers and make-up—or glam artistes, as they liked to call themselves—to get me to look like this. It took several hours sitting in a chair, too, and by the end of it, I was ready to tear my hair out. They ignored my polite requests to stop and continued about their tasks with a grim determination. It's only when I jumped up and yelled at them to leave the room that they complied. Apparently, you need to throw a tantrum for people to take you seriously. Maybe that's why stars get stuck with the label of being temperamental? You're treated like an object, and people forget you have your own preferences and emotions, and the only way to get through to people is to raise your voice.

"I wish we could be there for your first performance, but with Isla's wedding happening later today, it was too tight for us to make it."

"No, of course. You need to be there for Isla's wedding. Please apologize to her that I couldn't make it. I'll be there as soon as I get a break from the tour."

"How many cities are you covering?"

"Not sure. Maybe forty or fifty?" I reach for a paper towel and mop the sweat on my brow. There, almost as good as new.

"Did you say fifty?" she cries.

"Uh, yeah. In the next five months, of course."

"Jesus Christ, woman, you're going to do fifty cities in five months? That's ten cities in a month—"

"Two cities a week, give or take." I raise a shoulder. "Good thing the label sprung for a tour bus, huh?"

"You have your own tour bus?"

"Yeah, now that I have a band—"

"A band? You have a band and you never told me?" she screeches, and I flinch.

"Ouch, easy, I need to save my hearing, now that I'm earning a living from it and my vocal cords."

"What else haven't you told me?" The lines on her forehead deepen. "You have a band, and a touring bus, and three million followers online. Bloody hell, you're a certified star."

"You saw that, huh?"

"You mean the three million followers? A little hard to miss. Also, how else am I supposed to know what you've been up to? You refuse to keep in touch, don't answer my calls—"

"Just been busy practicing."

"Bullshit. I'm calling you out on that, Sol. You're telling me you've been too busy to text me and let me know you're okay?"

I flush. "I'm sorry, you're right, I—"

There's a knock at the door. "Hold on." I walk to the door and open it to find Rick. He holds out a package for me.

"Who's it from?"

He tilts his head.

"If it's from him, I don't want it." I'm about to shut the door when he plants his foot in the doorway, "You don't have to open it; just let me put it inside the room so I can say I delivered it."

I hesitate, then nod.

He strides in, places it on the dresser, then leaves.

"Who was that, Solene?" Abby asks.

"He sent me a package." I don't have to specify who 'he' is. We both know who I'm referring to.

"Aren't you going to open it?" She asks.

"I'm not sure."

"You know you want to."

I do, goddammit; I do. The sound of the crowd in the arena reaches me through the closed door. I pale, then glance at the package again. The clapping grows in intensity. My guts churn.

"You okay, Solene?" Abby's voice is concerned.

My heartbeat ratchets up. My pulse-rate spikes. I'm going to be performing live in front of all those people. *Oh, god!* Bile bubbles up my throat. I swallow it away.

"Solene?" Abby's voice reaches me, "You went pale."

"I... I'll be okay." I stumble toward the dresser, grab the package, take a breath, then another. *You're going to be fine. Fine. Fine. Fine.*

I pull the wrapper apart, then open the black velvet box, and stare at the piece of jewelry.

"Solene, what is it?"

I hold up a tiny rabbit-shaped figure attached to it between my fingers.

"He sent you a charm?" Abby's voice rises in excitement.

The box slips from my fingers. I fix the charm to the bracelet around my wrist—the bracelet *he'd* given me with an unsigned note which had simply said 'wear this' and I had, of course. I hold up my hand for her perusal.

"OMG, he's thinking of you," she cries out.

"Maybe." I rub my finger over the exquisite little bauble. The beating of my heart slows, and my pulse settles closer to its normal pace. My stomach, too, is behaving itself. Huh, seems the good luck charm is doing its job.

There's another knock on the door, then a voice calls out, "It's time, Ms. Sabatini."

41

Declan

"Why the fuck can't you tell her that you're here? She'd have wanted to know. She'd have felt reassured that you were here to support her."

"And that's exactly why I can't afford it." I peer through the floor-to-ceiling window of the VIP room. It's positioned above the cheering crowds that react to her every move, that sing along to the chorus of her song that went viral online. She prances about on stage in that silvery dress that hugs her every curve. And when she kicks up her leg, the strip of skin between the hem of the dress and the thigh-high boots she's wearing has the crowd going crazy. I curl my fingers into a fist and press my knuckles against glass.

With the lights focused on her as she moves, she's exquisite. And shimmering. A spark, a star, a flare of light that's a beacon in the dark night. She's entrancing, enticing, and after tonight, she's no longer mine. She belongs to the world, to her fans. She's going to go straight to the top, and I've always known it. She'll be the story that critics talk about whenever they want to refer to an overnight success.

She's the kind of woman dreams are made of. The kind who was never meant to be hidden away. All that talent, that stage presence, that ability to keep gazes fixed on her as she throws back her hair and belts out the song. With her hands clasped together in front of her, she's both demure and a seductress. A virgin and a whore. My whore. My cunt. My woman. No longer.

She belongs to them—the fans. And I did my bit in bringing her here. I allow my gaze to dwell on her features. Even at this distance, I think I can make out the curve of her lips, the sweep of her eyebrows, those luxurious eyelashes that she raises... *And fixes her gaze on me.*

I freeze. With the lights in her face, I know she can't see me. I'm sure of that. And yet, she tilts her head as if sensing my presence. She moves forward in my direction, arm outstretched. *Fuck, fuck, fuck. Impossible; she can't see me.*

"She can't see you," Rick confirms.

But her instinct must tell her I'm here. I can almost see the moment she changes her mind and turns away from me. She struts over to the guitar player. She places her hand on his chest, leans in, and he joins her in the chorus.

"Fucking hell!" Anger burns a trail down my gullet. My stomach ties itself in knots. Of course she's found someone else. That was the plan all along. But moving onto someone else so quickly... is not something I thought would happen.

I grab a bottle of water and throw it against the wall. The bottle bounces off and hits the floor, then rolls away. Goddamn, even my anger doesn't have an edge to it anymore. How pathetic have I become? Hiding here and watching her, then unable to give vent to my rage. I pivot and stomp toward the exit, Rick in tow.

He, mercifully, stays quiet as I head up the stairs and toward the heliport on the roof of the performance center. It's the only way I could make it here without losing time in transit. The helicopter will take me back to the private landing strip and then, from there, I'll take the plane back to New Zealand, with one more stopover.

I reach the door that opens onto the helipad, when Rick touches my arm. "You okay, Dec?"

I shake off his hold. "Why the fuck wouldn't I be?"

"It meant nothing what she did; probably just caught up in the performance."

"What-fucking-ever," I snap.

"Keep telling yourself that. You could prevent all this. Just let her know you're here, meet her once—"

"I need to get back."

"You made it all the way here. You just need to stay another half an hour, and the performance will be over," he says in a low voice.

"That's half an hour I don't have. I need to leave now if I want to make my next meeting."

He hesitates. "As your friend and head of your security, I have to caution you that the person you're going to see—"

"Yes, I know, he's part of an organized crime syndicate, blah, blah, I understand."

"Do you?" He folds his arms across his chest. "Dealing with men like him—"

"—will get me the rest of the funding I need for my film."

"I don't understand why you need that." He shifts his weight between his feet. "Wasn't the shooting well underway?"

"Half the investors pulled out. I've underwritten the expenses to the extent I could, but there's still a gap that needs filling."

"Isn't it risky—"

"To put my own money in the film? Hell, yeah. Spending it in a casino would be a better gamble. But this is the vehicle that launches me as a leading man, and if I don't have faith in myself, then what kind of an actor I am, eh?"

He searches my features, then nods. "You're determined to make this happen."

"Fuck, yeah."

He pulls out his phone; his fingers fly over the screen. My phone dings, and I pull it out to take a look at the details he sent me.

"Thanks, man."

"Don't thank me." He looks away and mumbles, "I hope to fuck I don't regret it."

"You're going to fucking regret this," Cade growls at me.

An hour from my destination, he and Knight called me on the plane. I almost didn't answer the call, then realized I couldn't evade them forever. I already missed our last two weekly catchups. If I missed this one, too, they'd probably call Rick and insist he have me call them back. I saved us all some time by taking the call. When I told them my plan, Cade was the first to explode.

"Not sure why you're against it, considering it's the kind of crowd you ran with not too long ago."

Cade's gaze narrows. "It's because I ran with a gang and got involved with organized crime that I know what you're doing is going to end with you paying a price."

"If it helps me get my movie made—" I raise a shoulder.

"You're not thinking straight, douchebag. So what if this production shuts down? There'll be others," Cade argues.

I shake my head. "No, there won't be. It might be decades before this director, and this script, and this kind of cast are able to get together again. I can't wait until then. I need this movie out. It's exactly what I need to take me to the top."

"Is that what you want? Making it to the top?" Knight asks slowly.

"You know I do."

"And you want it more than her?"

I hesitate.

"Do you?" Knight presses.

I blow out a breath. "Yes. Yes, I do."

There's silence, then Knight's lips curve. "You're doing a great job of fooling yourself, but I don't believe you."

"You can believe what you want; it doesn't matter. I'm going through with this. And if this is the only way I'm going to get a loan to keep the production running, then so be it."

"You're a motherfucking obstinate arse,"—Cade shakes his head —"but if you've set your mind on it—"

"I have."

"Let me come along with you to the meeting."

"No fucking way. You're the bloody captain of the English cricket team. The last thing you need is to be seen associating with the likes of this man."

"And *you* can afford it?" Cade narrows his gaze.

I raise a shoulder. "I don't have a choice."

"Yes you do," Knight draws himself up to his full height. "I'll finance the film."

I shake my head. "I'm not going to turn our friendship into a relationship based on money—" Knight begins to speak, but I hold up my hand. "You guys are my friends. And bringing money into the equation is the fastest route to losing our connection."

Cade turns to Knight, "Tell him how wrong he is, will ya?"

"Much as I hate to admit it, I understand what he means." Knight firms his lips, "Hell, I even respect it."

Cade gapes. "You're encouraging this harebrained scheme of his?"

Knight jerks his chin in my direction. "If you can't take money from us, how about the Seven? Or JJ, or even the Sovranos?"

"All of whom I count among my friends, and I will not be indebted to them," I point out.

"It's not a debt. They'd be investing money in your project," Cade growls.

I set my jaw "And there's less than a one percent chance of any of them seeing their money come back."

"It's the nature of being an investor." Knight narrows his gaze.

"Precisely, and given the high probability they'd never see their money again, I'm not going to ask people I've come to regard as friends to invest. No, it needs to be someone who not only has the money to take the risk, but if he were to lose the money, it wouldn't impact my personal relationship with them. It needs to be a purely business transaction. Also—" I prop my palms on my hips. "The person I have in mind for the investment has the contacts needed to fast-track the production on the ground."

"I changed my mind. Not only are you a motherfucking, obstinate arse, you're also a nincompoop," Cade snaps.

"Careful, or I'll think you care for me." I half smile.

He glowers. "You're determined to turn your life upside down, eh?"

I shrug. "Comes with the territory. Making movies is a high-stakes business. If I pull this one off, it'll change the course of my life." *Again. And in more ways than one.*

"You should take Rick with you." Knight leans forward on the balls of his feet.

I rake my fingers through my hair. That would have been my preference, too, but I'd rather he stay back and take care of Solene's security. There's no one I trust more than Rick with her safety. Other than myself, that is. And I can't be there with her, so this is the next best thing.

"It's best I do this on my own. If there's a price to pay, I'd prefer it be me rather than involving any of you."

"You're taking a big risk." Knight's forehead creases. "I'd rather you not do this, but if there's no other way—"

"There isn't."

Knight and Cade grow quiet. "If I can't stop you, then I'll back you, man," Knight says.

I glance at Cade, who regards me with an angry gaze. For a few seconds, I'm sure he's going to continue to voice his objections. Then, he jerks his chin. "Fuck that, if this is what you want to do, then I'm in your corner."

"But remember—" Knight lowers his chin to his chest. "If you don't call us within an hour of meeting him, we're on the next flight there."

"One-hundred million dollars. That's a lot of money." Nikolai Solonik, the New York-based head of the Bratva in the US, taps his fingers together.

Rick's a managing partner in the security agency run by Karina Solonik Beauchamp, who's Niko's brother, as well as my brother Arpad's wife. She wasn't happy when I told her of my plan, but finally agreed to help.

"It's a fraction of the kind of money you and I are used to dealing with," I drawl.

His lips curve a fraction.

"If it were that easy to drum up this kind of financing, you wouldn't be here."

"And if you didn't want to be a part of Tinseltown, you wouldn't have agreed to see me." I raise a shoulder.

He tilts his head, a considering look in his eyes. "You think that's why I'm entertaining financing your film?"

"To have your name up there as one of the producers of a possible Oscar-winning, box-office thumping movie? Fuck, yeah."

His smile widens. "You're not wrong. But there are easier ways of making money. In fact, as you and I know, there is a ninety-nine percent chance I'll never see this money again."

"And you know I wouldn't be here if I weren't ninety-nine point nine-nine percent sure about the bankability of this film." I cross my ankle over my other knee.

"You're here because, while you have financiers lined up and you're pouring your own money into it, you still have a gap you need to fill."

So, he's aware of the financing structure of my film. Just as I'm aware of how keen he is to find a legal route to investing his money. I tap my foot on the floor. "A gap right up your alley."

He narrows his gaze. "It still leaves a margin of doubt on the return of my investment."

"A risk well worth it for the kind of fame and entrée to Hollywood this movie could give you."

He drums his fingers on the table between us. "It's true, I've wanted to get a foothold in Hollywood for a while—"

"And to do it with the leading star in the industry? You'll never get this chance again, and you know it."

He stills his fingers. "I'll invest the money."

I lean forward in my chair. "But?"

He blinks. A look of respect comes into his eyes. "Smart of you to realize just the admission into Hollywood isn't enough for me to invest the money."

I hold his gaze. "What's your condition?"

42

A month later

Solene

"Champagne, I need more champagne." I glance up and down the long table. "Where is the champagne, anyway?"

We're at my friend Abby's wedding to Cade Kingston, captain of the English cricket team, and while I'm happy for her, I can't wait to put this event behind me and focus on figuring out how to revive my singing career. A career headed for a huge collapse, the likes of which only a pop star with a number one chart hit can face when the fans decide they don't like your music anymore.

"Uh, we wanted to avoid any accidents, so the champagne is on that table." My friend, Summer, points at the table at the far end of the room.

"Accidents?" Declan scowls at her, then turns to me.

I hold his gaze for a second, long enough for those blue eyes as unfathomable as the depths of the sea to widen. A-n-d there is the other reason I want to be as far away from this table as possible—my boyfriend. I haven't seen him face-to-face in a month, and I've been evading him since arriving at this wedding.

I jump up and head toward the bubbles. I reach for the bottle of champagne and begin to pour it into a glass. *Thud-thud-thud. Why is my heart pounding so fast? Thud-thud-thud. That's not my heart.* I turn to see why everyone at the table is yelling, but before I can fully turn, something goes sailing through the air, blocking my view. Not something, but someone, or rather, someone's dog. Isla's Great Dane Tiny snatches the bottle of champagne from my hand and turns it upside down with the head of the bottle somewhere down his jaw.

Whoa, that's some acrobatics. And whoever heard of a dog drinking champagne, or rather, a champagne-drinking dog? I'm so amused by him, I don't even realize I've lost my balance. The world tilts, and that's when I realize the result of the dog's bottle stealing tactic is that I'm falling, falling. I brace for impact, which comes.

Only, I don't hit the ground. I slam into something which feels even harder yet moves with me to soften the blow. Something which feels like a muscled chest. And when his arms come around me, and that familiar dark chocolate and coffee scent of his swirls around me, I allow myself to sink back against that tank-like expanse for a few seconds. During which time, the beating of his heart thuds against my back, his thick forearm is banded about my waist, and my hips are nestled against his pelvis, the thick column in his crotch stabbing into the valley between my butt cheeks. My thighs tremble, and a waterfall seeps out from between my lower lips. *Oh, god, it feels so good to be in his arms.* With his length supporting me, and his breath raising the hair on my head. His chest rises and falls, his breath coming in quick pants. He tightens his grip around me, and the movement breaks the trance I've fallen into. I push up and off of him, then jump to my feet.

"Get the hell away from me, you *stronzo*." I stab my finger at him. "I don't need any of your false concern."

"Wait, what?" Declan shakes his head as if to clear it. "It's not false."

"Tell that to your girlfriend, you *pezzo di merda*," I say in a voice so cold, so hard, that I can't stop myself from flinching.

He staggers to his feet. "What are you talking about?" He straightens, and keeps straightening, looming over me so I have to tilt my head back, then further back, just to meet those stupid, gorgeous, traitorous eyes of his. Eyes crowded with concern and confusion, and maybe, even… love.

No-no-no. I won't try to discern what his eyes are saying when he's never—not once in all the months we've been together—ever come right out and told me how he feels. I'm not going to second-guess him anymore. If he feels something for me, he'd better come out and say it, and then back up his words with actions. Otherwise, based on his actions thus far, I'll have to assume he's the self-centered bastard he's shown himself to be.

I shove aside the need to throw myself into his arms and tilt up my chin. "So, who's the woman I walked in on with you in your house?" I ask softly. I should be angry and raging. I should be spitting out the words at him. I should be losing my shit, but somehow, all I feel is a sense of calm. At least, I don't have to pretend. Like I did over the past month, trying to maintain the facade of a relationship to the media, to him, to myself, when in reality, we've been running on parallel tracks for a while now.

He blinks, then the confused expression on his features fades away. The crystalline blue of his gaze hardens to a dirty grey, so brittle, surely, it's going to shatter. Like my heart. He steps back, putting distance between us. A cool wind rushes in between us and I shiver. Goosebumps pepper my skin.

"You came to our house?" he finally asks.

"*Your* house."

"And you saw me with her?"

Oh, god. He's not denying it. He's not. I glance around to find our friends are following our exchange with interest. They're not close enough to hear us, thankfully. I take a step back, and it might as well be a thousand paces. That's how huge the distance between us already seems.

"Who was she?" I manage to force out the words through lips gone numb. My stomach churns, heat flushes my skin, and yet, I'm so cold. I wrap my arms around my waist. "Who was she, Declan?"

He looks away into the distance as if calibrating his response. His jaw ticks, and a vein pops at his temple. His shoulders bunch and I know, whatever he's going to tell me is going to change my future.

I sense the impending shock and brace myself, so when he opens his mouth and says, "I can't tell you," I'm almost not surprised. And yet, I am.

What did I expect him to say? That she's his wife? A girlfriend? The real love of his life? The reason he's been unable to make time for me as we've danced the transatlantic-long-distance-relationship-that's-been-going-down-the-shitter shuffle?

"You can't tell me?" I finally push the words out through lips gone numb.

He doesn't answer.

"You can't tell me who the woman I saw you talking to was? The woman whose shoulders you held; the woman who you consoled as she sobbed into your chest. Was she your sister? A cousin? A relative?" This is his chance to tell me it was all a stupid misunderstanding. That what I saw was completely innocent. That there's a perfectly logical explanation for why he was comforting her.

"Declan?" I whisper, hating how desperate I sound in the moment. Hating the fact that, although I thought I'd resigned myself to the fact that our relationship was slowly fading away, faced with evidence of it, I now realize I hadn't. I'd hoped we could set things right. That we could meet and talk things out. That we'd each apologize for being so focused on our respective careers. That we could come together and stay strong in the face of all the media scrutiny every time we're spotted together in public.

"Declan, tell me who she was?"

"I can't."

"What?" I gape. "You can't tell me who she is?"

He shakes his head slowly.

My heart begins to race. The fine hair on the nape of my neck rises. "Wh-why can't you?"

He shifts his weight from foot to foot. "Trust me on this. You don't want me to."

I swallow, then tip up my chin "I do trust you, Declan. You're the man who saved me from a Mafia wedding. You're the man who gave me a chance to pursue my dreams of being a singer. You gave me a place to stay in LA. You're the one who introduced me around to those in the business. It's you who gave me the confidence to release my first single. It's because of you, I followed my dreams. It's because of you, I found my voice. You created this new me. I owe everything I am to you, but I'd trade it all to find out what's going on."

He stays silent, our gazes still locked. But he doesn't say anything. *How can he not say anything? Can't he see I'm dying slowly inside? Why is not saying anything?*

He stays there for a few seconds more, then closes the distance between us. He places his palms on my shoulders, and I let him. I let him because he was supposed to be my happily ever after. My one true love. He was supposed to be the one. I thought, when I found him, I'd walk into the sunset with him. I thought I'd found my match. Maybe I was wrong.

"Are you in love with her?" My voice seems to come from far away. My throat is so dry I'm barely able to speak. *How could I even form those words? Where did I find the courage to blurt that out? How could I not?*

"Are you, Declan? Is it someone you met on the road? I know how isolating it is to be shooting for months on end. I know, I've been busy pursuing my career, too."

His eyes flicker, "As you should. You're a talented artiste. You owe it to yourself to share your voice with people."

"I'd rather sing only for you."

"You shouldn't treat your art with such disrespect." His hold on me tightens. "You're a star. You need to shine brightly, and nothing and no one should hold you back."

I frown. "What does that mean? Are you implying you're holding me back?"

His eyebrows knit. "You don't know what you're talking about."

"That *is* what you're implying. Is this because my song hit number one before your movie became the top-grossing box office smash you were expecting? Are you holding it against me that my career took off before yours?"

He hesitates, then shakes his head. "You're putting words in my mouth."

"It's not my fault my song was such a big success. You know that, right?"

"You need to own your triumphs, Solene," he says softly.

"I'd give everything to go back to when it was just you and me, and neither of us had seen the kind of success that would force us to spend so much time apart."

"You can't change what's already happened." He begins to lower his hands, and I catch hold of his wrists.

"What are you saying? Why are you being so defeatist?"

"I'm not the one looking back and wishing for the past. I'm not the one who's so quick to trade my hard-won success for love. But then, I forget how quickly you became successful. You didn't have to struggle like—"

"Like you? Are you saying because it took longer for you to get to the top of your game, your success is more relevant than mine?"

"That's not what I meant," he says through gritted teeth.

"Yes, you did." I try to pull away, but this time, he's the one who locks his fingers around my arms and holds me in place.

"It's your guilt at not being there for our relationship that's making you see and hear things when there's nothing there."

"Why should I feel guilty? You weren't there for me, either." I pull away, and to my surprise, he releases me and oh, god, he may as well as have slapped me. "Wait a minute. Are you saying I'm delusional?"

His jaw tics. "I'm saying, we need to stop trading insults and act more civilized with each other."

"And what about you refusing to tell me about that woman I saw you with? Is that being civilized?" I say hotly.

"That's being... Considerate of your feelings."

"If you were being considerate, you'd tell me who she was."

His gaze shutters. A pulse tics at his temple. He massages his temple as if he's got a headache brewing there. Good, he should feel some of the pain I'm going through right now.

"You know, deep inside, there's an irreproachable explanation to what you saw," he says softly, but there's an underlying intensity, a seriousness that penetrates to my core.

I swallow, "And I want you to say it."

"And I can't... Not— I just can't."

I curl my fingers into fists at my sides. "Why not, though? Why can't you tell me who she is? Why can't you share why she was upset and why you were consoling her?"

"Because it would hurt you."

The breath whooshes out of me. Until now, I held out hope it was nothing. That really, it was all a misunderstanding. We got our wires crossed. There's a perfectly simple explanation for what I saw. But something in his eyes, something in how he sets his jaw, how those beautiful lips of his thin, how he seems to retreat deeper behind that wall he puts up between himself and the outside world, tells me that, perhaps, it's too late. He'd rather not reveal the reasons why he was consoling that woman. He'd rather risk me being upset with him. He'd rather risk that secret driving a wedge between us than come out and tell me who she is and what she means to him.

"Why was she crying, can you at least tell me that?"

"That's not my secret to share."

I gape, "I'm still your girlfriend."

A series of expressions crosses his features, one after the other, too quick for me to understand what it means, and then he schools his face into a polite mask. "Are you?"

I reel back. "Wha—" I swallow around the ball of emotion in my throat. "Are you kidding me?"

He glances over my shoulder, and his gaze widens.

Seriously? "Declan are you listening?" I curl my fingers into fists at my sides. "We've been spending so much time apart, I'm not even sure if I know who you are anymore, and—"

He moves so quickly, I blink. The next second, he's thrown me over his shoulder.

"Hey, what are you—" I gasp. A flashbulb pops. He turns around, storms past our friends who've been watching the entire spectacle unfold, and marches inside the house.

43

Declan

"Let me go!" She wriggles.

I tighten my hold on her.

"What's wrong with you, Declan? What are you doing?"

"Trying to have a conversation without the entire world and their mother looking on."

"You're crazy." She struggles anew. "And was that a paparazzi's camera that took that picture?"

"Not even Sinclair Sterling's top-notch security can stop a paparazzo from getting through to get a piece of the both of us." Not that I'm surprised. Every time Solene and I get together, it results in a feeding frenzy from the news people. They've hung around outside my home in LA, followed me into shoots in the Australian bushland, trailed Solene's concert tour bus between states in the US. You'd think having Hunter Whittington, the Prime Minister of this country, in attendance at the wedding would result in the protective detail being upped so much it would prevent the paps? But apparently, not. Seems they'll risk being arrested just to get an exclusive pic of Solene and me.

As if reading my thoughts, Solene groans aloud, "Jesus, Declan, and you carried me out in front of them? We'll be all over the internet in a few seconds."

"We'll be all over the internet, one way or the other, anyway. If not now, then when you're spotted running back to LA, or when I'm photographed taking the next flight out to my shoot. In a way, that pap did us a favor. This way when it comes out that we—" I firm my lips.

She freezes; her body seems to turn to stone.

I take advantage of her temporary stillness and shoulder my way through the back door of Sinclair Sterling's townhouse, then up a flight of steps, and down a corridor. I shoulder open the door to the bathroom and that seems to rouse her out of her reverie.

"When we what—?" She asks in a low voice. "What were you trying to say?"

Fucking fuck, can't do one thing properly can you ass-wipe? I lower her to her feet. When she pulls away from me, I almost reach for her, then stop myself at the last moment. *See this through. You must see this through.*

"What was it you were trying to tell me, Declan?"

"That I saw the pap in the bushes and decided to give him a show."

She scowls. "You carried me out of there knowing the pap was right behind us?"

I shove my hand into the pocket of my pants, "You're aware how much in demand a joint picture of the both of us is. It'll drive speculation about the status of our relationship."

"Relationship?" She scoffs. "We haven't been in one for the last month."

I widen my stance. "And whose fault is that?"

"You're the one who was so busy with the PR for your upcoming release that you had no time to call me," she spits out.

"You're the one who embarked on a tour of fifty cities in five months." I force out words through a throat lined with razor blades, "And then you wonder why you're so tired you're unable to answer your phone whenever I call you?"

"I was focused on my career," she snaps.

"So was I."

We stare at each other, and the air in the bathroom thickens. Unsaid words, emotions, feelings press down on my chest, and my stomach churns.

Bloody fuck, it is partly my fault that this relationship has deteriorated to where it is. Open your mouth and apologize, you asshole. Tell her it's all your fault. Tell her you'll do everything possible to make it up to her. Tell her she's more important to you than your career. Tell her… you care for her. Tell. Her.

I open my mouth, but nothing comes out.

I can't do it. She's going to loathe me soon enough. She's going to tell me to fuck off and out of her life when I tell her who that woman is. Not long until she'll want nothing to do with me, but until then… Until then, I have these last few minutes with her, and I'm going to make the most of them.

I walk over to her, until the tips of my shoes brush hers. "I'm sorry I wasn't there for you more."

Her shoulders hunch, and some of the fight seems to leach out of her. "I'm sorry I didn't try harder to keep in touch."

"It's no joke, trying to live up to the reputation that a first hit song confers on you," I murmur.

"It's no joke, trying to follow up a hit movie with another. I know how much you need it to consolidate your reputation at the box office." She searches my eyes. "But I'm not sure I can look past your refusal to tell me what that woman means to you." She looks between my eyes. "Who is she, Declan? Tell me."

Tell her. Do it. Now. The band around my chest tightens, sweat pools under my arm pits. I glance to the side, then back at her, "You sure you want to know? Because once I tell you, there's no going back."

She pales. "Declan, please. Please tell me what's happening, because my mind is building all sorts of scenarios right now."

I hold her gaze for another second and memorize the openness of her expression, the beseeching look in her eyes, the thickness of her eyelashes, the little upturned nose, the obstinate jut of her chin, the way her lips part slightly, as she searches my face.

"Declan?" she whispers.

I squeeze my eyes shut and when I open them, she must see the resolution in them, for she tightens her fingers into fists. She begins to shake her head, and I know she senses what's coming even before I say a word.

I reach out and wrap my fingers around her wrists, before bringing her fingers to my mouth. For the last time, if this goes according to plan. I kiss her fingertips, then look into her eyes. "She's my fiancée."

She stares at me for a second, another, then chuckles. "Nice one. You said the same thing when you pretended to be engaged to Olivia. You don't think I'm falling for that one again, do you?"

Ah, you know me well, my little Rabbit. Apparently, I need to up my acting skills in order to convince you of my intent... Which is to make you hate me enough that you'll walk away from me. Which is to convince you to move on so... When you find someone who's right for you, you won't hesitate.

The thought of someone else holding her, touching her, kissing her—anger squeezes my guts. Shock compresses my chest, and it feels like I've been hit by a ten-ton truck. *Don't do it. Don't.*

I have to. I must. The break must be clean and final, so that she moves on with no compunctions. A sharp ache lodges in my chest. I ignore it and draw myself up to my full height. "You didn't think our relationship was for real, did you?"

She crosses her arms over her chest. "Stop. You're not fooling me."

"It's the truth."

She opens and shuts her mouth. "You're joking." She scans my features, and the seriousness of my intent seems to get through to her.

She swallows, then whispers, "You're *not* joking."

I slowly shake my head.

She pulls her hands from mine, and I can't stop myself from leaning forward. I breathe in her scent, taking it all way into my lungs, trying to hold it there so it's a part of my essence.

She backs away as a calculating look comes into her eyes. "If she's your fiancée, why didn't you bring her here?"

"She's busy. She has a wedding to organize." Then I say the words I know are going to seal the fate of our relationship. "*Our* wedding."

The color fades from her cheeks. "Y-y-y-your wedding?" She looks like someone just broke her heart—that would be me. I hurt her. Yes, I'm a bastard, but I'm doing it for her. I'm not good enough for her. This is the only way to make her hate me. *And she's never going to forgive you for this. She'll never want to have any kind of relationship with you after this. Which is exactly what I want, right?*

My stomach heaves, and I swallow down the taste of bile. I manage to keep all emotions off my face—*Acting!*—and look her up and down. "You didn't think I was going to simply forgive you for what your brother did to me?"

"My brother Diego? B-b-but I thought you said you d-didn't hold me responsible for that. I-I thought you'd p-put that b-b-behind us?"

She's stammering, and I know it's because she's shocked. She only ever stammers when she experiences high emotion. And right now, I'm putting her through something very traumatic. Only, I feel her pain as if it were my own. My lungs burn. I manage to take a step back, putting more distance between us. This way, I won't be tempted to touch her, to kiss her, to throw myself at her feet and ask her to forgive me for what I'm going to do to her. To us.

This is the right thing. It is.

I square my shoulders. I straighten my spine. "You thought I'd be willing to overlook that you accused me of forcing myself on you? That your brother and his men scarred my face and changed the trajectory of my life? It's taken me twice as long to get to where I am because of that. You turned my life upside down; you made me face the kinds of challenges that would have defeated anyone else."

"But not you."

"Not me. I was determined to keep going, to prove to myself, and to the world, that I could make it. And all that time, I knew, one day, I'd have my revenge for what your brother did. It's the one thing that kept me going through all of those rejections, those doors that were slammed in my face, those who thought I was never going to make it to the top spot in Hollywood."

"And becoming number one is so important to you?"

She's asking me the same question Knight did. And I know my answer now. *I know it's not.*

Nothing is more important than you. Nothing comes close to you. Nothing makes me happier than making you happy. Than seeing you happy. Than ensuring you're never subjected to the kinds of depraved acts I want to subject you to. And that's why I have to push you away from me. And perhaps, one day, you'll even forgive me for it. But even if you don't, that's fine.

I'm doing the right thing. This much, I'm sure of.

I set my jaw. "It is."

Her gaze widens. "So, when you told me you had feelings for me, you…"

"Lied."

"B-b-b-but why?" She swallows. "Y-you were so c-convincing."

I shrug. "Speaks volumes for my acting skills, eh?" I smirk, but it feels more like a grimace. I should be used to acting the villain, but this is too real, too painful.

She glances away, then back at me. "Which means—" She blinks rapidly. "Which means, you asked me to come with you to LA because—"

"I was planning my revenge for what your brother did to me, because of you. And when this opportunity came up, I had to take it."

"So, you planned the entire scene? You counted on me—"

"Walking in and finding me with my fiancée?" I nod. "In fact, I'm surprised how well it all came together. Perhaps I have a future as a director, too."

She pales even more. Her eyes shine with unshed tears, and my guts churn. *No, no, no, don't cry, Rabbit. Don't or I won't be able to go through with this, and I need to. For your sake, I need to. I absolutely cannot allow you to get close enough to me that I'll do what I've wanted to do to you since you came back into my life. I cannot allow you to become as depraved as I am.*

My chest hurts. I try to breathe but it's as if I've swallowed glass. I might have set out to make her hate me, but right now, I loathe myself in a way I would not have thought possible.

"You never meant anything you said?" she asks softly.

I tilt my head and let a considering look creep into my eyes. At least, I hope that's how it looks. *I've never had to act so contrary to what I'm actually feeling. I've never had to fight myself like this.* "Oh, everything I said in bed was true. I didn't have to fake the chemistry between us, and that made my job easier. Besides, you were begging for it." I chuckle. To my ears, it sounds like I'm choking. "Poor repressed Mafia princess, you couldn't wait to spread your legs for the first man who said all the right thing to you, and—"

I see her move, see her hand coming in my direction, but I don't stop her palm from connecting with my face. I absorb the blow, relishing the entirely too brief respite from the pain in my heart.

There's a low whirring sound, then another flashbulb goes off outside the window.

44

Solene

"You broke up with him?" Penny's fingers fly over the screen of her phone.

We're in my hotel room in London.

When the flashbulb went off, Declan and I turned in the direction of the window from where it had come. And there, hovering outside the pane, still taking pictures of us, was a drone.

"Motherfucking paps!" Declan stalked toward a chair, grabbed it, and flung it at the window. The glass broke, and with it, whatever last threads of connection that had linked me to him. I ran out of the bathroom.

"Solene, stop." He yelled after me, but I ignored him. I heard him swear, heard more breaking glass—guess there was more than one drone taking pictures. For once, I was grateful that the paps had intervened.

I ran down the steps, and straight into Penny and Mira.

Penny took one look at me and thrust my bag into my hands, hustling me out through the front door into her little Mini Cooper.

Rick chose that moment to come racing up to the car. I told him I was leaving. He took one look at my face, muttered something under his breath that sounded like, "dumb bastard," and simply nodded. He didn't ask a single question. He reassured me he'd follow me in his car and keep the paps from giving chase.

He made good on his word and bought me enough time so I could use my phone to call my team and arrange for a hotel room. A boutique hotel—chosen for the fact that it's not as well-known as any of the other five-star hotels in the city and because it's so discreet, it doesn't even have a website. Word of mouth only, and only in select circles—which I might not belong to for much longer, considering who I just broke up with.

As expected, Rick tracked me down via my phone. When he arrived at the hotel, I told him I'd broken up with Declan. He seemed unsurprised, but angry—and not with me. He told me he'd been assigned to me, so he'd follow my orders—for now. However, he's on Declan's payroll, and he's Declan's friend, so I know it's only a matter of time before I lose him, too.

Thank god I have Penny and Mira. If it weren't for them, I'm not sure what I'd be doing today. I met both of them through Abby, and after she started seeing Cade, it was natural for me, Mira and Penny to gravitate toward each other.

Now, Penny looks up from her phone. "You released a statement on your social media platform?"

Guess she's seen my post. Over the past few months, I've been posting steadily on my feed and amassed five million followers. Every time photos of Declan and me appeared, the #Declene fans went crazy, and the number of my followers swelled. I depended on them to get the word out for my tour. I've come to think of them as my crew, so it seemed only right to be the first to tell them about my break-up with Declan.

"Your followers aren't happy about it." Penny tucks her feet under her. She's on the settee pushed up opposite the bed where Mira and I are sprawled out.

I hunch my shoulders. "They'll get over it."

My phone vibrates and continues to vibrate. I already blocked Declan's number and told Rick in no uncertain terms that he has to keep that *stronzo* away from me. So far, he seems to be complying with my wishes. Though, considering how well he knows Declan, I'm not sure how long that will last. The buzzing stops, then starts again.

I stare at my phone that I placed screen-down on the nightstand.

"Are you going to get it?" Mira asks

"You don't have to." Penny glances up from her phone.

And how long am I gonna hide out? I'm a successful popstar. So what, if the man I thought I loved is a *stronzo*? I still have my career—barely, but I still have it—and it's time I prioritize it.

Which means, I better get my phone and see who it is. Not that I'm going to answer anyone at the moment, but maybe I should, at least, see who's calling? Tears prick my eyes again and I blink them away. I'm not going to cry over that *pezzo di merda*. I'm strong. I'm not going to hide. I'm going to face this...head on.

I reach over and slide my phone across the nightstand, then pick it up so I can see the screen. Twenty missed calls. Most are from Harry and Giorgina. Two from Olivia. I do need to call my sister back, but I don't have the strength to do that yet.

As for Harry and Giorgina? Ugh. I'm sure they're upset at my post. Even though Giorgina is Declan's PR lead, she and I have struck up a working relationship. We had to, considering being seen together—for me and Declan—was an important way for us to maintain our profiles. Especially as the distance had grown between us, we'd been communicating more and more through Harry and Giorgina.

I scroll over to my social media feed and blink. "Wow, this post is doing better than any I've put up in the past few weeks."

"Well, it's big news. You're the hottest upcoming singer, and you've announced you're breaking up with Hollywood's number one heartthrob. Of course it's going to do well." Penny throws her phone on the bed, then asks, "You going to tell us what really happened?"

I raise a shoulder. "I saw him with a woman in our— I mean, *his* house."

Penny looks at Mira, and a look passes between them. Then she turns to me. "What were they doing, exactly?"

"She was looking up at him with a serious look on her face. I was too far to hear the conversation. But then she started crying and threw herself into his arms." I swallow.

"And then—?"

"Then I was so upset, I ran out of there." I toss the phone face down on the nightstand.

"So, you didn't confront them?" Mira asks slowly.

"No, I was too upset. I'd seen enough."

"And that was a few weeks ago?"

I nod.

"And you haven't seen him since? Or spoken to him, or messaged him?"

"Not until I saw him at Abby and Cade's wedding earlier today." I reach for the miniature bottle of tequila I'd snatched from the minibar and twist open the cap. "Turns out, he's engaged to her."

"What?" Penny jackknives up into sitting position. "He's engaged to her?"

"Yep. He told me she's his fiancée and he never had feelings for me, so—" I take a sip of the tequila and promptly cough. *Ugh! I've just been dumped, the least I can do is drink alcohol properly. Isn't that supposed to be a rite of passage or something?*

Mira lowers her chin. "That doesn't sound like Declan. He might be an egotistical asshole—"

"Alphahole," I say bitterly.

"Alphahole," she corrects herself. "But he doesn't strike me as a someone who'd do that to you."

I scoff, "He's a good actor. He had us all fooled." Certainly had me taken in completely. I looked at him and thought he was the one. I can imagine how he'd be laughing right now to see me and know how easily he fooled me.

"That bastard." Penny glowers. "Did he tell you who she is?"

"Nope, we never got around to that. I slapped him—again—and the stupid paps intruded with their stupid drones hovering outside the stupid bathroom window where they probably got another shot of us."

"They did." Penny reaches for her phone and resumes her scrolling. "There are pictures of you slapping him all over the internet."

I flex my fingers. It should have made me feel good to get that second slap in, but strangely, the tortured expression on his face too closely resembled what I was feeling.

"Speculation is that one or both of you is having an affair." She peers up at me, a worried look in her eyes.

"I guess they're right. For a change," I grumble.

"Every time I saw the two of you together, you both seemed so much in love." Mira shakes her head. "I'm finding it very difficult to understand why he'd do this."

"He did it because he wanted revenge." I slump back into the pillows. Maybe I can pull the cover over my head and never surface.

Maybe I can pretend Declan and I never had that conversation. Maybe I can get on the next flight back to Naples and— I blow out a breath. Nope, I'm not going to do that. There's no way I'm going back. I have to move past this. Somehow.

"Revenge?" Penny blinks.

"Revenge?" Mira scowls at the same time. "What do you mean, revenge? For what?"

I look between my friends. "I first met Declan when I was seventeen."

"Seventeen?" Penny and Mira chorus, twin expressions of surprise on their faces.

I nod. "He was on a shoot in my hometown and saved me from some thugs on a beach. I fainted; he took me to his home. When I woke up, I saw him and thought he was the most beautiful man I'd ever seen. Of course I fell for him."

"Oh my." Mira blinks rapidly. I think she has tiny heart-shaped symbols in her eyes.

"Yeah, I know. So romantic, eh?" I say in a self-deprecating voice.

"And how old was he?" Penny tilts her head.

"He was twenty-one. He assumed I was eighteen. Of course, he was horrified when he found out how young I was. He hustled me home, and I thought I'd never see him again—"

"—but you did." Penny walks over to sit on the bed.

"He sneaked into my room to say goodbye. I seduced him into kissing me—"

"He kissed you when you were seventeen?" Mira yelps.

"Actually, I kissed him. And after a few seconds, he kissed me back. Only, my brother walked in on us."

"Oh no." She groans, then jumps up to her feet, "Wait, don't utter another word until I obtain more liquid refreshments to lend a suitable rosy glow to the proceedings."

Penny blinks. "Do you always talk like a nerd?"

Mira tosses her hair over her shoulder. "Don't you mean, a smutty nerd? People always assume I'm studious because I'm never without my Kindle. If they only took a peek inside the device..." She snickers, then walks over to the minibar in the corner and pulls out a selection of bottles.

She walks over to the bed, drops them in the center, then chooses one and holds it out to me. "You need more alcohol to lubricate your proceedings, which, girl, sound straight out of a romance novel."

"Do you think of anything besides smut?" Penny arches an eyebrow.

Mira snickers. "Is there anything more important than smut?"

Penny reaches over, grabs a bottle of whiskey, twists open the cap and takes a sip. "Not that I don't love spicy books, but now, I worry my expectations are so high that I'll never find a real-life boyfriend to live up to the ideal set by my book-boyfriends. Which basically means, I'm going to be single forever."

Mira snickers. "All the more reason to immerse myself in book-boyfriends and never let them go." She screws off the top of a bottle of vodka and holds it up. "What are we toasting to?"

Penny holds up her own—whiskey—and takes a deep breath. "To tales of the smutty kind."

"To the sisterhood of smut." Penny leans over to clink her bottle with Mira's.

"To not giving alphaholes the power to break your heart." I tap my bottle with theirs, then tilt it to my lips and chug down the liquor. The liquor burns its way down my throat, then hits my stomach, radiating warmth toward my extremities.

"Uh, perhaps you should slow down?" Penny murmurs.

"Nah, where's the fun in that?" The words come out slurred, but I don't give a shit. I need to forget the man I thought was my soul mate but who, clearly, isn't. "So, where was I?" I hiccup, then glance down at my bottle of tequila. "Oh, yeah. So, my brother's men beat him up. Which is how he got the scar on his forehead—"

"Which is hardly visible anymore," Penny scoffs.

"Not when you're blown up on a cinema screen."

Both of them wince.

"Yeah—" I hunch my shoulders. "It changed his career trajectory. Made it more challenging for him to get leading man roles in Hollywood."

"He seems to have done well for himself, anyway," Penny points out.

"Well, that's what I thought. That's what I thought he thought. I thought he'd forgiven me. Turns out, it was a pretense. He only pretended to forgive and to care about me to get revenge."

"This is bullshit. You were a kid. You can't be held responsible for what your brother did." Penny scowls.

"I agree. Not that it doesn't lend a certain romanticism to what happened, but surely, he can see you're not to blame for what happened?"

"Except, he does. It's why he made me fall for him, and then dumped me. So, he could break my heart in return." My nose tickles. A pressure builds behind my eyes. I sniff, then hiccup again.

"Here, babe, have some water." Penny walks around the bed, snatches up a bottle of water from the nightstand and offers it to me.

I hand the tequila to her and take a sip of the water. "Of course, all this drama has to happen now, when my career is faltering."

"What are you talking about?" She rolls her eyes. "You just came off an extremely popular tour— "

"The last leg of which they had to cancel because the last ten cities on the tour didn't have enough ticket sales." Yep, not even my five million followers were enough to ensure enough attendance toward the end of the tour.

"Probably because you took too much on. Fifty cities in five months is a lot for anyone," Mira reminds me.

"Not if my popularity had continued to rise, as planned." I drag my fingers through my hair. "And now, I've broken the news that Declan and I have split, which is only going to make things worse." I hold out my hand for the bottle of tequila.

"I really think you shouldn't drink anymore," Penny murmurs.

"Please? Just this bottle; then I'll stop."

She hesitates, and I make a sad face. "Please, pretty please?"

Her expression softens, then she hands over the bottle of tequila.

I take a sip and the alcohol burns its way down my throat setting off a warm glow in its wake. And hey, no coughing. *Take that, Declan-mother-fucking-Beauchamp. I don't care that I'm not legally supposed to drink. I can and will. And in style. I am my own woman now.* I wipe the back of my hand over my mouth.

"Now that my career is in decline, you'd think the media would give it a rest. But no, they can't wait to watch me crash and burn so they can dance all over the remnants of what was once my meteoric rise."

"Meteors do burn out." Mira sips from her bottle of vodka.

I purse my lips. "Are you implying I was always headed for a fall?"

"No, no, I mean you had a really quick overnight climb, and you can't always maintain cruising altitude, the aircraft has to come down at some point. Hell, even when you climax, you can't stay high on endorphins. You either slowly float down, or you crash down. And if you're lucky, you'll have a dick waiting for you to land on again."

Much as my heart is breaking, I can't help but burst out laughing.

Penny, who's just taken a sip of her whiskey, splutters, spraying the liquid across the bed. "Jesus, woman, you do have a way with words."

"Thank you." Mira flutters her eyelashes. "I owe it all to the Ph.D. in cliterature I'm studying for."

I laugh. "What about a diploma in smutology?"

"That's next." She quaffs more of her liquor then stabs a finger at me. "But you're the one who's leading by example, my girl. You've had such an eventful life and you're what, twenty-one?"

"Eighteen, though I feel much older in here, you know?" I rub the space over my heart.

"Aww." Mira scoots closer. "We're here for you babe."

Penny drops down on the bed and brackets me in from the other side. "Always. Consider this a circle of trust. We're your ride or die, huh?"

A ball of emotion clogs my throat, and my eyes burn. There's no reason for me to feel sorry for myself. So what, if my career is slowing down? So what, if my fans are pissed with me? So what if Declan—that *stronzo*—decided he wants to be with someone else? This is what I wanted. This is what I chose when I left Naples with Declan.

He didn't make any promises, except to introduce me around in LA to the right people. Which he did. Which is what jumpstarted my career. Which is how I became even more famous than Declan in half the time it took him to get to the top of the Hollywood box office.

I owe my career to him. I owe the woman I've become in such a short period of time to him. I was eighteen and had stars in my eyes, and an unwavering sense that he was my one true love, my future, my partner. That together, we'd climb the steps of our respective professions. That we'd support each other through challenges. What I hadn't counted on was each of us becoming the challenge the other encountered. I never thought the way I'd met Declan would become the reason for us to split. When I met him for the second time, he pretended to be engaged to Olivia. And now, he was engaged to someone else. If only, he were pretending now too.

Maybe this is kismet? Maybe this is what people mean by 'what goes around, comes around'? Another teardrop squeezes out from the corner of my eye.

"Oh, babe; it's okay to cry." Mira caps her bottle of vodka, tosses it on the bed, then throws her arms about me.

"Group hug." Penny, too, wraps her arms around the both of us.

I sniffle. "You two are crazy."

"You need a bit of crazy to distract you from whatever other craziness you're going through right now," Mira declares.

"You have no idea." I pull back.

The two of them look at each other, then at me.

"I still can't believe he'd get engaged to someone else." Mira rubs her chin. "Every time I saw pictures of the two of you together online, you two looked so happy and—"

I narrow my gaze, and Mira raises her hand. "Right, the media is not to be believed."

"The last few weeks, we've coordinated through his PR manager and made sure our schedules coincided so we could be seen together. This way, they'd leave us alone the rest of the time. It helped us play to the #Declene fans, and that kept us both relevant and top-of-mind with the media. Not that the pictures were all posed." *At least, not on my side.*

"And that was important? Being seen together?" Mira pushes up to sit cross-legged.

"There are #Declene fan clubs, and countdowns to our possible engagement. In fact, they've even dedicated a shrine to the two of us somewhere in Asia."

"They have not." Mira gapes at me.

"They have." I lower my chin to my chest.

"Not that it's creepy or anything. Okay, strike that. It *is* creepy." Penny takes another pull from her miniature whiskey bottle. "You're going to hate me for saying it,"—she pulls up her knees—"but I'm with Mira. I don't buy that he's engaged to someone else."

"I heard him, remember?" I pull up my knees and wrap my arms around them.

"But do you believe him?"

I frown. "I have no reason not to."

"But you've never seen them together before this or thought he was cheating on you?" Mira taps her fingers on the bed.

"No. I knew he was conflicted about us. We hadn't been calling each other that often, but I put that down to him being busy with the film. It never occurred to me he would look for another woman."

"And how did you find out he was in LA?" Penny supports her chin in her palm.

"What's with all these questions, eh?" I look between them.

They both exchange glances again, then Penny turns to me. "Humor us, babe. How did you find out he was in town?"

"We were supposed to have another planned photo-op with the paps. Giorgina mentioned Delcan might be at home, so I stopped by the house, hoping to see him. I thought we could go together. When I went upstairs, I heard something in his room. So, I went to say hi." In my mind's eye, I flash back to that day—how excited I was to see him again after so long, and how confused and heartsick I felt when I saw him with her. "That's when I saw them."

"Hmm..." Penny looks at Mira, who raises her hands.

"What? What is it?" I scowl.

Mira starts, "If this was a planned photo-op, he had to know you'd be coming home..."

Penny excitedly adds, "I think you need to test him on this."

"Why would I do that?"

"Because I think he wants you to believe that he's with someone else. He planned it—for you to walk in on him."

"What?" I drag my fingers through my hair. "Why?"

"Because he wanted you to break up with him," Penny exclaims.

"Well, it worked. I did break up with him. I never want to see him again." I shake my hair back from my face.

"But don't you want to find out why he'd do something like this?"

"No." I firm my lips.

Both of them look at me with matching expressions of sympathy, mixed with frustration and hope. Damn it, there's this big, fat hope shining in their eyes. Something I don't want to believe in. Something I can't afford to believe in.

"I think the two of you are clutching at straws," I mumble.

Mira raises a shoulder. "Maybe, maybe not, but I vote we find out."

Penny nods vigorously.

I sigh. "And how do you suggest we do that?"

45

Declan

"Nikolai Solonik. He's responsible for this?" Cade holds up his phone. He's referring, not to the fact that a photo of Solene slapping me is all over the internet, but the fact that she's pissed with me. As for the slap? I deserved it. If only, I'd managed to stop the picture from getting out, though. I took down the drone, but that didn't make a difference.

"Niko Solonik, the head of the Bratva? How are you involved with him?" a new voice asks.

I turn in the direction of the doorway, then groan when JJ Kane swaggers in. He used to head up an organized crime group—perhaps, he still does, though he claims to have legalized his businesses—so, no surprise he knows Nikolai. As if that's not bad enough, he's followed by Sinclair Sterling, the CEO of 7A Investments, the leading financial services firm in the country, and Michael Sovrano, the ex-head of the Cosa Nostra, now the CEO of CN Enterprises—which is still suspected of maintaining its links with the Mafia, though no one can prove it. Together, the three of them have formed an alliance, a result of Sinclair and Michael's wives being sisters. And JJ? Well, JJ likes to be the man about town. He loves playing the large-hearted, older statesman who's seen life—and who fell in love with a woman less than half his age—and who loves to give advice, especially on matters of the heart. As do Sinclair and Michael, since they are happily married and have also spawned offspring. Apparently, this makes them uniquely suited to counsel the rest of us single folk, or so they'd like to have us believe. I know, it's a lot.

"Okay, that's it. I'm not waiting around for you three to have a go at me next. I've heard enough of how you counseled Cade as he struggled through his romance with Abby—"

"And look at him, happily married now," JJ says in a sage tone.

"You mean, he's joined the ball and chain club the rest of you have taken membership in, but which I'm not interested in, especially not when I need to give my full attention to my career." I rise to my feet, when JJ closes the distance to my chair.

He grabs my shoulder and pushes me down. "Sit down, boy."

"I'm not your son who you can boss around. Oh, sorry, you can't boss him around, either, given you hooked up with his girlfriend." I smirk. "Awkward."

JJ sets his jaw. A nerve pops at his temple. For a second, I'm sure he's going to lose his temper, but then he seems to get a hold of himself. "You're fighting back. Good. You need to channel some of that aggression toward fighting for your woman."

"She's not my—"

"Not your woman. Is that what you're going to say?" Sinclair asks in a voice that's pleasant, but which hints at the cold ruthlessness he's well known for in boardroom circles, or so I've heard from my brother Arpad, who's one of Sinclair's friends and partners in 7A.

"What's it to you anyway?" I jut out my chin.

"I think the question to be asked is, Why is Nikolai Solonik involved in your life in any form?" Michael Sovrano's hard voice hangs in the air like a black cloud intent on pissing all over my life.

A-n-d, there you have it. Trust the ex-Don of the Cosa Nostra to get to the crux of the matter. Guess it takes a Mafia guy with the spirit of the Cosa Nostra running through the veins of his ancestors to suss out the problem here.

I shake off JJ's hold and spring to my feet. "I did not ask the lot of you to intervene, so back the fuck off."

"Aha, so it's not as out-of-your hands as you make it out to be, then."

JJ looks me up and down. "What did you barter with him, you motherfucker?"

I feel the blood drain from my face. "The fuck you mean?"

"You struck a deal with him. It's the only reason he asked you for what he did. Given what we saw earlier, with your woman—"

"Not my woman," *anymore,* I growl.

"—running out with tears streaming down her cheeks, it seems to have cost you dearly."

My heart pounds into my ribcage. The veins swell at my temples. Anger coils in my guts until it feels like I've swallowed a volcano that's bubbling and sizzling and threatening to blow at any time. I stalk toward the doorway but Cade—the traitor—is already there, blocking my way. He slams the door shut and leans against it. "You going to answer the question?" he asks softly.

"How much clearer do I have to be? It's none of your damn business," I snap.

"Afraid it is, ol' chap." Cade folds his arms across his chest. "You're a friend, the closest I have to a brother, other than Knight. I can't let you screw up your life, much as you seem to be hellbent on doing so."

The anger rears forward. The acidic notes of rage, combined with the blinding sense that I've fucked things up beyond belief envelops my senses. I ball my fingers into fists, then throw them up.

Cade lowers his hands to his sides. He rolls his shoulders. "You going to fight me on this, bro?"

My chest rises and falls, and my pulse thuds at my temples, behind my eyeballs, deep in my chest—where my heart once resided but which is now just an empty cavity because she took it with her. She's gone. And I can't change it. I've lost her, and it's all my fault. The realization crashes into my chest like a sledgehammer. The breath whooshes out of me. Just like that, the fight drains out of me, and I just want to curl into a ball and die.

"Fucking fuck." I hang my head. "She's too good for me. It's only right she walked out on me."

"No shit," interjects Sinclair. "They're all too good for us. Thank god they haven't figured that out."

The other men laugh with him, but I don't have it in me.

"What did you agree to do?" Cade's eyebrows knit.

"More to the point, what did Solonik promise you?" Michael growls.

I pivot, then stab a finger at him. "Shut the fuck up."

Michael's lips thin. His shoulder muscles seem to swell. "You're upset; it's why I'll allow you this one transgression." His black eyes seem to grow even darker. *He's a motherfuckin' snake, is who he is. Like I fucking care?* If not for the fact I need to be on camera in the next forty-eight hours, I'd swing at the man. Not that it's advisable to pick a fight with the man who's a legend in the underground world, and with the cops, as well.

"All right; back up, guys." JJ prowls over and stands between us. "Let's all take a seat, shall we?"

"Let's not," I growl.

He turns on me. "Sit down, dickwipe, and tell us what happened. We're trying to help you unfuck whatever the fuck you did. You've got the most powerful men in the country on your side. You don't want to lose this fucking opportunity to try to set things right."

I open my mouth, but he throws up his hand. "You need us. Don't even try to claim otherwise."

I draw in a breath, then another. Then force my muscles to unwind. Five-four-three-two-one. Some of the anger ebbs away. Fucking acting classes have their uses when you least expect it. I take a few steps to the side, so I'm no longer in the center of this very uncomfortable circle.

"Fifty percent of my investors pulled out of funding my movie. I needed to bridge the gap. So, I struck a deal with Nikolai Solonik."

"I fucking knew it," Michael snarls.

"The fuck were you thinking, resting dickface?" Sinclair Sterling snaps.

"That I needed to make another film and fast. And this time, I was going to source the funding. I was going to produce it, so I no longer had to hand over control to some prick..." I pause. The irony of my statement is not lost on me. "...who thinks he's the greatest creative brain alive, when in reality, all he does is destroy my role until I don't believe in the project anymore, and then it shows on screen, and you know what happens after that?" I make a sound like that of a plane falling out of the sky as I dive my hand to the ground. "Crash and burn, like my future."

"Or your love life." JJ scowls at me.

"It was a choice." I raise a shoulder.

"Did you do what I think you did?" The furrow between JJ's eyebrows deepens.

I shake my head. "Nikolai agreed to front the money. I had carte blanche with it. I could choose my own creative team, the cast, the script. You know what that means to an actor like me?"

"Like you won the lottery?" Sinclair drums his fingers on his chest. "What was the catch?"

I rub the back of my neck. "Nothing. At least, not then. He said he'd call in a favor and— "

Sinclair groans.

"—he did." JJ completes my sentence.

I throw up my hands. "If you guys already know everything, why am I even bothering to speak?"

"Because you're the shit-stain who gambled away your love for your career," Sinclair snaps.

"All I did was agree to an arranged relationship with the woman. One in which I'd get engaged to her, but there would be no real romantic relationship between us. And no marriage."

"Who is she and why the hell does he want you to do that?" JJ frowns.

"The fuck if I know. Or care." I raise a shoulder. "I secured my future."

"You lost your present." He reaches forward and slaps the back of my head.

"Hey!" I stiffen. "Watch out, old man; you're stepping across the line now."

"Stepping across the line? It's you who stepped across the line." He bites out the words with such force, spittle sprays from his mouth." Why did you not come to one of us for the money?"

Cade coughs. "My point exactly."

Traitor. I glare at him.

He raises his shoulders. "I did tell you so."

I dig my fingers into my hair and tug. "I will not take money from my friends to fund a venture. It's a sure-fire way to lose relationships." I glare between the men. "And don't tell me you don't agree."

JJ scowls.

Michael firms his lips.

Sinclair's eyebrows knit.

None of them say anything. "That's what I thought." I roll my shoulders to try to alleviate the ache that's settled between them, not that it helps any. "I saw an opportunity and took it."

"At what cost, though?" Sinclair tilts his head.

At the cost of my heart. At the cost of my living out the rest of my life knowing I'll never find anyone like her. Knowing I'll never feel like this about anyone else. Knowing I love her. My heart stutters. Goddam it, I love her.

I did the right thing in making her hate me. She deserves someone better than me, someone who doesn't share my proclivities. And every time I see her with another man, I'm going to want to kill myself.

I allow my lips to curl. "It's all or nothing. You get one opportunity to get things right. You get that one big, shining, tingling feeling once in your lifetime, and for me—" I slap my chest, once more playing the role of egotistical Hollywood film star. It's what my friends expect to see, after all. "This was it."

It was also the perfect opportunity to give her a reason to walk away from me and find someone more worthy. When I found out about the planned photo-op, I knew that was my chance. I figured, I could arrange things so she'd walked in on me with Niko's woman. This was the perfect opportunity to make her hate me. And when Solene told me what she saw, I knew my plan was working. I could use her insecurities to my advantage. I hated myself for even thinking it, but this could be the key to pushing her away. I had to use it. Of course, she wasn't buying the story I was engaged to someone else. I shouldn't have been surprised; we've played that game before. Which is when I decided to blame it on my desire for revenge for what her brother did to me.

Now, she hates me. I hate myself for making her hate me. I wish there had been a way to do this without hurting her, but I needed to make sure she'll never care for me again. I needed to prove to her that the me she fell in love with when she was seventeen, is not the same me today. I curl my fingers into fists at my sides. She's never going to forgive me for what I did. But as long as she has a chance to find the right man, and the kind of future she deserves, it will be worth it. Which makes me wonder. *Maybe the old me is hiding in here somewhere.* I shake my head to dislodge that thought.

Michael scoffs, "Coming to an understanding with the head of the Bratva, who's known to squeeze his opponents of their every last drop of utility... Do you realize how insane your plan is?"

"You should know; haven't you done the same?"

He opens his mouth to finish, but this time, I raise my hand. "No, let me finish. You know I'm right. This is the tactic you've used at every turning point in your life, and look where it's gotten you."

"I also got my head out of my ass long enough to marry the love of my life with whom I now have a child," Michael counters.

"Maybe that's not what I want." I thrust out my chest. "Maybe getting this movie done and racing it to the top of the box office is the future I want."

"Maybe you're as stupid as you come across." JJ leans forward on the balls of his feet.

"*Maybe* I want the lot of you to butt out of my life."

"We've established that's not happening. Deal with it," Michael says in a voice that brooks no argument.

A-n-d, my acting skills have never come in handier than now. Even my friends are willing to buy my act as someone willing to do anything to star in the movie that will catapult me to the top of my career. *Even Solene bought it.*

And it's true, that's why I decided to get Nikolai Solonik to invest in my film. And when he called in his favor, I struggled. I didn't want to agree. When it comes down to it, I didn't want to let Solene go, but I knew it was best for her. So, I embraced what I had to do, and when I realized I could use the situation to get her to walk away from me, I had to do that, too. *And why do I have to keep reminding myself I did this for her?*

All I have left now is this movie. Something I've worked for all my life. *So why am I not more thrilled about it? Why is it that, without her, nothing holds the same attraction for me?*

"Declan, are you listening?" Sinclair's voice cuts through my thoughts.

I glance between the assembled men, then square my shoulders. "I'm going through with this, and nothing you guys say can change my mind."

Sinclair opens his mouth to speak, when my phone buzzes. I ignore it, and it stops. Then, another buzzing sounds—Cade's phone, this time. We glance at each other, then he reaches for his phone, checks the screen and frowns.

"Hello?" He answers. "Yes, this is Cade Kingston." He listens to the voice on the other side, then pales. "How long has he been missing?"

46

Solene

"Oh, my god! I came as soon as I heard." I rush into the townhouse I left in a hurry just a few hours earlier. The girls and I had been on our third miniature bottles of alcohol each, when my phone rang with a call from Cade. I'd be lying if I said we weren't well on our way to getting wasted, but the news he gave us had the effect of sobering us up right away. We each downed a cup of coffee, brushed our teeth, then Rick drove us over.

I make my way toward the living room, Penny and Mira on my heels. Sinclair's whippet Max clatters toward me, his nails scrabbling on the wooden floor of the hallway. I pause to pet him, then glance up at Summer. "How is she?"

Summer shakes her head. "It was all so chaotic. The base called Abby first, and when they couldn't reach her, tried Declan, then Cade, who picked up the call. They're in the living room." She gestures in that direction.

Max moves onto Penny, who fusses over him.

I'm familiar with the layout of the house, for obvious reasons. I head down the hallway and toward the spacious living space. I walk in and, once more, appreciate the floor-to-ceiling sliding doors at the back which open onto the back garden where the reception was held earlier. The space is now dark, aside from some subdued nighttime lighting, and the wedding tent has been cleared, as has the table and chairs where we ate earlier. Hidden lights illuminate the bushes and trees and beyond that, in the distance, the lights of London twinkle.

Inside, there's a fire in the hearth, and on the wide sofa opposite, Abby is curled up with her legs under her next to Cade, who's holding her close. Abby no longer has her veil, and Cade has pulled off his bowtie, other than that, they are still in their wedding clothes. Abby's hair is down from the twist she put it up into earlier, and her eyes are swollen. She glances up at me, and her lips trembles. I rush toward her, sink down to my knees in front of the sofa, and take her hands in mine and whisper, "I'm so sorry, Abby."

"H-he's not dead. I know they're not holding out much hope, but they haven't found his body, so he has to be alive, right?" Tears roll down her cheek.

All I knew was that he was missing. This is the first I'm hearing it may be much more serious than that.

"The aircraft he was in went down inside enemy lines. They lost contact five days ago," Cade says in a low voice.

"Five days?" I swallow down the emotion that crowds my chest.

"They would have liked to wait longer before they called us, but there's been a leak to the press." Cade sets his jaw. "The news will be out—"

"It's out now." Declan holds up his phone from where he's standing propped up against the bar on the far right of the room.

Abby makes a noise at the back of her throat, and Cade pulls her even closer. "I know, baby, and I'm so sorry this is happening." He cups her cheek. "If I could do anything to take away the pain this is causing you, I would."

Abby swallows. "It must have happened just after we spoke to him. He wanted us to go ahead with the wedding. He wouldn't hear of us waiting for him. He must have had an inkling about... About..." Her features crumple. She pulls away from me and buries her face in Cade's chest.

"Shh, baby." Cade runs his hand down her hair. He's pale under his tan. "Please, don't cry. It kills me to see you like this."

She only sobs louder. Cade lifts her into his lap and begins to rock her. The tenderness in his gestures, the way he tucks her head under his chin, the way he holds her like she's the most precious thing in his life, makes the ache in my heart grow stronger. My ribcage feels too tight. A heaviness knocks at the backs of my eyes as I recall when Declan held me just like that. When he pushes her hair back from her cheek, it feels like I'm intruding on what's a very private moment.

I rise to my feet and back away. The hair on the back of my neck stands to attention. Before I can tell myself to stop, I turn my head. Cold blue eyes meet mine. The eyes that have graced the big screen and been celebrated by gossip magazines and his fan clubs. Eyes that have sent women around the world into a swoon. Eyes that glare at me like it's my fault Knight is lost in action. I blank my features before I hold his gaze and his jaw tics. All of the muscles in his body are coiled so tightly, he positively vibrates with rage. He pockets his phone, and that breaks the spell.

I turn and walk into the corridor, where Penny and Mira are talking with Summer. Max is no longer with them.

"Sinclair is with Michael and JJ in the study." Summer glances between us. "They're reaching out to their sources to get as much information as possible about Knight's situation. Her baby was fussing so Karma went home. The others, too, had to leave. I'll add you three to our girls' chat group so you can stay updated about Knight."

Another baby's cry sounds from the floor above. She looks upward, then at us. "I'm sorry, I have to—"

"Go, please, your little one needs you." I touch her shoulder. "We should probably leave, as well."

"Oh, please stay. I'm sure Abby appreciates you three rushing over; you all are such good friends." The baby's cries grow more strident, and Summer pulls away. "It's a year, and I'm still breastfeeding. I really do have to wean her away, but I'm not ready, you now?"

I nod. I haven't been in that position, but I'll take her word for it.

"There's food and drinks laid out in the kitchen." She turns to leave. "Feel free to stay as long as you want."

"Don't mind if we do." Mira tips up her chin.

Penny and I scowl at her, but she raises her hands. "What? All I'm saying is, it might be good for us to hang around a little longer—" She glances about the plush space. "If you remember, she said there were enough guest rooms—"

"There are." Summer smiles at us over her shoulder. "I'll get Jeeves to show you to them. Feel free to stay over. I know Cade and Abby, as well as Declan are."

Well then. If he's staying over, then I'm not. No way, do I trust myself under the same roof as him.

"Oh, and you don't have to worry about random paps. The security has been beefed up. Nothing can get through." She heads for the staircase.

"Thanks for the offer, Summer, but I think I'm going to leave."

"You sure?" She pauses and looks over her shoulder. "There's plenty of room for all of you." She includes Mira and Penny in her glance.

"I'm sure. I have an early flight out tomorrow and I'd prefer to get back and pack, you know?"

She hesitates then nods. "Whatever you want, Solene, and remember, we're here for you." She waves, then begins to climb.

Penny, Mira and I say goodbye to Abby, then pivot and head for the door with me in the lead.

"Solene?" Declan's voice reaches me, and a few seconds later, his heavy tread approaches. I stiffen and lock my fingers together. I will not turn. I refuse to give him the satisfaction of finding out he's unnerved me. I knew he would be here at the Sterlings' residence—he and Cade and Knight are the closest of friends—but I tried not to dwell on it. Abby's one of my closest friends, too, and I needed to be there for her emotionally.

Penny and Mira move forward to stand on either side of me. It's a show of support, and damn if I'm not grateful for it. I'm not sure if I have the strength to face Declan after the emotional rollercoaster of a day I've had.

Declan skirts our little group and turns to stand in front of me. He surveys my features, and whatever he sees there makes the frown on his face deepen. "You okay, Rabbit?"

I wince at the nickname, then school my features into a mask. I cannot allow him to see how much his nearness is affecting me. "I will be, when I don't have to see your face again."

His features tighten. He takes a step forward, but Penny steps between us. "She doesn't want to talk to you."

He draws in a breath, then narrows his gaze on me. "We need to talk."

"You heard Penny. I don't want to talk to you," I say through gritted teeth.

"I spoke with Giorgina a little while ago. I think it's important for both of our careers that you listen to—"

I step closer and stab my finger into his chest. "I don't fucking care, you *pezzo di merda*. You have some temerity trying to speak with me after what you did earlier. I fucking h-h-h-hate you." And there goes my stutter, revealing my emotions, dammit. A tear squeezes out of the corner of my eye, then another. The last thing I want is for that *stronzo* to see me breaking apart. I will not let him see how much he's affecting me with what he did. I will not let him watch me make a complete fool of myself.

I pull back my arm, haul my bag over my shoulder and say, "Let me be clear, Mr. Hollywood Star, I never want to see you again. *Capiche?*"

47

Three months later

Declan

"You have to try to see her again." Giorgina's voice floats up from the phone I placed on the floor next to the punching bag.

"Not sure she agrees with that," I reply as I continue to pummel the punching bag in the private gym set up for me in one of the trailers on location. We've been shooting in New Zealand for the last month. With the money from Niko Solonik coming through, and the remaining investors ready to play ball, I restarted the production, and this time, on my terms.

And every moment of every day, I've missed her.

I've thrown myself into my work, but not even being immersed in my dream project has gotten her out of my mind. The pain in her eyes when I told her I'd only pretended to be emotionally involved with her will live with me forever. I'm scum of the lowest order. Worse than the news-hungry paps who followed me around. A bottom feeder. That's me. No, I'm worse than that. I hurt her in the worst possible way. I went back on my word that I'd forgiven her for what her brother did to me. I hit her where it would cause the worst damage. And I did it, so she'd forget about me and move on—which is what I wanted, right?

Now she can find someone who'll treat her like the princess she is and not the whore I insisted on degrading her to every time we were together. Not someone whose perverse tendencies would debase her. Is it supposed to hurt so much to do something for the benefit of someone else?

She deserves better. So why is it that I can't move on from her?

"Declan, you still there?" Giorgina asks. A thread of worry laces her tone, a first from my hard-headed PR manager. It shows how distracted I've been since I walked away from my woman. I need to get my head back in the game. Need to move on. Need to get my act together and focus on my dream project.

I set my jaw. "I'm good." *I'm not.* The need to see her has grown daily. A throbbing, insistent ache that has infiltrated every cell in my body. At least, she's safe. I can take some solace in that. I know this because the security detail she employed in place of Rick was also vetted by me. Not that she knows that. She's also unaware that Harry is keeping me posted on her performances, and on whether she's seeing anyone else. She's not. That arsehole owes me, after all. It's the only reason I've managed to stop myself from jumping on a flight and going to her. To apologize and tell her how badly I screwed up. But she's better off without me, and that's what has stopped me. Now, if only I could focus on the movie before I screw it up beyond redemption.

"O-kay." She hesitates. "You do realize, it doesn't matter what you think she thinks. Question is, what do *you* think? Are you sure things are over between the two of you?" she asks.

I lower my hands to my sides. My breath comes in pants. Sweat flows down my temples and drips down from my chin.

"Absolutely." I grab my towel from the floor and wipe my face. "Regardless of what I think or want, whatever was between us is over. She already announced that to her audience," I remind Giorgina.

"It's true, the two of you haven't been seen together since, but all it needs is one well-placed photo-op and—"

"She'd never agree to it."

"But you'd be open to it?"

I pick up the phone, then walk over to place it on the bench pushed up against one wall of the room. "It doesn't matter." I begin my cooling down exercises. "I've hurt her enough. I'm not going to subject her to more of the media scrutiny that comes from our being seen together."

She frowns. "What happened between the two of you?"

Anger squeezes my guts. Anger at myself. That dull thud behind my breastbone, the one that hasn't faded since the day I told her I have a fiancée, ratchets up in intensity. "That's between her and me."

"I wish I could agree with that, but I'm afraid the flop of your last film at the box office says otherwise."

I pause, then drop down into a push up.

"And—" She hesitates.

"Go on, Giorgina, spit it out."

"The financiers of your existing project—not the Sovranos, but the rest—uh—they're thinking of pulling out."

I stay poised in plank position. "The fuck you talking about?"

"Sorry." I hear her swallow. "I know it's not ideal news."

"Their contracts are air-tight; they can't just pull out."

"And you and I both know, if they want to, they can find loopholes and do just that."

"I'll sue every last one of them," I growl.

"It's not going to make them invest the money."

I jump to my feet, grab the phone and squeeze my fingers around the device with such force the cover cracks.

"What's that?" Giorgina's voice rises in pitch. "You okay? Did you break something?"

"Not yet, but I'm going to." I begin to pace. "I'm going to find a way to get them to honor their funding commitment. I'm—"

"And they will, on one condition."

I rotate my neck, and my joints pop. "Nope. Whatever it is, no."

"But—"

"It's not happening, Giorgina."

"Will you, at least—"

I disconnect the phone and continue to pace. No way am I going to sit across from Solene and see the hurt and anger in her eyes, knowing I'm responsible for putting it there. I'm going to find another way to make this movie happen. I'm Declan-fucking-Beauchamp. I didn't get this far to watch my dream go up in smoke. There are no guarantees in Hollywood. Only a fraction of movies get made here, and an even smaller fraction of them get released. And a very tiny percentage of them are hits. I bet everything I have on this movie, including her, and I'm going to find a way to get it made... Without having to go to her for help.

My phone rings again. It's Cade. I accept the video call, and his face appears on screen. He's unshaven, dark circles under his eyes. He's wearing a faded sweatshirt, and by his surroundings, I gather he's home in London.

"Any news on Knight?" I pause.

He shakes his head.

"Fuck, he's been missing for three months." I wanted to help with the efforts to look for him, but Abby and Cade insisted I continue with the shooting. Between Sinclair, JJ and Michael, they mobilized both the law and those on the other side of the law to help with the search. They convinced me I wouldn't be able to add anything more to the efforts. Which is the only reason I've stayed here and continued to shoot.

It also gives me a reason to be far away from everyone I know. Including her.

He drags his fingers through his hair, so it stands up further. "There have been no demands made. No word from the other side as to whether he and his team are alive or not."

I rub the back of my neck. "Where did the flight go down?"

"They lost touch close to the border of Ukraine and Russia. He was part of a discreet team of British military personnel sent on a recon mission to Russia."

"Jesus."

He nods. "It's not looking good."

"He has to be alive. That bastard is hard to kill. He's been on dangerous missions before and survived. Remember how he went missing in the Middle East?"

"And resurfaced three weeks later." His jaw tightens. "It's been longer this time."

"He'll get through this. He'll be back." He has to. I need to believe in it.

Both of us fall silent for a few seconds then I rub my neck. "I wish there was something I could do. It feels wrong to be out here, working on my film instead of putting my efforts into finding him."

"What you can do is stay focused on making this movie. It's what you've worked toward your entire life. Knight wouldn't want you to take your focus off it now."

I bark out a laugh. “A movie that’s stalled again.”

“Again?” He frowns.

“This time, the financiers—not the Soloniks—want her to star in the movie with me. Apparently, our joint star appeal outweighs the clout I carry on my own.” *Whatever I do, there’s no getting away from her presence in my life.*

He looks at me with a strange expression. "I could have sworn you loved her."

When I stay silent, he nods. "I see."

"I didn’t say anything,” I growl.

"You don’t need to. You broke her heart, you dickhead.”

I shuffle my feet.

"You do realize, it’s time for you to make amends?” he says slowly.

I hold up my hand. "Let me guess. You want me to go all emo and 'fess up what I did, and then, you’re going to give me the kind of advice JJ, Michael and Sinclair gave you."

His lips quirk, then he shakes his head. "Nope."

I stare. "You’re not?"

"I’m not, because I have a feeling whatever you did is not something she’s ever going to forgive you for, even after you grovel."

I thrust out my chest. "I made my choice, and I’m going to see it through."

"But at what cost? You stand to lose the love of your life and your career."

"Not if I can help it."

He looks closely at me. "What are you planning, Declan?"

48

Solene

"So, this is what you've been planning?" I glare at Harry. He loosens the tie he's wearing around his neck—the one that makes him look like an overweight, about-to-have-a-coronary banker—and hunches his shoulders.

"I wanted to get you to meet him, and I knew you'd never agree." His chin quivers.

I scowl at him. "No way am I going to stay here and wait for that *stronzo* to arrive. Also, I'm sure he's late on purpose."

The hair on the back of my neck rises. I ignore it.

Harry blinks and mops his brow. "No, no, there was turbulence, and they had to take another route from New Zealand—a longer route—and stop to refuel, which is why he's running late, and—"

"The fuck I care. You can tell him to go stick his excuses where the sun don't shine."

"You can tell me yourself." That deep, dark voice of his shivers down my spine and coils in my lower belly. Shit, I should have left before he came. I should have run out as soon as Harry told me why he'd asked me to his office. *And shown him how much of a coward you are? He has no more influence on you. You're single, carefree, living your own life*—and trying to resurrect a career threatening to unravel as quickly as it shot me to the top.

Posts on my social media platform are no longer getting the kind of reach they enjoyed when I first starting posting. My last popular post was the one when I told the world I was breaking up with Declan. A lot of people left comments showing how upset they were. I also had those who supported me.

And then, the fan clubs turned on me, blaming me for the demise of the relationship. Apparently, I didn't have time for him. I was too career focused. I turned down his offer to marry me. Ha! The speculation doing the rounds was crazy. Maybe, eventually, he'll get around to announcing his engagement and that will take the blame off of me. Then again, maybe not.

That post continues to accumulate comments, but after that day, the downloads of my songs plummeted. I lost followers on my social media platforms, and the promoters of the tour decided they didn't want to bet on me again. Even the label, which had released my first album, the one that had netted them millions, decided to scrap plans for my next one.

Unfortunately, by the time the recording label and Harry had pocketed their percentage, there was barely enough left to cover my travel costs... And perhaps, buy a small condo. Not a single-family house, but a condo. Thankfully, I made enough from the record deal to retain my security team.

I suppose, if I really wanted to, I could have moved out, but it seemed more prudent to bank the money I made for the future. Besides, Declan is never around, so I have the house to myself. And since he hasn't been in touch with me, I assumed he'd given up on me. Unlike the paps, who continue to follow me around. Only, they keep asking me where Declan is. Apparently, they're only interested in shooting pictures of the two of us.

The only consolation is, according to Giorgina, Declan isn't faring better.

A thousand goosebumps erupt on my skin as I feel him move closer, then I hear his voice, "You okay, Rabbit?"

A shudder ladders up my spine. My throat closes, my pulse flutters. His footsteps come closer, and I slowly turn to find he's standing in front of me. His blue eyes snap on mine with the force of a gale wind. Tiny embers spark in parts of me that only he knows so well.

He rakes his gaze down my face, my chest, to the hem of my dress which ends mid-thigh, then the strip of skin bared above my over-the-knee boots which have become my trademark, down to my feet balanced on eight-inch-heels, then back up to my now flushed features. And the embers blaze into a fire that envelops all of me.

I take in his broad shoulders that stretch his sweatshirt. The sleeves are tight around his biceps and molded to his chest. In contrast, his waist is narrower. His jeans cling to his powerful thighs which flex as he walks in my direction. He seems to have grown broader since I last saw him. And hotter. The days' old growth on his chin only adds to that bad boy look of his. He's pushed up his sleeves and the sight of those veiny forearms of his sends lust shooting through my veins. Sweat beads my forehead.

I draw in a breath, and my lungs fill with the scent of him. He's sucked up all the oxygen in the room. My heart seems to hit my toes, then bounce back up to my throat. It only serves to remind me that someone carved out the space in my chest and turned me into a hollow shell of the woman I once was. Him. His presence makes me wish I could retake my heart and fill up the emptiness, even though I know that's impossible. I draw in a breath, trying to find my balance. *Merda!* I forgot the effect this man's presence has on me. No, I lie.

I haven't forgotten anything. I've merely managed to avoid facing the fact that every second of every day that I've spent away from him, thoughts of him have been a canvas against which I've lived my life. During the day, I've ensured I've been too busy to allow him any space in my mind. But in that time between night and day, when dawn hasn't yet broken over the horizon, when I've tossed and turned, and tried to quell the aching emptiness between my legs, when my chest feels like it's been stripped of the ability to feel, to hold a beating heart in it again, when despite my wanting to sleep, my eyelids have refused to stay shut, I've given up pretending I don't miss him and reached for the toy that has granted me only temporary relief.

It's never enough. Nothing can substitute for the stretch of my pussy as it fits around his cock, the feel of his skin on mine as we slide against one another, his breath intertwined with mine as he stares into my eyes, his lips grazing my cheek as he shares my breath and sucks on my tongue, and his heart beating against mine as I clutch him to me. Which is when I give up, sexually frustrated and unable to sleep, and walk down to the tiny gym in my basement and attempt to run from that scene of him with that woman which is seared into my brain.

"Where is she?" I glance around him. "Where is your fiancée?"

His jaw tightens.

"She's not here."

I roll my eyes, then scoff. "Shouldn't she be with you, supporting you, and all that? In fact, I haven't seen a picture of the two of you together yet on your social media or in the press. I'd have thought you'd want to announce it to the press."

A slow smile curves his lips. "You been stalking my social media, Rabbit?"

My cheeks burn. I shouldn't have said that. I should have shut the hell up. But as always, when I'm around him, the connection between my brain and my mouth seems to be tenuous, at best. I flip my hair over my shoulder. "I've been too busy for that."

"Really? Despite the last leg of your tour being canceled. Not to mention, your label dropped you. In fact, you don't know how you're going to find the money to launch your next record. Am I right?"

I pale. “Why are you being such a *carogna*? What's wrong with you?”

I have the satisfaction of seeing him glance away.

“Besides, aren't you the one who's run into funding difficulties, *again,* with your movie?"

His features harden. Then, to my surprise, he nods.

I blink. Wow, did he just admit his plans are not going as they should. Our gazes meet and hold. Those blue eyes of his darken to that indigo I know so well. The indigo that's haunted my dreams and appears in my mind's eye every time I close my eyes. The air between us thickens. Unsaid emotions seem to lace the molecules around us.

Someone clears their throat. I glance in the direction of the door to find Giorgina lurking inside the threshold.

She nods in Harry's direction. I turn around, and the guilty look on his face intensifies. "You planned this with her?" I snap.

"I, uh… Trust me when I say, it was important to get the two of you together in a room."

I draw myself up to my full height. "I thought I could trust you, Harry. I—"

"Don't blame him; this was my idea."

I turn on him. "You could have just called me instead of going to this length."

"Would you have spoken to me?"

I glance away, then shake my head.

"That's what I thought."

He looks past me at Harry and says, "Leave us."

Without a single protest, Harry uses his stumpy legs to propel himself past us and to the door.

Giorgina nods at me, then follows him out. The door snicks shut. I look past him at the door. I should leave. If I stay here, he's going to influence me into agreeing with whatever scheme he's come up with.

"Just a few minutes, Rabbit; that's all I'm asking for."

I huff.

"Please?"

I jerk my chin in his direction. "Excuse me, did you just say what I think you did?"

He chuckles. "Surprised?"

"You're saying the P-word, but I'm sure you don't mean it."

The smile vanishes from his face. "Just five minutes of your time; that's all I'm asking for."

"And if I don't agree?"

"You'll always regret it. You'll wish you heard me out because, in your heart of hearts, you know you want to hear what I have to say."

"What do *you* know about my heart of hearts?"

He looks down but seems to be at a loss for words.

I blow out a breath, then turn and stomp over to the sofa on the far side of the room. Harry might be a shyster, but his office is comfortably furnished. And it should be, considering the money he's made off of me. As has the label. I throw myself into the sofa.

Declan follows me more slowly and takes the seat across from me. His lips quirk, and there's a look on his face I can't quite interpret.

"What?" I scowl.

"I like what you've done to your hair," he murmurs.

"You mean the color?" I wind a strand of blue hair around my finger. His gaze follows the movement, and his throat moves as he swallows. Apparently, he's as affected by my presence as I am by his. And that shouldn't surprise me. Chemistry is the one thing we've never had a problem with. It's everything outside of that which never seems to line up. "I'd already colored it when we met at Cade and Abby's wedding."

"I wanted to tell you then, but—" he raises a shoulder.

"But you were too busy telling me about your fiancée."

"About that." He shuffles his feet. There's a guilty look on his face. A look I've never seen before, considering how cocky and confident this man normally is. "I broke it off," he murmurs.

"What?" I blink. "What do you mean?"

"Meaning, it was an arrangement. But I ended it."

"Excuse me?" A headache begins to drum at my temples. "What do you mean, it was an arrangement?"

"It's the kind you were in when we met."

I lock my fingers together in my lap. "Okay, stop it. We've been through this, remember? I already asked you if you were kidding me when you told me you had a fiancée—similar to how you pretended to be engaged to Olivia—and you told me that wasn't the case. You lied to me?"

Color smears his cheeks. He rolls his shoulders, then glances away. When he looks back at me, it's as if he's dropped the last barriers between us. As if he shrugged off that coat of ego he's worn so closely to his skin that it became part of him, but he's now torn it off and tossed it aside.

The person looking back at me is Declan—but not as I know him now. It's the Declan I met when he was twenty-one, and he looked at me and knew I was the one for him. He's looking at me like the woman he wanted me to be then, but who he's found now.

"If you remember, I didn't answer your question. I simply didn't correct your assumption." He shifts his weight from foot to foot. "I didn't have an engagement like when I pretended to be Olivia's fiancée so she could save face with Massimo. I had one a bit more like the one you had with Massimo, when your family arranged an alliance with a rival Mafia clan. Your engagement was an arrangement, as was mine. But you were genuinely expected to marry him to solidify the alliance, while I was expected to *act* as if I genuinely expected to marry her. Mine with Olivia was pretend, through and through. It didn't even last through one dinner because it wasn't as important to maintain the façade."

A thousand butterflies take wing in my belly. *No, no, no, don't go there. You can't let yourself hope. Not now. Not after he squashed all the joy out of you, and hurt you, and mis-used your trust, and made you believe you could never love anyone else again... but him.*

And that's the thing. Despite how he broke my heart I still am not over my feelings for him. *What does that mean? Why can't I move on from this man? Why is it that everything in me is holding out hope for him to explain his actions? Why is it that I still want us to be together?*

I throw up my hands. "What are you trying to tell me? Can you spell it out in simple English? My brain cells are dying here."

He blows out a breath. "I entered into an arrangement with the Bratva."

"The Bratva?" I stare at him. *Did he say the Bratva?*

"What for?" I burst out. "Why would you associate with an underground criminal organization?"

"I wanted access to money to fill the production gap for my movie. And if I pretended to marry her, Nikolai Solonik, the leader of the Bratva would loan it to me."

"Are you aware of the potential consequences of mixing up with the Bratva?" I throw up my hands. "How do you even know him?"

"He's, uh, family... In a roundabout way."

"He's family?" I stare. I left Napoli, hoping not to be associated with the Mafia in any way, and now, he tells me he's linked to the Bratva? "How is he family?"

"His sister Karina is married to my brother Arpad. That also provides me with a bit of a safety net. I knew he couldn't dick around with me—" He raises a shoulder. "And he had the money and the contacts I needed to accelerate the pace of production of the film on the ground."

My heart drops into my stomach, then flips back into my chest. My head spins. "If your financiers hadn't pulled out, none of this would have happened—which I still can't understand. Why would they do that? You're one of the most popular leads in Hollywood already."

He half smiles. "That's the name of the game. You're up one day, down the next, much like your own career."

I glance away. I don't want to show him just how difficult it's been. I made enough money from the sales of my first album, but given what's needed to produce the next one, and without the help of a label to cover the overhead, it's far more challenging than I thought it would be.

"You don't have to hide your thoughts. If anyone understands the fickleness of this business, it's me," he murmurs.

I still don't look at him.

"I know how difficult it was for you, after your tour got canceled." His voice grows even softer.

I swallow around the ball of emotion in my throat. "That must make you happy, right? Looks like you're getting even more revenge than you bargained for."

"That's not true, baby, and you know it."

"Do I?" I squeeze shut my eyes.

I hear the sound of footsteps, and the next second, he's squatting in front of me, his palms pressed into the seat on either side of me. I open my eyes, prepared to tell him off.

"I behaved abominably," he says softly.

"Ya think?"

"I'm sorry for what I put you through, truly. I never should have agreed to that arrangement. I thought it was the best thing to do for the both of us, though."

"You mean, my walking in on you with another woman was what you thought was best for me?"

"Yes," he agrees.

Che coglione! "I can't believe you're saying that."

"You don't understand."

"I do. You decided you wanted to put me through the worst time of my life. You thought making me think you were cheating on me... No, worse, making me believe you were going to marry someone else. That even while you were fucking me—"

"—making love to you," he corrects me.

"Fucking me," I repeat. "Even while you were *fuck-ing* me, you were thinking of another woman, all along."

His throat moves as he swallows. He shuffles his feet as if he's not sure what to say, then he squares his shoulders. "It's what I thought was best for the both of us."

Wow! I stare at him. I want to slap him for what he put me through. My fingers tingle. I want to claw at his face. I want to gouge out tracks in his flesh, so this time, when he gets scarred, it'll be because I wanted it. Because that way, he'll carry my mark. And every time he looks at it, he'll think of me, no matter who he's with.

A-n-d, I'm pathetic. I saw him with another woman—and yet, here I am, listening to him. I flatten my lips. "Who are you to decide what's best for me?"

"The man who brought you to this country and who started you off on your career?"

"A career which isn't going anywhere in a hurry, by the way," I snap.

"And I have a solution for that, too."

I take in his features, take in the serious look in his eyes. I've never seen him this determined, this intent on a goal. A shiver crawls down my spine.

"I don't want to listen to it. I'm not interested in the opinions of someone so fond of making decisions for me. Not when you're unwilling to give me a choice on what's best for me."

"Trust me when I say, I had your best interests in mind."

"Bullshit. You were thinking of yourself," I scoff.

"Not only," he objects.

I stare at him, expressionless.

He raises his palms. "Fine. I admit, I put myself first all this time. But no more." His gaze intensifies. "What I'm going to suggest is the best way—the most optimal way to get your career back on track. I've given it a lot of thought, and I wouldn't recommend it if it weren't going to benefit you in an exponential manner."

I hold his gaze, take in those piercing blue eyes, those flecks of silver in them which flash and brighten until it feels I'm adrift in space. This always happens. That hypnotic gaze of his seems to capture me, throw a net over my feelings, and bind me to him so I'm compelled to listen to him, and do what he asks of me. It's been like that since the moment I set eyes on him.

I manage to tear my gaze from him, and the breath rushes out of me. Managing to get a hold of myself I tip up my chin. "Why should I believe you when everything you've done so far has been designed to hurt me?"

49

Declan

"I'm sorry for what I did. I truly am. I knew I had to hurt you to get you to leave me, but I didn't realize how difficult it would be to do so. How much it would hurt me to see you hurt. And it was even worse knowing I was the one doing the hurting. How every time I tried to convince you that I was the kind of person you were better off without, it felt like I was tearing my heart out and trampling it underfoot.

She blinks rapidly then tosses her head. "Is that your excuse for everything you did? Is that why you were in your house, in your bedroom, consoling her, when you knew I was on my way to see you?"

"It's true. I told Giorgina I was home from the shoot, knowing she'd mention it to you. And I banked on your coming to talk with me, and I orchestrated it so you'd see us. But I had no idea she would be get so emotional and —"

She makes a noise at the back of her throat. Her green eyes flash. "You know what? Fuck that. And fuck you. And fuck whatever stupid idea you've come up with."

"Language," I growl.

"Typical double standard. You can swear aloud, but I can't. Well, fuck that, too."

"It's only because your gorgeous mouth was made for other things, baby."

She blinks, then the meaning of my words sinks in. Color flushes her cheeks. "How dare you?"

She slaps her hands against my shoulders, and the touch of her sinks through my sweatshirt and into my skin. My cock twitches. She must sense the effect her touch has on me for she swallows. "Let me go, Declan."

"No. Not until you listen to what I have to say."

"No, you listen to me. You had your chance and you screwed it up, and I'll be damned if I'm going to let you do that to me again."

Bam-bam-bam. My heart slams into my ribcage. My pulse rate speeds up. My insides seem to have been dumped into the blender, the way they're vibrating with apprehension. Fucking hell, from being at the top of my game to sinking to my knees and asking her to hear me out, I've swung from one end of the spectrum to the other. I shove aside my unease and school my features into a look of disdain. "If you don't listen to me, it's going to cost you."

"A-n-d, there you are. For a second there, I wondered if you'd changed, but clearly not. You still measure your worth and mine in money and fame and influence."

I blink. "So do you."

"But not to the extent you do."

"I don't know what you mean."

"Of course you don't. You've still got your sights on your career goals. On being number one. On becoming the most popular star in the world."

I lower my chin to my chest. "I've never shied away from my ambitions."

"And you've assumed it means as much to me to be the most popular in my field."

"And it did. You were hidden away by your family. You weren't given the opportunities to find out who you were. You didn't have the means to share your voice with the world. I gave you that chance. That springboard to showcase your talent to the world. To bare yourself and strike that chord with people who understood you."

She swallows. "And I'm grateful for that. If it weren't for you, I wouldn't have embraced who I truly am. I wouldn't have discovered how much I love to perform, how much I thrive on being on the same wavelength as my fans. How much I adore being able to share my creativity, my passion, my everything with the world, and have them reciprocate, but—"

"But?" I growl.

"But I don't want it to the extent you do. I'm not willing to sacrifice my truth, who I am, my words, the inherent reason why I began singing in the first place. I don't want to change who I am to fit in with the concept of what the world thinks I should be. I don't want a label dictating what I should sing. I don't want a partner who thinks he needs to protect me from whatever depraved tastes he has in sex."

I lurch back. "The fuck you talking about?"

Her lips curve a little. "You think I don't know how much you enjoy S&M? That you need to be dominant? That you thrive on seeing me submit to you? You think I didn't understand that the first time I went to the Club? You think I don't enjoy you being in charge?"

"You don't know what you're saying."

"Then tell me. Tell me why you had to go to such lengths, pretending to be engaged to someone else, knowing it would upset me and I'd break things off with you?"

I begin to rise to my feet, but she grabs hold of my arm. "Oh, no. You don't get to leave without talking to me."

I glare at where her fingers are locked around my wrist, then back at her. Her features pale, but she doesn't falter. Interesting. Apparently, the little rabbit has found her mettle.

"Let go of me."

"No."

"Don't defy me."

She tips up her chin. "What're you going to do, eh? Spank me?"

My gaze narrows. My balls throb. The thought of throwing her over my lap, revealing the creamy curve of her arse, then stamping her with my palm print sends my pulse rate through the roof.

"You'd better be careful about what comes next from your mouth, baby."

She makes a rude noise at the back of her throat. "You're all talk and no action, *baby*."

My vision tunnels. Adrenaline laces my blood. At the same time, a quiet descends on me. This, right here, is where I'm meant to be. Regardless of the issues with my career and hers, we're meant to be together. It's why I swallowed my pride to come to her. It's why I'm going to find a way to resurrect her popularity and mine. It's why… I'm going to give her one last chance to escape. I bend and peer into her eyes. "You'd better hop away, Rabbit."

She blinks rapidly.

"Wh-whatever do you mean?"

In her eyes is the knowledge that she's toying with me. That she's aware I'm dangerously close to the edge. That she's pushing me until I snap, but that she's past caring. So am I.

"If you don't try to escape, you'll always rue that you didn't even try."

She tips up her chin. "I'm not scared of you."

"You should be."

She leans forward until her nose bumps mine. "I'm. Not. Running."

"Neither. Am. I."

Those golden flecks in her eyes glow. Her pupils dilate until there's only a circle of emerald around the pupils.

"Last chance."

She pulls back her lips. "*Vaffanculo stronz—*"

The next second she gasps, for I've pulled my hand from her grasp, gripped her waist and flipped her over so she's kneeling on the sofa.

"What the fuck—!"

"You will watch your language around me."

"Go fuck yourself, you—"

I flip up the hem of the dress, which is too fucking short—and which I need to have a word with her about—but for now, it gives me easy access to her butt.

I yank down her panties and spank her.

She yells, tries to jump off, but I flatten my palm in the small of her back. "If you want me to stop, use your safe word."

"I don't have one, you *testa di cazzo*."

And that's the problem. "Choose one now."

She hesitates.

"You know what that is, thanks to your smutty books, so don't pretend otherwise. Choose. A. Safe. Word. Rabbit. Now."

"Unlucky," she bursts out.

Is this a reference to the good luck charms I've been sending her before each of her shows? The ones she's wearing attached to the bracelet on her wrist.

"Repeat it."

"Unlucky, you bastard."

I spank her butt again. She huffs.

"Use it if you really want me to stop, you get me?"

She nods, and I apply enough pressure on her back that she bends. She grips the cushioned backrest, then places her cheek between her hands.

"Hold on."

"What are you going to—" She gasps again, for I've slipped my fingers inside her.

"Oh, my god." She moans, then pushes back so her pussy slides up the length of my digits. I curve my fingers and her entire body jolts. "Oh, my god. Oh, my god."

I slap her butt. "Not even God can save you, Rabbit."

"Fuck you, you *pezzo di merda*, you—"

I slide my thumb inside her puckered hole.

She stiffens and falls silent.

Finally, fuck.

I push my fingers in and out of her sopping wet channel, and a groan falls from her lips. A fat drop of cum slides down her inner thigh, then another. "Fucking hell, you're making a mess for me aren't you, baby? You love my fingers inside you. You adore my cock in you. You can't wait for me to take your arse, can you?"

She groans, and mumbles something under her breath.

"What was that?"

I said, "Fuck you, arsehole."

I smirk. "What's that? Fuck your arsehole?"

She scowls at me over her shoulder. Her blue hair flows over one eye. The other one is fixed on me. A mixture of lust, need, and anger. Fucking hell. The sass in her. The way she stands up to me, dares me, challenges me to punish her, and then gives in to me… The entire cycle is an aphrodisiac that goes straight to my head, my heart and my balls. Every part of me wants her. Her scent. Her taste. Her anger. Her hate. Her love.

She must notice the emotions on my face, for her eyebrows draw down. "What's wrong?"

I swallow, then school my features into a scowl. "What's wrong is that you're still talking instead of orgasming."

Her gaze widens. "Wha—"

I remove my fingers from her, then push my face into her pussy.

50

Solene

"Declan!" His name has barely left my lips when he begins to eat me out. He grips my thighs and pulls them apart enough that I'd fall over, except he holds me in place as his tongue stabs inside my channel. He licks and sucks and bites, and to my horror, the orgasm wells up from somewhere deep inside.

"No, no, no." I shake my head and try to pull away. At least, I think I do. Only, my body decrees otherwise. Instead, I thrust my hips back and try to take more of his tongue inside my pussy. I begin to grind down on his mouth, and he obliges by licking me from my clit to my puckered hole. My eyes roll back in my head. I gasp, groan and whine. Sweat runs down the valley between my tits. My breasts swell. My nipples are so hard, so achy. And he must read my thoughts because he reaches up and pinches the right one. Hard. Shockwaves streak down to my core. My clit swells. Moisture pools between my legs and he slurps it up, then licks up my pussy lips. The pleasure waves inside me intensify, pouring over each other, growing in height, riding out and up my back, down my legs.

"Please, please, please." I'm not sure what I'm begging for, but he must understand, for he releases his hold on my nipple, only to pinch my clit and stab his tongue inside me. Then he slips his thumb inside my puckered hole, and the orgasm crashes over me. I cry out and dig my fingers into the cushions as wave after wave of ecstasy punches into my chest, bursts behind my eyes, and fills every cell in my body. My eyelids flutter down. Unable to hold on, I begin to slump, and have the sensation of being caught and carried. That delicious chocolate and coffee scent of his surrounds me. Without opening my eyes, I turn my head into his chest and inhale deeply, filling my lungs with Declan.

He places me down on what I'm sure is the counter in the ensuite bathroom, but I refuse to open my eyes.

"I need to clean you, baby." The vibration of his voice against my cheek is so reassuring. I've missed being held by him. Missed his scent and the way he surrounds me when he has his arms around me.

"Please, baby."

A-n-d, when he says the P-word, I can't refuse him. When he commands me, I can't stop myself from doing what he wants. And when he requests anything from me I…all but fall apart in my speed to comply. Either way, I'm fucked. I look up, and instantly, his piercing blue gaze locks with mine. He lowers his face, brushes his lips over mine and… I. Melt. I fall apart. Completely. A tear squeezes out from the corner of my eye. He instantly licks it up.

"Fuck, Rabbit. Don't cry."

"I'm not c-c-c-crying." A-n-d, cue the stammer. It's largely under control, except when I'm overwhelmed with emotions. Like now.

I begin to pull away, but he grips my chin. "You don't ever have to hide from me."

"I'm not hiding."

"Your stammer is a part of you, baby, and I fucking love it. I love every little thing that makes you... You. Your imperfections, your weaknesses, your faults are what attract me to you. I fucking adore every part of you. I wouldn't want you any other way."

My cheeks flush. He used the L-word. My heart somersaults into my throat. He used *the L-word*. Also, it's the first time he's referring to my impediment. To be honest, I never talk about it. My parents pretended everything was fine, and so did I…by turning to singing. When I sing, I'm not a confused Mafia princess turned popstar with millions of online followers who're quick to pass judgement on me. I'm simply a woman who bows to the muse inside. Who becomes the muse and channels this incredible gift so the world can hear it. Singing gave me the courage to be what I am. Just like he did.

I tilt up my head; he lowers his and brushes his mouth over mine. Soft, sweet—sweeter than any kiss we've shared before. Sweeter than any touch of his before. He stays there, savoring me, sharing my breath. Heat vibrates out from his touch, lighting up the nooks and crannies of my body that I'd forgotten even existed. A shiver oscillates up my spine, and a groan vibrates up his chest.

Our lips cling, he swipes his tongue across my mouth, and I gasp. Instantly, he pushes forward, and I widen my legs to accommodate him. The tent in his crotch presses against my clit, and I whimper.

"Fucking hell, baby, those noises you make drive me out of my head." He bites down on my lower lip, and I shudder. Then he licks my mouth, and my pussy quivers. "Fuck me, Declan."

His lips curve against mine. "I will, I promise, but first we need to speak."

He tears his mouth from mine, then hesitates and kisses me hard. "Don't look at me like that, baby."

"Can't believe you turned me down."

He scowls. "Does this look like I'm turning you down?" He thrusts forward, and the roughness of his jeans, combined with that baseball bat-sized erection he's sporting, rubs up on my still-bared clit. My thighs clench.

"Does it, baby?"

I shake my head.

"I promise, I'm going to satisfy you completely. But first, we really do need to speak." He leans over, runs the water and washes his hands. Then holds a washcloth under the tap, before squeezing it out and pressing it between my thighs. The slight burn in my core fades away, and I sigh. He kisses my forehead, then drops the washcloth in the bin. Stepping back, he pulls my panties up, then straightens my dress over my thighs.

"You're not wearing such a short dress again."

"What?" I blink.

"That dress—" He jerks his chin at my thighs. "You may wear it at home, for my pleasure, but when you go on stage, you'll dress like I want you to."

"Excuse me?" I gape at him. "Did you just ask me to change my look?"

"What's wrong with that?" He helps me down from the counter, then looks me up and down. "Also, now that we're together—"

"Hold on—" I throw up my hand. "Who said anything about being together?"

"You just allowed me to shove my fingers knuckle deep inside you. And by the force with which your pussy clamped down, I'd say you were very happy about it, too."

"It was *one* orgasm," I snap.

"And there'll be more to come. No hurry, huh? Now that we're going to be acting together in my film."

"Wait, what?" I blink. "I'm not acting in your film."

"Yes, you are."

I laugh. "You're delusional. Besides, I don't know anything about acting."

"What about the lessons you've been taking over the last few months?"

I frown. "How did you know that—" I smooth out my eyebrows. "Harry told you."

"He also mentioned you were looking for a role, and this one is tailor-made for you. Besides, the publicity around the two of us being seen together will propel not just our two careers forward, but also spur the movie on all the way to box-office success."

"You have this all worked out, don't you?"

"Of course. You and me? We're gold, baby. Our fans want to see us together. Think about how much organic traction we'll get when we announce we're together again."

"But we're not."

"We will be," he says with such confidence, I'm almost convinced myself.

Then, I shake my head. "Not so fast. There you go again. Making decisions for me without my consent."

I try to move away from him, but he reaches out and cups my cheek. "That orgasm there, the way you fell apart around my fingers, how you came so hard every part of me could feel the thrums of pleasure that trembled up your spine, how your cum dripped down your thighs and coated my fingers…" He brings his fingers to his nose. "Even though I washed my hands, I can still smell your sweetness on my skin."

My toes curl. My traitorous pussy instantly grows wet again. *No, no, no. I'm not falling for this. I'm not going to trust him; not again. Not after how he went out of his way to shatter my heart.*

"Why did you pretend you were engaged?"

He blows out a breath. "It's not important."

"And that's part of the problem. You think you can make decisions for me, and you don't trust me enough to tell me why you went to all that pretense. If we were really getting together again, if you really wanted me in your life, you would tell me."

He sets his jaw. "That has nothing to do with what I want for the two of us."

"That has everything to do with the kind of future you see for us."

Footsteps sound outside the bathroom, but we both ignore them.

"Also,"—I square my shoulders—"there's one more thing I—"

"There you are. I've been looking all over for you," a new voice says from the doorway.

Declan instantly moves so he's between me and the new arrival. This should be fun.

The new guy looks between us. "Solene, what are you—"

"Leave, we're busy," Declan growls without turning around.

The man hesitates. "But—"

"Didn't I tell you to leave?" Declan pivots, walks over to him, and grabs him by the collar. "You're pissing me off."

"Hey, hold on." The man looks from Declan to me, then back at Declan. "You okay, Solene?"

"Of course she's okay," Declan growls.

The man blinks. "I'd prefer to hear that from Solene."

"You heard it from me, now fuck off."

The man frowns. "Not without her."

"The fuck you mean?"

"I was just about to tell you." I walk up to them, then slide my arm through the other man's and smile widely. "Declan, meet my boyfriend."

51

Solene

"I assume that was about making him jealous?" Finn glances up at the rear-view mirror.

He's my new bodyguard, the one Rick recommended when he left. I knew there was a chance he'd report back to Declan, but Rick assured me Finn wasn't part of Declan's team. My instincts were right for he's every bit as good as Rick at his job.

"Was I that obvious?" I squeeze the bridge of my nose. *What was I thinking, putting that out there?* I hadn't meant to say it, but when Declan had assumed I was getting back together with him—just because he gave me another orgasm—something inside me insisted I push back. And the look on his face was priceless. The nerve of him, to presume I'd do his movie with him and help him with the publicity for the film.

Of course, he has a point—many points, actually. I'm looking to diversify into movies. Giorgina raised the idea with me, and while I initially disregarded the idea, the more I thought about it, the more I realized it makes sense. I mentioned it to Harry who not only supported it but also began to speak with studios about it.

Time is of the essence. I need to lock down the right role while my name is still top-of-minds for my fans. Sure, the most loyal ones won't forget about me, even if I don't release an album for a while; but much as I hate to admit it, most of them will move onto the next big thing unless I do something. And quickly.

Which means, releasing another album through my own label. I need a little time to finalize the lyrics and write new material for it. In the meanwhile, acting in a movie is perfect to buy me time, keep money coming in, and keep me alive in the public consciousness. So, his suggestion makes sense. I hunch my shoulders.

The way he assumed I'd simply fall in with his plan, acting with him —he knew it, too. And being seen together with him is exactly what's needed to keep me relevant. Argh! His suggestions are so perfect, so spot on. Then, he had to go and spoil it all by assuming I'd just agree to whatever he suggested... Suggested. Who am I kidding? It was more like an order.

And his confidence, thinking I'd comply with whatever he wants is, annoying... And hot. It's such a turn on. It made me want to agree. Made me want to drop down on my knees in front of him and ask him to have his way with me. And that innate response from deep inside me, somehow, did not shock me, and that made it worse. Not to mention, his assumption I'd change my style of dressing on stage for him. How dare he think I'd say yes to that, like a good little woman? And yet, why did I also feel a flush of heat at his possessiveness, that he doesn't want anyone else to see me dressed in such a revealing fashion? I run my fingers down my strands of hair and tug. The pain clears a swathe through the thoughts in my mind.

"To me, but he didn't realize that." Finn eases the car through the late-evening traffic.

"I'm sorry; it was a spur of the moment idea." I lock my fingers together. "I wanted to do something to unnerve him."

"And going by the shock on his face, you did."

I still remember the way Declan's jaw dropped. For a few seconds, he went silent. The dominant alphahole himself, taken by surprise. Imagine that. Then, he recovered long enough to glare down at where I had my arm linked through Finn's. He set his jaw, and a vein throbbed at his temple. His shoulders swelled, and I swear, he grew physically bigger. It's as if there's a Hulk hidden somewhere inside of him that I never sensed before. The one he seemed very close to unleashing. I knew it was time to high-tail it out of there, so I hustled

Finn out of the room. And thought we'd escaped. Except, Declan was right behind us.

"This isn't over, Solene," he growled.

I cuddled closer to Finn, then turned to glance at Declan over my shoulder—just in time to see the muscles at his jaw flex. The man was grinding his teeth so hard, it wouldn't surprise me if he cracked a molar. One can only hope. His biceps flexed. He curled his fingers into fists at his sides, and if we stayed there for one more second, I'm pretty sure a fight would have broken out.

So, I took the coward's way out. I gave Declan a mock salute—just like the one he gave me when he was on that motorcycle—and had the pleasure of seeing his eyes widen in surprise. Then I turned and ran out of there, pulling Finn along behind me. To my surprise, Declan didn't follow. To my relief, Finn didn't protest. We made it to the parking lot and out of there in minutes. And I still can't wipe the grin off of my face.

I'm safe from Declan's anger… For now. So why has my heart not stopped beating so hard? Why are my palms still damp? And why is my pussy still throbbing in reaction to how pissed off Declan was? Angry Declan is almost as hot as possessive Declan. Angry Declan means he'll throw me over his lap and spank me, and then have his way with me.

My core clenches. My panties dampen further, and I can't stop thinking of how he licked me there. He didn't come, either. His entire focus was on my pleasure. On me. On making me his. I wrap my arms about my waist. The way he made me come, then took care of me made me go weak in the knees, and in the heart. He definitely has feelings for me, even if he refuses to admit it, that *stronzo*.

"Solene, I asked you a question."

"Eh, what?" I glance up and meet Finn's eyes in the rear-view mirror.

His lips quirk. He's one fine specimen of a man, with his thick lashes, dreamy eyes, high cheekbones and broad shoulders that almost equal Declan's. He's almost too perfect. Unlike Declan's flawed countenance, that makes him so much more rugged, so much more attractive. Sadly, Finn prefers men. Not that he'd do anything for me, even if he were straight. Which is another reason why I told Declan he was my boyfriend.

"There are paps on our tail, so I'm going to try to lose them, okay?"

I glance out the window, then behind me, but all I see are rows of slowly moving cars approaching a traffic jam.

"Are you sure?"

He scowls at the side-view mirror. "That van's been tailing us since we left Harry's office."

"Shit, how did they know I was there?"

"They probably waited outside, hoping to spot someone, and then saw you."

I blow out a breath. "Do what you have to do to lose them."

He throws the car into reverse and backs up. The car behind us honks. He ignores it, then turns the steering wheel and pulls out into the next traffic lane. Brakes screech, there's more honking, and someone yells. He steps on the accelerator, and the car leaps forward as he pulls into the breakdown lane, passing rows of gridlocked cars. The traffic begins to ease. That's when he spots an opening and slides in. The car behind applies its brakes, and the driver rolls down his window, shows us the finger and yells at us. But we're in and moving.

"Jesus, you drive like a maniac."

He laughs. "There have to be some fringe benefits of being an ice-hockey player huh?"

"So why did you give that up?"

The smile vanishes from his face. "That's not a story I like to share."

"Fair enough. I get it. Some things are tough to rake up, huh?"

He nods. We drive past the next intersection and pick up speed. "So, you and Declan Beauchamp— are you getting back together?"

52

Declan

"There's no way she's getting back with you after this," Rick smirks.

"Fuck you, arsehole." I throw up my fist, but he evades me. He rams his fist into my side, and I stagger back. He follows it up by kicking my feet out from under me. I go down, manage to roll as I hit the padded floor, then spring up. He feints, and I move to the side, then land a blow to his stomach. He coughs and slides back, recovers just as fast, and hits out. I duck again, then land a punch in his shoulder. It slows him down long enough for me to strike out again. But he evades me. The two of us circle each other, panting, sweat sliding down my temples, my bare chest.

Rick bares his teeth. "For someone who's been so focused on going after what he wants, you've sure made a mess of both your career and your personal life."

Anger thrums at my temples. My guts churn. *She has a boyfriend. She has a fucking boyfriend. How didn't I know about this?* There has been no mention in the media or on her social network feeds. I'm not embarrassed to admit I've been stalking them. *No, it's not possible.*

"He can't be her boyfriend," I say through gritted teeth. I'd been too shocked by her revelation; it's the only explanation for why I let that douchebag with her leave the building still alive. That, and the fact I couldn't very well kill him in front of Solene. And kill him, I will. "I'm going to flay his skin from his flesh, then cut off his dick and feed it to him and throw him down a ravine where he'll never be found."

Rick smirks. "You checked out his credentials before I confirmed him as her security detail."

"And now, she claims he's her boyfriend." I curl my fingers into fists at my sides. "I'm going to kill him."

This time, Rick bursts out laughing. Bastard cackles like I cracked a joke.

"The fuck is wrong with you?" I leap forward, knowing he's provoking me, knowing I'm going to make a mistake, knowing I need to keep my calm so I can decide on a course of action. I know it, but that doesn't stop me from throwing up my fists. He easily sidesteps then punches my side, following it up with another. When I stagger back, he kicks my legs out, and I hit the floor.

This time, I stay down. "Fucking freestyle." I pant.

"You can say that again. Good thing your face is off limits, else I'd have knocked you out."

"Keep dreaming."

He shakes the sweat from his face, then holds out his hand. I grip it, and he hauls me to my feet. "Seriously though, what are you going to do about it?"

"What you're going to have to do is apologize to her and ask her very politely to star in your next movie." Giorgina's voice reaches me from the doorway. As one, Rick and I turn to find her gliding across the floor and toward the padded ring in the center of the gym.

"The fuck is she wearing?" Rick growls.

I take in the skirt suit she has on and shrug. "Seems fine to me."

"It's too fucking short."

"Huh?" I narrow my gaze on her, then nod. "That's what I told Solene."

"That's why she decided she was with Finn?"

"That arsewipe was your choice," I growl.

He nods. "Which is why what you said earlier, before you lost your cool and attacked, is true."

"Didn't lose my cool."

He scoffs.

"And what did I say, anyway?"

"That he can't be her boyfriend."

"Huh?" I pause. "I'm not following."

"Me neither." Giorgina walks up to the platform, then tilts up her chin. "How could you make such a mess of things?"

"For once, we agree." Rick smirks.

Giorgina flicks a glance in his direction. Her gaze sweeps over him, and her cheeks heat. For his part, Rick goes completely still. Tension coils under his muscles. Something thickens the air between them. *Jesus.* Apparently, there's something there. Something I wasn't sure I noticed before. Not that I care. This is their problem. I have enough on my fucking mind, with my woman swanning around town on another man's arm.

"The fuck are you talking about? Care to cut out the games and spit it out?" I glare at Rick.

He manages to stop eye-fucking my PR manager long enough to say, "He has a boyfriend."

"Who does?"

He tugs on the knot of the laced-up glove with his teeth, then pulls it off.

"Finn."

"The fuck is Finn?"

Despite not having taken a hit to the head, my brain cells are clearly not firing properly, for Giorgina gets it first. "Her so-called new boyfriend."

I scowl at her. "How do you know?"

"It's my job to know these things before anyone else. Also, social media." Giorgina waves her phone at me.

"And"—I turn to Rick—"he's interested in men?"

"He is," Rick confirms.

"Hmm." I unlace my gloves and drop them on the floor, before moving forward and snatching up her phone. There, on the screen, is a picture of that motherfucker Finn with his arm around Solene, shielding her from paps as they walk into a restaurant. The headline screams:

Solene with new beau. Is this the end for #Declene?

. . .

Tension grips my shoulders, and I squeeze the phone with such force the cover cracks.

Giorgina yelps. “Hey, don’t destroy my phone.”

I glare at Rick. "Either way, he’s a man and he has his arm around her."

"He was doing his job, protecting her from the paps," Rick offers.

"That’s my—" I firm my lips.

"Your?" Rick asks with great interest.

I show him my middle finger, and he smirks while shaking his head. "Can’t believe you fell for that."

"I had no reason to believe otherwise." I lean over the ropes and hand the device back to her.

"Guess you really pissed her off, huh?" Giorgina narrows her gaze on me.

"Fuck!" I unwind the boxing tape from around my fingers, then hurl it to the ground. "Fucking fuck."

Rick and Giorgina exchange glances.

"What?" I snap.

Rick rolls his shoulders, then shakes out his arms. "You’re not going to like this."

"Spit it out, man."

"Giorgina and I spoke—"

I scoff. "For the first time, I suppose.”

He flushes a little, and when I glance at Giorgina, she looks away.

Apparently, they’ve spoken more than just about me. Hmm. The two of them definitely have the hots for each other. Again, not my concern.

"Go on," I jerk my chin in his direction.

"You need to speak with Solene," he finally murmurs.

"You think?"

"And ask her to—ah—"

"You need to ask her to get back in a relationship with you," Giorgina bursts out.

"What makes you think I haven’t asked?"

"A fake relationship."

I shake my head. "Hold on. I need to ask her to pretend we’re in a relationship?”

"Exactly so."

I squat down and tug on my hair. "You do realize the two of us have a checkered past when it comes to fake relationships? We met when I pretended to be engaged to her sister. Then I pretended to be engaged to someone else in order to make her hate me. And clearly, I succeeded all too well, for now she's pretending to be in a relationship with someone else."

"But you've never faked being in love with each other," Giorgina points out.

I lower my hands. "That's because I don't need to pretend."

She stiffens. So does Rick.

"So, you're finally admitting that—"

"I love her? Of course I do. Why the hell else would I turn my life upside down?"

Giorgina's features soften. "Aww, that's so sweet."

I wince. "Not the word I'd use in connection with me."

"Beneath all that bluster, you're a softie. Unlike—" She stabs her thumb in Rick's direction.

"Hold on, what do I have to do with this?"

"You provide an interesting benchmark, is all," she sniffs.

"I beg your pardon?" He scowls.

"Oh, my god, can you pull out that stick from up your ass and advise your friend?" she cries.

Rick looks taken aback. "What did I do?"

"Nothing, and that's the problem." She stamps her foot. My normally calm and collected PR manager actually stamps her foot. "As for you, Declan. You're my client, we've worked together for many years, and I think I know you well enough to say you can't afford to lose her. You need to find a way to convince her to take you back and you two need to do this movie. You need each other. #Declene is magic. Break it up, and there's nothing."

Turning, she walks out.

In the silence that follows, I lay back on the boxing ring floor and stare up at the ceiling. Not that there are any answers there.

Rick leans over me. "I wouldn't agree with that women if it were a life and death situation, but in this case, I'm afraid she's right."

I groan. "The fuck am I gonna do now?"

Rick throws himself on the floor next to me. "What's the one thing that will make her agree?"

53

Solene

"If he thinks that's going to make me agree to this utterly stupid, asinine scheme, he's completely wrong." I prop my hands on my hips and scowl at Harry. My manager's wearing a collared polo today, which stretches over his portly girth. Paired with his jeans, which are freshly ironed—enough that they have a crease running down the center of each pant leg—and his brand-new, still-white sneakers, he resembles a cuddly koala bear. Only thing is, I've heard him negotiate on the phone with labels and tour operators, and the man can turn into a shark in an instant.

"And what made you invite me to a golf course to have this discussion? More to the point, why did I accept this invitation?" I glance around at the miles of green, the undulating hills, the pool of water, and beyond that, the tree line. Not that I have anything against greenery. I love greenery… When it's created by Mother Nature. Give me overgrown gardens over curated flower beds, wood mulch-filled allotments over manicured lawns, and untamed pines that soar to the skies, instead of rising-to-the-same-height eucalyptuses. I sigh. Guess I'm home sick.

When I left Napoli, I never thought I'd want to visit the city again. It's not that I miss my family—other than my sister. It's more that sense of belonging that I yearn for. The one I find now with my friends in London. The little time I've spent with Penny, Isla and Mira is the only time I've felt like I have someone in my corner. Sure, I talk to them often on the phone, and I visit London whenever I can, but it's not the same as hanging out with them on weekends.

When I first came to LA, I had Declan. Even if it was for only a few days, he was there, and his presence helped me acclimatize to a new city. Then I was touring, before coping with the fallout of the tour. Now that I'm trying to create again, my mind is free to wander, and it doesn't help that it keeps returning to him.

Someone clears their throat. I shoot Finn a sideways glance. He's standing to the side with my golf bag parked in front of him. His lips are quirked and the look in his eyes indicates he wants to say something.

I narrow my gaze on him, and he waggles his eyebrows. Our relationship since he came on board has developed into that of siblings. Finn's one of those people I felt immediately comfortable with. With Rick, I ensured there was a distance because he was on Declan's team. Finn, though, is the kind of brother I'd have wanted Diego to be. Tears prick the backs of my eyes. Jesus, why am I crying about Diego now? When he died, I was shocked, sure. But then, I only felt an overwhelming sense of relief.

Now, for some reason, I'm remembering the time when Olivia, Diego and I were kids. When our father was alive, and we were a family. When Diego was happy to play with me and Olivia, despite being older than the both of us. He'd spent hours attending our tea-parties and allowing us to pull his hair into a ponytail, and even letting us apply ma's cosmetics on his face. This was before he took his role as the heir of the Camorra. When our father died, everything changed. Overnight, Olivia and I lost our childhoods, and Diego became the man of the family, taking his duties very seriously. He, too, lost a father and went through his own journey, which was not kind to him. It's why he was so determined to make an arranged match for Olivia—before she reminded him she had our father's blessing and took off to pursue acting—and then he focused his attention on me. It's why I was so scared of him, enough that I pretended Declan had forced himself on me when Diego walked into the room. And then, everything went to shit.

Somehow, I can trace the reason for my standing on this golf course in LA, arguing with Harry about the scheme he's outlined to me, to the day I lost a parent. It put things in perspective. It doesn't matter what you try to control, life has a way of taking you where it wants you to go, and you have to make the most of the situation.

"You should consider what he said." Finn folds his arms across his chest. "I'm your security detail; it's not my place to voice my opinion, but"—he raises a shoulder—"I think it might help you get another perspective from a friend."

"And that would be you?"

His lips curve. "I hope so. In the months since I joined your team, I've watched you work hard. I've seen you go from being at the top of your game to someone who's back at the starting line. Such highs and lows are what get to people. Most cannot cope with it and pack up and leave."

I chuckle. "Your point being?"

"You've managed to stay level-headed through the ups and downs. You were happy when you were riding the charts. And you picked yourself up quickly when your concerts had to be canceled. You have a good head on your shoulders, Solene. You have the strength to cope with the highs and lows. You're in this for the long run."

"But?" I lower my chin to my chest. "There's a but there somewhere, isn't it?"

He leans forward on the balls of his feet. "But I'm with Harry on this one."

"You are?" Harry bursts out. "Can you convince her, please, that this is the way forward? She must accept Declan's offer. This movie is going to be the re-launching pad for the both of you."

"Do you really believe that?" I turn on him.

He opens his mouth, and I stab my finger at him. "No, really. No manager talk. Don't blow smoke up my ass. Do you think this movie will even get made, let alone, be a hit?"

"Yes and yes." Harry nods with so much enthusiasm the long hairs he plasters down over the bald spot on his head come loose and fan about. A giggle wells up my throat. My lips quiver. I glance at Finn who flashes me a humorous look.

"It's your call, Solene." He raises a shoulder.

"You think I should do it?"

"I think you should follow your instinct."

Somehow, that's worse. I'm not quite sure what my instinct is telling me at this stage. I place the golf ball on the tee, then widen my stance, bending my knees slightly. I raise my golf-club, hit the ball, and it whizzes up through the air, beyond the body of water, and toward the tree line.

"Whoa, and you said you've never played golf before?"

I shake my head. "I'm a quick study, though."

"Let me go get the ball." Finn turns toward the golf cart, but I stop him. "I'll get it."

"You sure?" He turns. "I can do it."

"Nah, you hang out here with Dirty Harry, I'll get it. Also, I can do with the exercise." And with time out to think about my options.

I jog toward the tree line. I hear Finn say something to Harry, then their conversation fades. A slight breeze ruffles my hair, and birdsong wafts over me. The rustle of leaves grows louder, and I enter the small grove of trees. I slow to a stop, searching the grass. I increase the perimeter of my seeking eyes until I reach the shrubs. I take in my surroundings again. Nope, can't see the ball. I blow out a breath, then head for the bushes, push aside the leaves, and forage in the undergrowth.

The hair on the back of my neck rises. A shiver runs down my spine. I straighten, looking around. I'm in a small clearing. A gust of wind blows the hair across my face. I push it aside, then commence searching through the brush. A flash of white peeks out through the vegetation on my right. "There you are!" I bend down, reach for it, but I can't touch it. "Oh, whatever." I drop to my knees and crawl through the scrub. My fingers stroke against the shell of the ball. I lean in closer, snatching it up. "Gotcha."

"I'd say so."

"What the—?" I fall face-forward into the greenery, then flip over onto my back. I tilt my head up, meet the gaze of the man standing in front. "What are you doing here?"

54

Declan

"I just need a minute of your time."

Her features flush. Her lips flatten. She makes no move to rise up. "I don't want to talk to you."

"But I need to speak with you."

She tips up her chin, "We can't always get what we want or need. Time you realized that, Mr. Heartthrob-Wannabe."

I arch an eyebrow. "You've been stalking my social media feeds again, Rabbit."

"I fucking hate it when you call me by that name."

"That's not what you said the last time I made you come."

Her cheeks flush. Her lips tremble. Those emerald eyes of hers flash with a mixture of anger and helplessness and lust. Oh yeah, she can try to deny it, but her body recognizes its master. I stalk over to stand over her, then hold out my hand.

She glances at it, then at me. Juts out her lower lip in that expression which hints at that stubbornness in her. The one I noticed the very first time I met her, when she was trying to fight off those men on the beach in Napoli. We've come a long way since then.

I've faced my inner demons, had to find that core of resilience in me, had to challenge the devils that pre-occupied me during the time I was fighting preconceived notions of what a leading man in Hollywood should look like. I broke down barriers—I was fortunate to have the money and circumstances on my side. And it's one of the reasons I'm attracted to her.

Like me, she's had to overcome her impediment and break free of the situation holding her back. I always knew all she needed was the chance to thrive. To share her voice with the world, and they'd see what I recognized. That she's special, unique, and her voice is a window to the beauty inside of her. Talented, alluring, and magnificent. She holds people's attention because she's stunning, exquisite, ravishing, bewitching, and all mine.

Only I know her hidden insecurities. That she's sick with nerves before every concert. That she yearns to break free of all constraints. That she hates being tied down. She's a free spirit, my Rabbit. And also, an old soul. She has that innate goodness inside of her which makes her want to trust people, which makes her believe the best in them. Which is why, despite the fact that her brother never allowed her to embrace her talent, she came to his rescue when I began to beat him up that day in her room. It's what made me stop and led to his men thrashing me instead. And I hated her for so long for that...

But now I understand she did it because it's the kind of person she is. Loyal, tender-hearted and caring. It's why she accompanied me to LA when I gave her the chance. That, and the fact that she loves me. Or at least, she loved me before I shattered her heart. And now, it's up to me to make it up to her. To give her what she wants... What she doesn't know she needs... Yet.

"Take my hand, Rabbit." I lower my voice to a hush. Narrow my gaze. I infuse just enough dominance into my tone, and she shivers. Her pupils dilate, a tell-tale sign she's turned on. Could I bring her to orgasm with just my voice? Hmm... something to try out.

"Take my hand. Now."

She grabs my palm. I haul her to her feet, then reach down and lock my fingers with hers.

Her gaze widens, and her lips part. She swallows, leans forward, I hold up my hand, with the white golf ball locked between my fingers. I throw it over my shoulder and take a step forward, until the tips of my boots brush against her sneakers. My chest brushes against her breasts, her nipples standing at attention, little buttons of delight waiting for my delectation. The thickness at my groin stabs into her belly, and she shudders, then tilts her head back so her gaze is fixed on mine. I tuck a lock of her gorgeous hair behind her ear. The pulse at the base of her throat speeds up. I cup her cheek. She draws in a breath, then turns her face into my palm. She kisses the base of my thumb, and my heartbeat grows erratic.

"I'm sorry, baby. So sorry for what I put you through."

She stills then turns her face to stare at my chest.

"When I'm around you, I don't think straight. And when I'm away from you, I'm so preoccupied by thoughts of you, I don't think straight anyway."

She smiles slightly, which is a plus, eh?

"I know you don't want to be with me anymore."

She scoffs.

"That possibly you don't trust me anymore."

"Whatever gave you that idea, I wonder?"

"That you don't believe me when I say being together is exactly what we both need at this stage."

She holds up a hand. "You can't charm me into wanting a relationship with you."

"I agree."

She blinks. "You do?"

I nod. "It's why I'm proposing that we pretend we're together."

"Eh?" She peers up at me. "So, we—"

"Are seen together. Which will affect an instant boost to both our profiles. Meanwhile, you accept the role in my film, and the publicity from our joint sightings is going to give us both the hit we need."

"The hit you need, you mean?" She scowls.

"The one that's going to give you the money you need to launch your own music label."

She purses her lips. "This is an insane scheme. Besides, I have a boyfriend."

"Finn's your security detail. Also, he's interested in men."

She flushes.

I curl my lips. "Nice try, though."

"Did it make you jealous?"

"What do you think?"

"I think you were shocked to realize I have options."

I lower my hand and curl my fingers into fists. *Your only option is to prostrate yourself on the floor. Back toward me, butt in the air, part your arse cheeks and take everything I give you. Your only option is to bend for me. To become my willing slave. The sweet pussy that I'll bury myself in whenever I want, and you'll receive every drop of my cum and be happy about it.*

I draw in a breath, another, and force my heartbeat to slow down. To disperse the adrenaline that threatens to overwhelm my blood flow.

"Your option, if you don't accept my proposal, is to spend years trying to find your way back into the mainstream."

She stiffens. A myriad of expressions flits across her features. First shock, then hurt, followed by that familiar jut of her chin, which tells me she's going to be stubborn about sticking to her position on this. How I fucking love her obstinacy. How I wish she'd give in this once?

She tosses her head. "Maybe I don't want the kind of popularity I enjoyed. Maybe I'm happy doing this slowly, at my own pace."

"And risk being forgotten by your own fans?"

"They won't forget me." She sets her lips together, but there's a spark of doubt in her eyes. *Good.*

"Sure, there'll be those who wait for your next album. But you and I both know, unless you find a way to stay in the headlines, it's going to be an uphill struggle for you."

She rubs her temple. "Why do you have to be so logical?"

I smirk. "Just one of my many superpowers, baby."

She scoffs, "If you're trying to convince me—"

"The beating at the hands of your brother's men led me to the kink lifestyle."

She stills. "Excuse me?"

I step back from her, not because I want to put distance between us, but because it's the only way I can avoid being distracted by her beauty. It's the only way I can tell her what I should have shared a long time ago—rather than gaze at her beauty which, to be honest, would be my preference.

"After they beat me up, Knight and I got on a plane back home—"

"Wait, Knight was with you?" She frowns.

"He saved my life. If it weren't for him, I might not have made it that night."

She looks stricken. "I'm so sorry about that. I had no idea it was that bad. I mean, I know your face was scarred"—she glances at my forehead—"but to think you may have—"

I hold up my hand. "The wounds didn't seem that bad, but by the time the flight landed in London, I had collapsed. They rushed me to the hospital. They discovered I had internal bleeding. They had to operate on me urgently. I was in an induced coma for a week."

"Oh my god." She pushes her knuckles into her mouth. "Why didn't you tell me?"

I raise a shoulder. "Seemed beside the point. The damage had been done. I came out of the coma and needed to have therapy, and I recovered all bodily functions. However..." I look away, then back at her. "It would seem, the blow to my forehead resulted in something called Emotional Blunting."

She lowers her hand. "What does that mean?"

"It's when your ability to feel emotions and express them gets restrained."

"You're saying your ability to feel emotions is—"

"Dulled. It makes it difficult for me to identify what emotion I'm feeling. It makes me appear as if I don't care about things or other people, but that's not true. I simply have difficulty showing it. I can feel the emotions, but often, I'm unable to connect with them or recognize them, so I'm unable to express them."

She stares at me, then realization dawns. "And you're an actor. Your job depends on emoting, on being able to bring dialogues to life by showing emotions."

I laugh, and the sound is toneless. "You can imagine how much of a shock that was. It took me a year, and seeing several doctors, to get a diagnosis. Meanwhile, the inability to understand what was happening to me, combined with the scar on my forehead which, even after plastic surgery changed the way I looked and began limiting my roles, meant I was spiraling into depression.

"Knight and Cade were there for me. They saw me through it. I refused to meet them for months, and it was Knight who showed up at my place and pulled me out of my funk. He forced me to see a therapist who helped me through the aftermath. I learned how to understand the emotions I'm feeling and react appropriately. How to translate the emotions into expressions others can understand."

"Oh..." She opens and shuts her mouth. "I wish you'd told me that earlier."

"I didn't want to share what I went through. Doing that seemed like it would break down yet another barrier between us, and I wasn't sure I was ready."

"But now, you are?"

I nod.

She takes a step forward, and I'm sure she's going to touch me, but then she seems to get ahold of herself. "And now you're able to emote on screen?"

"That's the easier part. It's more of a science when you're playing a role. You tap into specific emotions inside yourself and embody them. The writers give you the words to say, and that's why it was much more straightforward to rewire my brain. Turns out, giving voice to your expressions with people in real life is far more difficult to retrain because you have to put your feelings into words yourself. I've been largely successful, though I can't say I'm completely the same as I was earlier."

She nods slowly. "That makes so much sense. I often wondered why you felt different—harder to reach, more removed from your feelings. I wondered why you often came across as unemotional, why you didn't ever share how you felt about me and our relationship. I put it down to growing older and the experiences you faced getting where you are, and some of it down to your being a man. But now that you've told me what really happened, it's so much easier for me to connect the dots."

"That incident with your brother's men did change my life, and for a long time I was bitter about it. I wanted revenge. And when I saw you again that day at the restaurant, I knew it was my opportunity. Except, somewhere along the way, I realized it wasn't your fault, either. And I must admit, it left me unsure of what to do next.

"For so long, the need to avenge what happened to me was a driving force in my life. And then, it wasn't there anymore. Instead, I turned my attention to my career. It's all I'd had for such a long time, so it was easy to fall back into it. Which is why, when the funding for my movie fell through, I decided to put in my own money. When that wasn't enough, I approached the head of the Bratva for help and struck the deal with him. When I broke off the engagement, Niko wasn't happy."

She frowns. "The Bratva are dangerous—as much as the Mafia, if not more."

I hold up my hand. "He's still investing in the movie."

"He is?" She stares at me.

"I explained the situation to Niko. He's not happy, but he agreed to go through with the funding. I owe him and he's going to call me on it, but I'll cross that bridge when I come to it."

She pales. "This is insane."

"One needs to do insane things to fulfill one's dream. It also means

this movie needs to be a hit, at any cost. Hence—" I look at her meaningfully. "I need you in the film."

She rubs at her temple. "Ugh, I don't even know what to say to that."

"Say yes, and that you'll make a joint statement with me to the press. The resulting publicity will help the launch of the movie."

She shakes her head. "After everything you told me, it's not like I can refuse you, either."

I nod slowly. I'd been counting on that. *Am I using what her brother did to me to coerce her to buy into my plan? Yes. Am I an opportunistic bastard? You bet. Am I doing it because it's the only way to get her to be by my side? Abso-fucking-lutely. And I don't regret it one bit.* "There's one more thing."

"O-k-a-y?" She eyes me warily.

"You saw me at the Club—"

She cuts her palm through the air. "And realized you were a Dominant."

I allow my lips to quirk. "The spicy books sure are increasing the range of your vocabulary, Rabbit."

"You trying to put off what you were going to confess?"

I blow out a breath. *Am I that transparent? Am I truly deflecting? Why am I unable to share who I truly am with her? Am I that worried about losing her? Yes, I am. But I owe it to her.* If I have any hope of a relationship with her, I need to tell her what my expectations are from her. Telling her about my preferences, while suggesting we embark on a fake relationship. Yep, I recognize the contradiction. But I have to work with what I have. I've gotta take this slow, gotta find a way for her to be with me and not turn me down completely. I shift my weight from foot to foot, then square my shoulders.

"I am, actually. I told you already about my reduced capacity to feel emotions. Indulging my kinks helped to amplify what I was feeling, so I could differentiate my emotions better, and that aided me in recognizing them. It's why the BDSM lifestyle played an important part in my recovery."

She frowns. "Not sure what you're saying."

I widen my stance. "The lifestyle helped to intensify my response to sex, so I could actually feel something. Kink was the only route to actually sensing something, other than the blank flatness inside me. During the time I was depressed, I began frequenting BDSM clubs. It helped me feel. It kept me going. And even after I relearned how to recognize and express my emotions, I stayed with it. When I am a Dominant, I have control over my emotions in a way I can't find in any other part of my life. It's why being a Dominant is more the real me than any other role I might play in life."

She surveys my features. "So, when you're being Dominant, you're…"

"I'm at my most genuine. It's the only time I'm being truly me."

She blinks. "Hold on, did you just confess to another weakness?"

"My only weakness is you, Solene."

She swallows. "I'm not sure how to react when you do away with that boss-man facade you normally wear."

I laugh. "I like that name, but I prefer you call me Sir or Master."

Her breathing grows choppy. She's aroused. Despite telling her how much kink means to me, how much the lifestyle is a part of me, she's not running away from me. She's not disgusted or scared—maybe a little scared, but that's good. It means she's present and aware, and that's important for what I'm going to propose. It's what gives me the courage to say, "I prefer you sink to your knees every time I enter a room."

Her cheeks heat.

"I prefer that you're naked, that you widen the space between your knees, hold open your arse cheeks, show me all your holes, and ask me which is my preference."

The pulse at the base of her throat increases in tempo.

I prefer that you take your orders from me, you leave your choices to me. I want to become your entire world. I want to hide you away from everyone else and protect you and care for your every need and show you how beautiful it can be between us, is what I want to say; but I love her independent spirit. It's what makes her who she is, so all I say is, "I want you to do as I ask of you, when I ask it of you, except when you're on stage."

Her pupils dilate, and a trembling grips her. She stares at me, unable to look away, and if I'm not mistaken, she's aroused.

"Are you turned on, Little Rabbit?"

55

Solene

"I am." I nod. And for once, I don't stammer, even though my heart's soaring like the high-pitched tone of a soprano in my chest.

He seems somewhat taken aback, then his eyes flash. "I want you to submit to the lifestyle with me. I want to be able to wake up with you and fall asleep with my cock buried in your sweet, hot pussy. I want to play with the rosette between your arse cheeks until you're able to take me there. I want to fill all your holes, Rabbit."

Liquid heat sears my veins.

"I want to look into your eyes as you come for me. Want to bend you over and fuck your pussy, then take you from behind."

Sweat beads the valley between my breasts. My core clenches.

"I want to make love to you until you whine. Want to shag you until you scream my name. Want to feel the shape of my cock embraced by the column of your throat as you swallow. I want to—"

He bends until he's eye level with me. "Want to show you how it is to be dominated by me, worn out by my demands on your body, floating high on the endorphins that comes from release, shattered as you're completely consumed by me."

A thousand little fires ignite under my skin. I'm so wet, I can feel my cum trickling down my inner thigh. My breasts hurt, my nipples so hard I could surely drill through glass.

"Declan, what are you doing to me?"

He leans in and pushes his forehead against mine. "Nothing I don't want to do to myself."

We stare at each other for a few seconds, then footsteps approach on the other side of the tree line. "Solene?"

"It's Finn." I begin to pull away, but he grips the tops of my arms and holds me in place.

"So, what do you say Rabbit? You willing to give this relationship a chance?"

"You mean the fake relationship or the Dom-sub one?"

"Both."

I glance between his eyes, seeing the intent in his. The seriousness. The helplessness. He's not sure I'm going to agree. Oh, he's trying to portray a confident front, as evidenced by the set of his shoulders, the firmness of his jaw, the steadiness of his hold on me, but his gaze gives him away. Those startling blue eyes are so dark, they seem like clouds before a storm. His grasp tightens, and a gasp escapes my lips. "You're hurting me."

"It's only the start."

"If this is you trying to convince me to agree, then—"

"Is it working?"

Before I can answer, there's a crashing through the undergrowth, then Finn emerges in the small clearing.

"Solene, you okay?"

Neither Declan nor I look in his direction.

"Solene?" He moves forward and Declan holds up his hand. "She's fine. You, on the other hand, are going to miss a few teeth if you come closer."

Finn stiffens. "She's my—"

"Principal, and you're her security detail. I'm aware."

"So, you know I can't leave until she assures me she's fine."

I draw in a breath, then slowly nod. "I'm good."

"Are you sure? I can stay," Finn murmurs.

Declan's jaw tics. His left eyelid twitches. A sure sign that he's pissed off. Funny how, even after all these months apart, I'm so tuned into this man. He opens his mouth, but I shake my head, "I'm good, Finn. Honestly. But I'd appreciate some privacy."

Finn hesitates, then turns and leaves.

In the silence that follows, Declan glares at me. "Don't fucking say his name again," he growls. A muscle pops at his temple. His shoulders seem to swell. He's doing that impersonation of a very angry alpha male, which is both a little scary and also a turn on.

My nipples harden into points of desire, and my pussy clenches. And still, he doesn't move. He's only getting angrier by the second. He opens his mouth, probably, to chew me out, so I do the only thing I can think of to shut him up. I close the distance between us and touch my lips to his. He stiffens but doesn't move. I share his breath. Draw in that masculine scent of his that I've carried in my memories. His eyes are still open, and I stare into those silver sparks hidden between the darker flickers in his irises. Mesmerizing, enthralling, drawing me in.

I sway forward and my nipples brush his chest. His shoulders bunch, and his chest planes seem to toughen until they seem to be carved from concrete. My mouth dries, my throat closes, and still, he holds me spell-bound. He seems to be carved out of stone, but his lips—oh, his lips are so soft. I bite down on his mouth, and a jolt shoots through his body. A small sound of satisfaction escapes me. I lick the drop of blood that beads his lip, and a growl vibrates from him. The tension leaps off of his body, the air around us so thick with our emotions, our lust, the absolute need to immerse in each other, my head spins.

"Declan," I whisper. Not sure what I want. Or what I want to say. Or what I'm waiting for. His approval? His permission? His orders? Why do I get such an unhealthy satisfaction from wanting to please him? And why do I keep resisting this innate urge to satisfy him?

"Declan?" I swallow, and his gaze intensifies. The tendons of his throat pop in relief. He looks like he's struggling with an internal quandary. Like he wants to throw me on the ground and bury himself between my legs. But at the same time, he's holding himself back from touching me. And it's because I sense that internal clash, because I also sense his confusion, the fact that he's baring himself to me for the first time—all of it causes a softness to invade my chest. I raise my palm and cup his cheek.

"Don't," he says through gritted teeth.

"Don't touch you?"

"Not until you tell me if you're going to agree to my stipulations."

"So, you want me to plunge right back into a relationship—"

"A fake relationship," he growls.

"A fake relationship, but a Dom/sub arrangement that's not fake?"

His eyes open and he glares at me. Whatever had been troubling him a few seconds ago has been resolved, and once more, he's the hard, confident man he's grown into. "That's what I said."

I frown. "So let me get this right, we're going to be fucking, and spending most of our time together but to the world you still want us to portray that we're in a fake relationship?"

"Exactly," he nods.

"O-k-a-y, since our relationship is 'fake'—" I make air-quotes with my fingers, "Does that mean I'm allowed to fuck other men?"

"Fuck no."

I throw my hands up. "So how, exactly, is this a fake relationship?"

"Because at the core of our relationship is our Dom/ sub agreement which is transactional. There are no other feelings or emotions involved except for my need to control you."

"You mean, you want me to hand over control to you?" I glance away.

He pinches my chin and applies enough pressure, so I have no choice but to turn to look at him.

"I want to show you who I am," He looks between my eyes. "Want you to trust me enough to give up your choices to me. Want you to believe in me enough to let me pleasure you and satisfy you and show you how it could be between us."

I take a step back, and he lets me go. I miss his touch already, which is as crazy as this so-called arrangement he's proposing. I lock my fingers, then set my jaw. "I left behind my childhood home and my family because I never again wanted someone else to tell me what to do. I moved away from everything familiar because I needed to be in control of my destiny. And yet, you want me to give up all of that to you? You want me to give up my power to you?"

"You're wrong."

"Oh?" I scowl.

"It's me giving up my power to you in this arrangement!"

I scoff. "And how is that?"

"By handing over choice to me, you are charging me with taking care of you. You're charging me with overseeing your welfare, your pleasure, your needs. You're placing the onus of your wellbeing on me. You're landing the task of steering your happiness on me. It's a responsibility I take very seriously. To ensure you're satisfied with my every decision, every action I take on your behalf. And underlining it is the fact that you have the power to say no. You can use your safe word anytime, and I will stop."

I open my mouth, but he raises his hand. "And if I push things to the extent that you use the safe word, it means I've failed you. It means I didn't gauge your requirements correctly. It means I'm not delivering to your expectations in which case, you can leave. So, the onus is on me to deliver. I may be in charge, but it's you who has the power, not me."

I trace his features, trying to understand everything he just outlined.

"So outside of when I'm performing, you're in control?"

He nods.

"Can I have friends? Can I go out and do things without you?"

"Sure you can, as long as I agree to it."

"Eh? That sounds like I have no freedom at all."

"If you want more freedom, all you have to do is ask, and we'll discuss it until we reach an agreement that works for both of us."

I blink. "You make it sound so easy."

"It is, as long as we keep communicating. Also, you'll find, little Rabbit, the intense pleasure and the multiple orgasms you derive from our arrangement will more than make up for your perceived lack of free will."

Madonna Mia, he said the O-word, and my pussy instantly dampened. Is there a direct connection between the filthy words he spews and my cunt, or what? And I must admit, the confidence with which he handles my body, the way he makes me come, how he touches me, holds me, caresses me, punishes me... All of it is something I miss. Something I crave. Something I want in my life. The pressures of being in the public eye means I constantly have to make decisions about what to say and do. To have the freedom not to in my private life, to give up that choice to him, knowing he'll make the right choice for me... is ... Freeing. Even if I can't admit that aloud... Yet.

I fold my arms across my chest. "And you won't direct what I wear when I'm on stage?"

A muscle over his jawline tics. The pulse at his temple picks up speed. Also, he's doing that whole gritting-his-teeth-with-such-force-that-he's-going-to-crack-his-molar thing. Anger vibrates off of him, and the atmosphere seems to close in on me. It's a little frightening but also, so hot. I squeeze my thighs together.

Of course his gaze drops to the delta between my legs. Ugh, now he knows even his anger has the effect of turning me on. I hop from foot to foot, and that's when he raises his gaze to mine. "Okay," he growls.

"Okay?" I tilt my head. Then because I can't resist the urge to push at his control further, I ask: "So you're okay with my wearing clothes of *my* choice on stage?"

He nods then makes that growling sound at the back of his throat, the one that seems to arrow straight to my core and makes me drench my panties further.

"So, I can wear the dress I had on the last time we met? The one you said I should only wear at home for you?"

He looks like he's going to refuse, then slowly dips his head. "On one condition."

56

Declan

She's agreed this far. At least, in principle, she's not against the Dom/sub arrangement which, I'll be honest, is what I worry about more than the fake relationship. The fake connection between us which could help rescue my career... and hers. And it's important her future is secure. For the first time since I embarked on this journey of becoming the top-billed actor in Hollywood, my goals don't matter.

And why was I so keen on that objective anyway? Was it to get the approval of my father? He's never begrudged me my dream, but somewhere deep inside, I've always felt I'd let him down. Like he views my career as frivolous.

Sure, my brother Arpad is running the company on behalf of my father. And neither of them have ever compelled me or guilt-tripped me into feeling I shouldn't pursue my own dreams, but I've always felt I was being disloyal to my family by striking out and wanting to make it on my own.

In that way, she and I are similar. We left behind everything known and wanted to be the masters of our own destinies. Only... I want more. I want her sighs, her acceptance, her consent... Also, her defiance and her strength to hold her own against me. I want to show her how much pleasure I can wring from her body. I want her submission. I want her. More than I've ever wanted anything in my life. More than the success I've craved, more than the adulation from my fans, more even, than the recognition of my peers... And coming from an actor, that's something. We are narcissistic, self-focused, and obsessed with ourselves. I'll do anything to feed my ego... Or rather, I would have done anything to feed my ego...

Until I met her. Now, I want her pleasure, her orgasm, her comfort, her love... I'm focused on her gratification. Obsessed by thoughts of how to fulfill her. Of how to ensure she enjoys this new association between us. I'll do anything to feed her rapture. To stoke that craving I've sensed in her. I'll set the world on fire if it means I can seduce her into submission.

"Declan?"

Her voice cleaves a path through the noise in my head. I zero in on her, and everything else fades. I go down on my knees and bring her hands to my lips. I kiss her fingers, then pull out a ring and slide it onto her finger.

She stills. "Oh my god, what are you doing?"

"Something I should have done a long time ago."

"B-b-b-but, that's an—"

"Engagement ring, to make our relationship seem genuine this time around. We've come together and apart so many times, this is what sets our connection apart this time. So the press believes it."

She flutters her hand this way and that, her gaze fixed on the ring. She hasn't taken it off, so that's a start.

Her lips part. "It's platinum." She glances at the rabbit engraved on top with an emerald set into it, and when she bites down on her lower lip, I know she likes it. She looks over at the tiny figurines on her bracelet, then at the markings engraved into the ring. The light reflects off the tiny emeralds set around the perimeter of the band. She blinks, then swallows. "Are th-those symbols etched into the ring?"

I nod. "One each for the ten shows you missed and for which I couldn't send you charms."

She rotates the ring on her finger. "A cloverleaf, a dolphin, a rainbow, a ladybug, a horseshoe, a dreamcatcher, a key, a ladder, a jellyfish and—"

"A shooting star."

She swallows, then glances at her bracelet where the twenty charms I sent her before each of the twenty shows she performed are attached.

"And that's not all."

She tilts her head. "There's more?"

"I have another gift for you."

She holds up her hand sporting my ring. "I haven't said I'm accepting this one."

"Aren't you?"

She stares at her ring, her gaze contemplative. "And it's all for show?"

I narrow my gaze. "You don't think I want to actually get engaged to you?"

"Of course not," she scoffs.

"And you want to explore the dynamics of our Dom/sub relationship." It's not a question. I know she does. It's written on her face. Whether she accepts it aloud or not—her parted lips, the flush on her features, the dilation of her pupils—all of it indicates she's curious about what this arrangement entails.

"Turn around."

"Excuse me?" She scowls.

"Turn. Around. Rabbit," I say in a low voice that has enough edge to it that she knows I'm serious. She hesitates, then slowly turns her back to me.

I pull off the sweatshirt I'm wearing and spread it out it in front of her. Then I place my hand on her shoulder and apply enough pressure, so she sinks to her knees—her tender skin protected from the dirt by the cloth.

"Unhook your shorts and shove them down," I order.

A shiver grips her. But she pushes her shorts down to her knees.

"Now, bend over on your hands and knees."

She instantly complies. *Fuck me, the sight of her bent over, revealing her panties-covered butt drains the blood to my groin.* I reach over, squeeze her arse cheeks, and a whimper escapes her. The sound goes straight to my head. My balls tighten. My heart stutters. Only she has a direct link to my heart and my cock. And I need to finish what I set out to do before I lose control and take her right here. Which is not how I want our first time together after our time apart to be. There's time for that. Time for her to want me so much, it'll be her begging me to fuck her. Until such time, I'm going to do my best to get her there. I yank down her panties, and she gasps.

"What are you doing?" She glances around. "We're in the open."

"Relax, Rabbit, this will take only a minute."

I pull a velvet box from my pocket, and slide out a tiny, cone-shaped device. From my other pocket, a tube that I squeeze into the valley between her arse cheeks.

"Whoa!" She clenches down. "What the hell are you doing?"

I glare at her. "You can always say no and walk away right now."

She narrows her gaze.

"What's it gonna be, Rabbit? You going to stay or leave?"

She mumbles under her breath.

My lips twist. "I didn't hear you."

"I said, I'm staying, you *pezzo di—*" She gasps as I push the plug into the rosette between her butt cheeks.

"What the—" She flinches, then bears down on the intrusion. "What did you do?"

"Does it hurt?"

She shakes her head slowly.

"Is it uncomfortable?"

"How do you think it feels?"

"I think that's an easy fit compared to what's coming."

She gapes at me. "I can't believe you just said that."

"What're you gonna do about it, little Rabbit?" I palm the growing tent between my legs, and her gaze drops there. I massage myself through the fabric of my pants, and she draws in a sharp breath.

"What're you doing?" she says in a breathless voice.

"No more questions." I pull out a tissue, clean her up, then tug up her panties. I stuff the soiled paper back in my pocket before pulling up her shorts. "You may zip yourself up now."

She does so, then jumps up and around. "You're going to leave that thing in there?"

"It's for your own good." I smirk.

"How the hell is something stuck up my *culo* a good thing?"

"How else am I going to stretch your tight little hole so when I finally take you there you can accommodate all of me?"

57

Solene

I gape at him. An expression I, apparently, seem to wear a lot around this... this... complicated, frustrating, sexy as hell, alphahole. "B-but... It's distracting."

"You'll get used to it."

I pout. "It's... weird. And unnatural. And what is it with your obsession with anal anyway?"

"What's not to like about it? It's your tightest hole. It's forbidden. Besides, you're still a virgin there."

"Technically, that little thingy you stuck in me is there before you."

"Technically, that little thingy, as you say so eloquently, is only a quarter of the way in."

I gulp. A bead of sweat slides down my temple. "You're trying to scare me, aren't you?"

His smirk widens. "Am I succeeding?"

"Of course not." Not that I'd ever admit if I were, which I'm not. Okay, I might be a little. But I've read enough about the act in my spicy books to know it might be a little painful, but ultimately, the orgasm I get from it is going to be much more intense.

"Good." He closes the distance between us until that gorgeous scent of his wraps around me, along with the heat of his body which, together, is doing funny things to my insides. He cups my cheek. "You're incredible, Solene, and I can't tell you how much I appreciate you agreeing to star in my movie."

I take in the genuine emotion in his eyes, the softness around his lips as he holds my gaze. Despite everything, why does it feel so right to finally be on the same side as him? "Why are things between us always so complicated?" I place my hand on his.

"If things had been too simple, we might not have appreciated how right it feels to finally do this together."

His thoughts echo mine, and again, I shouldn't be surprised. Underneath all that push-pull, we've always been on the same wavelength. Largely.

"So, what's next?"

"Now, we head out there and tell your manager that we are together. Then, we let ourselves be spotted around town, all casual-like."

"So, we let the speculation build?"

He nods. "Meanwhile, we get through the shooting. Closer to when the movie is done, then we do a more formal video of the two of us together."

"Which will help with the launch of the movie."

"You okay with that?"

"I'm not surprised you have it all planned out, but somehow, I wish things were a lot more spontaneous between us."

He flashes me a grin. "I got you covered there."

I blink. Whoa, that full-wattage smile of his is so rare. It transforms his face and hits you straight in the solar plexus. My heart does a funny jump in my chest. Also, there's something a little mean about that smile that I don't quite trust. "What are you cooking up?"

"More like what do I have vibrating up?"

"What do you—" There's a buzzing between my butt cheeks. I jump. Then squeeze down on the thing that's going a thousand miles a second in the most intimate of my spaces. The oscillations streak out. There must be a direct connection to my clit, which throbs and swells. My pussy lips clench which, in turn, pushes me to bear down on the damn thingy, which restarts the cycle all over again.

"Oh, my god, this is—"

"Spontaneous enough for you, baby?" He looks closely at me, trying to discern just how much it's affecting me.

"Not quite what I had in mind." Another whimper boils up. I bite down on the inside of my cheek to stop it from escaping. "How long do I have to wear this?"

"Until I allow you to remove it."

"Which is when?"

"When I let you."

"But you're going back on set— "

He shakes his head. "I'm not."

I still. "So, it's you and me under one roof again?"

"It'll reinforce the story we're together."

"Convenient for you, huh?" I scoff.

His gaze grows intense. "Convenient for both of us that you never moved out. I wonder why that is, Rabbit? Why is it that, despite making enough money to afford a space of your own, you stayed?"

I hunch my shoulders. "It seemed more sensible to save the money I'd earned—which by the way, wasn't enough to buy a home."

"You could have moved into an apartment?"

I roll my eyes. "With even less to deter the paps from getting to me?"

"You retained your security team, they'd have kept the journalists at bay," he points out.

I stare at him. "Fine, okay, if I really wanted to, I could have moved out, but I didn't have the time. I was constantly touring. I was never home long enough to— " I jump because that damn thing between my legs buzzes again. My pussy instantly moistens, and my clit swells until I'm sure the wetness is seeping through my panties and onto the seat of my pants.

"Stop that."

"Don't lie to me, Solene. Why did you never move out?"

"I told you, I was too preoccupied with other stuff, I— " I clench my teeth to stop the shudder of sensations that burst up my spine. "Stop it."

"Not until you tell me the truth." He holds up a little gizmo in his right hand. So that's responsible for the waves of heat that swell under my skin.

He lowers his thumb to touch the button on the gadget, and I throw up my hand. "Okay, fine, you win. It's because I didn't want to. It was something that made me feel connected to you. And despite the fact you were acting like an arse"—I don't react to his raised eyebrows—"I couldn't bring myself to leave. It's the first home I've known in LA, and I couldn't see myself anywhere else."

"And?"

"And what?"

"Complete what you were going to say?"

I shuffle my weight from foot to foot. "And nothing. That's all."

His thumb touches the button, and I shake my head. "No, no. Not that, please."

"Then tell me, Solene. Tell me why you stayed, even after you thought I was with someone else."

I flinch but can't look away from those piercing blue eyes of his. "I couldn't leave because, deep inside, I didn't believe what you told me, okay? I thought—"

"You thought?"

"That we'd get back together, you *stronzo*. You *fetente,* you—" He reaches over and pulls me to him. I allow him to wrap his arms about me and hold me so close I can bury my nose into his shirt and fill my lungs with him.

"I really am sorry for putting you through that. I wasn't thinking straight."

"You broke my heart," I sniffle.

"I promise, I won't do that again."

"I'm not sure if I believe you."

He leans back and notches his knuckles under my chin, so I have to tilt my gaze up to his. "Then it's up to me to disprove that, isn't it?"

"This is going to be so good." Giorgina claps her hands together. "Of course, when you break up again, that will give rise to another round of publicity, and—"

"We're not breaking up," Declan interjects.

"We're not doing this again," I say at the same time.

Declan stares at me; I don't look away. Something passes between us. So basically, we've both agreed our relationship is fake, but we're not breaking up. By the intensity in Declan's eyes, I know he knows. And considering I can never hide my thoughts from him, he knows I know. So—what does this mean? Honestly, I'm not sure.

Giorgina looks between us. "Okay. So now that you are back together, we can make it official on social media, and—"

"No." Declan raises his hand this time. "I've outlined how it's going to be this time, and I'm not changing my mind.

She blows out a breath. "This is big news. It's best you drive the narrative by putting out a statement."

"No, keep them guessing. We're going to let them see only what we're willing to share."

"That's one heck of an engagement ring." She jerks her chin toward my left hand. The weight of the band on my left finger balances out that of the bracelet with the charms on my right hand. I'm wearing the marks of his ownership on me and in me. What does that say about me?

"Thanks," I murmur.

"You going to do a post with that?" she encourages me. "It's one hell of a newsworthy update to your fans."

I look at Declan who shrugs. "That's up to Solene."

I blink. I thought he was going to dictate every aspect of my life off stage. Guess there are some things he's happy to leave up to me.

"What do you say, Solene?" Harry pushes down his hair. He's seated on a chaise. Giorgina's in a chair, with Rick not far from her. He's Declan's security detail but he might as well be Giorgina's shadow, the way his gaze keeps moving back to her. Finn is positioned near the door, his body language alert, as always.

After Declan and I returned from our little tryst, Finn drove us back, with Harry following. I can tell the sight of him pisses Declan off, but Finn's been a good addition to my team. Besides, Declan knows Finn isn't interested in me that way. So, he really has nothing to be glowering about.

"Solene?" Harry prompts.

"Eh, what?" I yawn suddenly. "Sorry, it's been a long day." And the emotional ups and downs have tired me out faster than I imagined.

"Why don't we let my fiancée decide after a good night's sleep, huh? It's been a tiring day, and she needs her rest now."

Harry nods, then jumps to his feet. Clearly, he can't wait to get away. Not that I blame him. Between Declan's grumpy countenance and the unsaid emotions between Giorgina and Rick, it's a pressure cooker environment in here.

He bobs his head at me. "I'll message you the dates of your

upcoming shows. The venues are nowhere as big as those on your tour, but it's a chance to keep performing."

I rise to my feet. Declan stiffens, but I ignore him. I walk toward Harry, knowing Declan hasn't taken his gaze off of me, but whatever. I can't allow his glowering presence, and the fact that he is now my Dom, change how I interact with others. "You did well, Harry. And actually, I prefer smaller venues. It's more intimate. A chance to strike up a personal relationship with the people in the audience, you know?"

Harry flushes, then nods with enthusiasm. "You're a good kid, Solene, and for what it's worth, I'm happy you and Declan are together. That man's name carries clout, but together, the two of you are catnip for the press, for your fans and I'm sure, for movie-goers, too."

I blow out a breath. "I sure hope so, Harry."

He nods again at everyone, then turns and walks out.

Giorgina, too, rises to her feet. "That's my cue." She scowls at Declan. "Don't go off and do things I wouldn't do."

"Have I ever?" Declan smirks.

She rolls her eyes, then turns and walks past Rick, who angles his body in her direction. He takes a step forward before stopping himself.

Declan blows out a breath. "Oh, for fuck's sake, man. Why don't you leave with her?"

Rick draws himself up to his full height. "You don't know what you're talking about."

"Oh yeah?" Declan leans back and throws his arm over the back of the settee. "So why do you look like something crawled up your arse?"

I shoot him a dirty look. Did he say that on purpose? He flashes me another of those killer grins, which has me clamping down on said thing that's between my ass cheeks. His grin widens like he knows exactly what's happening down there. I glower at him. He pats the seat next to him. "Sit down and relax, little Rabbit."

I flush a little at his using my nickname in front of the two men, then walk over and sink down onto the chaise… On the side farthest away from him. He arches an eyebrow at me, his only reaction to my having disobeyed him. *Ooh, does that mean he's going to punish me later? I hope so.*

He turns to face the two men. "With Solene and me combining forces, it makes sense to have the both of you coordinate our security detail. Rick can continue to be on my team, and Finn on Solene's, and since you two know each other, you two can work out the rest of the formalities."

Finn jerks his chin in my direction.

Once more, Declan's muscles seize up, then he seems to get a hold of himself.

"I'll do a survey of the perimeter before I leave for the night." Finn turns and trots off.

I turn to Declan, but before I can speak his phone buzzes. He pulls it out, and his forehead furrows. "It's Cade," he tells Rick before putting it on speaker.

"Is Rick with you?" Cade's face appears on the phone

"I'm here." Rick walks over to stand behind Declan.

"You have news of Knight?"

Cade's features are serious. "They think they've got a lead on him."

"They?" Rick asks.

"The combined forces of JJ, Michael and Sinclair. They set up a task force focused on tracking down his whereabouts, and they think they've come up with a lead."

"Where is he?"

"It's confidential. I can't reveal that over the phone, but they're waiting to confirm the veracity of the lead."

"So, he's alive?" Declan lowers his chin to his chest. Worry is reflected in his eyes. His jaw tics in that familiar fashion that tells me he's stressed.

"They think so." Cade rubs the back of his neck. "The need to get to him sooner than not, else the impact on his psyche of being a prisoner of the enemy for so long is going to be catastrophic."

"Fuck!" Both Declan and Rick swear aloud.

"They're putting together an extraction team as we speak."

"I want to be in on it," Rick intervenes.

"It's not your specialty. The team will consist of highly-trained people who've delivered on challenging missions in the past."

Rick straightens. "I need to do something."

"You two be ready for when Knight is back. He'll need all our support."

"I'll do anything for him, you know that," Declan growls. "But Cade's right. We need to leave this to the experts to increase the chances of his getting out alive. Also, I need you here, Rick."

Rick hesitates.

"I know this is not exactly the kind of gig you anticipated when you were discharged from the military, but I'm counting on you to keep us both safe."

Rick rolls his shoulders. "You're blowing smoke up my arse, Pretty Boy."

Declan winces at the nickname, but before he can reply, I pipe up, "He's not. We do need you. Wait until news of the two of us gets out; it's going to be mayhem."

58

Declan

"It's fucking mayhem." I glance toward the doorway of the bookstore where we've spent the last half an hour.

We spent the night in different rooms. I didn't insist she move in with me, which she seemed to be relieved about. Which, in turn, pissed me off further, for reasons I don't want to analyze. When I walked into her room, it was to find her standing with her back to the mirror over the vanity table. She'd stripped off her clothes and was peering at herself over her shoulder.

The sight of the rabbit-shaped emerald glittering from between her arse cheeks, once again, turned my knees to jelly. A spurt of heat shuddered up my spine. I'll never get over how erotic and forbidden and right it felt. To have her wear my mark on her, *in her,* makes me feel like the luckiest man in the world.

I walked over to stand in front of her. Our eyes met in the mirror. Her pupils dilated instantly, and her breath grew choppy. I slipped my arms about her, then slid my hand down to ease out the butt plug. Her knees buckled, and I held her close, supporting her weight. She turned her face into my chest and inhaled deeply, as if storing my scent.

When she seemed more stable, I kissed her forehead, and though it hurt like hell to leave her there, aroused and wanting—I swear, I all but came in my pants as I held her soft body so close—I forced myself to leave.

We met for breakfast, which I served her. I made sure she ate everything on her plate, then I'd slipped the plug back between her arse cheeks and guided her out of the house.

In the first of our agreed-upon sightings by the press, I decided to take her back to the bookstore I bought for her and which I refuse to sell, despite the fact I could do with the extra money to put into the film. It's more important to have a place where she can go if she wants to buy her smutty books, anywhere in the world. Besides, the beneficiary of all the knowledge she gleans from the spicy books is me, so I can hardly complain.

I expected for there to be a lot of interest around our first sighting. What I hadn't realized was the sheer number of reporters who'd turn out to get a picture of us. Now, I step in front of her, wanting to shield her from the crowd of paparazzi gathered outside the double doors of the store.

"Whoa, all of them are here for us?" She peers around me.

"It would seem that way." I shift to the side once more, trying to block her from the sight of the journalists. Which is crazy. She's a figure of interest. One of the top-selling pop-stars in the world. She's going to be performing in front of people soon.

When I asked her to join me in LA, I knew it was only a matter of time before the world would want a part of her. I knew it, and I encouraged her to embrace her future. Hell, I'm the one who introduced her to Harry. So why do I want to wrap her up in cotton wool, and hide her away? And fuck her, and keep her high on endorphins, and never allow anyone else to set their gaze on her? I knew this was coming when I asked her to pose as my fake fiancée in front of the press. I knew I'd hate sharing her with anyone else when I asked her to be my sub, but the extent to which this would be tested by her fame is not something I considered.

Did I make a mistake asking her to be such an integral part of my life? Did I fool myself into thinking I can keep an emotional distance from her—enough to allow the world to be part of her life, too?

Clearly, I didn't analyze this enough. I didn't conceptualize the enormity of what I wanted. It's only now, hearing the excited cries from the throng of reporters and seeing the distant flashes going off, that I realize, once again, I've landed her in the eye of media attention.

And that was the entire reason for this charade. To turn the spotlight on the two of us so it can benefit the film and her career, but goddamn, if I don't want to call it all off and take her home and never let her leave. Which is crazy. This is the life I chose. This is what she deserves for her talent. I have no right to deprive her of this chance to resurrect her career. This is the right thing to do, to allow her to explore the heights of fame, and the influence and power it brings with it. To step aside and let her shine. I bunch my fists at my sides, force my muscles to relax, then angle my body enough so I don't block her from view. But goddamn, I can't allow her to be seen completely. I can't. I hold out my hand.

I sense her stiffen. The seconds stretch, then slowly, she places her much smaller palm in mine. A shiver of relief courses through me. I link my fingers with hers. Outside the double doors, Rick stands shoulder-to-shoulder with Finn. Rick looks at me over his shoulder. I nod, then lead Solene through the doors, and the flashes go off. She inches closer to me, and I wrap my arm about her, drawing her into my side. Rick and Finn bracket us on either side as the journalists fire off questions:

"Are you two together, Declan?"

"Solene, are you no longer with your bodyguard?"

"Solene, did you pretend to be with your bodyguard to throw us off track?"

"Declan, is the two of you getting together a publicity stunt?"

I throw up my hand, and the crowd quiets. Then I twine my fingers with those of her left hand. I slide my other hand into my pocket and brush my fingers across the device. Next to me, she gasps, and I see her shiver.

She turns to me, but before she can speak, I lower my head and close my mouth over hers. I draw off her breath, draw in the words she was about to throw at me, tilt my head, and deepen the kiss until she melts into me. I pull her close and kiss her for a second longer, aware of the flashbulbs going off around us. Then, I tear my mouth from hers and survey her flushed features. She raises her heavy eyelids, a mixture of lust and anger swirling in hers. Just how I like her. Defiant enough, yet ready enough to fall apart under my ministrations. I step back, then lift her palm, and more flashes go off. They bounce off the diamonds on the ring, until the entire space around us seems to be haloed in light. I hold up my hand again, and they fall silent once more.

"Does that look like a publicity stunt?" I snap.

The questions start up again:

"When did you get engaged?"

"How did he propose, Solene?"

"When's the wedding date?"

Fucking hell. There's no satisfying this crowd, is there? At a glance from me, Finn and Rick push back the journalists. A path clears, and once more, I wrap my arm about Solene, hold her close, and shield her as much as possible as I guide her toward the waiting car.

Rick holds the door to the passenger side open. She slides in, followed by me. Rick throws himself into the seat next to the driver, and Finn, who's taken the driver's seat, steps on the accelerator and sets off even before Rick's door is completely shut. The noise fades. We leave them behind, and Finn steers the car forward. Silence descends.

Solene's hand is still in mine. Her palm is sweaty, her breathing erratic. I turn to find she's staring straight forward, a dazed look on her face.

"You okay?" I murmur.

She nods, then shakes her head. "I don't know, to be honest." She raises her hand to her hair, her fingers trembling.

"It's okay, baby, I'd never let them get to you."

She laughs a little. "Somehow, I believe you. I knew they'd be interested in pictures of the two of us. Hell, I've faced crowds of twenty thousand during my tour, but they were at a distance. There was always a separation between them and me. With the paparazzi though—" She shudders. "They're so close. It's like they want to crawl into your skin and get a piece of you."

"Hey, look at me."

She tips up her chin, and our gazes lock.

"I'll never let them hurt you. I'll always be there to protect you, I promise."

She half smiles. "I do believe you. Not sure why, but I do. Especially after that stunt you pulled back there."

"You mean this?" I slide my hands into my pocket and touch the device.

Instantly, her back curves, and she pushes out her breasts, the nipples already beaded and visible through her blouse. Fucking hell, I don't want to share her, and yet, I'm proud of how much I'm able to affect her. That I can push her arousal to fever pitch by the flick of my fingers. When her breathing finally slows, she lowers her chin. "You're not playing fair."

"I love to catch you unawares."

She pouts. "I can never predict what you're going to do next."

"It's why you love being with me, baby."

She tosses her hair over her shoulder. "I shouldn't allow myself to be this weak with you."

"You can be anything you want with me, Rabbit."

She glances ahead at the two men in the front seat.

I hit the button and privacy screen rises. "There, now they won't see or hear anything."

"You always get your way, don't you?" She shakes her head. "Why am I not used to the kind of influence you have over others? I thought I'd tasted fame and the ability to hold power over others, but you take the ability to wield authority to a whole new height."

I allow my lips to curve. "It's who I am, baby."

She snorts. "Can't accuse you of being modest."

"I didn't get to where I am by being modest."

She nods slowly. "You wear power like it was made for you. You hold dominance in every angle of your body, in every pore on your skin, in every glare, every breath, every step you take. Your presence is a weapon made to make others bend to your will."

"Just as long as I have you in my power, I don't care about anything else."

She looks into my eyes, then chuckles, the sound nervous. "You really mean it."

"Of course I do. Fuck the world. Fuck my career. If I can have you with me, if I can bend you to my will, if I can make you submit to me, if I can satisfy you, and arouse you, and take you to heights you've never been, if I can coax you to trust me, and push you out of your comfort zone, and discover the woman you truly are inside, then I'll have fulfilled the reason for my existence."

The pulse at the base of her throat picks up speed, and her lips part. "Oh my god. That was so… romantic. I shouldn't think it to be so. I should be frightened of what it means when you declare your intent with such ferocity, but somehow, I'm not."

"Good." I tug her even closer. "Are you ready for the next stage?"

59

Solene

"Are you going to tell me what the next stage is?" I look across the table at the man seated opposite me. We're at Declan's home in Malibu.

The sound of the waves crashing on the shore is a distant yet comforting hum. A gull screeches from somewhere overhead. The infinity pool stretches out, seeming to lead straight to the setting sun that slips slowly down the horizon. The sky is streaked with reds and purples. Intensely sensuous colors to halo an intensely sensuous man. Declan's wearing a white button down and black pants. His hair is slicked back, his jaw freshly shaven. Which is a pity. Not that I don't like him this way, but I prefer the whiskers on his chin which chafe my skin when he draws it across the sensitive skin of my pussy.

I squeeze my legs together, and the feel of my thighs against the smoothness of my sheath-dress sends a burst of sensations up my skin. He laid out a thong that was barely there, and the glossy, satiny, white dress—that I'm wearing— on my bed. I saw them as soon as I came out of my shower, and while there was no message from him, it was clear he wanted me to wear them. And now, I understand why. The whisper of the fabric on my skin adds to my arousal, as if his proximity isn't enough to rouse me to fever pitch. I scowl at him.

As if sensing my perusal, his lips curl. Then he slides his hand inside the front pocket of his shirt. I stiffen and wait for the inevitable vibrations that will send those familiar shivers undulating up my spine. Wait. Wait. He withdraws his hand and places a small hourglass on the table.

"What's that for?"

"You wanted to know what the next stage is?" His lips curl.

I glance at the hourglass, then up at his too-pleased face. Bet he has another of his BDSM-related surprises up his sleeve. "*Stronzo.*" I glower at him.

His smile widens. "Oh, ye of little faith."

"You don't get to say that, considering you pulled that little stunt in front of those journalists. What if I'd—"

"You'd...?"

"You know... arrived."

"Arrived?" He blinks.

"Get with it. That's how you refer to 'coming' in polite company." I make air-quotes with my fingers. "Not that you're polite company, but considering you made the effort—" I gesture to the table between us set for dinner for two, complete with cutlery, plates, wine glasses, sparkling wine chilling in a bucket, and roses and candles with wind protectors placed over them.

"Arriving, coming, cumming. Call it any name you want, but before the night is out, you'll be calling out my name as you indulge in all three verbs."

Heat flushes my skin. My nipples harden. He pours himself a glass of the Prosecco, then puts away the bottle.

"What about me?" I gape.

"You're still not old enough to drink in this country," he reminds me.

I tip up my chin. "Can I have a tiny sip, please?"

"Have I ever failed to cater to your tastes, Rabbit?"

His housekeeper—who's also an amazing cook—wheels out a cart laden with food. She parks it next to the table, then turns to Declan. "Anything else this evening, Mr. Beauchamp?"

"That will be all; you may leave," he says without turning to look at her.

"Thank you, Charlotte," I call out.

She flashes me a smile, then turns and walks off.

"Her name's Charlotte?" He frowns.

"You didn't know that?"

"Why would I know that?" His eyebrows knit.

"Why wouldn't you? She's worked for you for five years. Also, she's a Michelin-star chef."

"I pay for only the best."

I rub at my temple. "Your ego knows no bounds."

He throws up his hands. "I've barely been here the last five years. I bought the house because it was a good investment and it made sense to have a base in LA. I also have a home in London, and I'm thinking of buying a place in Naples."

"Naples?" I still.

"Would you like to have a place to stay when you go back and visit your family?"

I place my hands in my lap. "You're not making any sense. Why would you buy a home in Naples?"

"Why wouldn't I?"

"You know why; our engagement is a fake."

"And the press is going to try to prove that, too. The only way to hold them off is to show how much I care for my fiancée. In fact, I'm so in love with her, I've splurged on a heritage house in her hometown."

"So, it's all for show?" I ask slowly.

"And for investment. I'll rent it out."

"Of course you will. Can't pass up a means to increase your wealth, huh?"

"You bet." He leans forward in his seat. "Any more questions?"

"Just one."

He tilts his head.

"Where's my Prosecco?"

"Coming right up." He takes a sip from his flute, then rises to his feet. He walks around to stand beside me.

"What are you—" He plants his big palms on either side of my mouth, then squeezes with enough pressure that I open my mouth. He lowers his head and trails the sparkling wine into my mouth.

My stomach tightens, and my pussy contracts. Bubbles warmed by his mouth pop on my tongue. The taste of lemon, pears, green apple... and him fills my palate. He releases his hold on my face, and I swallow. The liquid slides down my throat. It feels like I swallowed a part of him. He watches the movement of my throat, and his blue eyes darken to that indigo I'm so familiar with. The one that indicates he's turned on.

"Open," he growls.

Before I can comply, he grabs his flute, takes another sip, dribbles it into my mouth, and wraps his fingers around my throat as I swallow.

"You're so fucking sexy, Rabbit. It makes me want to turn you over and take you right-fucking-now."

Before I can respond, he releases me. Then he straightens, walks over to the food cart and slides my plate in front of me. "Eat."

I glance down and exclaim, "*Spaghetti a la Puttanesca*? My favorite? How did you know?"

"I know everything about you, Rabbit. I take my role as your Dom very seriously."

I peek up at him from under my lashes. What do I make of this complex man? Now I know that the distance I sense in him is not of his making. Now, I know that, although he seems dissociated from the moment, in reality, he's very engaged. His focus is always on me, even when I'm not aware of it. During the time I was upset he wasn't in touch with me when we were apart and I thought he was focused on his career, even then, I didn't feel alone. It wasn't until that day I came home to find him with that woman that I felt a distance between us.

Have I forgiven him for that farce? I'm not sure. At the very least, I gave him a taste of the anger, jealousy and helplessness I'd felt by pretending to be with Finn. I couldn't resist when he invited me to experiment with the power exchange in our relationship. Blame it on my fascination with spicy books. Or on the fact that I hold the power in our association. *I do hold the power. I do.* I remind myself of that as he nods toward my plate. "Eat."

The power in that one word sends another burst of anticipation up my spine. I dig into the food and take a mouthful. The tangy flavors of tomatoes, the bite of garlic, the zing of capers, the saltiness of anchovies—all of it bursts on my tongue. It also makes me miss the taste of him that clung to the bubbles. He watches me, his own food untouched.

"Aren't you eating?"

"Watching you appease your appetite is enough to satisfy mine."

"Oh." I pause with my fork halfway to my mouth. "You mean that don't you?"

One side of his lips quirks. His cold blue eyes sparkle with a fire that scorches as it chills me. The hair on the back of my neck rises. Goosebumps pop on my skin. I bring the fork to my mouth and slide the tines of the fork between my lips. He watches with utmost focus as I pull it out, then place it back on my plate.

"You need to eat some more."

"I can't." I lean back in my seat.

"You're going to need your strength," he murmurs in a low voice.

I can't stop the nervous giggle from bursting out. "You sound so serious."

"That's because I am, Rabbit."

"B-b-but I'm full," I whine.

"Not as full as you're going to be when I take your arse."

60

Declan

Her gaze widens. "You said that on purpose." She stabs her finger in my direction.

I raise a shoulder. "Maybe I said it because I like to see that innocent girl I met come to the surface. Maybe I said it because I like seeing that mix of fear and lust in your eyes? Or maybe it's because I like seeing you getting aroused by the thought of my cock in your virgin hole, but fighting it and trying not to show it and failing."

Her breath hitches. The tell-tale pulse at the base of her neck begins to beat faster. I toss back the rest of the Prosecco, then push back from my chair. I walk around to stand in front of her then jerk my chin. "On your feet, little Rabbit."

She tips up her chin, then slowly rises.

"Good girl."

She flushes. *Fucking hell, this praise kink of hers is going to destroy me.* It's going to bring me to my knees and have me pushing my nose into the delta between her legs in seconds. I'm greedy for her scent, her taste, the feel of my dick being strangled by her tight little hole. The need to take her, own her, possess her overwhelms me. She wears my ring, she's mine to do with as I want. Mine to possess. Mine to take. Mine to fuck until I'm seared in every cell in her body. I reach over to push aside her plate. "Turn around; grab the edge of the table."

"Wh-what…?" She stutters.

"Don't make me ask twice, Rabbit."

She holds my gaze for a second, then slowly lowers it, before turning and gripping the table.

I step back to admire the flow of the dress over her arse. Through the almost transparent fabric the valley between her arse cheeks is visible. The blood drains to my groin. I'd hoped to wait a little longer. I'd wanted to, at least, feed her dessert before I took her, but the sight of her bent over and waiting for me with such supplication has the blood gushing through my veins. My heart somersaults in my rib cage. My thigh muscles flex. I need to have her. Right fucking now. I close the distance between us and flip up her dress. The creamy globes of her arse thrust out proudly, and nestled between them, the emerald-encrusted rabbit sparkles. My breath catches in my chest. My throat goes dry.

"You didn't wear the panties I placed out for you?"

She looks at me over her shoulder. "Do you like it?"

"I'm going to have to punish you for your brattiness, baby."

She swallows, then her lips curve, "Maybe I'm counting on it, hmm?

"Maybe I can't help but enjoy the mix of lust and out-of-control expression you're wearing right now. Maybe—" She gasps, for I've reached forward and pulled out the plug in one smooth move. Instantly, she whines in protest. The sound goes straight to my cock.

I reach over, grab the olive oil and drizzle the cold liquid down the valley between her butt cheeks.

"Oh, god, oh, god. I really was stupid for taunting you, wasn't I? I'm not ready for this, I'm not." She wriggles her butt.

"Want me to stop?"

She opens her mouth, presumably, to say yes. I smirk, and her eyes glint with anger.

"Do you, baby?"

She hesitates, then slowly shakes her head. *And fuck, if every cell in my body doesn't seem to spring to attention at that.*

"Say it," I order.

She swallows then juts out her chin. "I don't want you to stop."

Satisfaction fills my chest. My heart thunders in my ribcage. "You sure?"

She nods again.

"I'm going to try my best to ease this, but it's going to hurt."

She swallows. "I trust you."

I blink. A melting sensation fills my chest. Heat flushes my skin, and a thousand little fires light up my blood stream. "You shouldn't. Not me, not anyone else in this town. The only person you should trust is yourself."

She chuckles. "A little late to teach me that lesson, when I'm laid out with my *culo* bared to you." Then she gasps, for I slip in a finger into her rear end.

"Oh, god," she groans.

I stay still, allowing her to adjust to the intrusion. "How does it feel?"

"Good." She inhales sharply when I begin to move my finger in and out of her; in and out.

Right about now, the discomfort should begin to fade, and little sparks of sensation should take its place, and—

"Oh… oh, wow." She sighs in pleasure.

"Not what you expected, eh?"

"It's… It's…"

She huffs, for I've slipped in a second finger. She stretches around me, the muscles quivering under her skin.

"Deep breaths, Rabbit. In and out. With me."

She follows my lead, takes in a breath, exhales. And another. And another. Her back curves, she arches up on her toes and pushes out her butt, chasing the feel of my fingers. Her body jolts, then she tugs on her wrists, but I tighten my hold. I move closer, and the fabric of my pants chafe against her legs. Goosebumps pop on her skin. "More." She moans. "Please, more."

I slide in another finger, stretching her further.

"Oh, god," she gasps.

"I'm here, baby." I lean over and press my cheek to hers. "I'm four fingers inside you. Up to my knuckles, and fuck, if it isn't the most salacious sight. Ever. You're a gorgeous, beautiful, willing slut, aren't you, Rabbit?"

She whines, then clenches down on my fingers. My heartbeat accelerates even further. *Bam-bam-bam.* It echoes the pulse beating in her core. I twist my fingers, and her eyes roll back in her head.

"It's too much. I'm too full," she whispers. A trembling oscillates up her legs, and that's when I pull out my fingers.

"Wha—" She flutters her eyelids open, and I hold her gaze.

"I'm going to fuck you now."

61

Declan

I replace my fingers with the crown of my shaft, and her breath hitches. Nervousness pours off of her, and a trembling sensation shudders up her spine.

"Shh, baby." I push her hair over her shoulder, baring her neck, then curl my fingers about her nape. Instantly, she settles. She peers at me from the corner of her eye, and I can see my desire reflected in them.

"Take a deep breath," I order.

She does. And as she releases it, I slip through the ring of muscle that was resisting my entry.

She gasps. Her lips part. Color sweeps up her shoulders, her face. I hold onto her wrists, locked behind her back, giving her time to adjust.

Then, because I can't help myself, I bend and kiss her temple, then whisper my nose around the shell of her ear. The tension drains out of her. I rub my cheek against hers, and a moan spills from her lips. I release my hold on her neck only to skate my fingers down her spine, down the valley between her cheeks until I reach her pussy. I strum her clit, and she shudders. I slide my fingers down her pussy lips, and she parts her legs wider. I slip another centimeter inside her, and she groans.

"I'm too full; it's too much."

"Not enough. Take all of me, baby."

"I can't," she whines."

"You can. You will." I slip my fingers inside her cunt, and she moans. I curve my fingers, striking that part deep inside her that makes her clamp down on my cock. My blood pressure shoots up, sweat beads my temples, and I dig my heels into the ground. I need to go slow. Wait until she's fully adjusted to my size. I begin to rub her clit in earnest, and her back bows off the table. Moisture drips down her inner thighs. Her inner muscles relax. I tilt my hips and slide all the way in, and she stills. "You're doing so well, Rabbit."

I slide my fingers in and out of her pussy, and a whimper leaves her lips.

A trembling starts up her legs, up her thighs. The pulse beating at her temple goes into overdrive. She squeezes down on my fingers and on my cock, and I know she's close.

"Don't you dare come, Rabbit."

She whines. "But I'm so c-c-close."

"You won't come until I give you permission."

She scowls, but her trembling recedes. Her body knows how to obey me, and the fact that she's still able to hold her own against my will is so fucking hot. I slide another finger inside her pussy, and she whimpers.

"How does it feel?"

"I'm so very crammed. You're surrounding me, you're overwhelming me." A tear drop squeezes out the side of her eyes and I lick it up.

"You're so tight. So hot. You feel incredible." *You feel like home.* I pull out until I'm poised at the rim of her entrance. Then, holding her gaze, I piston my hips forward and bury myself all the way to the hilt.

She throws her head back and her eyelids flutter down, and I begin to fuck her in earnest. The next time I impale her, her body lurches forward. The entire table moves. A plate falls to the ground and shatters. But I don't stop. I fuck her pussy with my fingers and her arse with my shaft. Her thighs tremble, her hips jut out. She curves her back and writhes under me. Which only allows me to sink even deeper. A trembling screeches through me. "Fucking hell." I pick up my pace, slam into her over and over again. Her body shudders under me, and this time, I know we're both climbing that hill. Together.

"Open your eyes, baby."

She opens her heavy eyelids, then turns and fixes her gaze on me over her shoulder. I pinch her clit, then thrust into her with such force, the vibrations zip up my spine straight to my heart.

"Come with me, right fucking now."

She opens her mouth in a wordless scream, and her body bucks. Moisture gushes out of her, bathing my fingers as she slumps onto the table. I grit my teeth, watching as she flutters around my cock and quivers in the aftermath. Sweat pours down my back, and I continue to fuck her through the convulsions. Color flushes her face, her hair streams out across the table, and I pick up speed. In-out-in. I sink into her, hitting a spot deep inside her that sends goosebumps cascading over her skin. Then I cram myself inside her one last time and dig my teeth into the curve of her shoulder as I empty myself inside her.

I stay poised over her, my shaft still buried inside her, not wanting to move, licking the marks I placed on her neck. Her eyes are shut; her breathing evens out. I watch her face, taking in her relaxed features, the smoothness of her forehead. I press my lips to the top of her hair then pull out of her. She murmurs but doesn't stir when I scoop her up in my arms and carry her up to my bedroom.

"Where are you taking me?" she slurs.

"Gonna clean you up, baby."

I run the water in the bathtub, and when it's full, I ease into it, settling her between my legs.

"That feels so good." She nestles into me, and I proceed to wash every inch of her, before attending to myself. When I'm done, I step out of the tub and walk over to where the towels are kept. I ease her to the floor, and she yawns. "I love feeling your hands on my body."

I pause, then dry her, before scooping her up in my arms. "Are you sore?"

"A little, but it's fading already." She yawns again.

"I'm sorry, I didn't use a condom. I'm never careless but when I'm around you, I'm unable to hold onto my control."

"'S'alright, 'twas the wrong hole."

62

Solene

I hear him bark out a laugh and I crack my eyes open. OMG! Did he just…? "Did you just laugh?"

"Apparently, I did."

He seems as surprised as I am.

"Was what I said funny?" I manage to force out the words, then spoil the effect with such a loud yawn, my jaw cracks.

"You're incredible, you know that?" he says in a soft voice.

I snuggle into his chest, enjoying the scent of him that curls around me. Loving the fact that we're both naked and in bed together. In his bed together. Reveling in how his gaze is fixed on my features. How, with his tousled hair and his relaxed jaw, he seems so much more like the man I first met. "You're gorgeous," I murmur.

"And you're exquisite."

I raise my hand and cup his cheek. "I like you like this."

"Like what?" His tone is amused.

"All sprawled out in bed like a big lion that's replete and has—"

"Fucked his mate?"

I blink, a blush crawling up my face. *Madonna Mia,* why does that sound so hot to me?

"Am I your mate, or is that the power of the anal speaking?"

He blinks, then throws his head back and roars with laughter. OMG, the sight of Declan Beauchamp, the hottest commodity in Hollywood, the alpha male every woman wants in her bed, guffawing aloud with laughter, with his features alight with mirth, and his massive shoulder muscles bunching, and his chiseled chest planes heaving as he laughs and laughs, is a sight I'll carry around in my head forever.

"Umm, was it that funny?"

"It was on the head… of the butt plug, no less."

"Har, har," I deadpan.

"You're a fucking delight, baby." He pulls me closer. "How did I survive all this time without you?"

"Very well, apparently, given your plan for world domination."

He scowls. "You make me sound like a Bond villain."

I raise a shoulder. "You did manage to play him well in your last movie."

"Touché." He cups my cheek. "Having you in my arms makes everything else pale in comparison."

"A-n-d, another confession." I place the back of my hand on his forehead. "You're not running a temperature. It's definitely the power of anal which has loosened your tongue."

I lower my hand, but he captures it and brings it to his mouth, kissing the ring on my finger.

"Your every hole has so much power over me, baby. Your every glance fells me. Your scent laces my dreams. The touch of your body is a yearning that pulses through my every waking moment. It's your body, of course, which holds me captive. But it's your ability to give, your wholeness, your willingness to try new things, your generosity of spirit, your artistic expression that comes through in your words, your voice that soars on the wings of angels… It's all of you that entraps me… Willingly."

Tears prick the backs of my eyes. My heart flutters in my chest like a caged dragonfly. "And now I realize why you're so powerful on screen. When you tap into that part of you that connects to your emotions, it's everything."

A teardrop rolls down my cheek. He dips his head and licks it off.

"Sweet, always sweet. Everything about you is like nectar on my tongue."

"Now that's an exaggeration," I scoff.

"Don't believe me?"

I shake my head, then scream when he tosses me on my back and climbs in between my legs. He slides down until his head is poised over my melting core.

"Ready, baby?"

"F-f-for what?" I swallow.

"For your pretty pink pussy to be consumed by me?"

My core clenches. I'm not ashamed to say my arousal pitches through the roof. That tell-tale fire sparks low in my belly. I try to close my legs but end up pushing into the sides of his biceps, for he's planted those broad shoulders between my knees.

"And if I say no?" I whisper.

"Oh, sorry; did that sound like a question?" His cold blue eyes spark, then he bends and licks me from puckered hole to slit, in one long, smooth swipe.

"Oh, god!" My eyes roll back in my head. I dig my fingers into his hair and tug. A growl rumbles from his mouth and across my pussy. My core shivers. I feel a fat trail of cum squeezes out from between my thighs. He licks it up, then begins to eat me out in earnest. He flattens his tongue up my pussy lips, again and again, then circles my clit. "Declan!" I scream.

Another rumble of sound emerges from him, this time, one of satisfaction and greed. So much greed. It chafes across my nerve endings, and my brain cells seem to melt. He hooks his arms under my knees, pulls me up, tilts me to the side, arranging me just so, and then he stabs his tongue inside my pussy. In-out-in. My entire body jolts. I writhe around, trying to pull away, then push up, trying to ride his tongue, wanting him to fill that emptiness that rolls about inside me, needing him to put me out of my misery, to quench this hunger that squirms inside of me.

"Please, please, Declan," I beseech him to take me to the edge and push me over so I can soar and fly and find that glimmer of brightness over the horizon that beckons to me. That calls to me. That— I gasp when he fondles the rosette between my butt cheeks, then moan when he slips his thumb inside, only to screech when he bites down on my clit. He tugs on the engorged nub, and sparks of sensation ricochet up my spine and flare behind my eyes. My orgasm sweeps up from my toes, swirls about my hips then roars over me. That's when he pulls back and replaces his tongue with something bigger, more blunt, heavier, thicker… Everything I wanted.

"Look at me."

I raise my heavy eyelids, and his deep blue gaze instantly holds mine. He looks deeply into my eyes, and I swear, I come right then. The intensity with which he holds my gaze, the way he plants his elbows on either side of me, looming over me, bracketing me with his heat, pinning me to the bed with his cock, which throbs and extends and grows impossibly big inside me, turns me into a squirming, melting, liquefying mass of need.

It grows bigger in my belly, until it fills my chest, my throat, extends to my extremities. Until I'm one throbbing mass of sensations. And yet, he stays there, poised at the rim of my slit, holding me down with the sheer force of his presence. Then he propels his hips forward and slams into me in one smooth stroke. My entire body jolts, and my back curves. I thrust my breasts up, and he locks his lips around my nipple. He tugs on it, bites down on it, causing a thousand fires to arrow down to my clit.

Every part of me he touches seems calculated to rouse me even more, spiraling my need higher. He pulls out, then thrusts forward and into me with enough force that the headboard slams into the wall. I dig my heels into his back, throw my arms about his neck and hold him close enough that the *bam-bam-bam* of his heart mirrors the sped-up beats of mine.

He raises his head and holds my gaze again. His blue eyes deepen in color to the indigo that I associate with him. His features are flushed, his jaw tight. Sweat beads his gorgeous shoulders from the effort of fucking me. A physical reminder of just how hard he's taking me, and that turns me on even more.

I squeeze my inner muscles, and his cock seems to push back. It thickens further, crowding against my inner walls. It's as if we're engaged in a silent struggle, the result of which will decide if I've been subsumed by him. And I don't want to give in. If I do, I'll lose the part of me I've held onto all my life. The part that kept me going all those years when my brother and mother insisted my future role was that of the dutiful Mafia wife. When I agree, on the face of it, appeared docile and unthreatening, only to write out my thoughts and my frustrations into words. The very words which are now recognized by the world.

They sensed who I was inside. A girl who yearned for approval. A woman who wanted to be everything for her man. Who'd satisfy him, while finding herself through him. Who'd hold the power, yet willingly hand it over when he commanded me to.

He must sense my internal struggle, for he slows. He pulls out, and this time, sinks inside me inch by inch, forcing me to feel every ridge, every pulsing vein that graces his cock. I want to... Need to let go and yet...

I can't. I can't. I yank on his hair, and his shoulders seem to grow larger. His jaw tics. His chest muscles swell. He grabs my arm and twists it over my head, then the other. He shackles my wrists with one large hand, then peers into my face and growls, "You're going to come with me."

"No." I shake my head. "No, no, no."

"Yes, Rabbit."

He begins to pound into me. Slamming into me, pulling out, thrusting into me at just the right angle so his pelvic bone hits my clit. He slides his hand between us, circles the part where he's joined with me. "You. Are. Going. To. Come."

"No," I pant, my resolve melting inside me. The hardness I gathered, somewhere along the way as a defense against what my family wanted from me, begins to melt. He's not the only one who changed since that day we met on the beach. I had to. I just hadn't realized it. Not until now. Not until the sweat slides down his temple, clings to his chin then plops down on my cheek. Not until he squeezes his finger inside my channel. I open my mouth to groan, but no sound comes out. The unbearable pressure of having his thick digit and even thicker cock inside me at the same time...is a kind of fullness I never imagined possible. He releases his hold on my wrists, then shoves his large palm under my butt, and when he slips it between my butt cheeks, I moan. *Too much. Too full. Even more than when he'd fucked my back hole.* "Declan," I gasp.

"Come with me, baby. Come right now."

Holding my gaze, he pulls out, and this time, when he propels into me, he brushes my cervix, and I shatter. The climax sweeps through me. I'm aware of someone screaming; I know it's me. But it's as if I'm floating above my body, watching his shoulders pull back, then release, and again, as he buries himself inside me. Then, just like that, I'm back in my body. Shudders grip me. I slump into the bed as he continues to fuck me through the aftershocks. Then his gaze narrows, the blue of his irises dilating until there's only a ring of indigo around the circumference, his big body shudders, and his features contort. He lowers his head, buries his teeth in my neck, and with a groan, empties himself inside me.

63

Declan

I taste the coppery taste of her blood and realize I've broken her skin. I lick it off, soothing the chafed area. Her body slumps, and when I take in her face, I realize she's asleep. I lower my lips to hers, then kiss her closed eyelids.

A melting sensation fills my chest. My stomach feels like the bottom has dropped out of it. My knees tremble, and my ribcage hurts. It feels like I've run a marathon, when all I've done is fuck my Rabbit. I gaze at her sleeping figure, my dick nestled contentedly inside her. If I could, I'd crawl inside her skin and live there happily.

For the first time since I was diagnosed with emotional blunting, my mind feels calm. Not empty, but calm. And there's a subtle difference. It's more than post-coital glow, more than my balls feeling the aftereffects of having been drained, it's… As if, for the first time in my life, I'm back in my skin.

I allow myself to gaze at her for a few seconds more, then pull out of her. A mixture of my cum and hers slips out. I didn't use a condom… Again. And this time, it was the right hole. I push the mixture back inside her, then rub the rest of it into her inner thighs. She smells of me and that's the way it should be. She belongs to me. My rabbit. My fiancée. My submissive. Mine.

I right myself, then spoon her from behind. She snuggles back, the curve of her arse pushing into my cock, which instantly thickens. I've fucked women before, but never been ready to go again so quickly. When it comes to her, I'm insatiable.

I lock my arm about her waist, tuck her head under my chin and hold her. For the first time since I asked her to come with me to LA, I am able to decipher my feelings for her. I want this relationship to be real. I want her to be my fiancée in every sense of the word. I want to teach her the pleasures of true submission. So far, she's complied, but not without protest, and that won't do. I need time to show her the absolute joy that comes with giving herself up to me. Today was a start.

The way she took me in both of her holes, the way she fell apart around my cock each time, the sheer peace that the Dom part of me finds in her pleasure cannot be replicated anywhere else. I recognize it. Now, all I need to do is convince her of it. I need to find a way to win back her trust after how I broke it. I need her to…

Come to me, in her own time. I need to give her space to pull apart what she feels for me. I need… her to need me. To give herself up fully to me. And she will. As we work on the movie together, I'm sure there will be occasions to show her just how good we are together. Meanwhile, I've bound her to me in the best way possible. Now, all I need to do is give her a chance to recognize how good we are together, too.

Her breathing evens out. I stay spooning her for a few minutes more. Bury my nose in her hair and inhale her scent. My eyes close. The curves of her body sink into mine. She sighs in her sleep and cuddles closer. Her butt pushes into my already lengthening cock, and that's when I realize, I need to leave before I fuck her again.

I need to get back to work on the movie, need to ensure everything goes according to plan, that this relaunches her career and brings her the acclaim she deserves. Which, in itself, is a contradiction. I don't want to share her with the world, yet I want her talent to shine. I want to hide her away and be the only person who can look at her; but I also want her to be recognized by her fans. It's a conundrum that's going to haunt me. I don't know how I'm going to resolve it. But I can't deny her this chance to reach the top of her game. I want it for myself, so how can I deny her from having it?

I slide my arm out from under her neck, then slide back and off the bed. She doesn't stir. I watch her for a few seconds more. Her breathing deepens. I tuck the sheet up under her chin and around her, then turn and grab my clothes. Slipping into them, I grab my phone and head down the stairs. I step out onto the patio overlooking the infinity pool, and beyond, at the vastness of the ocean. For a few seconds, I enjoy the crash of the waves, the feel of the breeze on my lips. When your emotions are dead inside, it's amazing how sensory perception can take over and give you a chance to feel... Just differently. I dial Cade's number and am not surprised when he answers on the first ring.

"The team's been assembled. They're formulating a plan before going in," he says without preamble.

"You trust them?"

He hesitates, then: "I trust JJ, Michael and Sinclair, and if they say this group can do the job, then yeah, I trust their opinion on this, too."

I rub the back of my neck. "How's Abby?"

"As well as can be expected, under the circumstances. Sinclair and Michael's wives, and JJ's girlfriend have formed a support group around her. If it weren't for them, I couldn't have allowed myself to be away and involved in the planning." I hear the gratitude in his voice.

"I wish I could be there."

"You're there, at the other end of the line. I know, no matter what, you'll always pick up the phone when I call. And this, despite facing the most important project of your life."

"You mean the movie?"

"That, too."

I shake my head. "When did you get so wise on relationships?"

"Since I had to get my head out of my own arse and realize nothing's more important than Abby."

"I envy your clarity on that."

"You have Solene. You're in love with her. There's no other truth in your life."

"There's my career and hers," I protest.

"Red herrings. Distractions. And you know it."

"You don't know what you're talking about, man." I roll my shoulders.

"Don't I? You know what I gave up to be with Abby."

"And do you regret it?"

"Not for one second." Someone calls out his name in the background. "Right. The team's regrouping to discuss strategy; gotta go."

I disconnect the call, then call my pilot. "Ready the jet. I'm on my way."

64

Solene

"This is bullshit. He tells me he wants me in the movie with him, but not only am I not on set with him, but he's gone and left both of you behind to watch over me? What am I, five?"

Not to mention, he implies he wants to win back my trust but then ups and leaves without telling me. And that, after fucking me so deeply I can still feel him inside me. All I have is a text message from him saying he'll call for me when it's time for me to shoot.

Every time he's inside me, he seems to come undone. Our love-making is intense and earth-shattering. Each experience is different and confirms to me that we are meant to be together. He must sense it too and that's why he takes off. He's, clearly, running scared.

"Well?" I scowl at Rick and Morty—oops, I mean Rick and Finn. The two look at each other, then Rick raises his shoulders. Finn glowers at him. They scowl at each other for a few seconds more—how strange. Apparently the two of them aren't happy with this latest development, either. Finn is the first to look away.

"It's only temporary." Rick holds up his hands. "Only until he's readied everything on set."

"Stop making excuses for him." I stab my finger at him. "And stop patronizing me. I'm not a child. There's no reason he couldn't have told me this in his own words before he hopped a flight and ran off. Also, why are you with me? Why are you not with him? Aren't you his security detail?"

He shuffles his feet. "Declan was insistent we both stay here to protect you."

"From what?"

Finn rocks forward on his feet. "From your fans. From anyone who gets overeager about getting close to you."

I turn to Rick. "He's a bigger star than I am. You'd think he'd want you with him, Rick." Finn's just an inch shorter than Rick. And where Rick's heavily muscled and seems to spend all his spare time in the gym, Finn's got the build of a runner. Lean and streamlined. They're a good contrast for each other, including in their personalities, with Rick's dark, bad-tempered looks and Finn's more laid-back, outgoing personality. Rick rubs the back of his neck. "Declan's the boss. I do as he says."

"But the two of you are friends."

"We are. I was in the military with Knight. He's the one who introduced me to Declan. So, we do have friends in common." Rick's features darken even more. Talking about Knight must remind him about his friend's predicament.

"Any word on Knight?" I ask.

Rick runs his fingers through his hair. "Cade confirmed they have an extraction team in place and are drawing up plans to go after Knight."

I nod. I was there for that call. "I know you want to be there—"

"But I need to leave it to the experts. I'd only get in the way. Besides, my skills are of better use here doing my job."

I roll my eyes. "You mean, updating Declan about my whereabouts, don't you?"

"I take my role seriously, and if that means keeping Declan informed about where you are so he can focus on his movie, then yes."

I stare at him. "You're very loyal toward him."

He rolls his shoulders. "He's a good guy." He hesitates. "I was in a bad place in my life after I left the military. Knight, as you're aware, stayed on, but… things happened, and I decided to leave."

Finn stiffens. I shoot him a glance, to find he's staring at Rick with a look on his face that I can't quite decipher.

"Knight asked Declan to check in on me, as he was worried. He and Cade came in search of me, found me in a bad way. If he hadn't intervened, I wouldn't be standing here. So yeah, I owe him."

Finn shuffles his weight between his feet. He opens and shuts his mouth, then seems to change his mind and flattens his lips. O-k-a-y, the dynamics here are making my head spin. But whatever is going on between Rick and Finn is their business. I have problems of my own. Not the least of all, the fact that after that wonderful night we spent together, when I was sure he had feelings for me, when I thought the way we'd made love was the start of something different between us, when I thought—I trace the stone on my engagement ring with my finger—our engagement meant something more than the vehicle to kick-start our careers...

Turns out, nothing changed for him. If it had, wouldn't he have called me before he flew out? Or left me a message? Or called me from the plane? He could call Rick but not me, apparently. He left and took the butt-plug with him. The muscles of the rosette between my ass cheeks clamps down on the empty space. Goddamn him, but I miss that intrusion, which is so weird. I was sure it was an invasion of my privacy, but I guess it was also a way to stay connected to him. Anyway, I don't mind my privacy being invaded, as long as it's by him. I turn away from the two men and walk over to busy myself with the music sheets I've been working on.

Only good thing with this up and down relationship with Declan? I have enough inspiration to write the lyrics for my next few songs. Seems the best way to free the muse is to be on an emotional rollercoaster. Harry put me in touch with a new producer who's going to work on my next album with me. We're in his studio, and for the first time since the cancellation of the last leg of my tour, I can't wait to get started.

My throat tickles and I end up coughing. Finn looks at me with concern, then brings me a glass of water. "You okay?"

"Of course. I'm probably dehydrated, is all." I take a sip of water, cough again, and end up emptying the entire glass.

The two of them exchange glances—their interaction is completely professional, with both of them wearing their security detail faces.

"*Madonna Mia*, you guys, there's no need to worry. See, I'm not coughing any more. No need to go bothering Declan about it." *And if I've coughed on and off the last couple of weeks, it's nothing. Okay not nothing, because it's persistent. And it has interfered with my singing, and to be honest, I'm worried about it. But no way, am I going to make a big deal of it.* It'll only make Rick inform Declan right away and then he'll be all up my business, which I don't want right now. I'll get it looked at... As soon as I finish the tour.

"You sure you're okay?" Rick frowns.

Luckily, the producer enters the room.

"There you are!" I hold up the sheaf of paper with my lyrics. "I can't wait to get started."

"Have you called to tell him you're upset with him for leaving without talking to you?" Penny eyes me with concern from my phone screen.

After I finished the session with the producer, which had gone really well. So well, in fact, I'm going back in the studio and recording my next song tomorrow, which is unheard of. But hey, when everything comes together, you don't question it. You thank your muse and keep going.

The new producer is brilliant. He has experience, having worked with some of the biggest names in music, yet he's also enthusiastic and knows exactly when to back off. He's patient enough to let me have my say when it comes to arranging the vocals. If anything, he helped me hone the tune. A few tweaks and it sounds even better than what I envisaged. Which is exactly the role of a producer. I can't wait to get back to the studio tomorrow.

I came home—to Declan's home, that is—and went up to my room. And then I missed him even more. Which is when I called Penny. Not wanting to disturb Abby, who's stressed enough over Knight, or Isla, who seems to be in a perennial honeymoon phase with her new husband Liam, Penny was the logical choice to turn to. She must feel the same way; she's been messaging me over the past few weeks, as well.

Summer added both of us to the online wives and girlfriends chat-group she created, but the women there are involved with men who are close to Declan, and I don't really want to share what I'm going through there. Besides, most of them there are married or in stable relationships, like Lena with JJ, a-n-d I'm not sure they know what it's like to be single and gripped with anxiety about the state of your relationship.

"Solene, did you hear me?"

"Yes, I heard you. And no, I'm not going to call that *stronzo*. Why should I, when he's the one in the wrong? Again."

She nods slowly. "I suppose you're right. And I agree with you. It's confusing when he blows hot then cold. I guess it's naive of me to think it's easy to put things right by making the first move. But then, this is why I never want to be in a relationship. It feels like so much work!"

"It is, but I guess I'd miss these ups and downs, too—"

"No. Seriously?" She cries.

"No, but..." I cough, then clear my throat. "When I think of a life without him in it, it feels so empty, you know?"

"You have it bad for him, eh?"

I cough again, then reach for a glass of water and drink from it. "I've had it bad for him since I saw him on that beach."

I place the glass down and take in her pinched features. "Don't worry about me. I survived this far, and I will going forward, too."

"Of course I worry about you. You're my best friend."

"Aww, thanks, babe." I flash her a grin. "Enough about me; what about you? How's the auditioning going for the musical?"

"Nowhere," she says with a jaunty flick of her hair.

"Nowhere?"

She raises a shoulder. "I'm changing course."

"What does that mean?"

"I'm studying to become a chef."

"A chef?"

"I've always loved food, and I got tired of going to auditions and never getting call-backs. Also, I got accepted to study cooking in one of the leading schools in London, so—"

"OMG, that's great news."

"It is, except for the fees. It's going to put me in debt, but I'm hoping I'll be able to pay it back with my first job. After all, good chefs are always in demand, right?"

"You're excited about this, huh?"

"I am." She bounces on the balls of her toes. "I love new beginnings. Love this feeling that comes with starting something new."

"And I love that about you. If only I weren't the type to see things through to the end. It's a disease—one I can't seem to get rid of."

She surveys my features closely, "You talking about your pop-star career or your Hollywood beefcake fiancé?"

"Fake fiancé. And both, I suppose." I rub at my temple. Goddamn migraines. I've never had one in my life. And now, I seem to get them every other week. I'm sure it's the stress of having to cope with the demands of my career.

"That ring doesn't look fake." She gestures to the ring on my finger.

"Yeah, he had to make it look good for the media, you know."

"Those pictures of you, and the post you put up that day with the two of you looked very convincing."

Yeah, I finally got around to sharing the news on my social media feeds, and whoa! My views, which had been on the decline, jumped through the roof. This post is at a million views and counting. Which, in turn, increased the visibility of my other posts. My feed is humming with comments, mainly positive ones from my fans.

So, Declan's idea of jumpstarting my career with the fake engagement news had been on the nose. Additionally, his follow up announcement that the two of us will star together in his next film went viral. It's simply a statement from him without photos of either of us. But he, or rather, his PR team, tagged my social media handles. Between that and my own viral post, I'm suddenly the darling of the internet again. Only this time, I'm taking everything slowly.

I'm not attaching too much importance to what the fans are saying. Everyone is happy for us and for the upcoming movie, and that's great, but now I know how quickly things can change. My focus is on recording my songs and putting together my next album. That's what I am at my core; it's what I enjoy doing. Facing the camera comes naturally to me—apparently, it's easier for me to act a part than be myself—so I'll do the movie with him and then… Then, we'll see.

My heart sinks into my stomach. Damn, it's going to be so difficult to walk away from him after this. But I'm going to have to find a way. Even if it kills me. A flash of pain stabs at my left temple. I wince and rub at it. Then reach for the ibuprofen and swallow it down with a sip of water.

"You okay, Solene?" Penny asks again.

"A nasty headache, but it'll fade soon enough, I'm sure."

"You need to rest up a little, you know? Take it easy. Enjoy the ride."

I laugh. "I love that you're so chill."

"And I love that you're so focused. If I could, I'd be more like that instead of running after every shiny new project I find exciting."

"But I love your zest for life, Penny. Oh, and the fact that you also dyed your hair."

"Yay!" She holds up a strand of her pink-tinted hair. "Twinsies."

I tug on a strand of my blue streaked one. "Not quite, but close enough. Twinsies."

She lets her hair slip through her fingers. "So, what are you going to do now?"

65

Three weeks later

Solene

I'm doing what I'm best at. Seated on a stage with the spotlight on me, in a room packed with people looking at me. The rest of my band is in shadows for this song. It's one of my newer, unreleased compositions, and this is the first time I'm testing it out in front of an audience. To be honest, I like playing to these smaller groups of spectators better. I can sense their reactions more, understand what they're responding to, or not. There's more of a dialogue happening, and while I can't see their faces due to the lights, I'm tuned into their feelings which, in turn, feeds my spirit.

This… this is what I wanted that day when I jumped out of my bedroom window and wandered on the beach after midnight. When I raised my head into the breeze and began to sing. Pretending I was center stage with a throng of listeners holding onto my every word. When my voice rose and fell, and their response with it.

This is power. A hypnotic connection that links me to them, a silvery thread that I yank on, and they respond to, a channel of communication so public, and yet so private, between me and each one of them. I'm singing for myself, for them... For him. More than anything, for him. He's not here, but he remembered me. I know, because he'd sent me another charm.

This one is an Egyptian ankh. *Is there a day he'll run out of ideas for them?* I need to ask him. The next time I see him, I won't waste a moment. I'll question him right away, before it gets too late. I close my eyes, open my mouth, and let the music pour through me. I'm but a channel for this gift that I download from the ether. An instrument for my muse to shine through.

Since I was five, I've known I was going to be a singer. For a while, I lost sight of my dream, thought it was unachievable—until he came along. He was the first to recognize my talent. I wrote during the time he was missing from my life, but those songs are nowhere as good as the ones I'm writing now. It wasn't enough just to be missing him. My muse thrives on the angst sparked by our interactions. Every time he's appeared in my life, it's resulted in pain, and a depth of feeling which leaves me breathless. He uncorks these living sentiments inside of me—so visceral, so real, so tangled, until he comes along, and each individual strand of emotion inside me separates so I can feel each distinct sensation. They swell my eyes and overflow as I let the notes spill out. And with it, that ever-present, scratchy, nagging ache in my throat, which has only gotten steadily worse.

I've nursed it with painkillers, doubling the amount as the tour continued. I have only three weeks during which I can tour. Three weeks in which to test out my new material with the audience. Three weeks, ten cities. Playing to audiences of not more than a thousand each. It's the perfect way to test and get feedback.

I push away the pain, ignore the sweat dripping down my temples and my back, and bat away the dull, recurring ache in my side. I can do this. I must do this. I will myself to flow with the music, to immerse myself in the words. The love I hope to have, the one that's almost within grasp but which always eludes me.

Why is it always the wrong time for the two of us? Why can we never see eye to eye? Why is it that, while we're on the same wavelength, we never manage to meet each other halfway? More sweat pools in my armpits and drips down my arms. My head spins, but I don't stop singing. *Why is it that he cannot see that the only thing that matters is us? Why have we hurt each other so much? Why? Why?*

My fingers slip on the microphone. I open my mouth, but no sound comes out. The pain behind my eyes, in my throat, and at my back come together in a perfect trifecta that takes my breath away. I gasp. I try to lift my eyelids, but they seem to be weighed down. The music rises to a crescendo, and I manage to croak out the last line. Then the instruments stop, just as I wrote it. At the peak. The climax. Unfinished. There's no climb down for me. No redemption. Nothing except the darkness that rushes up to greet me. I lose my hold on the microphone, which hits the ground a second before I slump over.

66

Declan

"So, she's on her tour?"

"Yep." Rick nods at me from the screen of my phone.

"And she got on the flight okay?"

"She didn't want to use your private jet but, as per your instructions, I ensured there were no flight tickets available on any commercial airline."

"I knew I could count on you." I push up the barbell on the bench-press. I'm lifting double what I usually do, which is foolhardy, but fuck that. I need to find a way to reclaim my focus and stop my mind from wandering to her in the middle of tasks. And the only way to do that is to push myself. To challenge myself, until I have no choice but stay in the present and keep my attention razor sharp.

"How long you going to do this?"

"What?" I lower the barbell until it's parallel to my chest. My biceps strain; my shoulders scream in protest. I grunt then begin to push up the weights. *Slowly. Slowly.*

"Use me to keep you updated on her movements."

"It's what you're paid to do."

"And you know I do it, but not for the money."

"Yeah." I straighten my arms, still holding the weights. My arms shudder, and my chest hurts. There's a catch in my side. Sweat pools in my palms. The barbell begins to slip, and I lower it back into its cradle with a thump. My muscles release the tension they were holding, and pain slices through me. My breath comes in hard pants. Spots of black dance in front of my eyes.

"There are easier ways of killing yourself than with your own exercise weights."

"Har, har." I groan as I straighten to sitting position. "And wouldn't the press have a field day with that."

"Speaking of which, you could have warned her before posting the news about your movie together."

"I don't need permission from her," I growl.

"I thought you were past this shit, man. When are you going to pull your head out of your arse and do the right thing?"

"I am trying to do the right thing here." I snatch up a towel, then wince when my muscles protest. "Shit, I think I might have pushed it a little too hard."

"You think?" He sneers.

And that, coming from calm and collected Rick, gives me another pause. "What's crawled up your arse?"

"The fuck you talking about?"

"I'm supposed to be the ornery one here, not you."

"Yeah, well. You've paired me up with that arse-hat, Finn. What else did you expect?"

"First, you're the one who said he was the best person for the job."

"Well, he is." His scowl deepens.

"Second, you seemed to know so much about him, I thought you two were buddies."

"Fuck no. I barely know the guy."

I stare at him. Something's bothering him, all right, but fuck if I have time to get into it right now. "You'd better resolve whatever animosity there is between you and Finn. I want no gaps in her security."

"You're doubting my professionalism now?" he snaps.

"You're the best there is. It's why I want your attention focused on her. I need to make sure she's okay."

"The fuck don't you do that yourself, man? She doesn't need her security detail babysitting her. She needs her man."

I tighten my grip about my towel. Not a day has gone by in the past few weeks when I haven't asked myself this question. I flew back to New Zealand to prep for the shooting of the film. Now that Solene and I are back, so are most of the sponsors.

"I need a few more weeks to get everything in place before I send for her."

He glares at me.

"What?" I scowl back.

"You're pussyfooting around this. It's not like you, man."

"I'd like to see what you do when you're in my situation."

"Not happening; not anytime soon," he scoffs.

"That's what Cade said, and look at him now."

"He's one pussy-whipped bastard. But damn if I don't envy him having found the love of his life. Something which you, too, have by the way. So don't waste the opportunity, man."

I toss the towel aside and rise to my feet. "If you're done with your sermonizing, I need to get back to my work out."

He blows out a breath. "Just don't leave things too long." He cuts the call.

I stare at the blank screen for a while longer. Am I leaving things too long? Am I being a coward here? Nope, I've done everything to ensure her career and mine take off. I'm making sure we don't sacrifice our dreams. Sure, we're in love… I haven't told her that explicitly. But she should realize it after how I made love to her that last time. Right? Hell, it was the most moving experience of my life. The kind a man doesn't forget easily. And I saw her emotions in her eyes. She loves me, even though she hasn't told me so. Nah, we have time. Once she's here, and we're done shooting the movie, which shouldn't take more than two months, everything will be on track. Then, we can plan a real wedding in the run up to the premiere of the film, and fuck if that won't benefit the both of us.

So, this is what you've been reduced to? Playing the PR machinery like a loser? Bending your life to feed the machinery you once loathed? The same machinery also built me up, though. It gave me the fame, the power, the control I craved. And once I release this movie, I'll have achieved the one thing I feared was out of reach. I'll be unstoppable after this. I begin to work out again, when my phone vibrates with an incoming FaceTime call. It's Solene.

I reach for it, then stop. If I talk to her now, nothing is going to stop me from getting on the next plane to her. And right now, I don't want that. I need to stay on track. Need to get the shoot set up so I can bring her over. This time, I can't let things slide. This time, I'm going to deliver for both of us. I sink down into a push up, when the phone vibrates again. And again. I reach over and punch the red button disconnecting the call, then I switch it off.

I'm still at the gym an hour later when the director of the film barges in. He waves his phone at me. "You need to see this."

Even before I've snatched the phone from him, I know it's her. My heart leaps into my throat. A screeching sound fills my ears. I glance at the phone screen in time to see her topple over. She sprawls on the floor next to her stool and mic stand. Her blonde hair streaks across the dark wood floor in an obscene parody of sun rays lighting up a cloud-heavy sky. The camera zooms in on her features, so pale, those heavy lashes a dark fan against her cheekbones. Her lips—those soft sumptuous lips, slightly parted, as if she's asleep. But she's too pale, too still. Is she even breathing? That screeching sound between my ears turns up until it's vibrating from me, around me, cloistering me so I can barely breathe.

"Breathe, dammit!" I roar.

The sound of yelling fills the screen, the camera wavers, then cuts off. I stare at the blank screen, unable to understand what I've just seen. The piercing sound in my head fades, leaving me with complete blankness for a second. Then, the sounds around me penetrate the place I've fallen into. I toss the phone at the director and reach for mine on the floor. Switching it on, I call my pilot. "Ready the jet! I'm going to my fiancée."

67

Solene

I'm cold, so cold. A shiver runs down my spine, traveling all the way to my feet, then bounces up the front of my legs. A chill wracks me. My teeth chatter. I bring up my knees, curling them into my stomach, trying to keep in the warmth, but pain cuts through my side. I gasp. The shivering intensifies. *I'm cold, so cold. So lonely. Where am I? Where is he? Declan? Why aren't you here with me? Dec—*

"Shh, baby, I'm here now."

As if my thoughts have conjured him, I hear his voice in my ear. The next second, warmth heats my back. What can only be his big body curves around me. Heat wafts off the hard muscles that spoon my back. I instantly push my ass back until it connects with a familiar thickness.

A groan rumbles from him. "Fuck, baby, don't do that."

A weight descends about my middle, and he pulls me even closer. As if trained, I lift my head, and he slides his other arm under my neck. The heat intensifies, sinks into my blood. The chill finally dissipates. I stop trembling, let the sleep pull me under.

I come awake with a start. The scent of antiseptic that teases my nose, and the beeping of machines around me tells me I am in a hospital. The last thing I remember is trying to fight off the pain in my body and then, nothing. At least, the pain in my body seems to have ebbed somewhat. I open my eyes and still.

Facing me are dark, sooty eyelashes that block out those startling blue eyes from the world. For the first time, I watch him unobserved. I've never seen him sleep before this. How strange is that?

He's always awake, doing something or glaring at me with that cold-fire gaze that makes my knees buckle. That makes me want to sink to my knees and beg him to have his way with me. It's so distracting, I'm often unable to string my thoughts into sentences around him. I'm too busy trying to cope with the overwhelming emotions he raises in me. That complex need of wanting to be with him, to sink into him, to welcome him into my body, to allow him to have his way with me.

But I fight myself on this. I fight how he makes me feel. How he makes me want to conform to what he wants me to be, to be the kind of woman I thought I left behind. I didn't want my family to tell me what to do but when he does, I like it; and I can't explain it.

I feel needy and weak when I'm with him, yet he also makes me feel safe and secure.

There's nowhere else I'd be rather than by his side, but he makes it so difficult for us to be together. It started because I was too young, too immature to stand up to my brother for him. But he was older than me, and he should have known better than come to my room when I was alone. What my brother did to him was unpardonable, but I've apologized to him for that. Declan says he's forgiven me, yet he keeps hurting me. And a part of me knows that's because of his issues. If only I could get through to him. If only he'd let me get through to him. If only there were a way to start all over again. If only...

Tears prick the backs of my eyes, and it's crazy, really, that I should be crying now, when so much has happened between us, but I'm unable to stop the tear that slides down my cheek.

"Don't cry, Rabbit."

I still.

He flicks open those eyelids, and his powerful gaze settles on my features like the warmth of the early morning sun.

"You weren't sleeping, were you?"

He doesn't reply. He simply continues to take in every angle of my face. Without touching me, he manages to make me feel his phantom touch over my eyebrows, down my nose, under the curve of my lip.

I swallow. My pulse picks up. That familiar heat slides like honey down to the place between my thighs.

"Declan," I whisper.

He raises his hand and cups my cheek. "I'm sorry I left you like that. I'm sorry I didn't stay in touch. I'm sorry I didn't ask you to come with me earlier. I'm sorry... so sorry, baby."

I frown. "Where's this coming from?"

"I'm going to ask you something, and you're not going to deny me this."

I look between his eyes. The look in them is so serious, so unlike anything I've ever seen before, a shiver of apprehension runs up my spine. "What is it?"

He swallows. For the first time, I sense Declan-motherfucking-Beauchamp is uncertain, and that fills me with apprehension.

"You can tell me, baby." I place my hand on his, then turn my face into his palm and kiss it. When I look back at his face, he's shut his eyes. There are hollows under his cheekbones, and he seems to have lost weight since I last saw him. Also, when did he get here? "When did you get here?" I ask aloud, then glance around the room. "How long have I been in here?"

"You've been out for almost an entire day."

"Whoa." I shake my head. "Guess I was really run down, eh?"

He brings his other palm up to frame my face. "Remember, I told you I would take care of you?"

I nod.

"Clearly, I've been doing a shit job of it. I'll never forgive myself for this."

"For what?" I smile a little, but when he doesn't reciprocate, that weird sensation in my belly intensifies. "I feel fine now. All the aches and pains seem to have disappeared, and I'm sure I can be back on my feet really soon."

"There's something you need to know, baby."

"Okay, now you're really scaring me."

The skin around his eyes tightens. "I'll do anything for you, Rabbit. I'd give my life up... I will give my life up, if that's what it takes to get you back on your feet."

"Now, now. Surely, there's no need for such a dramatic gesture, and —" I nod slowly. "Now, I see what you're doing."

His eyebrows knit. "You do?"

"It's that last quarter of a smutty book, when the hero realizes he's been wrong all along—which of course, you have been—"

"Of course," he murmurs with a small smile.

He smiled. OMG, it's a teensy smile, but still… He smiled, so things can't be that bad, eh? "— and decides the only way to win the heroine back is to grovel. That's what this is, right?"

"You're right." He nods slowly. "You're always right, baby. Only, this is not *only* the groveling—a part I have yet to master—but this is also something more I want to do for you."

I blink. "So, this is your... Grand gesture?" Yep, reading those smutty novels has also provided me with the vocabulary to express myself.

He leans in until his nose bumps mine, until his breath intertwines with mine, and those long, thick eyelashes of his tangle with mine. Until I can make out the individual sparks in his eyes—a dizzying mix of blue and silver. Until his lips are so close, I can taste him on my palate. Until his features seem to soften and wear a look I've yearned to see on his face. *Mine. Mine. Mine.* He couldn't proclaim it louder if he shouted it out. Funny how, sometimes, the unspoken word can be so much more powerful. And coming from a word-slut, that's saying something.

"You could call it that. You can call it by any name, as long as"—he pushes his forehead into mine and looks deeply into my eyes—"you promise to accept it."

68

Declan

"No, absolutely not. I'm not going to accept this from you. No way." She folds her arms over her chest, which only makes her tits push out against the hospital gown. I know she's not wearing a bra under that. I know because I wasn't able to stop myself from palming them to soothe myself to sleep. After I crawled into bed and pulled her into my arms so I could share my warmth with her. She instantly settled, and in a practiced gesture, she pushed her butt into my crotch, which notched up my need for her further.

I'm never going to be in the same space as her and not want to be buried within her hot, tight hole. I'm never going to not be able to think of her every moment I'm away from her. I'm never not going to want to protect her from the world. Never be unable to want to shield her from the attention of everyone else. It's not in my DNA to rein in that possessive side of me. It's who I am. And it's time we both accept it.

"Yes, you are."

"No. I'm not." She tips up her chin.

I had her moved to a hospital suite as soon as she'd recovered enough. Strong enough, that is, to be able to be transferred, not strong enough to find that streak of adamancy in her that has brought us to loggerheads so many times before.

"This is not a negotiation, Rabbit. Nor a request. This is a fucking order." I glare at her, and she holds my gaze for a second, then another. Then her lips quiver, her eyes grow brighter, and a teardrop slides down her cheek. I bend my head and lick it up. "Please, baby. Please, let me do this for you."

She shivers. "Don't do that."

"Why not?"

"I don't like it."

"Your body says otherwise." I palm her tit, and the telltale hardness of her nipple stabs into my palm. I tilt my head at her, but she's not impressed.

"Don't change the topic with sex."

"There's no topic to change, because you're going to accept this from me."

"You mean, your kidney?"

"Yes."

She laughs, but it sounds hollow.

My heart feels like it's going to break through my chest. "No, baby, I'm not going to let you give up. I'm not going to let you wallow in self-pity or get depressed. We identified the problem and found the solution. Now, let's just implement it, shall we?"

She rubs at her temple. "How can you always reduce everything to cold, hard logic?"

"It's what I'm best at."

"It's a lot to take in." She begins to look away, but I pinch her chin, so she has no choice but to stay focused on my face. And to look into my eyes. Which is one way of ensuring she complies with what I have in mind.

"It is a lot. And I blame myself for things getting to this stage."

She scoffs. "It's hardly your fault I was ill with a streptococcal infection that led to needing a kidney transplant. It's a one in one-thousand chance that this could happen." She hunches her shoulders. "Just my luck that point-zero-zero-one percent settled on me."

"And the chances are even lower that I'd turn out to be a tissue match. But here we are. I want to do this for you. I order you to let me do this for you."

She squeezes her eyes shut. "Isn't it enough that you suffered from what my brother did to you? Now you want to put yourself through something potentially life-threatening, and—"

I place my palm over her mouth. "I'd sacrifice myself over and over again for you. It's the only thing I can think of to do to make up for how much I hurt you."

She glances away then back at me. "Are you saying these things because you think that's what I want to hear, or do you mean it?"

"What do you think?"

"I think." She swallow, "I... I..." She shakes her head. "I want to believe you mean it, but after everything you did, I'm not sure what to make of it."

My heart slams into my ribcage, and my pulse rate shoots up. I roll off the bed then sink to my knees.

"Wh-wh-what are you doing?" She begins to sit up, but I grip her shoulder and gently apply pressure, so she sinks back against the pillow. "What are you doing, Delcan?"

"Trying to show you how sorry I am for everything I put you through. As you know, I'm not good at expressing my feelings, Rabbit, but I'm going to try."

Her eyes fill with more tears, and she blinks them away. "You don't have to do this."

"I do. I know you think I'm donating my kidney because, well, who wouldn't in my situation—"

"There are many who wouldn't, and—" She begins to speak, but I hold up my hand.

"Please let me speak. Let me do this. Please, hear me out, baby. Please."

She bites the inside of her cheek, then nods.

"I know I treated you horribly. I shouldn't have accepted Nikolai as my investor. Shouldn't have agreed to pretend to be engaged to his rival's daughter. Shouldn't have planned it so you walked in on us. Shouldn't have broken your heart. Shouldn't have decided for both of us that it was the right thing to do to alienate you, so you'd leave me. I broke your heart when I did that. I should have trusted you enough to share everything with you. And then, after finally coming clean to you, I shouldn't have left you and gone on the shoot."

"Why did you do that, Declan? After you told me about your deal with the Bratva, and how being beaten up by my brother's men affected not just your physical appearance but also your emotional state-of-mind, after sharing how the BDSM lifestyle helps you get in touch with your feelings… After all of that, you still left me. How could you do that?"

Pain slices through my chest and spreads to my extremities. My stomach heaves, a pressure drums behind my eyes. It's as if every part of me is slowly coming alive. The sensations that have been suppressed inside me for so long seem to be clawing at my insides and tearing their way out.

"I'm so sorry for what I did. I'll do anything to make it up to you. I'd burn the world down for you, if I could. I'd go to the ends of the earth, I'd... Give up my career just to see you happy and healthy and safe. Let me do this for you, baby, please. I beg you."

"And then what? You'll give me your kidney, and then things will go back to being as they were? We'll recover, and you'll take off again without telling me?"

I wince. The pressure behind my eyes builds until I'm sure my eyeballs are going to burst. "Never. I'm never going to leave you again. I'll never forget how it felt to see you collapse on that stage. To see your prone body and be so far away and not be able to do anything to help you. I'm never going to put myself in a situation where I'm not there for you." I take a breath, then continue pushing out words through a throat that's constricting. "You're the most important thing in the world for me. You're more important than the very air I breathe. You're it for me, baby. And I won't let even death take you away from me." I blink, and her gaze widens.

She reaches up and touches a finger to my cheek. When she holds it up, moisture clings to her fingertip.

"Declan, you're crying," she whispers.

Another tear joins the first. I touch my other cheek, and my finger comes away wet. I'm speechless. All I can do is nod.

"After what you told me about your feelings being dulled… I didn't think you could express your emotions, let alone shed tears."

"Neither did I," I whisper. "I've never felt as deeply as I do now, on my knees in front of you, begging you to give me a chance to save your life. Please, baby, let me do this for you, please?"

69

Declan

"She refused you?" Cade gapes at me from where he's seated opposite me. We're at the cafeteria in the hospital. After she turned me down, I was too shocked to say anything. Yep, the man who's known for delivering impactful one-liners on screen found himself dumbstruck. She turned me down and it was as if someone had struck a red-hot knife through my chest and twisted it. And I felt every second of it.

Emotionally, there's still that familiar screen between me and what I feel, but everything seems sharper, more in perspective. Like someone wiped the screen so I can sense everything with more clarify. The therapist I worked with told me if I received an emotional blow intense enough, it might kickstart the breadth of sensations I'd be able to express. And perhaps that's what had happened.

Perhaps the shock of her denying me this opportunity to come to her aid caused a trauma intense enough to rival the blow I took to my head. The pain in my chest deepens, and I rub at it. I wanted to stay with her, no matter that she didn't want to look at me, but the nurses came in to check on her and shooed me out.

I wandered out of the room and found Cade waiting for me. He took one look at me and hustled me down the stairs and to the canteen, where he pushed me down into a chair, then placed a cup of coffee in front of me. Now, I wrap my hands around the cup and stare into the murky depths.

"You okay?" Cade frowns.

No, I'm not. I never will be. I'm going to lose her, and there's nothing I'm going to be able to do about it. The pounding at my temples intensifies. A drop of moisture plops into the cup and I stare at it. *Apparently, I'm crying again.*

A flash goes off somewhere off to the side, but I don't look up. I don't fucking care if a pap takes a picture of me crying and splashes it all over the internet. I don't care if it's bad for the action hero image I'm going for. I don't care if it ends my career. I don't care... About anything but her.

"The fuck—" Cade jumps to his feet, but before he can head for the pap, I hear the sound of a scuffle, then the pap's voice protesting. His voice fades, and silence envelops me.

I glance up to find Finn hauling the journalist away. Rick jerks his chin at me, then follows them to the entrance of the cafeteria where he parks himself. I look around, noticing, for the first time, that the place is virtually empty. Except for a lone doctor in scrubs who's on his phone in a corner, and two nurses who are eating at another, there's no one else. One of the nurses watches me with empathy in her eyes. She gives me a small smile, then goes back to her food.

"Fucking paps. They must have been tailing me, which is how he tracked you down here," Cade growls.

I go back to contemplating my coffee.

Cade clears his throat. "It won't be long before news of Solene's condition gets out to the press," he murmurs.

"Not if I have anything to do with it," I say grimly.

"You can delay it, but you and I both know, it's only a matter of time before the news is all over the media."

I grip my coffee cup tighter.

"So, what are you going to do about it?" he asks.

"What do you mean?"

"So, she turned you down… What are you going to do about it?"

"What can I do about it?"

Familiar voices reach me, and I glance up to see Michael and Sinclair making their way toward me. JJ pauses to speak with Rick. Both turn in my direction. Then JJ claps Rick on the shoulder and follows in Michael and Sinclair's wake. Michael turns around the chair on my left and straddles it. Sinclair slides into the one on my right. JJ hauls a third one over to our table, and plants it between Michael and Cade before seating himself.

"So—" He leans across the table. "Where were we?"

I scowl between the three of them, not liking where this is going. Knowing this is an intervention, and unable to say anything to cut off their monologues before they start.

I raise the cup of coffee to my mouth, only Sinclair snatches it away before I can take a sip. Some of the brown liquid splashes onto the table in front of me. A slow burn starts at the base of my neck, but I ignore it.

I reach for one of the two cups of water Cade placed between us, but Michael snatches it and holds it out of reach. I reach for the second cup of water, but JJ gets to it before me. He drains the water, crumples the paper cup, and tosses it onto the table. The burn turns into a flash fire that ignites my entire body. I jump up with such speed, my chair crashes to the ground.

I hear a gasp, then out of the corner of my eyes, I spot Finn escorting the two nurses and the doctor out the door. He steps out and slams the door shut behind him. I crack my neck, then face down the men, none of whom have moved from their chairs.

"Sit down." Michael nods toward my chair.

"Fuck you," I growl.

Sinclair yawns. "Sit the fuck down, if you know what's good for you."

I show him the bird.

Cade barks out a laugh. When I glare at him, he wipes the smile off his face.

"Good to see you're behaving like the loser you are." This from JJ. I throw myself across the table and at him, only Michael and Sinclair move as one. They each grab one of my shoulders, haul me back and to my feet, and drag me through the space between the tables and chairs behind us to throw me against the wall.

My back smashes into the hard surface. Pain zips down my spine to my feet, then bounces back up to meet the burning sensation at my nape. It's like a lit match to fuse, and every cell in my body sparks. I growl and charge forward, but both men grab me and hurl me against the wall again with such force that bits of plaster from the ceiling float to the ground. My back screams in protest, my bones feel like they've been tossed around in a rollercoaster, and sparks of red fly behind my eyes.

I shake my head to clear it, begin to straighten myself— Only, I'm tossed back into the wall, over and over and over again. I hear a crack, then an entire section of the ceiling crashes to the floor on my right. Suddenly, I'm released.

I draw in a breath and my lungs burn, but it's nothing compared to the agony that I feel in every breath I take. My entire body goes numb, then spasms, then goes numb again. The pattern repeats until I'm panting in earnest and seeing double. The specks of darkness in front of my eyes close in on me. I resign myself to falling unconscious, when water drenches me. I gasp and snap my eyes open to find all four of them staring at me.

Michael places a jug of water on the table next to him, then narrows his gaze on me. "Better?"

I'm never going to get fucking better. When I don't reply, Sinclair grips my shoulder. I shake it off.

"You're going to have to man up and do the right thing here," he snaps.

"You think I haven't tried?" I take a step forward. My back spasms, the pain slices through me, and the darkness tries to overwhelm me again, but I shove it aside. I find my focus, take a deep breath, then another, and will the pain to subside. When it turns down a notch, I take another step forward. "I offered her my kidney; she refused."

I don't need to bring them up to speed, I know Cade messaged them, which is why the fuckers arrived here. I wish they'd stayed out of my business, but at this stage, I'm beyond caring. I simply want... Her to accept my kidney.

"What are you going to do about it?" JJ rises to his feet and walks over to stand in front of me. "You going to moan and cry about the fact that she turned you down, or you going to find a way to convince her?"

I scoff, "Like I haven't tried that."

"Try harder, *stronzo*," Michael drawls.

"Clearly your persuasion skills need polishing up if you can't convince your woman to do what's good for her," Sinclair taunts.

"You losing your touch?" JJ closes the distance to me and grabs my collar. "You can't sway your submissive to do the one thing that would save her life? You're going to lose her, you bastard, you absolute good-for-nothing turdstain. You're a fucking loser. A piss poor excuse for a man. A failed Dominant. An alpha who's lost his power, you—"

Something snaps inside of me. I twist my torso, break his hold, then snap my head forward. I connect with his nose, and blood blooms from his face. I stagger back, then throw my head back and roar. "I will not let her die. I will not. Will. Not." I turn, then crash my head into the wall again and again.

I'm grabbed by my shoulders and pulled back. This time, Sinclair and Michael half-carry, half-drag me back to my chair, which has been rightened. They thrust me into it, then stand on either side of me.

Cade takes in the blood dripping down my face and winces. "You're not pretty anymore, I'm afraid."

Good. It's this focus on my countenance that made me want to avenge what her brother did to me. It blinded me to the fact that I'd fallen in love with her the moment I saw her singing on the beach. I found her again, only my ego stopped me from doing the one thing I should have done all that time ago—I should have bound her to me and never let her go. I should have told her how much I loved her. How much I cared for her. How much I want her—need her—yearn for her to be in my life. By my side. To be mine.

JJ draws in a breath, then sits back in his seat, "It's not too late."

70

Solene

It's too late. I'm going to die. I'm never going to be able to sing again. I'm never going to look into his eyes and see them blaze as he says—

"Solene, I love you."

I snap my eyes open, and his gaze holds mine. Blue, deep, intense, like I'm looking into the cold heart of hell... or the frozen tableau of a bird caught in mid-flight. I blink, and sparks of silver flare in their depths, then golden flares ignite. A tear drop squeezes out from the corner of his eyes, joining the streak of dried blood on his cheek.

"Wha—" I raise my gaze to his forehead and take in the bandage over where his scar would be. My head spins. My throat dries. "You're hurt?" I rasp.

"I hurt you more. I deserve this, and everything they did to me."

"They—?" I lean back and notice he's dressed in scrubs. Another bandage peeks out from the neckline. "What happened? Did you get into a fight?"

"Something like that." One side of his lips quirks, but his smile doesn't meet his eyes. He squeezes my hand, and that's when I realize he has my palm clasped between both of his.

"I love you, Solene."

I jerk back, pull my hand from his, and to my surprise, he lets go. I study his battered countenance. "This is going to play havoc with your movie."

"They'll accept me the way I am. Or not." He raises a shoulder. "I don't fucking care."

I bite the inside of my cheek. "But this is your dream movie. You've worked so hard for it, and if it fails, you have so much at stake."

"The only thing that matters to me is you, and until you're well, I'm not leaving your side."

My heart feels like it's filling my chest. I've waited so long to hear his words and yet, now that I am, I'm not sure I believe him. He must sense my discomfort, for he rises from the chair then sits on the bed next to me. He reaches for my hand, and I let him grasp it in his much bigger palm. He raises it to his mouth and presses his lips to my knuckles. "I love you, Rabbit, and you know it."

I flush, then turn away. "You don't have to say that to me because you know I'm going to die."

He freezes; his entire body seems to turn to stone. He's so still. Has he stopped breathing? I raise my gaze to find his features wearing an expression of such anguish, my breath catches in my chest. I can't look away, can't unsee the desperation in his eyes, the hopelessness, the love. The love. So much love. I squeeze my eyes shut. "Don't—" I swallow. "Please, don't."

"I'm sorry, I don't mean to overwhelm you with my declarations, but I'm desperate, baby."

I half laugh. "First, I see you cry. Then, you turn up with your face hurt—something I know is likely career-changing for you, and I know how much your career means to you. And now you say you love me. You have to admit, it's a lot."

He doesn't reply; the silence stretches. My nerve-endings crackle with the building tension. Finally, I can't stop myself from opening my eyes again. I take in the expression on his face—this one so tender and filled with so much yearning. And love. Again. Love. Love. Love. Love. He may have said it. But seeing it on his face, in his gaze, in how he holds my hand… I know he means it.

"It's not fair. You're such a good actor, you're convincing me that you're in love with me."

He winces, then lowers his chin, "I deserve that and more. I deserve every single name you call me and more. I deserve—"

"Us."

He freezes, then slowly shakes his head. "You don't have to do that. You don't have to give in to me. I know I can be persistent and controlling and dominant and—"

"An alphahole."

"And I'm sorry for everything but that last one."

A-n-d there he is. A fierce rush of... pleasure? Need? Hope? All of it fills my chest. "Just as I was getting worried about you, too," I murmur.

He raises his gaze to mine, and once more, those blue eyes which have always seen through me, and known me, and recognized me, capture mine.

"I'm still me. There's no getting away from that. But I'm going to change for you. I'm going to make sure my actions show you how much I love you. That I can't live without you. You're my breath, my soul. My very being is you, and if you die, my soul will die with you."

A tear slides down my cheek, mirroring the one that trails down his face. I tug on his hand, and he leans in until his nose bumps mine.

"I love you." He looks between my eyes. "Only you. Always you. Forever you. Let me do this for you, baby, please."

"Do I have a choice?"

"Always. You'll always have a choice, except"—his gaze intensifies—"when it comes to safeguarding your life, and when it comes to our bed."

Oh my god. I choke out a laugh, and more tears roll down my cheeks.

He raises his head and kisses first one eyelid, then the other. "Your sight is mine." He kisses my nose. "Your breath…" Then my lips, my chin, the pulse that flutters at the base of my throat. "Your breath is mine."

He raises his head and looks deeply into my eyes. "Your body is mine, baby." He reaches between us and cups the flesh between my thighs through the hospital gown. "Your pussy is mine. Your heart, your soul—"

He releases my hands and places his palm on my breast. "Your gorgeous tits, your very breath, your every thought, your hates, your discomfort, your stutter, your quick temper, your beautiful voice, your gorgeous eyes, your soft skin, your heart, your soul, your every touch. Your hopes. Your every dream. They are mine. Mine. Mine."

His. His. His.

"You're crazy," I say softly,

He nods. "For you."

My lips twitch. "And obsessed."

"Never claimed otherwise."

I squeeze my eyes shut, then open them. "This is insane. The doctors made it clear that the person donating the kidney has a more difficult time than the one who receives it." I hold up my finger. "Reduced life-expectancy, for one."

"I'd rather lead a shorter life with you in it than a longer one without you. I've already told you that my life is nothing without you being part of it, baby. I live for you. To be with you."

"Then, there's nerve damage, chronic pain—"

He raises a shoulder. "All of it is a small price to pay to see you well and happy. And on your feet."

"But you're hurt." I stare pointedly at the bandage that peeks up from under the neckline of his scrubs.

He scoffs, "It barely hurts. Nothing is going to stop me from donating my kidney to you."

"The medics might say otherwise."

"Like I'd let them."

My lips quiver, and I manage to keep them from curving into a smile. "It's going to mean your dream project is delayed," I murmur.

"Woman, haven't you heard a word of what I've been trying to tell you? All that matters is you."

Once more, he brings his face close to mine, until we share breath. "I thought working on this film and taking on this role—which could have finally made me the highest-grossing actor in Hollywood—was the culmination of all my dreams, but I was wrong. My most important achievement has been meeting you, knowing you, seeing you blossom into the incredibly talented artiste you are, watching the world recognize your potential, embracing my love for you. I have loved you from the moment I met you. You're it for me. You're the only woman for me, baby. Since I saw you, there's been no one else but you. It's only ever been you."

Heat flushes my cheeks. His eyes are so clear, I'm drowning in them, and this time I won't be able to— No, this time, I don't want to save myself.

And because I know I hold power over him, I can't help adding, "You sure you're not saying it because you think I'm going to die?"

His breath catches, then he glares at me. "Never say that to me. There's no life for me without you. I'm nothing without you. You're my sun, my moon, and my stars. My complete universe. And I will never, ever let anything happen to you. I promised you, remember?"

Tears pool in my eyes, and heat spreads to my chest, my stomach, my feet, until all of me is tingling with sensation. "You take your promises seriously, don't you?"

He nods.

"You're a stubborn *figlio di puttana*."

He chuckles. "Only you can call me a son-of-a-bitch and make it feel like you're singing me a love song."

I huff. "You really do love me?"

He nods. "Even before I met you. I just didn't know it then."

A giddy sensation spins around in my chest, my head, at my pulse-points. I've turned into a kaleidoscope of hope, of faith, of a trust that, finally, things will turn out all right.

He reads my thoughts because, of course he does. "It will, I promise." He brushes his lips over mine. "I love you, baby. I'm doing this for you. *For us*." He plants his arms on either side of me on the bed. "This is a non-negotiation. The deal is done. I'm giving you my kidney; end of discussion."

I hold his gaze, then reach up to touch the scar on his forehead. "I really am sorry for what my brother did to you."

"No more apologizing, baby. That part of our life is over; done with. The most important thing now is your health. To get you back on your feet and fully functional. Then in my bed, with your legs spread wide open, and your tight, pink pussy ready and willing for all the things I want to do to it."

I roll my eyes. "And you were doing so well."

His smile widens. "So, it's decided?"

71

Four weeks later

Solene

"Whoa, my feed is going crazy." I take in the likes, comments, and views that multiply by a factor of a hundred, if not a thousand, by the second. Just ten minutes ago, the post stood at a hundred thousand likes. It doubled to two hundred thousand and is gaining momentum. The comments are all positive—like *all* positive. "I've never seen anything like this."

I hold up my phone where I'd posted a photo of Declan and me—in identical hospital gowns, with tubes running from our noses, IVs stuck in our arms, disheveled hair, and twin expressions of happiness, sheer adoration, and love… Yeah, we're wearing what one of my fans has called the #DecleneDelight

And then there was the #AngstyDeclene hashtag that trended when the pap who'd got a picture of Declan with a tear rolling down his cheek in the hospital cafeteria published it and the fans jumped on it and shared it all over social media.

Both are cringeworthy hashtags, but they've caught the imagination of my followers and his. My follower count has catapulted, as has his. We kept the news of the twin operations a complete secret, except for our closest friends. And even then, we told them not to come over, but instead, stay focused on the rescue efforts for Knight.

There was no stopping my sister Olivia, nor Declan's brother Arpad, though.

They came over to be with us during the operation and only left a week ago… After making the two of us promise to visit London and see them very soon. The good news is, the procedure was a success, and both of us are on our way to recovery. It also means, neither of us has any other commitments, at least, for another month.

I urged him to get reconstructive surgery on the new scar on his forehead, not because it bothers me, but because I know how he feels about scars, but he refused. He insisted the audience must accept him as he is. He also shared how the wound was self-inflicted, as well as how his friends knocked him around until they knocked some sense into him —his words, not mine. I was shocked, and honestly, a bit amazed they showed up to help him, even if they were a bit violent, and he insisted it was a good thing. That it spurred him to return to my hospital room and share his feelings with me... Which is why we're here, together.

Declan's team of lawyers ensured the insurers cover the delay in shooting the film. The result? Even the hard-nosed financiers of the project were pacified enough to wait. The even more important result? This is the longest ever we've both been in one place, under one roof and in each other's company. It's also the happiest I've ever been, and the most relaxed I've ever seen him. Speaking of, the most handsome, most charismatic, most striking, heart-stoppingly dominant man in the world continues to stare at me without speaking.

I flush. "What?"

"Can't I admire how gorgeous my wife to-be is?"

"So, our engagement is real after all, I take it?"

His beautiful, puffy lower lip curls. "Did you ever think otherwise?"

"So why didn't you ask me to marry you for real? Why that entire pretend-to-be-married-so-it's-good-for-our careers thing?"

"Because it was… It is good for both of our careers?" He smirks.

I peer at him from under my eyelashes. "You're a cocky bastard."

"Your cocky bastard."

I chuckle. "You're also in a very good mood."

"I'm here in our bed, with my beautiful and utterly ravishing fiancée, and I have nowhere to be for, at least, the next week. What's not to be in a good mood about?"

He folds his arms behind his neck, and his biceps bulge. I take in that beautiful neck of his, those shoulders, those cut muscles of his chest —which haven't lost any of their edge, despite the fact he hasn't been able to work out for the last three weeks—the white bandage at his side which is a twin to the one I sport on mine.

"How are you feeling?" I ask softly. It's been three weeks since the operation in which they took the kidney from him and immediately transplanted it in me. I opened my eyes, and the first thing I wanted to know was if he was okay. The doctor in charge of the procedure laughed and told me he did the same when he regained consciousness. Prior to the surgery, he'd also insisted—no, demanded—that he be wheeled into the recuperating room with me so we could recover from the operation side-by-side. The team in charge wasn't happy, but after an internal consultation, they agreed. Considering a part of him is inside of me now, there's no way they could have kept us apart.

"How are you feeling?" he shoots back.

"Getting stronger every day." I smile.

He traces the curve of my lips with his eyes, and it's as if he's touched me. Then he leans across the bed and does so with his fingers. A shiver runs down my spine, my nipples tighten, and my pussy clenches.

"Darling Rabbit, you need to behave. I'm not going to fuck you until you're completely, one-hundred percent back to normal; you know that."

I pout. I know. I understand why. But also, I don't want to understand why. I toss my phone aside, then crawl over to him. Pain radiates out from the site of where they cut into me, but I ignore it.

"Soon we'll be sporting matching scars, huh?" I throw my leg over his waist and place my pussy exactly over that swollen portion at his crotch.

"Jesus, what are you trying to do, baby?" he growls.

I wriggle until my wet panties, which are wedged inside my melting slit, are framed around his rapidly swelling cock. "What do you think I'm trying to do, baby?"

That slow curve of his lips is in evidence again, my heart flutters. My stomach feels like I've swallowed an entire flock of hummingbirds who are fluttering and trying to break out. "I want you," I murmur.

"You have me." He places his massive hand on my hip. "You had me from the moment that angelic voice of yours reached me on the shore that day."

"You know exactly the right thing to say to me, don't you?" I lean over and place my lips over his. "I can kiss you, can't I?" I murmur.

"I suppose that's allowed.

"And this?" I swipe my tongue across his mouth, and when he parts his lips, I slide my tongue over his. Soft and sweet and dark and... everything. The taste of him is better than any Michelin-star meal.

His hold on my hip tightens, and I can't stop the satisfaction that slithers through my veins. I deepen the kiss, and he allows it. He lets me suck on his tongue and lick across his teeth and moan into his breath. When I bite down on his lower lip, it's as if a shock of electricity zings down his body. He hisses, then clamps his other hand around my neck. I try to kiss him again but am unable to do so because he's holding me away.

"But I wanna." I scowl.

"And you will. You can have my tongue and my cock and my fingers all over you and in you. You can have your thighs squeezed around my face as I devour your cunt."

Heat surges under my skin.

"You can have your nipples pinched and your tits massaged as I fuck them, you can have your slit stretched around my cock as I stuff myself inside your tight hole, as I caress the space between your arse cheeks and make you come with such intensity, it'll be close to a religious experience."

The heat extends to my toes, my fingers, and my scalp, until every part of me is on fire, and my very breath seems to have turned into a thousand tiny sparks that infiltrate all of my cells and make me writhe around on his cock.

"You can have it all, baby. After you're better."

"But I'm so horny," I whine.

"Horny huh?"

I nod. "What are you gonna do about it?"

72

Declan

"This, baby. This is what I'm gonna do."

I slide down my sweatpants, then grip her hips, and position her exactly over my swollen cock. I thrust up and into her, hitting the exact center of her core, brushing over her throbbing clit, and sliding into the hole of her slit, which hasn't stopped dripping since she crawled over to me.

Her eyes roll back in her head. She grips my wrists, throws her head back, exposing the sweet column of her throat, the sensuous turn of her shoulder, and the thrust of her breasts with the engorged nipples that stab through the fabric of her camisole.

I wasn't kidding when I said I intend to follow the doctor's rule to the letter. No physical exertion for my baby. Doesn't mean I can't find a way to make her come, with me doing all the work. A slight discomfort crowds my side—the site where they took my kidney. Where I'm proud to display the mark of life. The life that I could offer her.

How many lovers can say they shared their life with their soulmate, literally? The fact that I could do this for her is my privilege. And my honor. It's the one good thing I've done in my life. The media thinks it's selfless—I say it's the most selfish thing I've ever done. I did it for myself. So I could have her with me, at my side, in my life. I wasn't kidding when I said I would have died for her. But this is so much better. To live with her and watch her flourish again, thanks to a part of me that will be part of her—which will connect me with her forever. I am the luckiest man alive.

"Declan, I am so close."

She lowers her chin and looks at me from between her hooded eyelashes. Her skin is flushed, her lips parted. The dark circles under her eyes are almost gone. We're still under observation, and she'll be on medication for the rest of her life, but we'll grow old together. And she'll be able to perform again, once we get the all-clear.

It's a second chance, the kind that makes me feel humble and appreciative in a way that I've never felt before. My heart swells in my chest. The emotions that have always felt at arm's length away seem so much closer now. I increase the pace of my thrusts. My cock feels like it's about to stab right through the crotch of my sweatpants. My balls grow heavy. The blood drains to my groin, and I grunt.

She leans over me, her glorious hair a curtain about us. "I love you," she gasps.

"The time in my life when I didn't love you was when I was the most bereft."

Her eyes soften. Her chest rises and falls. The next time I piston my hips up and into her, I hit that sweet spot inside her exactly, and she gasps. A trembling grips her, and I know she's about to— "Come for me, baby," I order, and she does. I continue to rub my erection against her slit as she moans and cries out, and with a final whimper, slumps forward. I lower her to my chest and wrap my arms about her waist. "Sleep, Rabbit. We're together now."

Two months later

"You sure you're up for this?" I hold out my hand to my fiancée.

She glances up from the smutty book she has open in her lap. "Thought you were always up for this?"

"I see you're getting bratty, Ms. Sabatini. Time you were taught a lesson, hmm?"

Her grin widens, and color flushes her cheek. "What did you have in mind, Mr. Beauchamp?" She flutters her eyelashes.

"Jesus, baby, when you use that tone of a voice, I'm tempted to drop everything, throw you over my shoulder, and march you right back home to our bed."

"That would make the crowd of reporters out there very happy." She stabs a thumb in the direction of the doorway. We're back in the bookshop I purchased for her. The one I refused to part with, even when selling it could have meant bridging the gap in the capital needed toward financing my film. I would never consider parting with it; would have done everything in my power to keep it. Other than our bed, it's the one place where she's most happy.

After the doctors pronounced her well on the mend, I set up a reading corner for her in a back room of the bookshop. It's next to the main shop floor with the books, with French doors that lead out into a private garden. I changed the parking lot behind the bookshop into an oasis of greenery. Away from prying eyes, I furnished a comfortable loveseat, arranged with blankets and cushions, then added a fireplace opposite so she'll always be warm. Then I slipped in a coffee and tea bar and arranged for her favorite biscotti to be stocked. Now, she reaches for one and bites into it. "These are delish. I forgot to thank you for arranging to have them in the shop."

"Everything you love under one roof," I note with satisfaction as she crunches down on the confection and swallows it.

"Including you." She goes to brush off the crumbs, but I circle my fingers around her wrist. I squat down in front of her, bring her fingers to my mouth and lick off the traces of the cookie.

"Yum." I lick my lips.

Her gaze grows heavy. "You're doing that on purpose." Her voice is breathless.

"Doing what on purpose?" I tease.

"Drawing my attention to your gorgeous lips, knowing I'll never be able to resist the call of your sexy body."

I reach for a napkin, pat her fingertips dry, then flick the waste into the trash can.

"You didn't answer me, baby," I murmur.

"What was the question?" Her tone is distracted, her gaze still fixed on my lips.

"Keep looking at me that way and we're never leaving this room."

"Nothing wrong with that." Her mouth curves.

I take the book from her lap and slide it to the side. When she parts her legs, I lower my head and press my nose into the space between her thighs. I inhale deeply, and the sugary-sweet scent of her pussy goes straight to my head and to my cock, which instantly swells. "Fuck, Rabbit, I need to bottle the scent of your cunt and carry it around with me."

"And then how will you relieve your are-you-happy-to-see-me-shaped baseball bat in your crotch?" She reaches between my legs and squeezes my shaft, and I almost come in my pants.

"Woman, you're a menace," I grumble.

"You taught me well, Tiger."

I blink. "Tiger, huh?"

"You call me Rabbit; figured it was time I came up with a name for you," she says in an innocent voice.

"Hmm." I sit back on my haunches—my head, my heart, my soul still full of her scent, her taste, her very essence. These weeks we've spent locked in my house have been the best of my life. And if I could, I'd simply stop the production of the movie and devote the rest of my days to keeping her high on post-coital endorphins. But I need to keep her in the style she deserves. More importantly, I need to ensure she gets her chance at reviving her career. I cannot—will not deprive her of this. "I'm rather partial to you calling me Lord or Master."

She rolls her eyes. "Of course you are."

"Yep, definitely time."

"For what?"

"For now, it's going out and facing the press."

"Which should be a breeze, since I'm with you." She raises a shoulder.

"So much confidence in me, hmm?"

"Always, Tiger. Always."

"I'm keeping count of the number of ways you sass me, and I'm going to return it to you with interest," I say in a low voice.

A shiver runs up her spine. She leans in until her nose brushes mine. "I'm counting on it."

"You two ready?" Giorgina's voice says from the doorway.

Neither of us looks away.

"The crowd is getting restless," Harry's voice pipes up from somewhere in the same direction.

I rise to my feet, and this time, when I hold out my hand, she takes it. I pull her to her feet. Once more, I scan her features—the lack of black circles under her eyes, the healthy color of her cheeks, her pink blouse and skinny jeans teamed with Doc Martins. On her right wrist she wears the bracelet with the charms I've given her. On her left hand is the engagement ring. All pieces of jewelry that I gave her. And inside her is a part of me. I touch her side. "How does it feel?"

"It doesn't hurt at all." She smiles. Then, in a move that mirrors mine, she presses her palm against my side. "How does it feel?"

"Don't feel a thing anymore." So, maybe I'm lying a little. Maybe the lingering pain in my side is one that may never go away. It's similar to the pain of a phantom limb, the doctor told me. It might fade with time, or grow worse, or neither. So, I might need to take painkillers until I find a better way to manage it. But it's worth every bit of inconvenience, every twinge that grips me when I move, every bead of sweat that slides down my spine as I entwine my fingers through hers and turn to face our managers lurking anxiously by the doorway.

"You sure you're okay?" She tugs on my sleeve.

I glance down at her. "As long as you're by my side."

Her eyes light up. "I'm a sucker for romance, and you know it."

"I'm just getting started, too, baby."

We grin at each other, and I know the look on her face echoes the complete adoration on mine. And I probably look like a sappy, pussy-whipped *stronzo*, but fuck that. My Rabbit is fine and back on her feet, and the happiness and satisfaction I get from knowing I played a role in that is the most satisfying feeling in the world.

Giorgina clears her throat. "Shall we?"

73

Solene

The flash of lightbulbs going off is blinding. I should be used to it by now, but the months I spent away from the media recuperating have made me forget how full-on the paparazzi can be. After I posted the picture of the two of us on my social media feed, I put away my phone and so did Declan. Harry and Giorgina monitored the online feedback and kept us posted. We warned our friends and family we were going underground until we felt ready to face the world, which was yesterday.

After days of being immersed in each other, getting to know each other's tastes even better, and talking about everything we loved and hated about our lives, our pasts, and our futures, as well as spending hours, sometimes, sprawled out on the couch in front of his infinity pool simply reading, I feel like I may know this man better than myself. I also feel rested. In no little part, because he refused to let me do a thing. He insisted on bringing me anything I needed, and when I protested that he'd been through a difficult procedure, too, he finally relented and allowed his staff more access to me. Plus, Rick and Finn were always close by not only to look out for us, but also to ensure we never lacked for anything. Between them, Giorgina, and Harry—who showed a side of him that went beyond simply the money-grabbing shark I thought he was when I first met him—we found ourselves in a little bubble of contentment we didn't want to burst. We kept postponing the inevitable, until yesterday, when he decided to take a swim. It was the first of any kind of physical activity since the doctor had pronounced him fit.

I watched his powerful arms cleave through the water and realized he is, indeed, at one hundred percent in terms of his recovery. He hoisted himself up and out of the swimming pool and shook the water from his hair. Framed against the glorious California sunset, with the reds and oranges streaking the sky and highlighting the tan of his skin, I knew it was time.

When I pointed it out to him, he was reluctant to accept it, but I insisted. I told him I couldn't wait to get back to work—which is both true and a lie. True because I can't wait to start singing again, but also a lie because I don't want to leave our little slice of paradise.

I also know it's important to get the movie started. I know he feels it's going to be important for my career, but really, it's more important for his profile that we do this movie together. Of course it will benefit me. And yes, #Declene will also boost the earnings from the film, but he's the star here. A real, genuine, Hollywood A-lister. And since this is his first time in a leading role where he doesn't play a villain, there's already a lot of anticipation around it.

Sure, my presence helps. The story of us, coming together for this movie, both on screen and in real life, as well as his organ donation to me… All of it is going to stoke the public's need to see the film.

But first, the movie has to be made. There's no putting off the fact we have to venture out of our happy space.

I urged him to think about restarting the production. He thought it over and told me I was right. That he'd been putting it off but there are people whose livelihoods depend on the shoot kicking off. He can't put it off anymore. As one, we agreed not to delay things further. We'll get things rolling with a short press conference today to crank up the PR machinery.

As I take in the sea of journalists who've turned up to listen to us—and with such short notice—I know we've made the right decision. If we waited any longer, interest might have fizzled out. Any less, and they might not have been this hungry for information. Nope, we timed it just right. Doesn't mean it's any less nerve-wracking to confront the wall of faces.

He must sense my nervousness, for he pulls me into his side as we pose for the photographers. There are no chairs for us to sit. Instead, we decided on keeping it very casual. We're standing in a space in the middle of the shop, surrounded by rows of books.

And can I tell you a secret? All the shelves in this section now hold smutty books from my favorite Indie authors. All catalogued by author and by levels of spiciness. OMG! It's something he surprised me with. He'd ordered all the books himself, after doing some online research. Then engaged extra help to have them arranged in a format he knew I'd love. I squealed when I discovered it. To think, there was a time when I wasn't allowed to read my favorite books, and now I'm surrounded by them. And it's all thanks to this incredible man. How lucky am I, eh?

I wrap my arm about his waist, and his familiar scent, his touch, the heat from his body, all of it more familiar to me than my own, wrap around me. I can't stop myself from turning my face into his chest and rubbing my cheek against the soft cloth of his hoodie. In response, he bends and kisses the top of my head. Which only makes the flashes from the cameras intensify. It seems to go on and on, until Giorgina steps in front of us. On either side, we're bracketed by Finn and Rick. They're far enough away not to be in the frame, but close enough that they can step in to intervene, if necessary, while Harry's lurking off to the side. Giorgina puts up a hand, and the flashes finally fade away.

"Declan and Solene have a statement to make."

There's a murmur from the crowd.

"That is, once you settle down." Her voice is firm. She thrusts out a hip, slaps her hand on it and taps her foot shod in six-inch stilettos. I wince. The woman's a hard arse.

"You look good yourself, Gio," one of the reporters calls out.

She tosses her hair over her shoulder. "Flattery will get you— everywhere." she flashes him a smile. The man winks at her, then drops to his haunches and takes a shot of her.

"Okay, that's enough." Rick steps between them.

"Hey, man, you're ruining my shot," the paparazzo whines.

"I'll ruin more than that if you don't back off, buster." Finn plants himself next to Rick. The combination of the two of them shoulder to shoulder in front of Giorgina makes me exchange a look with Declan. He shrugs. "I have no idea what that is."

"Hmm." I glance up to see Giorgina walk forward and tap the men on their shoulders. They move aside, and she steps in between them.

"They have a point. If you can step back, we can start the proceedings, and that's what you're here for, eh?"

Giorgina turns to look between the two security guys. "If you two can also get back into place, perhaps we can get this show on the road?" Her voice is laced with impatience.

"You okay?" Rick looks her up and down.

"He shouldn't have stepped out of line," Finn points out.

"And shit happens; deal with it. I don't have time to argue with the two of you. Let's get on with it."

Finn doesn't look happy. Rick looks like he's going to beat up someone. Then, he seems to get a hold of himself. Without another word, he moves away to one side while Finn moves to the other.

"Okay, you guys are on." Giorgina nods in our direction, then moves aside.

Declan lowers his arm, then once again, weaves my fingers with his. "Thank you for giving us some breathing space as we recuperated over the last few weeks." He nods in the direction of the journalists. "Solene and I cannot begin to tell you how much we appreciate it, and the chance we've been given to start all over again, in more ways than you can imagine."

74

Declan

"Do we have to leave this room?" I lock my fingers behind my neck and watch my Rabbit slip on a pair of white cotton panties.

She laughs. "Our friends and family—including your grandmother—have arrived. I'll say, yes?" She thrusts out her hip and plops her hand on it. "Did you have other plans?"

We're in a townhouse Solene and I bought not far from where the Seven, Michael and JJ live. I didn't need to be in Primrose Hill, but given everything we've been through, and the fact that she'll have to be on medication for the rest of her life to manage the effects, it feels reassuring to buy a house in the same locality as my friends.

I take in her creamy breasts, her narrow waist, and the scar that marks her as mine. Her white knickers can't hide the shadow of the cleft between her thighs. I can't forget it leads to her pretty, pink pussy where I've spent so much of my time. And still, I can't get enough of her. I narrow my gaze, and she tilts her head. "I'm not sure I like the look in your eyes."

"Oh?" I throw off the cover which has already begun to tent at my crotch, then push my legs over the side of the bed. I rise to my feet, plant my palms on my hips, and mirror her stance.

She drags her gaze down the expanse of my chest, to where my cock stands up proudly against my lower belly. Color smears her cheeks. "*Madonna Mia*." She brings her palms up together in praying position over her chest. A very Italian gesture, and one very appropriate in this case.

Allowing my lips to curl, I grip the base of my shaft and massage the column to the top. She licks her lips, and her nipples grow so hard they must, surely, hurt. I widen my stance, and she lowers her arms to her sides. Then, without looking away from my thickening dick, she slides her panties down her legs before straightening and kicking them off.

"Come here," I order.

She instantly moves closer, until she's standing in front of me. Her chest rises and falls, and she curls her fingers into fists.

"Do you want to suck my cock?"

She nods at once. No hesitation. That elusive trust between us, the one I didn't think I'd ever find, the one I hoped she felt, thought she felt, but which was never the all-encompassing, complete confidence that shimmers between us now. It's a tangible connection between us.

"On your knees. Arms behind your back. Keep your mouth open, tongue depressed, so you can take me down your throat."

And that's why I'm able to say aloud the thoughts that crowd my mind. The commands, the dictates, the primal urge to steer her to suit my needs, the intrinsic necessity to satisfy her through satisfying myself, is something I no longer need to hide. She understands me now, in a way I never thought anyone else could. But then, she's my submissive, my only, my other half. The woman—the only one—who holds the power to slay me. To make me bend to her will, should she choose.

It's her choice as she sinks to her knees now. Her choice to hook her fingers behind her back. Her choice to open her mouth, pushing down her tongue and baring that sweet, hot, hole perfect for my cock. I dig my fingers into the back of her hair and tug just enough for her to pant. Her pupils dilate, and a shudder grips her.

I stuff my erect cock into her mouth until it hits the back of her throat. She gags, and the resulting suction squeezes my balls. My thigh muscles spasm, and I almost come right then. That's how it is with her. Doesn't matter how much I've fucked her mouth, or her pussy, or her arse, I always want more. I'm like a horny teenager unable to hold myself back with her. I pull out and stay balanced on the rim of her lips. She breathes in through her nose, then licks across the sensitive skin at the crown of my shaft. Heat from her touch sears my veins. My vision doubles, and my heartbeat escalates.

"Fucking hell, Rabbit, what you do to me."

I curl my fingers around her throat, then push forward and down. The feel of my cock sliding down her gullet sends a fire of possessiveness streaking through my body. I pull out again and begin to fuck her face in earnest. Her breathing grows labored, and her breasts swell. Sweat beads my shoulders, as I pick up my pace. My balls draw up. "I'm coming, and you're going to take every drop, baby, you hear me?"

A ripple runs down her body. Her pupils dilate further, until the circle of green around the black almost disappears. And that's so fucking erotic, so hot, I can't stop myself. With a growl, I empty myself down her throat. I pull out, then bend and haul her up into my arms.

She wraps her legs about my waist, and I kiss her. I absorb the taste of myself on her, I suck on her tongue, sample every inch of her sweet mouth. She melts into me. She twines her arms about my neck and pushes those gorgeous, fleshy breasts of hers into my chest. My cock instantly thickens again. With a growl, I turn and drop her on the bed. She bounces, legs still spread wide, her eyes so big, they seem to take up her face. "I'm going to fuck you now."

Without giving her a chance to react, I place my knees between her thighs, then throw her legs over my shoulders. I fit my cock into the opening of her melting slit. With one tilt of my hips, I'm inside her. I groan aloud. So does she. She's stretched around my cock, bent almost double, and it's the sweetest sight I've ever seen. I plant my arms on either side of her and allow her to adjust to my size.

Each time I take her, it feels like the first time. The clamp of her pussy around my cock, the tightness of her channel around me, the way her inner walls flutter around my shaft... All of it is a mixture of heaven and the kind of hell that comes with needing to hold back until we're both at the very edge. I curl my fingers around her throat and squeeze. A moan spills from her lips. She grips my wrist with her tiny hands, the difference between her fairness and my tanned skin, and the slimness of her digits in contrast to my much thicker wrist highlight the difference in size between us. It's arousing, and exciting and so indecent, my cock thickens further inside her.

"Dec-lan," she gasps.

"What do you need, baby?"

"You. I want you." She digs her fingertips into my forearm. "Fuck me, Tiger."

75

Solene

My nickname for him sends him over the edge. His hold on my throat tightens, and he begins to fuck me in earnest. Each time he slams into me, my body moves up the mattress. The entire bed shakes, and he still goes at it. He stuffs himself into me over and over again. There's a look in his eyes I've never seen before. A determined look, one of focus, of absolute certainty and lust and need and trust and everything I ever hoped to see on his features and feel in him.

All of it swirls together in one perfect storm of love. It has to be love. This intense, tearing me apart sentiment that builds the pressure behind my eyes and between my legs as he pounds into me over and over again. Our gazes are locked. And I whimper and gasp and moan as he fucks me thoroughly. He squeezes down on my throat. I draw in a breath, and my lungs burn. Spots of black flicker around the edges of my eyesight. Then he hammers into me again, hitting that spot deep inside me that only he can find. And when he releases his hold on my throat, the oxygen pours into me, and I ignite. The climax crashes over me, and still, he doesn't look away. He holds me with his gaze and his cock as I fall apart around him. His jaw is hard, and a pulse beats at his temples.

He continues to fuck me through the aftershocks. Then a muscle ticks above his cheekbone, and with a low groan, he follows me over the edge. Liquid heat bathes my insides. I open my mouth, and he fits his over mine. We kiss deeply, our gazes still locked, my ankles entwined about him. His muscles tremble, the planes of his back move, then he pushes his forehead into mine. We stay that way for a few seconds more. He's consuming me. He's inside me in every way.

"I'm yours, only yours." I swallow.

"And I yours." He rubs his nose with mine. "I love you, Rabbit."

"And I want to spend every moment of my life with you."

"I'm going to make that happen," he swears.

"No more separations."

"No more staying away from each other," he agrees.

A teardrop squeezes out from the corner of my eye, and he licks it up. "What's that for?"

"Happiness?" I brush my lips over his. "I—"

A pounding at the door cuts me off. "You two coming out anytime soon?" a woman's voice hollers.

"That's Penny," I groan.

"Everyone is waiting, and we all know what you two are up to, including grandmama," she yells.

"Grandmama." He winces.

"Told you we shouldn't have kept your grandmother waiting," I point out.

"I can hear you guys whispering, by the way," Penny calls out.

"We're coming. We'll be down in a bit, I promise," I yell back.

There's silence, then the sound of her footsteps recedes.

"We really have to be getting back," I murmur. Then just because I can, and because he still hasn't told me everything, I squeeze my inner walls around his still erect cock.

His gaze widens. "Woman, the hell you doing?"

I peer into his eyes. "Trying to get you to tell me why she was crying."

"Why who was crying?" he gasps.

"When I walked in on the two of you at your place, why was she crying?"

His chest rises and falls. He searches my features. "You're not going to let that go without finding out, are you?"

I shake my head.

His lip curves on one side. "You're fucking obstinate woman, and that's one of the things I love about you."

"Are you trying to change the topic, because—"

"She was crying because she was pissed off with Nikolai. She needed to confide in someone, and I happened to be there."

I tilt my head, take in the sincerity etched into his features. "She's in love with him?"

"I can neither confirm nor deny that."

"So, she *is* in love with him."

He half laughs. "That's something you'll have to ask her. Or Niko."

"And I'm going to see them when?" I pout.

"He's an investor; he'll be there at the premiere of our film. And if I'm reading the situation correctly, so will she. I—"

I clench down on him again, and this time, a pulse leaps at the base of his throat.

"You're going to pay for that, you realize that?" he growls.

"Can't wait." I absolutely adore the effect I have on him. I've seen how he never lets me out of his sight, how he follows me with those gorgeous eyes every time I'm in the same space with him. I also know he tracks me through my phone and that, at least, one of the charms he gave me has a tracker... But somehow, I can't get upset with him. It's his way of watching out for me, of caring for me, of ensuring we're always connected. Also, he agreed to return the favor.

I touch the locket he wears around his neck on a silver chain. It's a twin of the one he gave me to wear as a charm. A tiny locket with a strand of hair from each of us entwined. There's also a chip embedded in it. This way, I can keep track of where he is. If that sounds a little obsessive, well, that's too bad. This is what makes us happy. And that's all that matters, right? I reach up and kiss him.

He deepens the kiss until we're both panting. He tears his mouth from mine. "If it weren't for the thought of Grandmama waiting to see us, I'd have told everyone to fuck off and shown you just how much I love you."

"We have to go," I manage to force out through my sex-addled brain. "But first, I need to shower."

"No shower."

"Eh?" I blink. "I smell of—"

"Me—and I want it that way."

"You look good." Penny looks me up and down.

"Thanks?" I laugh.

"No, I didn't mean it that way. I mean, you're glowing, and you look in love, and not like someone recovering from a procedure—oops." She claps her hand over her mouth. "I'm always talking before thinking. Don't mind me. My brain has a very loose connection to my tongue. I mean, ugh! Ignore me!" She flushes and falls silent.

Mira and I burst out laughing.

"Don't worry, I know you don't have a spiteful bone in your body," I chuckle. Now Giorgina, on the other hand, I can never tell if she's being spiteful on purpose or not. But then, since our procedures, and all the social media interest around it, she's been nothing but supportive. So beneath all that cattiness is a genuine heart. It just takes a lot for her to show it. Of course, that doesn't seem to deter Rick. Or Finn, given how I've caught him looking at her. Apparently, he broke it off with his partner and is also single now.

He told me he's equally into men and women... Which makes sense. He has the kind of appeal that cuts across sexual preferences. There's something about that guy that appeals to both men and women equally. Of course, that piece of information does nothing to assuage Declan. While Finn and Rick both still lead on our security detail, he's made it clear to me he doesn't want to see me alone with Finn again. We're going to have to work out what that means, but there's still time for that. Probably after we finish shooting the film in New Zealand. The preparations for it are all complete.

We wanted to meet our friends and family before we left though, as we're not going to be back for a few months, at least, and definitely not until the shooting is complete.

"How do you feel about traveling and getting back to work?" Penny asks.

"As long as I'm with him, I'm good." I glance past at her to find Declan looking at me. He's sitting next to a woman with gray hair that flows to her shoulders. Her features are lined, but her gaze is sharp. She's wearing a silk suit that seems to have been cut especially for her. Seated at the same table is a man who looks like a slightly older version of Declan. That must be his brother Arpad. And the woman next to him holding the baby must be his wife Karina. Arpad looks at her with an expression of complete devotion on his face.

And when I turn back to Declan, it's to find him looking at me with a similar expression—of love and tenderness and adoration and so much more. Something flares between us, and I find myself walking away from the girls. Declan, too, rises to his feet. We meet in the middle of the room, and he wraps his arms about me and pulls me into him. He kisses my forehead. "I missed you."

76

Declan

"Anyone would think you two had been apart for years instead of minutes," a man's voice interrupts us.

Fucking JJ.

"Ignore him, baby." I pull Solene closer. She giggles and snuggles into me.

"Not that I don't understand the hardship of being away from the one you love..." he offers.

"You called, darling?" A young girl in her early twenties walks over to join us.

"My heart always calls to you." JJ wraps his arm about the girl's waist.

"I'm Lena." She beams at us. "Congratulations on the upcoming movie and the successful recovery. You two look so cute together."

"So do you," Solene replies.

"It's good to finally meet you, Lena. My condolences" —I point at JJ—"for this guy."

She laughs and snuggles in closer to him as he rolls his eyes at me.

I rub tiny circles over Solene's upper arm. Goosebumps flare over her skin. My heart swells with an emotion I now identify as love, my cock with lust, and the rest of me— Well, the rest of me is filled with a sense of calmness, tranquility, a sensation I know people call contentment. I didn't think I'd ever be lucky enough to have her in my life. And I have my friends to thank for helping me win her back.

JJ, Michael and Sinclair, with Rick's help, ensured the hospital canteen was fixed in the shortest possible time. They sponsored free food for the day for everyone to make up for any disruption. They also donated to the hospital to fund staff facilities. It alleviated any worry I might have had about the damage we inflicted on the hospital premises.

Cade walks in. He's unshaven, his hair mussed. His fingers are threaded through Abby's, and she looks just as tired. She spots Solene, and her eyes light up. Solene pulls away from me, and both women embrace.

"Abby, I'm so happy you're here!"

"Me, too." Tears pour down Abby's cheeks.

"Abby, are you okay? Is everything okay?"

Cade closes the distance to her and pulls her into his arms. "She's overwhelmed," he murmurs.

Unable to stay away, I walk over to Solene and circle her shoulders.

"What's wrong, Abby?" Solene scrutinizes her friend's face.

"Nothing's wrong." Abby's lips curve a little. "Everything is going to be fine." She and Cade exchange looks. And something in their faces, the hope and the relief, and the slight dread, alerts me. The hair on the back of my neck rises. "Are you talking about—"

"Yes." Abby looks over her shoulder. "Yes." Her eyes shine. She opens and shuts her mouth. Cade glances in the direction of her gaze; so do the rest of us. Silence descends upon the room, broken only by Abby's exclamation, "Knight!"

Cade releases her, and she darts past us and throws herself at the man who's entered the room and is standing uncertainly inside the doorway.

"You're home!" Abby throws her arms around Knight, who stands stiffly.

His hair is overgrown. He's bearded, with a few gray hairs peeking through the strands. It's a visible sign of how much he's aged in the months he's been held by the enemy. There are hollows under his cheekbones, and he sports a bandage over his left cheek. He's wearing a crisp, white button-down and slacks, which is markedly different from the military fatigues or jeans and T-shirts I've seen him in.

Abby buries his face in his chest and weeps, but Knight doesn't make any moves to console her. He stands there with no change of expression on his face. Cade and I exchange a glance. Cade gives a subtle shake of his head, then approaches the brother and sister. "Shh, babe, your brother needs time to acclimatize." He places his hands on Abby's shoulders and coaxes her back.

"I'm sorry I broke down like that—" She wipes her face. "I'm happy to see you, big brother."

Knight's expression softens a little. He clears his throat. "It's good to see you, too, Abby."

Abby makes a choked sound. "I was so worried about you. I thought I'd lost you, I—" She begins to weep again, and Cade pulls her into his arms. She wraps her arms about his waist and begins to sob. Her husband pats her hair. He glances up at Knight, who's watching the proceedings with a slightly confused look on his face. Finally, Knight shakes his head, then reaches over and pats Abby's shoulder.

"Cade is right. I need a little time to adjust back to civilian life." He winces, then adds in a soft voice, "Permanently."

"Permanently?" Penny cries out. All of us turn in her direction, and she flushes.

"I mean, uh... Of course you want to leave the force after what happened. I mean, it's not easy being a prisoner of war." She cringes. "Did I just say prisoner of war? That is the official term for what you were, eh? Oh gawd, now I'm putting my foot in my mouth. I mean, I have verbal diarrhea. Ugh, those two scenarios don't go that well together."

Knight's entire body goes on alert. Tension thrums off of him. He narrows his gaze on her.

Penny shakes her head, then squares her shoulders. "Okay, let me try again. What I was trying to say was, you must have loved the military, surely, and thought of it as your calling to join it, so to leave it? That must be agonizing, no matter the circumstances."

Ouch, that's not something I'd have chosen to say at this juncture.

Silence follows her outburst, Penny flushes further. "Oh my gawd, somebody kill me."

This time, it's Knight who winces.

Penny slaps her forehead. "Oh shoot, what am I thinking about, prattling on about killing and dying and—" She waves her hand in the air. "Forget I said that. You probably have PTSD from just hearing me blathering on like this, huh?"

I gape at her, as does everyone else in the room. When I risk a glance at Knight, it's to find his face wearing a dark expression. Interesting. I've never seen my friend this worked up.

"Oh, no, no, no. Did I say the P-word? I'm not supposed to say the P-word." Penny shuffles her feet. "No, no. Forget I said it."

Knight glares at her. The veins on his neck pop. He seems to be holding himself in check, barely.

"What are you doing here anyway? Shouldn't you be in debriefing or whatever it is you have to do once you're rescued?" Penny waves her hand in the air.

Knight's features grow hard, then he seems to force himself to relax. "I debriefed with my superiors before I flew in."

"O-k-a-y." She swallows. "And therapy? Shouldn't you have gone straight into therapy?"

Someone—JJ I think—clears his throat. Mira giggles nervously. All of it is lost on Penny and Knight who're too involved in... whatever it is that's unfolding between them. Like spectators in a tennis match, all of us turn to Knight in anticipation of his reaction. He does not disappoint.

His eyes narrow. "What did you just say?" he growls.

A-n-d all of us look to Penny. The tension between them ratchets up. Penny must sense it too for she shifts her weight from foot to foot, then tilts up her chin. "It's just… I wondered if you shouldn't acclimatize to people in phases and—" her voice peters off. Utter silence descends upon the room.

Penny hunches her shoulders, then flashes him a smile. "Sorry, sorry, I'm so sorry for being so indiscreet. I don't normally have such a non-filter. I mean, no, I normally don't have much of a filter, but I'm being especially filterless today. It's all your fault."

Knight blinks.

She stabs a finger at him.

"Yes, sireee, it's your fault. You make me nervous. Am I the only one who's nervous?"

She glances at the rest of us and must not see any help forthcoming for she turns on him. "But seriously, isn't therapy the best way to give yourself a chance to adjust back to civilian life?"

"Are you saying you'd rather I had not come to meet you and"—he jerks his chin in the general direction of the room—"our friends?"

"No, no, I was only concerned that it might be too much for you to have descended here in the middle of a group of people when you've spent the last six months being tortured and—" She squeezes her eyes shut, then snaps them open. "Oh, my gawd! That's it. I have officially reached the end of my tether. Can't take me out anywhere, eh?" She laughs weakly.

Someone in the room begins to chuckle—it's Cade, Abby's husband. He quickly turns it into a cough. JJ guffaws loudly, and shoots Penny a thumbs up sign. Sinclair looks between her and Knight, then smirks.

That only seems to annoy Knight even more. His gaze intensifies, and his jaw tightens further.

Penny tips up her chin, "Right, then. Now that I've made a complete earthworm of myself, can someone point me in the direction of the door?"

Mira's lips twitch. "Uh, Penny, did you say earthworm?"

"Yeah, you know, since I don't like to swear. And I'll take my torn Chucks—which, by the way, are the same as Converse. Did you know that? I didn't. I had to, uh, Google it and— Oh, my god, I'm doing it again. I'm jabbering on." She hunches her shoulders. "Can we pretend that didn't happen?"

A nerve pops at Knight's temple. "To answer your question, I'm good. I might have been locked up and tortured for six months—"

She swallows.

"—but that's only made me stronger. It's exactly what my job prepared me for. A job I've since given up. And now, I have a question of my own." He looks her up and down. "Who the fuck are you?"

To find out what happens next read Knight and Penny's story in The Wrong Wife

Read an excerpt

Penny

"You're home!" My friend, Abby throws her arms around her brother Knight who's prowled in the room. His hair is overgrown, and his beard is threaded with a few gray hairs. Huh? Knight definitely didn't have gray hairs the last time I saw him. But then, he hadn't been captured by the enemy and held for six months as a captive, either. Not that he looks any less desirable. He's lost weight, but that only adds to his appeal. There are hollows under his cheekbones, and a bandage over his left cheek which only adds to that dark and dangerous look he always carries around with him like a coat of armor. He's tall enough to tower over me.

At six-feet five-inches, and with shoulders that block out the room behind him, Knight looks mean and lethal. He looks like the soldier—or maybe secret agent—he's supposed to be. Abby told me he works for the British government. A real-life James Bond meets Jack Reacher with thick, dark hair, brawny biceps which stretch the white button-down he's wearing, tailored slacks and formal shoes.

The last and only time I saw him was when he was about to ship out on his mission. He was dressed in army fatigues, and he kissed Abby on both cheeks and hugged her tightly, his affection for his sister apparent. He promised to be safe and held her tenderly as she held back her tears. His tenderness seemed at such odds with his thick muscles and larger-than-life persona that I melted.

I haven't been able to get his piercing green eyes out of my mind. Or the strength in his shoulders, the sculpted planes of his chest, barely contained by his shirt, or the way his pants molded to his thighs, not hiding the bulge at his crotch.

No, I wasn't looking at my best friend's brother's crotch. Okay, maybe I was. Just a fleeting glance. I only peeked, promise. But—oh, my—the size of that impressive package between those tree-trunk like legs sent a pulse of heat straight to my core. I swear, I drenched my panties, then pretended it didn't happen. Not that he noticed any of it. He consoled Abby, then left.

Within weeks, I heard of his being captured on his mission and held behind enemy lines, before finally being freed.

Now, Abby buries her face in his chest and weeps, but Knight doesn't make any moves to console her. He stands there with no change of expression on his face.

Cade gives a subtle shake of his head, then approaches the brother and sister. "Shh, babe, your brother needs time to acclimatize." He places his hands on Abby's shoulders and coaxes her back.

"I'm sorry I broke down like that—" She wipes her face. "I'm happy to see you, big brother."

Knight's expression softens. He clears his throat. "It's good to see you too, Abby."

Abby makes a choked sound. "I was so worried about you. I thought I'd lost you, I—" She begins to weep again, and her fiancé Cade pulls her around and into his arms. She wraps her arms about his waist and begins to sob. Cade pats her hair. He glances up at Knight, who's watching the proceedings with a slightly confused look on his face. Finally, Knight shakes his head, then reaches over and pats Abby's shoulder.

"Cade is right. I need a little time to adjust back to civilian life." He winces, then adds in a hard voice, "Permanently."

"Permanently?" I cry out. Then flush as every single person in the room turns to look at me.

We're at our mutual friend Solene's engagement party, so I know many of the people in the room. Not that it stops me from wanting to slap my hands over my face and pretend I didn't just say that. Instead, I draw in a breath and flash a bright smile at my audience, because, uh, that's basically what they are, and that's basically what I do when things aren't going my way. I curve my lips and draw on every last sliver of positivity inside me because when you think positively, positive things happen. Right?

"I mean, uh... Of course you want to leave the force after what happened. I mean, it's not easy being a prisoner of war." I cringe. "Did I just say prisoner of war? That is the official term for what you were, eh? Oh gawd, now I'm putting my foot in my mouth. I mean, I have verbal diarrhea. Ugh, those two scenarios don't go that well together."

I shake my head, then square my shoulders. "Okay, let me try again. What I was trying to say was, you must have loved the military, surely, and thought of it as your calling to join it, so to leave it? That must be agonizing, no matter the circumstances."

Silence follows my outburst. Everyone is still staring at me with varying degrees of shock... horror... pity? My cheeks feel like they're on fire. "Oh, my gawd, somebody kill me."

This time, it's Knight who winces.

Ugh, nice one. I slap my forehead. "Oh shoot, what am I thinking about, prattling on about killing and dying and—" I wave my hand in the air. "Forget I said that. You probably have PTSD from just hearing me blathering on like this, huh?"

His features darken.

"Oh, no, no, no. Did I say the P-word? I'm not supposed to say the P-word." I shuffle my feet. "No, no. Forget I said it."

Knight glares at me. If I thought he couldn't appear more pissed off, I was wrong. Because his shoulders swell, the veins on his neck pop, and even his hair seems to thicken and stand on edge. Waves of rage vibrate off of him. Cold rage. The kind that, surely, heralds the coming of a storm or a nuclear explosion. The air between us thickens. The hair on the back of my neck stands on end. An arrow of heat zips straight to my core.

Huh? Do I find his anger hot? Why do I find his show of rage hot? And sexy. And erotic. Surely, it's because I'm tired and on edge, since I barely slept most of last night. Knowing your short-lived career as a junior chef is over and wondering how you're going to pay your bills can do that to a girl.

Then, because I never did know when to shut up, I prattle on. "What are you doing here anyway? Shouldn't you be in debriefing or whatever it is you have to do once you're rescued?"

His features grow hard, then he seems to force himself to relax. "I debriefed with my superiors before I flew in."

"O-k-a-y," I swallow. "And therapy? Shouldn't you have gone straight into therapy?"

His eyes narrow. "What did you just say?" he growls.

His hard voice lights up my nerve-endings. Every pulse point in my body seems to drum in tandem. I shift my weight from foot to foot, then tilt up my chin. "It's just... I wondered if you shouldn't acclimatize to people in phases and—" my voice peters off. Utter silence descends upon the room.

I hunch my shoulders, try to imitate a turtle tucking its neck back into its shell. Although, by the way his gaze is locked on me, I know I'm still very much visible. I turn up the wattage of my smile. "Sorry, sorry, I'm so sorry for being so indiscreet. I don't normally have such a non-filter. I mean, no, I normally don't have much of a filter, but I'm being especially filterless today. It's all your fault."

Knight blinks.

I stab a finger at him. "Yes, sireee, it's your fault. You make me nervous. Am I the only one who's nervous?"

I glance around, taking in the various expressions of surprise and amusement that the rest of them wear. "But seriously,"—I turn on him—"isn't therapy the best way to give yourself a chance to adjust back to civilian life?"

"Are you saying you'd rather I had not come to meet you and"—he jerks his chin in the general direction of the room—"our friends?"

"No, no, I was only concerned that it might be too much for you to have descended here in the middle of a group of people when you've spent the last six months being tortured and—" I squeeze my eyes shut and flatten my lips, then count from five-four-three-two-one. When I open my eyes, everyone is still staring at me.

"Oh, my gawd! That's it. I have officially reached the end of my tether. Can't take me out anywhere, eh?" I laugh weakly.

Someone in the room begins to chuckle—it's Cade, Abby's husband. I scowl at him, and he turns it into a cough. Another man guffaws loudly. When I look at him, he shoots me a thumbs up sign. Huh? He's older than the rest of us and a friend of Cade's. Guess he must see something I don't? The man standing next to him, also tall and broad, with intense looks—Abby mentioned he's the co-owner of the leading financial services company in the country—looks between me and Knight, then smirks.

That only seems to annoy Knight even more. His gaze intensifies, and his jaw tightens further. Jesus, he might just crack a molar, or ten, at this rate. He folds his arms across his chest, and those massive biceps of his stretch the sleeves of his shirt. And this is when he's leaner. He was an absolute beast when I first saw him. The kind who'd gift Beauty a library because she likes to read.

I've set my standards high for what I want in a man, but lord above, this man tempts me. He does look like a beast, though. A very mad, very grumpy, very sexy beast. I widen my smile—mainly to hide the fluttering of my heart and my pussy, which seems to have developed a sudden plumbing problem, what with all the moisture sliding through my slit.

Ignore it. Ignore the little fires that have popped under my skin. Ignore the bead of sweat that runs down my spine.

I tip up my chin and glance around at my friends, "Right, then. Now that I've made a complete earthworm of myself, can someone point me in the direction of the door?"

Mira's lips twitch. "Uh, Penny, did you say, earthworm?"

"Yeah, you know, since I don't like to swear. And I'll take my torn Chucks—which, by the way, are the same as Converse. Did you know that? I didn't. I had to, uh, Google it and— Oh, my god, I'm doing it again. I'm jabbering on." I hunch my shoulders. "Can we pretend that didn't happen?"

A nerve pops at Knight's temple. "To answer your question, I'm good. I might have been locked up and tortured for six months—"

I swallow.

"—but that's only made me stronger. It's exactly what my job prepared me for. A job I've since given up. And now, I have a question of my own." He looks me up and down. "Who the fuck are you?"

Knight

"Penny." She flashes me a big smile, her blue eyes sparkling. She thrusts out her hand and approaches me. "I'm Penny."

I purposely cross my arms over my chest. Her face falls, then she lowers her hand and manages to smile again. *Fucking hell, did she swallow sunshine and rainbows today?*

"It's okay, I know who you are."

I glare at her.

Some of the color fades from her cheeks. Her smile finally switches off, *thank fuck.*

"It's fine, you don't have to talk or anything. My ma says I can keep a conversation going all on my own."

She pushes a strand of pink-colored hair behind her tiny ear. Her heart shaped face has high cheekbones, a turned-up nose and a plush bow shaped mouth that's currently moving again. I tune her out and focus on the dress that drapes over her narrow shoulders—also pink. What a surprise, eh? It dips low enough at the neckline to hint at her ample cleavage.

Cleavage I've been trying to keep my gaze off of since I slipped in the door. The only reason I'm here is because I knew my sister would be anxious to see me.

It's been forty-eight hours since I was extracted from hell. During that time, I was flown to a military base in Germany and debriefed. After a quick shower and five hours of sleep, I was ready to be transferred home. They insisted I speak with a shrink, which I initially refused. I finally agreed to it after being told I couldn't return home without doing it, since they needed to ensure I was of sound mind.

After that, I sat through a meeting with my superiors. I must have said enough to convey to them that I was quitting. They were not happy. Not only because I'm one of the few soldiers to escape from being a captive of an enemy state known for beheading people on screen. Just the fact that they didn't immediately do that to me is both a mystery and a guilt-trip I'll carry with me forever. Especially since two other members of my team were killed in front of my eyes.

This is exactly why I always insisted on working alone. A dictate that worked well for me. Until this particular mission, where my orders were to go in as part of a squad. Fucking hell. I had a bad feeling about it from the beginning. But orders are orders. One doesn't disobey them when they're handed down from the highest authority in the country.

Like a good soldier—and ultimately, that's all I was, regardless of the fact that I was part of the secret service—I answered the call of my motherland. And almost died. That I'm standing here today is, in no little part, due to the crack-extraction team my friends put together to get me out of the purgatory I was trapped in. Black, darkness, pain, and a sense of hopelessness were my constant companions. In some ways, I'm still stuck in that coffin-shaped hole they stuck me in. In some ways, I'm still stretched out on that table while my enemies waterboarded me, before sticking electric rods onto my extremities and—

"Hey, you okay?"

I scowl down at the slip of a woman who's waving her hand at me? "You, uh, you blanked out there for a second."

I glower at her. Upturned nose, big blue eyes, skin that looks soft enough to give way under the impact of my palm. Plush lips which, when parted, would reveal a heart-shaped hole that would be perfect for my cock. I blink.

Where did that thought come from? Women like her, who seem to be made from spun sugar, usually dissolve when faced with a light rain. With her ample breasts, tiny waist, and hips the perfect size to hold onto when I bend her over and fuck her, she's exactly the kind of woman I need to avoid.

She'd never understand the darkness I carry within me. The agony that comes from having your life ripped apart. My ideals shattered. My goals revealed as a mistake. Everything I believed in, every opinion I've held, every interpretation of my hopes, my resolves... All of it, a mirage.

I wasted my life for the greater good. I wanted to contribute to my community, to my country, to my fellow humans. Something I held close to my heart since the day I became conscious I had the capacity to make a difference. All bullshit. All of it a mistake. A fallacy. I was fooled; I deluded myself. It took a stay behind enemy lines for my blinders to be removed.

From now on, I live… for myself. I'm going to join the ranks of those who pursue power, who make money. It's the only tangible thing, a stake in the ground. There are no shades of grey when it comes to money. It brings with it the influence and the power I craved.

I'm never going to be helpless the way I was in that hole in the ground. I'm going to live life in complete control. And that means, never allowing anyone or anything close enough to make me feel again. Emotions are raw, and real, and have no place in my future. There's only me and my born-again vision. Which definitely does not include the likes of a curvy, wide-eyed, innocent-gazed vixen.

I turn away from her, then walk over to my sister. I take Abby's hand in mine, then bring it to my mouth and kiss her knuckles. "I'm sorry for what I put you through. I'm sorry I missed your wedding. I'm sorry I spent so much time away from home. All that is in the past. I'm back now, and I intend to make amends."

Abby smiles through her tears, then she pulls her hand from my grasp and hugs me back. "Oh, Knight, I'm just happy you're safe and in one piece."

Am I though? I manage a tight smile, which seems to convince her enough that she steps back. She pats my cheek. "It really is wonderful to see you, Knight."

Cade, her husband and my best friend, pats my shoulder. "Good to have you back, mate."

I tip my chin in his direction, then turn to JJ. "Thanks for helping to put together the extraction team."

"Sinclair and Michael also played a part in this." He's referring to the two men who stand on his either side. Sinclair Sterling, is one of the Seven who co-owns 7A Investments, and Michael Sovrano, is the ex-Don of the Cosa Nostra. Perhaps still is, though he claims to have gone legit.

JJ, himself, is the head of an organized crime syndicate in the UK who also professes to have moved to the right side of law. The three of them represent the kind of morally grey men I once detested. Men like my father. Men who are ruthless and exploit the system for their own selfish ends. Men who value power and money over anything else—other than the women in their lives, and apparently, their friends. I mean, they came together to help me.

Once upon a time, I'd have passed judgment on them. I'd have said they were the reason people lost hope in each other and the future.

Now, I understand this is the only way to be. I might have had a vision about contributing to the greater good. Now, I know the only good that makes sense is the kind that benefits me directly. Sure, I'll extend it to include my sister and those who'd helped me out, but that's where I draw the line.

Money, power, control of my own fate. Those are my ultimate goals. Good thing my father's a billionaire and can't wait for me to take over his company. "I owe you both," I tilt my head toward Sinclair and Michael.

JJ searches my features. "Did the team arrive too late to save you?" he asks slowly. He seems to see something I've been desperately trying to hide from everyone else. He's a bit too observant for my tastes.

I scowl, then pretend I don't understand what he's implying. I widen my stance and shove my hands into the pocket of my slacks. "I'd already escaped from where I was being held. It was perfect timing when I ran into them. If not"—I raise a shoulder—"we wouldn't even be having this conversation."

Silence descends on the group, then JJ nods.

"Anytime you need to talk..."

A-n-d so it begins. Everyone I meet feels the need to contribute. They all think they know what I went through, that their words are going to help fill the gaping hole where my soul once used to be. They have no fucking idea. He probably means well—and these are my friends, and I should be polite—but fuck that. If they really are my friends, they'll know I'm not in the right space for niceties. I grunt before turning away and raising my hand at Abby and Cade. "I'll be in touch."

Then, because I can't push back the noise that fills my head anymore, I turn and stalk out the door, down the hallway, past the uniformed staff who're placing drinks on trays, toward the front door. Shouldering it open, stopping myself from taking the stairs two at a time, I walk down the steps at a steady pace and down toward where my car is parked. I lean against the trunk, draw in a breath, then another, and will my racing heart to slow down. Coerce my pulse to climb down from the insane speed at which it's galloping.

I've come to realize something very quickly; I don't like being indoors or in any kind of space with a crowd of people. Not that the room inside was crowded. Indeed, I know most of the people there. I saw the concern on their faces. Noticed the questions in their eyes.

Their worry was a thrum in the room, and it repelled me. I don't want their pity. Their scrutiny. Their agitation on my behalf. I want to deal with what I've been through on my own terms. As I feel is right.

Leaving the army was the first step. I need to keep going and assume the reigns of the empire I turned my back on for so long. I—

"Hey, soldier?" That same cheery voice that grated on my nerves earlier has, apparently, followed me out here.

I square my shoulders. Turning my back on her, I round my car. My chauffeur appears and holds the door open for me. I'm about to slide in when there's a tug on my sleeve.

"Uh, can I call you Knight?"

Penny

"I mean you're my best friend's brother, so I assume it's okay to call you by your name?"

He pauses but doesn't turn around. He also doesn't get into the car, which I take as a positive sign. *And why am I here? Why didn't I let him leave? What force compelled me to run out of the room, follow him outside, and try to engage him in conversation, when he barely acknowledged me earlier?*

Maybe it's the fact that he barely spent a few minutes in that room. Enough to let everyone know he's safe and to thank his friends for their help rescuing him. He acknowledged Cade and Declan—his closest friends—and then he left. He might be out of the warzone physically, but mentally, it's clear he's anything but in the clear.

He cut a solitary figure as he turned and stalked out. Taking with him that strange edginess that gripped me from the moment he locked his gaze on me. It was like being at the business end of a tractor beam. One that pinned me in place, robbed the breath from my lungs and the moisture from my throat, sending it to other parts of my body. One that also sent a pulse of exhilaration up my spine. A sure sign that I hate him. But it also made me feel alive. Like I was coming out of a prolonged holding pattern. Like I only ever existed before—biding my time, flitting from one interest to the next, trying to forge a career, trying to find something that caught my attention. Then I saw him.

Maybe it's fanciful thinking. I mean, the man doesn't even like me. But that inherent need to soothe tumbled to the fore. He's in pain. He's lonely. He's still in a state of shock. I'd go so far as to say he's still a prisoner, and I can't let him leave. Not yet.

So, I followed him out and caught him as he was about to step into the car. Which he hasn't yet done. But he hasn't turned around to face me either. I shift my weight from foot to foot. The grey-haired chauffeur looks between us, a question on his face.

"Hi, I'm Penny." I flash him a wide smile. Because that's what I do. When I'm embarrassed, I smile. When I'm angry, I smile more. When I'm in the wrong place at the wrong time, like right now, I smile the biggest smile I can muster. Because isn't being optimistic and happy supposed to make things better?

"Rudy." The older man smiles back and takes my hand. "Are you coming with us, Ma'am?"

"No," Knight snaps, before I can reply.

It speaks! So, all he said was a single word. And it's that one word in the entire English language that's the epitome of negativity. Still, that's progress... Of a sort. I think. It's how I choose to take it, anyway.

Rudy steps back, looks between us again, then nods. "I'll give you two some privacy." He sits down in the driver's seat and closes the door.

Knight makes a growling sound at the back of his throat. My toes curl. All of my nerve-endings seem to spark at the same time. All because this monster of a man makes a sound like a rabid beast. *No, no, no, I can't compare him to Beast.* That's my very own secret fantasy, and I'll never find anyone who can fulfill that. Certainly not, this bad-tempered, angry, snarly savage of a man. *Oh, but barbarians give the best orgasms. Eh? Why did my mind go there? Also, he's my best friend's brother, so that makes him off-limits or something, right?*

Of course, Abby is married to her brother's best friend which is slightly different but in the same territory...

I clear my throat. "Okay, I guess I'm going to go. I don't even know why I came after you. I mean, not *after you* after you, but just... after you. It's just, you seemed a little lonely, and maybe that's just my imagination, and really, it was stupid of me to come and ask if I can do anything to help. Not that I've asked you yet. But I couldn't stop myself from following you out. Not *follow you* follow you, just... I was right behind you and—"

I gasp, for he's pivoted around and is glaring at me again. Green, green eyes. Sparks of green and gold and blue circling each other, chasing and ebbing and flowing like the northern lights. I've never seen the phenomenon in real life, but if I did, I'm sure it would look like the vivid green that pulses and throbs and storms in his irises. Then, just like that, it's gone. Banked. Vanished. To be replaced by a sheet of emerald so hard, surely, it could cut me off at my knees.

The impact of his gaze is so intense, it's like a ten-ton truck slamming into my chest. I stumble back and would fall, except he shoots out his arm and grabs my shoulder. The heat of his touch sizzles to my core. My fingers tremble. My pussy clamps down and comes up empty. My nipples are so hard, they hurt. *They hurt.*

I'm certain he reads my mind, for he drops his gaze down to my chest. Instantly, I blush. I chose this dress, knowing it shows off my tits. I'm a big girl, and I've never hidden it. I like my size. I like my hips. My fleshy thighs. The little rolls of fat around my middle. Most of all, I like how my tits are perfectly round and how they jiggle when I walk. I'm a plus-sized girl, and no one is ever going to make me feel bad about it.

He looks down at my blouse for so long, a million butterflies take flight in my stomach. I try to pull away, but his grip tightens. Slowly, he raises his gaze to mine. I see a mirror of my surprise, and something like… loathing. Something so intense, I take another step back.

His eyebrows draw down, then he releases me so suddenly, I stumble again. This time, he doesn't right me. Instead, he pulls a handkerchief from his pocket and dusts his hand. *He. Dusts. His. Hand. What a… cretin.* He makes that growling sound at the back of his throat again, and my panties dampen. Just like that.

Okay, so he's mad. I get it. I'd be, too, if I'd been taken prisoner by my enemies. And then come home, only to be harassed by a woman like me who talks too much. And yeah, he's a hero. Media speculation is that he's going to be knighted by the monarch of England. *Which would make him a Knight knight? Would he be called Knight Knight?* I chuckle.

He scowls at the amusement on my face, and his green eyes blaze. That nerve that throbs at his temple is joined by a vein. The muscles of his shoulders bunch. He looks like he's going to burst out of his shirt any moment. *Would that make him Knight Hulk?* My lips quirk. *Don't laugh. Do. Not. Laugh.* Instead, I say, "It's not good to bottle all that rage inside, you know. It can lead to an early grave." The words are out before I can stop them. *Oh, my gawd! What's wrong with me?*

I lick my lips. His gaze drops to my mouth. Something flashes in those dark eyes. Something that sends a pulse of heat shooting through my veins. I shift my weight from foot to foot.

"Uh, I'm sorry, I didn't mean to talk about dying again. Honestly, especially because—"

He abruptly turns away from me, ducks his head inside the car, slides inside and pulls the door shut. The car drives off, leaving me gaping after him. *What the— He just drove off? And without saying a word to me? Did I mistake that flash of lust in his eyes earlier?* There's no mistaking the hate I glimpsed there, of course. He doesn't like me—I sensed it in the room, and the way he glowered at me, you'd think he had something personal against me. Except for the fact I've only ever seen the man once before today. Which begs the question: *Why did I feel so compelled to follow him out?*

"What are you doing out here?"

I turn to find my friend Mira walking toward me.

"I— uh—" A gust of wind blows the hair back from my face. A chill of foreboding slithers down my spine. "I—uh—thought I forgot something."

"You mean this?"

She holds up a bag. I stare at it for a second, then realization sinks in. "Yes, exactly. I forgot my handbag." I take it from her and hook it over my shoulder.

"You ready to leave?"

"You're no longer training to be a chef?" Mira takes a sip of the hot chocolate, then places the mug on the tiny breakfast counter which demarcates the living room from the kitchenette. We shared a ride here and decided to have a drink and decompress. Neither of us wanted to go out, so we opted to come back to the tiny apartment we share. It's a recent development, but when my last landlord asked me to leave with less than a month's notice, Mira—who'd been looking for a flat mate—asked me to move in, and I agreed.

"Turns out, the hours are too long, the pay is shit when you're starting out, and not much better later, and you don't even get weekends free." I glance down into the depths of my herbal tea. Why the hell did I chosen chamomile? I hate the taste, but it's supposed to be soothing, and I could do with a little of that right now. I squirm around on the bar stool, trying to find a more comfortable space.

Mira looks at me with curiosity. "You okay?"

"Why wouldn't I be?"

"You look a little peaked."

"It's the changing weather. Spring into Autumn, the days drawing to an end earlier. I mean, I do like the turning of the leaves, but I much prefer when it's warm and sunny."

"Hmm..." She taps her fingers on the table. "You're a shit liar."

"I'm not lying." I take a sip of the chamomile tea and almost gag.

"You don't have to drink that, you know?"

"I do." I hunch my shoulder. "My ma always used to say there was nothing chamomile tea couldn't make better."

Her gaze softens. "How is she doing?"

"Well, she recognized me when I saw her, so it was a good day." The slippery sensation of chamomile fills my mouth, and I force myself to swallow it. Maybe the more I do the things I don't like, the more God will reward me with the things I want. It's a strange logic, but one that has been drilled into me, thanks to the nuns who ran the school I went to. The same nuns who forbid swearing and thinking about sex and boys. It was a strict upbringing, but a happy one. For all the singing of religious hymns at morning assembly and the talk of sacrifice, there were also some upsides.

For me, it was an innocent, carefree childhood. My mother worked two jobs to keep a roof over our heads, but she also ensured I never wanted for anything. Our home was filled with love and happiness. My mother was my best friend, right until the day she collapsed in our living room when I was eighteen.

She was diagnosed with early-stage dementia. I put off going to university so I could support her. She was disappointed by my decision but didn't have the strength to fight me on it. Thankfully, I managed to get help from our local council and move her to a home where she's been for the last five years. Her condition has been steadily deteriorating, and the council went through budget cuts and can't cover her costs anymore. So, I need money. Fast. And here I am, unable to hold down a single job.

"I'm sorry, Penny." Mira reaches forward and grips my hand. "I wish there was something I could do to help you."

"You're allowing me to stay here and pay a fraction of the money I should be paying in rent. I think you're doing a lot already."

"I have a job. I can support the both of us." She raises a shoulder. "Besides, if I'd refused to accept any money from you, would you have moved in here?"

I begin to object when she stops me with a raised brow.

"That's what I thought." She lifts her mug of hot chocolate and slurps it up. "You make a mean hot cocoa. Also, I'm the beneficiary of your cooking experiments, so I'd say I got the better end of the deal."

"That's you, being generous. I'd hardly qualify my little cooking forays as worthy of getting to stay in this apartment in Central London." I glance around the tiny apartment. What it lacks in space, it makes up for in light. It's on the top floor of a four-story apartment, with skylights that allow the sunshine to stream in. And it's in the heart of Soho, which is as prime as you can get, in terms of real estate locations.

"You don't give yourself enough credit."

I laugh. "If you mean the cooking, I really do like it. It's just that I prefer it as a hobby, cooking at my own pace, rather than being packed into the pressure-cooker environment of a kitchen run by a professional chef."

"That bad, huh?" Her tone is sympathetic.

"It took the joy out of cooking. I realized, very quickly, it's not for me."

"It's good you realized it early, huh? This way, you can move on, instead of investing your life in a career you don't like?"

I take in her features. "Are you referring to yourself when you say that?"

"Who, me? Nah!" She places her palms together in front of her. "I mean, the big boss of my company is a jerkass, but I don't have much to do with him, so it's all right. I like what I do, so that's a positive."

"I wish I could find a career I love. I'm twenty-three and still trying to work out what I want to do with my life."

"You have plenty of time to work that out," Mira assures me.

"But my mother doesn't." I swallow down the ball of emotions that blocks my throat. "I need to find a way to keep her in the home. She's comfortable there. Everyone knows her and is kind to her. If only I could find a job that I could hold onto, I— "

As if summoned, my phone buzzes with an incoming text message. I glance at it. "It's from Abby," I murmur.

"Oh, what does she say?"

I read the message again, then hold up the phone for Mira.

Abby: I have the perfect job for you

TO FIND OUT WHAT HAPPENS NEXT READ KNIGHT AND PENNY'S, BEST

FRIEND'S BROTHER, FAKE RELATIONSHIP, BOSS-EMPLOYEE ROMANCE IN THE WRONG WIFE

WANT MORE DECLAN AND SOLENE? HERE'S YOUR BONUS EPILOGUE

Solene

"So, you're the woman who's trapped my grandson?"

Grandmama looks me up and down. Her silver hair is cut in a blunt cut that ends just below her chin. She also has a fringe which, along with the pink Chanel suit she's wearing and the pearls on her ears and around her neck, gives her a very chic and professional look. From what Declan tells me, she's the chairperson on the board of the family business; the same business which his father and older brother are the CEO and the CFO of. And it's not only in name. She still insists on working remotely twice a week and attends all the board meetings.

Apparently, his father and brother, while being the day-to-day leaders of the company, still need her sign-off for business deals when the value of the transaction totals one billion or more. A-n-d he'd told me that with a straight face.

My fiancé comes from a very wealthy background. Which makes the fact that he wanted to work hard and build his career in Hollywood on his own even more impressive. Now, it makes sense why he was so adamant that he didn't want to borrow money from any of his friends to finance his film. When you're born with a silver spoon in your mouth, either all that wealth goes to your head, or you turn your back on it and make a bid to shake off the shackles of your trust fund and forge your own fortune. And he does have a trust fund. Only Declan has never wanted any part of it.

Early on, he recognized that the money would only hold him back. I asked him if he'd ever been tempted to dip into the fund for producing the film. He thought about it and confirmed that he'd been tempted, but then remembered he'd promised himself he would make it to the top in Hollywood, in a leading role, on his own, without the help of his family. And if he had taken the easy way out, he never would've forgiven himself.

The fact he was willing to risk so much by going to the Bratva instead made me realize just how proud he is. And he has courage in his convictions, and perhaps, he's fearless. Or he's very foolish. Or a bit of everything. Bottom line, he believes in himself, and he's never lost confidence in his own abilities; and that made him even hotter.

As I stand here, subject to his grandmother's scrutiny, he shuffles his feet. I shoot him a sideways glance and find his eyebrows drawn down. His jaw is set. He seems a few seconds away from stepping in front of me and growling at his Grandmama, and that's a scenario I need to avoid at all costs. This is my first time meeting his family, and the last thing I want is for me to be the cause of any animosity between him and his grandmother.

Declan and I are in our new townhouse in London, at the get together we arranged for our friends and family. Our friends have left and now, it's only his grandmother and us.

"Well? You have anything to say for yourself, girl?" His gran frowns. "Or are you waiting for his approval to speak? Is your relationship that old-fashioned, or are you as feisty as you appear on stage at your concerts?"

"You've seen one of my concerts?" I burst out.

She blinks. I don't think she meant to reveal that. But then she waves her hand in the air. "I saw a clip of it on the news."

"And what did you think?"

"You were"—she narrows her gaze on me—"impressive. A shining light on stage. The camera loved you. The fans adored you. You have the kind of presence that will rivet generations to come."

"Oh." Tears prick my eyes. "Thank you." I take a step forward, and when I reach the table where she's seated, I hold out my hand. "I'm Solene. I am your grandson's fiancée and yes, I did trap him."

She tilts her head.

"But only because he wanted to be."

"Hmm..." She drums her fingers on the table. "And what about you? Did you want to be trapped, as well?"

"Absolutely," I say without hesitation. "I'm not sure if Declan mentioned it, but we first met when I was seventeen and he was twenty-one. It was love at first sight, for the both of us."

"Love at first sight, huh?" She glances from me to Declan. "You didn't tell me that."

Declan shoves his hand into the pocket of his pants. "Didn't know you were interested in the details."

"You're my youngest grandson. Your marriage will be the last in the family I'm going to attend. Of course I'm interested." She snorts.

"You're going to live long enough to attend your great-granddaughter's wedding."

Grandmama's expression softens. "When you get to be my age, your mortality stares you in your face every second you're awake. You see the morning and give thanks to the universe for allowing you to see another day."

Silence descends on our little group. The tears I thought I'd managed to blink away make another appearance. "I, more than anyone else, understand the sentiment behind your words. If it hadn't been for your grandson, I wouldn't be here today."

Declan wraps his arm about my waist and pulls me closer. Grandmama takes in the two of us and her expression relaxes even more. "So, this is not a made-up-relationship, for the purpose of PR and such?"

We both stiffen, then Declan barks out a laugh. "Trust you to hit the bulls-eye with your observation." He tightens his grip around me so I'm all but melting into his side. "I admit, that is how I coerced her into agreeing to get engaged to me. But then I made full use of the opportunities afforded—"

"He convinced me what we had was real." I lean my head against his chest. "Something I already knew, but I was waiting for him to realize it, too. And when he did, when he told me what he felt for me— More importantly, when he showed me just how much he loves me and that he'd do anything for me and for our future together, I couldn't not believe him anymore." I turn my chin up and my gaze locks with his. "I love you."

Declan

"There has never been a time in my life when I didn't love you. My heart knew you existed. I was searching for you, and when I found you, I never should have let you go. But I was younger and more foolish. I didn't appreciate what I had; not like I do now." I cup her cheek. "I'll love you until my last breath, and after that. In every life we live, you will be mine, only mine."

I lower my head and brush my lips over hers. She sighs into my mouth, and her lips cling to mine. I know my grandmother's watching us, but that doesn't stop me from entangling my tongue with hers. I wrap my arm about her waist and pull her closer. She trembles, then grips my shoulders and holds on. The blood drains to my groin—little surprise there. Only with this woman, am I always ready to go. Always ready to sink inside her warmth and stay there forever. I step back, press my forehead to hers. "Forever," I whisper.

My grandmother sniffles. I glance sideways to find her brushing a tear from the corner of her eye. "Grandmama, are you— "

"I'm good." She pulls out a handkerchief and dabs at her cheek. " And yes, I did cry. A little. But the love I sense between the two of you is real and tangible and it's everything that life is about." She rises to her feet and walks over to us.

Still keeping my arm around my fiancée, I turn to face her. She reaches up and pats my cheek. "You've found your soulmate. I can't tell you how happy that makes me. As for you, young lady— " She leans in and kisses Solene on her cheek. "You're beautiful inside and out and— "

"—much too good for my son, but it makes me so proud that you're joining our family," a familiar voice announces.

I glance over my shoulder as my father swaggers into the room. Philippe Beauchamp, current CEO of the Beauchamp group of companies—one of the leading producers of wine in Europe—looks much younger than his forty-nine years. He's wearing his normal uniform of a white button-down shirt with a grey suit, having returned from the office where he attended a meeting he hadn't been able to put off. The man looks the same as I remember him growing up. Sure, his hair is threaded with grey at his temples, and tiny wrinkles stretch out from the corners of his eyes when he smiles—none of which seems to put a damper on the appeal he carries for the opposite sex. He prowls toward us, then half-bows. "I'm Philippe Beauchamp— "

"Declan's father." Solene flashes him a smile. "And I'm— "

"Solene, my future daughter-in-law, and the woman who redeemed the soul of my good-for-nothing son."

Solene laughs lightly. She holds out her hand, and my father takes it in his. His touch is gentle as he bends and presses his lips to her knuckles. She sighs.

I can't stop the frown from crowding my forehead. "Okay, that's enough, old man."

My father straightens before raising one eyebrow in my direction. "You're protective of her. I approve." He flashes her another smile, then releases her hand. *Finally, fuck.*

"How did you get so lucky to get this angel to agree to have you?"

I scoff, then push her slightly behind me to protect her from my father's gaze. Not that I don't trust him. He's a flirt and has had no dearth of girlfriends over the years. None of whom he's ever brought home. It was only after Arpad and I left home that he decided to be open about his affairs. He allowed himself to be photographed with the models he so seems to prefer—most less than half his age and totally in love with him. Not that he keeps any of them.

The man has the kind of reputation that once made me want to compete with him. That's one of the reasons I left home and wanted to make it on my own. Now, I have my own woman, and strangely, that edge of competitiveness I've felt with my father seems to not be relevant anymore.

"You're right." I lower my chin. "I am lucky to have her. And every day, I ask myself what I did to deserve the love of this gorgeous woman." I glance down to find she's looking at me with shining eyes.

"Aww." Solene stands up on tiptoe and brushes her lips over mine. "You're making me blush, baby."

"And that makes you look even more beautiful, baby."

My father clears his throat. I glance up to find he's watching us with a bemused expression on his face.

"What?" I scowl.

He holds up his hands. "Nothing."

"Out with it," I snap.

He rocks back on his heels. "Can't say I thought I'd see the day when your career would take a back seat, but I can't say the look doesn't suit you. In fact, I'd say the two of you are positively glowing." He takes a step back as if he doesn't want to be infected by this so-called 'glow' he's alluding to.

"You worried it might be catching?" I tease.

He laughs. "Nope. Finding a woman and settling down is the farthest thing from my mind."

"It's time you did, though," my grandmother huffs. "Both of your sons have found the loves of their life. The business can practically run itself on its own. What are you waiting for?"

My father blinks. "Now, mother, I'm not getting married again."

"Nonsense. You're not even fifty, and given the variety of women who throw themselves at you, I'd say you've got more than enough choices."

"First,"—he holds up his forefinger—"those women are not the kind I'd ever bring home to my family, and second"—he holds up a hand

—"I've been there, done that." He nods in our direction. "I've brought up my sons; I've paid my dues."

"So, you don't want to be in love again?"

"No." Philippe draws himself up to his full height. "Once was enough. And I wasn't a stellar husband then, or a father, for that matter."

"I beg to differ," I protest. "You were always there for Arpad and me when we needed you."

"I could have been there more. I was too busy growing the business."

Grandmama cuts in, "And now, you've amassed enough money and power—"

"Does anyone have enough money and power, mother? If that were the case, you wouldn't still be coming in to attend board meetings."

Grandmama scowls. "I'm there because it gives me a focus in my life, as you well know. That company is also my husband's legacy, and—"

"And we welcome your presence on the board," Philippe says gently.

Mother and son exchange a glance.

"You're stubborn," she huffs.

"So are you."

"So is he." Solene taps my chest. "And persistent. Thank god for that."

All of us laugh.

"Don't think I'm going to forget about this little discussion," Grandmama waggles a finger at Philippe, "I'm letting it go for now. Doesn't mean I'm not going to bring it up again, you understand?"

Yep, you guessed right, Philippe will get his own Age Gap romance soon, so look out for it. Meanwhile, you'll meet Declan and Solene again in The Wrong Wife, Knight and Penny's story

Read Cade and Abby's, brother's best friend, fake relationship romance in The Agreement

Read Daddy JJ's, age-gap romance in Mafia Lust

Read Michael and Karma's forced marriage Mafia romance in Mafia King

Read Sinclair and Summer's fake relationship billionaire romance in The Billionaire's Fake Wife

Read Olivia and Massimo's second chance romance in Mafia Obsession

Want the suggested reading order for the Seven and The

SOVRANOS? THEY ARE PART OF THE SAME WORLD AND THEIR STORIES INTERTWINE FROM THE PROPOSAL ONWARD.

YOU CAN FIND THE SUGGESTED READING ORDER AT HTTP://WWW.AUTHORLSTEELE.COM

From L. Steele

PS – I want to hear from you!

Hello I'm L. Steele and I love watching movies. I'm also fascinated by celebrities and how they seem to play out their entire lives in public. The price of fame, eh? But also, I'm intrigued by how they seem to follow their hearts—in terms of their breakups and falling in love and breaking up and trying again. It always makes me wonder how much of is real and how much of it is planned with a view to generating PR around their next big project. It was this as well as Taylor Swift, #Bennifer and #Jelena who inspired this story.

I tapped into Taylor Swift and how she talks about coming up with her best songs when she has the most angst in her life (normally after a break up). As well Solene on stage is very much inspired by Taylor Swift on stage and her confidence and her presence and charisma and everything!

Also I wanted to write a story in which #Jelena had an HEA and of course it was going to much spicier. And did Declan and Solene put me through the wringer! Declan, in particular, had me going—*What are you doing? Why are you doing this?* But he had a reason... After all, the meaner they are, the harder they fall, and this story only confirms that. I love Declan and Solene so much!

Please do review the book on Amazon, Goodreads, and Bookbub, as well as on TikTok and in Facebook reader groups. Reviews and recommendations from you entice other readers to pick up the book, too, and that encourages me to write more and faster!

Don't forget to follow me on TikTok and Instagram.

Want to be the first to know when my next book is out? Sign up for my newsletter on my website http://www.authorlsteele.com

CHRISTMAS ROMANCE BOOKS BY L. STEELE FOR YOU

Want to find out how Weston and Amelie met? Read The Billionaire's Christmas Bride HERE

Want even more Christmas Romance books? Read A very Mafia Christmas, Christian and Aurora's story.

Read The Pretend Christmas Bride - Edward's HEA story.

SPICY BILLIONAIRE ROMANCE BY L. STEELE FOR YOU

Read Daddy JJ's, age-gap romance in Mafia Lust HERE

Read Edward, Baron and Ava's story starting with Billionaire's Sins

NEWS

Join L. Steele's Newsletter for news on her newest releases at http://www.authorlsteele.com

ABOUT THE AUTHOR

Hello, I'm L. Steele.

I write romance stories with strong powerful men who meet their match in sassy, curvy, spitfire women.

I love to push myself with each book on both the spice and the angst so I can deliver well rounded, multidimensional characters.

I enjoy trading trivia with my filmmaker husband, watching lots and lots of movies, and walking nature trails. I live in London.

facebook.com/AuthorLSteele
x.com/Author_L_Steele
instagram.com/authorl.steele

ACKNOWLEDGMENTS

Edited by: Elizabeth Connor
Cover Design: Jacqueline Sweet

Huge shout out to my patreons Giorgina Meduri, Rachel Kroeplien, and Anna. You gals are my very own personal cheerleaders and I couldn't do this without you!

And to everyone in L. Steele's Team Facebook reader group, you guys are awesome!

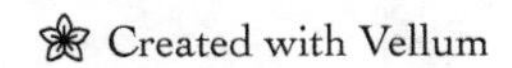
Created with Vellum

Printed in the USA
CPSIA information can be obtained
at www.ICGtesting.com
LVHW011046150524
780224LV00018B/977